Patricia Fawcett

Patricia Fawcett, who came from Preston, Lancashire
and spent several years in the Lake District, now lives in
Barnard Castle in the North Pennines with her scientist
husband. She has three grown-up children.

SCEPTRE

A
Family
Weekend

PATRICIA FAWCETT

SCEPTRE

A CIP catalogue record for this book is
available from the British Library

ISBN 0 340 65806 1

Typeset by Palimpsest Book Production Limited,
Polmont, Stirlingshire
Printed and bound in Great Britain by
Cox & Wyman Ltd, Reading, Berkshire

Hodder and Stoughton
A division of Hodder Headline PLC
338 Euston Road
London NW1 3BH

For my sons Neil and Peter

Part One

1

Charlotte Crabtree woke on the Friday of the birthday weekend to the sound of chirping outside her bedroom window. Those damned birds! One tree, the only tree for miles in this dump of a district, one tree and it had to be outside her window. If she'd known when she took the tenancy of the flat that the owner of the shop below thought he was Balaclava Street's answer to some TV gardening buff, she would never have moved in.

As well as keeping the tree, he had dug up most of the paving slabs in the long narrow yard and planted an herbaceous border. In midsummer, roses, honeysuckle and sweet peas climbed and trailed and rambled in a scented delight over the whitewashed walls, hanging baskets dripped with fuchsia, red and pink geraniums were potted and tubbed. Not one square inch escaped his green fingers.

A curved path led to what was once the outside lavatory but it was now looless, a miniature garden shed. It might be an oasis amongst the cheerless back-to-back red-brick streets but it had all gone to his head and, occasionally, he did conducted tours through the yard. On Sundays, thus disturbing her one really free day. Sundays she usually spent in bed.

It was too late. She was wide awake. Chill, she drew the duvet up to cover her nakedness and snuggled down, keeping a wary distance from the man sleeping beside her. She didn't want to start him off again.

Oh, why was life such a pig! It was going to be one of those sort of days when she spent the whole time feeling sorry for herself and she wasn't having it. Hastily, she snuffed out the tears that were welling up. She still loved that bastard Max and that was the cause, no two ways about it, of her misery. Having your husband walk out on you was bad enough but when he went into the arms of another woman, it was pretty near unbearable. The only thing in *that* woman's favour as far as Lotty could see was that she was supposedly a neat and tidy sort and Max would approve of that. She couldn't see that she would be any better in bed. God, she and Max had been fantastic sometimes.

Fantastic, and the comparison with this slob of a man lying beside her was pathetic. Kevin was about as exciting as a science teacher sounded he would be, his mind stuffed to distraction with chemistry equations or whatever, suffering from terminal dullness with his tweed jackets and wide-eyed specs. He was hopeless and she'd only done it to get her own back on Max.

She'd acted as childishly as the kids at school. No . . . that wasn't even true because some of them had ninety-year-old heads on their shoulders. Streetwise most of them but short on brains they could actually use for academic purposes. Kevin had been the only male member of staff who was even remotely fanciable and she had homed in on him six months ago, flirted in a way that now disgusted her. No wonder they all thought she was one smear of lipstick away from being a tart. What on earth had she done it for? She had egged him on until, in the end, he had of course taken the bait as any normal hot-blooded male would.

A six months hole-in-the-corner affair and it was getting beyond a joke. Way beyond a joke. How the hell his wife didn't know about it was beyond Lotty too. Admittedly, Beverley spent a lot of time with the children at her mother's house looking after her sick father, so that gave Kevin plenty of opportunity to spend nights, or part of nights, here with her. It stank. She was sure the entire school, including the worldly-wise fifth form, knew, even though she and Kev did their best to be discreet.

And now she was pregnant. Ironic after she and Max had tried for so long. Max must have a low sperm count and slob-face here obviously a normal one. He had three young children already, aged three, two, one and there was no way she was going to spring this baby on him. No way. A discreet abortion was what was called for. She didn't like babies. And if she told Kevin she knew exactly what he would say. He would go serious on her and talk about leaving his wife and she couldn't let him do that. She had never meant him to do that. For God's sake, she had never meant to break up a happy little home.

It had started out as a little harmless fun and she had no intention of spending the rest of her life linked to a balding, weary science teacher. In any case, she couldn't stand the name Kevin. When was a man of any importance, any great intellect, called Kevin?

Very carefully, keeping very still, so that she did not wake him or, worse, arouse him, she turned her thoughts to the coming weekend at Fernlands. She hoped her mother had got the birthday card or she would be in the bad books again, the naughty child. She supposed she should have put a first-class stamp on it to make sure but, on principle, she only used second. Her sister Sonia's card would have a first-class stamp on it, of course, and it would be an exclusive expensive card from Harrods' card department if they had such a thing. She wouldn't know. She couldn't remember the last time she had visited London. Sonia, offhandedly, usually invited her to come along anytime she chose but Lotty knew she would die on the spot if she turned up on the classy doorstep. Sonia was one helluva snob.

How could she and poor Beth possibly compete? Beth didn't have two pennies to rub together. Beth was marginally worse off than she was *and* she had to cope with Martin, that bible-ranting husband and those creepy kids. John and Paul. Thank God they weren't at Dockside Comprehensive. They'd go a bundle down there. They reminded her uncomfortably of Uriah Heep, sidling up to her. 'Why don't you go to church on Sundays, Aunt Lotty? Don't you have any best clothes, Aunt Lotty? Mummy says you mustn't swear, Aunt Lotty. Smoking will kill you, Aunt Lotty.'

Sod the pair of them. What was it about kids who caught religion too soon? Religion was not for kids. Religion was for older people hedging their bets. Her mother had never gone in for it and, rather surprisingly, because she wasn't the sort to have strong opinions about anything, she stuck to her guns on that one.

She glanced at Kevin as he made an anxious sound in his sleep, a frown on his brow. No wonder. Cheating on his wife. Beverley was either blind or playing it cool. He kept saying it was the first time he had done anything like this, expecting Lotty to offer sympathy and some miraculous way out of their dilemma.

Longing for a cigarette but deciding it was sure to wake him, she considered the implications of the visit to Fernlands. Would mother guess? Her mother was perceptive in her gentle way, certainly no fool. Her mother was the master of the probing, searching question. It was just possible she might guess Lotty was pregnant, but doubtful.

She was going to have to ask for help, financial help, with the abortion. She would pretend it was for furniture to do up the flat. Mother would approve of that because she was always on about how grotty it was.

Mother was a darling and she always forked out for all of them, Sonia and Beth included and of course their brother William. William had always got anything he wanted, mother's beautiful blue-eyed son, the fourth child, the afterthought.

Lotty sighed. She didn't like to ask but needs must on this occasion and the sooner the better. The longer she left it, the nastier it would be. She knew it was all high tech these days and she was going to a private clinic that a dear discreet friend had told her about but she still didn't fancy it.

Would Beth guess? She might but, even if she did, she could rely on her not to breathe a word. One thing about Beth, her word was her word. She had been surely destined to be a vicar's wife. She would no doubt try to dissuade her from having an abortion but she was onto a loser there. Lotty's mind was made up.

Sonia would not notice. Sonia wouldn't take a second glance at her the entire weekend other than to click her dismay at her choice of clothes and wrinkle her nose if she caught her smoking. Sonia was no problem.

On the other hand, Sebastian was. She'd always half fancied Sonia's husband. If she wanted all hell to break loose, she should have gone for an affair with Seb when Max walked out. He was willing. She saw that in those smouldering eyes of his. He was probably bored with Sonia for she had no warmth in her at all. Cool and calculating that was Sonia.

Sebastian and Charlotte. Yes . . . it went together a good deal better than Lotty and Kev.

'How do you put up with those birds? Noisy devils.' Kevin's eyes were still closed, his breathing regular, his hair, what was left of it, ruffled. Just for a moment, a dangerous moment, she felt a fondness towards him. He hadn't known what had hit him, poor love, when she seduced him that first time.

'It's like living in the country,' he said, opening his eyes and smiling at her. 'Without the advantages.'

'There aren't any advantages,' Lotty said crisply, slipping out of bed and into her old dressing gown before he got any ideas. 'I hate the country. Did I ever tell you I used to live in the country when I was little? The Lake District actually. My mother still lives there. She's lived in the same house for thirty six years. No sense of adventure, my mother.'

'Whereabouts exactly? I like it up there. Me and Bev went on our honeymoon to the Lake District.' He frowned, realising it was a bit off to mention that. 'Sorry . . .' he muttered, 'I didn't think.'

Lotty managed a laugh. He was hardly known for his tact, old Kevin.

'She lives right beside the lake. Between Bowness-in-Windermere and Newby Bridge.' She sighed and a vision of Fernlands appeared, its beautiful gardens sloping to the water. 'Classy place, Kev. You should see it.'

'Sounds lovely. Any teaching posts going in that vicinity?' he enquired with a grin. 'Would you like to move back?'

'No fear. I couldn't get away fast enough. It's depressing in winter when all the visitors are gone and far too busy in summer when you haven't got room to breathe. Speed boats, pleasure steamers, you name it, all zooming past at the bottom of her garden. Not a chance of sunbathing starkers. Tourists are a bloody nuisance if you ask me. Mother loves it up there but I'd go spare, Kev. Terrific views, I suppose, but bugger all else.'

She sat on the chair by the dressing table, rummaged amongst the pots of make-up, tissues and talc for her cigarettes and lit one, inhaling deeply. God, that was better! The first cigarette of the day was really something.

Still facing the mirror of her dressing table, she watched

as Kevin elaborately arranged himself into a sitting position, reflecting that pale hairs on a man's chest were nowhere near as sexy as dark ones. Max was dark. Italian looking. Dark as midnight and handsome with it. Rather like Sebastian.

She tossed Kevin the cigarettes and fell silent, studying her reflection soberly. Christ, she looked a mess! She was naturally pale but she was even paler than usual so that her huge brown eyes looked waif-like. She had lost weight recently instead of gaining it and she didn't like the boniness of her shoulders, the hollows in her cheeks, the shadows under her eyes. Her deep-brown hair was good though, shining and heavy and slightly curly, falling way past her shoulders. Max had always loved her hair, twisting it in his fingers, running his palms through it, stroking it. Every time they had a row, she threatened to have her hair cut. It was always a good starting point for a row, threatening to have her hair cut.

She pushed at it absent-mindedly, wondering if now was the right time to say what was on her mind. Be honest, there would never be a right time for it. She might as well get it over with, and, if she said it now, it would all be resolved by the time she set off this afternoon for mother's. If they quizzed her about a new man in her life, she would have no need to mention Kevin because he would be in the past.

'I've been thinking,' she said, casting a glance through the mirror before turning to face him, adjusting her dressing gown so that she was decent. He looked sleepily rumpled, somehow innocent, which made it all the harder. 'Look Kevin . . . we're being stupid, aren't we, you and me? I know we've tried to be discreet but how can we hope to keep it quiet? People are talking. Can't you feel everyone's eyes on you at school?' She shrugged as she caught his puzzled look. 'Maybe it's my imagination or a guilty conscience, I don't know and I don't know either why the hell it should bother me but it does. Be honest, it's just a matter of time before your wife finds out and you know you don't want to hurt her and the kids. No . . . let me finish, please. I think it would be better all round if we called it a day.'

She couldn't bring herself to call the woman by her name. Beverley. Kev and Bev. The ultimate naffness. 'We'll make a clean break,' she continued, seeing that he was momentarily struck dumb. 'I don't want you to come back here again. And no more meeting in our cars in that lay-by. It's just too juvenile for words. It's all over.' She waved her cigarette in the air with a flourish. 'Finito, Kevin. Sorry.'

'Hey . . . hang on, you can't do that.' He took an anxious drag of his cigarette, flushed in that peculiar way that very fair people flush. 'What's brought this on, sweetie? You seemed okay last night. I didn't hear any complaints.' The worried grin subsided into a sort of leer.

She should have complained. She eyed him with exasperation. 'Just because I spring it on you doesn't mean I haven't been thinking about it for ages. It's just not going anywhere, is it, and it never will.' She hesitated, worried that he might start making a commitment to her, thinking maybe she was angling for one.

'Forget it,' she said quietly, 'I don't intend to have a post-mortem on it and nor should you. Okay . . . so it was a bit of fun while it lasted . . .' She hated to say that for it had meant something at first otherwise, if it hadn't meant anything, she really *was* a tart. She turned away from his hurt little-boy look, staring upwards instead at an interesting crack in the ceiling that looked like a map of Italy. A big cobweb softly draped the corner, a curled-up spider suspended from it.

The room, let's face it, was a disgrace. The whole flat was a disgrace. Sonia wouldn't be able to find anywhere clean enough to place her designer-clad bottom and Beth would have the disinfectant and mop out before she was through the door. Beth was like that. One of life's tidy-uppers. Even when she was a little girl, her room had always been spick and span.

Fernlands, their house by the lake, was huge and they'd all had their own rooms. Sonia, the eldest, had bagged the best of course, one of the big ones overlooking the deep dark waters of the lake but she had liked her room looking out from the front of the house towards the road and the wooded slopes opposite, the really untidy room sandwiched between Beth's and little William's.

Beth had an equally large house to look after now up in one of the grey-slated villages in the hills and, without any help, kept it neat as a pin even with the boys and a couple

of goofish dogs. But then, what had poor Beth to do all day
except visit the sick, open bazaars, count the collection or
whatever it was vicars' wives did. She and Max had laughed
at Beth's earnestness, the manner with which she needed to
extract Martin's approval for everything she did. An engaging or
dopey trait, one or the other. Beth couldn't help it if she seemed
to be an irritatingly perfect wife and mother, just what Martin
deserved. Lotty dismissed thoughts of her sister and returned to
the matter in hand. Infuriatingly, Kevin was still anchored in
bed, his pale whale-like body irritating her more and more.

'There's no kind way of saying it, is there?' she continued,
alarmed to find she was hard-pressed to stop herself from crying.
'Just go, Kevin. For God's sake, go.'

'Right. I don't need telling twice.' He was in a huff, scrambling
naked out of bed, putting his specs on first before comically
having to search through the pile for his clothes that were heaped
and entwined cosily with hers. He put them on, fumbling with
the buttons of his shirt, while Lotty watched his every move.
He was very angry, face tightly compressed, cheeks pink, eyes
bright. 'It's goodbye then . . .'

She managed a laugh. 'Don't be so melodramatic. We'll see
each other soon, won't we, at school? When we do, it has to be
strictly business. Okay? No accidental touching. No meaningful
looks. Is that quite clear?'

'Of course, Mrs Crabtree. You needn't treat me like one of your
class. I understand perfectly.' He was now cool in his anger, tying
the laces of his battered Hush Puppies, not looking at her. 'As
a matter of fact, darling, it's crossed my mind too that we'd be
better going our separate ways. Beverley's so trusting and the last
thing I want is to risk losing my kids. I can't believe I've done this
to her.' He loosely tied his tie, picked up a bulging briefcase and
started fumbling through the pockets of his jacket.

'Here they are, you twerp!' Lotty tossed him his car keys,
grimacing as she heard his footsteps going downstairs, a distant
door slamming, his car starting up. Thank God for that! Men!
When would she learn? She'd had enough of men to last her
a lifetime.

After a quick shower, she dressed in her navy teaching suit,
wearing it with a cream blouse. She twisted her hair into its usual

workaday chignon, secured it, and pulled a face into the mirror. She looked almost presentable. The ladder in her tights was way up so nobody would see that and her knickers were frayed but nobody would see *them*.

Picking up her briefcase, she had to step over various items that had found their way onto the floor. She couldn't see the sofa for a heap of newspapers, a complete week's worth. Surveying the room grimly, she vowed she would go to town on this lot when she got back from her mother's. She would throw practically everything out, particularly anything that reminded her of that husband of hers. When the divorce was through, she would revert to her maiden name. Charlotte Howard. Miles better than silly Crabtree. It had taken some considerable time for her to consent to a divorce as she had at first ridiculously given the bastard time to come to his senses, but now that it was pending, she couldn't wait.

She climbed into her current heap and drove out of Balaclava Street through a maze of narrow cobbled streets to the school. It didn't exactly have 'Grotty, Gritty Northern Comprehensive' stamped across it but that's what it unfortunately was. A solid shiny red-brick effort with tacky crumbling add-ons, it had nonetheless a faintly reassuring air about it. The children wore a uniform, a dingy olive and cream that toned nicely with the interior paintwork. Lotty steered a cavalier path through a pack of late stragglers and parked neatly beside Kevin's rusting Metro. She did not give it a second glance. Head high, she marched into school. She was going to make a fresh start, lay Max's ghost once and for all.

There was just the tricky problem of the abortion to sort out first.

2

Sonia Matheson took her responsibilities as eldest child very seriously. She had decided some time ago that, when the time came, she would shoulder the burden of looking after mummy. And that time was now. She had no doubts that mummy would make a fuss for she was strangely independent in her quiet way but it was ·all organised or very nearly with the final papers awaiting signature. Their solicitor was a good friend but, even so, was beginning to press them, ever so slightly.

Mummy was coming to live with them when they moved to the house in France. She would be absolutely thrilled. They'd always gone to France on family holidays, weeks of lazing about on sunny campsites. The memory prodded and she found herself smiling. The sunnier climate would be good for her mother. She seemed healthy enough, for her age, but Sonia assumed she must have rheumatism for everyone over fifty seemed to. The hotter weather, the warmer winters, the drier climate generally would be ideal for keeping that at bay. Fernlands was beautiful, true, but it rained such a lot in the Lakes.

'You're quiet, darling,' she said now to Sebastian, taking her eyes off the road a second to glance at him.

'I'm tired,' he muttered, giving a huge yawn. 'Jet-lagged. I could do without all this family jollity this weekend.' He rubbed his long legs to get some circulation into them. 'You know I like to relax at home when I've been away on a business trip. That Atlantic flight knackers me these days.'

'It *is* mummy's birthday,' Sonia reminded him gently. 'We've always made a big thing of her birthday. Just think, once we move to France, this will all be a thing of the past, won't it? The rest of the family can come to visit us instead.'

He snorted his doubt. 'Nothing's signed yet,' he said. 'I wish you weren't so confident that she'll agree to it. I still think we should have discussed it with her before taking it to the lengths we have. Our house is as good as sold. It's just as well they aren't in any great hurry to complete. Suppose your mother hates the idea? What do we do then? We are relying on her to chip in the extra cash, aren't we?'

'Don't be defeatist. She'll adore it,' Sonia said, powering the big car up the hill to overtake a lorry. They were just passing the university, almost at Lancaster, and once there, it wasn't too far up to Kendal and their turn-off. Pretty good roads from then on with just the last bit left to negotiate on the difficult narrow twisting road that passed right beside the house and the lake. She hated this part of the journey up the M6 and she couldn't expect Seb to share the driving, not when he'd just got in from the States.

'A real chateau,' she went on enthusiastically. 'Mummy will be sold on that. With an enormous garden she can potter about in. You know how she loves gardening. And her own private suite . . .'

'A granny flat surely?'

'Please don't call it that,' Sonia said sharply. 'Leave the talking to me, Seb. I know her better than you and I shall simply say that, as she's getting older, now is the right time to sort things out for the future. It's no earthly use waiting until she's really old and decrepit and then wishing we'd done something about it earlier. Now is the best time to uproot herself and start afresh and where better than France? The chateau's an absolute bargain, too, we can't let it slip through our fingers. I don't care how bad the housing market is, Fernlands will sell in a flash. It will make an excellent guest house and the setting is just breathtaking.'

'My point exactly . . .' he said drily, 'She won't want to move.'

Sonia ignored that. It was the travelling that had put him in this pessimistic frame of mind. 'All that this means,' she went on undeterred, 'is that we'll be having our share now instead of after she's gone. I have to make mummy understand that without sounding too money-grabbing. It will have to be handled delicately. You know how she hates to discuss her money.'

He laughed. 'You're so sentimental, my love,' he said. 'Have you considered what your dear sisters and William will think about the idea?'

'They will love the idea,' she said firmly, 'They need their money *now* and William can hardly complain, can he? He's had more than his share already. She's always giving him money. How do you think he funds these trips abroad? Certainly not from busking with his guitar.'

'He plays that guitar quite well, although I see what you're getting at. He'll still expect his share though, a quarter, and you're a fool to think otherwise.'

Sonia sighed, feeling him glance her way. She nodded irritably as he suggested she pull in at the next services for a coffee and a break. Seb was going to be no help this weekend. A hindrance rather. Mummy needed careful handling because she liked Fernlands. She had often told them how she and daddy had fallen in love with it the very first time they saw it. The view of the lake from its wide windows was calm and relaxing, changing from one season to the next, and she would certainly miss that. They'd moved into Fernlands just before she, Sonia, had been born and thirty six years was a long time to be looking out of the same windows, trudging down the same drive.

But mummy would love the house in France. If she could only persuade her to visit it, then that would be that. She would fall in love with that too. As chateaux went, it was modest, more of a country house, but it was still officially listed as a chateau and would be fantastic on her letterheading. Perfect for her rapidly expanding business. You had to be blusteringly enthusiastic about the European connection these days and she wasn't going to be left behind. She was hell-bent on being at the forefront. She was going to set up an English design and decorating service and the chateau would be a living advertisement of what she could do. Splendid airy rooms. A flagged floor in the kitchen. Space. Lots of it. Mummy's suite was off a long corridor, tucked away, completely private, so there was no danger of them getting under each other's feet.

She would have to be firm. She was determined that mummy

was not going to end up in some dreadful nursing home where they mixed up the teeth, wore each other's dresses and, worst of all, played bingo. And she, Sonia, was the only member of the family with the foresight to prevent that happening. Lotty couldn't even look after herself properly. No wonder Max had left her. Lotty was a slag. And poor Beth had the family to contend with as well as her weight problem and, in any case, mummy couldn't stand Martin and all the pious utterings. Or those two rather odd boys. William didn't count because he was never around.

It was therefore up to her and she would not shirk her duty. She would have mummy to live with them and, eventually, when she got really old, she would employ a full-time nurse to look after her. Mummy need have absolutely no fears on that count.

She pulled into the motorway service area as Sebastian had requested and switched off the engine, flexing tired fingers.

'You go for your coffee, darling,' she said, reaching for a glossy magazine from the back seat. 'I hate these places and I don't want to get this skirt dirty.' She thought of sticky-fingered monsters as she watched a car nearby spew forth a trio of the horrors. Thank God she didn't have children. This finely pleated skirt had cost a bomb, from her favourite Italian designer's spring range.

She leafed through the magazine, not concentrating, her eyes on Seb as he strolled in that sexy way of his to the café, palest blue cashmere sweater slung over the shoulder of his navy silk shirt, navy jeans a touch tighter than they ought to be at his age. He was nearing forty although he didn't look it.

Sonia gave an involuntary shudder. Growing old was something she was determined to delay as long as possible and that was why she went to such lengths to dress well, that's why she was obsessed with her skin-care routine. Anxiously, she cast a glance in the driving mirror, her doubts disappearing as she looked upon an unruffled complexion. Her wide-set hazel eyes were her best feature and she played up to them accordingly. She wore her straight hair in a deceptively simple bob, the brown lightly teased with streaks of gold. Discreet jewellery and subtle perfume were her accessories. She was almost as tall as her husband, slender, the leggy one of the family, the gawkiness of youth long gone replaced by sheer elegance. Elegance had escaped the rest of the family, with the possible exception of mummy who played a teasing game with it.

She wondered how the meeting in New York had gone for Sebastian didn't discuss business much, knowing that she was bored with the computer technology he promoted so success- fully in his company. She also wondered if this thing with his colleague Jessica was over. Seb must think her a fool not to have noticed. Well, he wasn't getting away with it as easily as that and that was one of the reasons she was intent on dragging him off to France. He would have to spend more time working from home then and there would be much less opportunity for sly after-hours meetings with the delectable Jessica. Although, knowing how ladies were apt to buzz round her husband, Sonia was resigned to having to fight off the local mademoiselles. She allowed a small smile to escape. She didn't mind that much. It was nice to be married to someone so wonderfully attractive as Sebastian and didn't he always come back to her in the end? He was safe with her and proud of her too. It was good for his image to have a wife who was so successful although she had to work hard that she didn't come over as more successful than he. His male pride couldn't stand that.

She glanced at her watch, willing him to hurry. They still had a big chunk of the journey to complete and she wanted to relax a bit before the others arrived. Lotty would be late as she could only do about twenty miles an hour in that silly little car. Pity about Max . . . she had quite liked him, had happily picked his brains on occasions about paint techniques and the like.

As usual, they would have to sit down tonight to one of mum- my's fabulous meals. There would be so much to catch up on and they would have to try not to get up each other's noses too much. She must remember not to mention Max for that would upset Lotty. Nor daddy for that would upset mummy. Nor any connec- tions with weight problems for that would be upsetting for Beth.

She was going to wear a coffee-coloured silk blouse and a chocolate brown velvet skirt. Nothing too elaborate, the sort of items you could easily acquire in chain stores at a fraction of the price she had paid. It didn't seem quite fair to rub it in to Lotty and Beth that she had so much more than they.

3

Beth Bennett put the final stitch in the lilac sweater and held it up in triumph. Mother would love it. It was just her colour. Mum was a pastelly sort of person with her gentle fairish colouring. Of all of them, William took after her in appearance with his blonde, blue-eyed looks. The rest of them favoured father and she herself, unfortunately, had also inherited her father's weight problem. Despite the fact that he had been a GP he had been unable to control it and, in the end it had got him, no doubt contributing to his somewhat premature death from a massive heart attack.

She cast a careful look over the sweater, checking there were no glaring mistakes. It was an intricate pattern but she had enjoyed knitting it. Of course it would not compare with the piece of expensive jewellery Sonia would bring but it was the thought that counted surely and mum would appreciate the amount of time she had spent on it.

She glanced at the clock in the family sitting room which also doubled as her workroom and stood up, causing an immediate reaction from Ben and Dixie who had been slumbering at her feet.

'Not yet, you two,' she said fondly as they padded behind her into the kitchen. 'After our coffee . . .' She poured fresh water into their bowls and they lapped it up whilst she prepared coffee for herself and Martin. He liked to work undisturbed until eleven o'clock and then he enjoyed a break with Beth in his study. It was their special time. The boys were at school and it was an opportunity to discuss whatever was on their minds without interruption.

She carried the tray through the tiled hall to the study, smiling at her husband as she closed the door behind her.

'Finished?' she enquired as he pushed papers aside on the big old desk. 'Am I in the way?'

'How could you be in the way, kitten?' he asked with that wonderful smile of his, the smile that transformed his usually serious face. That smile did things to her. It never failed. 'Have you finished the masterpiece, the birthday present?' he asked, rushing across the room to make space for the tray on one of the low tables. Beth nodded, subsiding gratefully onto the comfortable chair that faced his desk.

She looked round happily. She loved this room, a very flowery room, especially loved the clever way she had furnished it with very little cash, loved the pretty linen and embroidered cushions. She had made the curtains for the windows out of inexpensive cotton lining fabric edged and trimmed with a pretty print so that the overall effect was quite striking. Padded covers on the window seat made it a pleasant place to sit. If there were thin bits on the carpet, they were hidden under cheap bright rugs.

The windows overlooked the back garden. A mature garden filled with flowers, its walls sheltering the more delicate plants. Not that far as the crow flies from her mother's, the village was several miles off the Windermere to Kendal road approached by a dizzily steep narrow hill, marooning them sometimes during the winter frosts, but the awkward access made it so peaceful and Beth adored it. They were encircled by gentle hills, peace and quiet. Such a haven. Martin divided his time between the church here and a couple of other churches in other villages. With only occasional part-time clerical help, it made him extremely busy.

'Thank you, dear.' She took the cup of black coffee from him and declined a biscuit. She was trying to lose weight again. She had always been the plump one but she had gradually ballooned since Paul's birth and she was determined to do something about it.

'I can't say I'm looking forward to this weekend,' she said as they settled into their routine chat. 'Sonia can be such a put-down and I always end up feeling sorry for Lotty. She puts on a brave face but she's still in love with Max. I can feel it in my bones. Isn't it so sad for them, darling?'

He sipped his coffee, a large bearded man with a strong voice that easily reached every nook of the church. A touch over-zealous some of the congregation felt.

'It is sad,' he agreed with a little smile, 'But, knowing how resilient she is, she'll be getting over it by now I should think. She's the sort who will bounce back, Beth.'

'I'm not sure, Martin. They seemed so close. In their way.'

'Let's wait and see, show that we're fully supportive and sympathetic and be prepared to listen to her. If she wants to talk, she will talk.' He gave a sigh, biting into a digestive biscuit. 'I'm afraid I'm going to be busy this weekend. There's a wedding tomorrow and of course Sunday is Sunday.'

'Shall I bother to ask them to come to church on Sunday?' Beth asked, exchanging a quick smile with him. 'After last year's fiasco . . .'

Martin made no comment, merely widened his smile. He had a wicked sense of humour that few people knew about. The boys were just like him, not quite how they might appear on the surface. On mum's birthday last year, the obligatory family visit to church had been not far short of a disaster. Lotty had done it deliberately, miffed that they had more or less forced her along. She had turned up, walking past the surprised congregation, wearing a tartan mini-skirt and short leather jacket, her hair caught up with a red ribbon. A slash of lipstick to match. Sonia on the other hand had been far too regal, sweeping down the aisle late, dispensing small smiles on either side, in a buttercup yellow suit and wide-brimmed hat. The twenty-pound note she had fluttered into the collection plate had remained startled amongst the more usual fifty-pence coins. Martin's congregation was tight-fisted to a man.

Mum had looked uncomfortable as she always did in church, embarrassed by the fawning attention she received from people who had been father's patients. Mum was such a private person and it worried Beth that she seemed to spend more and more time alone at Fernlands. True, she had never been one for socialising but she needed to get out more, meet people, before she stagnated completely.

'Do you want me to listen to your sermon?' she offered, her

hand straying and withdrawing from the biscuits, 'I've got heaps of time. I'll take the dogs out later.'

He didn't need to be asked a second time. He reached for it and began. Beth followed the words closely for a minute and then felt her attention wandering. She got up and walked over to the nearer window, kneeling on the window seat and staring out at the serenity of the garden.

They had so much when others had so little and she ought to be truly thankful. Why then, did she feel so . . . restless? She didn't like to bother Martin with worries about money but sometimes she was absolutely sick of all the juggling she had to do to make ends meet. How they did it she had no idea.

The boys went to prep school, day pupils only, but the fees were still moderately high so that took a huge chunk of their income, eating away at the small inheritance she had received when dad died. She was proud that they didn't owe anyone a penny. She made her own clothes, most of them, and she knitted all their sweaters. She had been most offended when Sonia had sent her what amounted to a clothes parcel last year, full of designer cast-offs. She had sent them promptly to Oxfam.

It was, she supposed, satisfying, spiritually satisfying, that she should cope so admirably. She kept a well-stocked fruit and vegetable garden, tended it herself, and they ate frugally but pleasantly for she was an expert at eking things out. She managed a seasonal part-time job, too, cleaner and caretaker of several holiday cottages nearby but that didn't help much financially, and she had to make sure she had time to help with the parochial duties involved with looking after the three small parishes.

Guiltily, hearing Martin's voice droning on, she tried to listen. Oh great . . . a sermon about personal sacrifice . . . how very appropriate! Things would get easier eventually and the boys had dad's money in trust for them for when they came of age but in the meantime . . . years and years of stretching the money to impossible lengths was beginning to pall. What wouldn't she give for the chance to just go and buy herself a complete new wardrobe of expensive pretty clothes? Surely God wouldn't begrudge her that one small pleasure?

'What's the matter?' he stopped suddenly and looked hard

at her. She never had been able to keep secrets from him. 'Something troubling you? You can tell me, kitten.'

'Nothing,' she muttered and then, seeing his face, 'It's just . . . I wish I looked nicer for you sometimes. Had something new to wear.' She tugged at the spotlessly clean but elderly blouse she was wearing, thinking of Sonia's tailored collection of tops. Sonia was always colour co-ordinated from top to toe. Apparently, her wardrobe was numbered and duly rotated, whatever that might mean. 'What am I going to wear for dinner?' she asked helplessly.

'Get yourself something new if you like,' he said, adopting that vague look when money was discussed. He had no idea how much or little money they had for she dealt with the purse-strings. They couldn't *afford* a new dress for her.

'Cheer up, darling . . .' He was at her side in a flash, pulling her towards him. 'You always look beautiful,' he said softly, tilting her face and gently kissing her. 'I never even notice what you're wearing. All I see is my beautiful wife.'

All the same . . . Beth tried a smile, didn't quite succeed. She was not looking forward to the weekend and that made her guilty, too, because she ought to be. After all, she and Lotty and Sonia didn't see each other very often and it was unforgivable that she was dreading it.

She had no idea how the birthday weekends had started or why it was deemed necessary for her and Martin to stay a couple of nights at Fernlands when they lived so close. Mum liked to have them all under the same roof, that was it, all cosily back in the nest. All except William that is. Beth wondered briefly which roof he would be sleeping under this weekend. A roof under the stars in some romantic far-off country, that's where he would be.

The pressing immediate problem was, what was she going to wear this evening for dinner? She supposed it would have to be the purple print dress again, the only smart dress she possessed. Mum always insisted on dressing smartly for dinner. These weekends followed a set pattern. Tonight was the sitting down in the dining room in some splendour night and tomorrow, Saturday, was an informal buffet or, if the weather permitted, up-market barbecue.

Tonight therefore was the night for getting dressed up. The boys would wear their school blazers and Martin his best suit and a clean white shirt and she would wear the purple dress. Her sisters would remember it for didn't she drag it out every single time?

She left Martin to it, dutifully pronouncing his sermon thought-provoking, and took the dogs for their long awaited walk which would take them through the village, over the stile and onto the pathway that edged the field where they could run about at will. She kept her smile on for the benefit of the villagers as she walked down the little street, past the church, past the pub and the grocery store that was just about holding its own, thank God, and a boon to the older villagers. The post office had disappeared last year but such was progress . . .

It was a pretty little village, blooming at this time of year and, as she walked by, she chatted, making appropriate pleased comments about the gardens, authoritatively discussing the merits of various plants, reminding people of various church activities coming up, smiling, consoling where necessary. All pretty basic workaday stuff that she and Martin could do standing on their heads. She knew what the villagers thought of her. She had once overheard a snatch of conversation in the little shop shortly after she and Martin had moved here, replacing the old much loved vicar who had died after forty years service to the little community. A hard act to follow.

'. . . that nice wife of the new vicar. Dr Howard's daughter you know. Remember Dr Howard? He practised in Windermere. Dropped dead suddenly a few years back. Well . . . she's the youngest of his daughters. Elizabeth. Yes . . . a nice girl . . . a bit on the plump side.'

4

'See you soon,' Laura Howard smiled and kissed Don, shooing him off and waving as he set off in his Range Rover. A quick stop at his home in Grange-over-Sands and then he was off down to Manchester to catch a shuttle to London. She would miss him these next few weeks whilst he was away on business. This evening he flew out to Hong Kong and he had wanted her to go with him but she had said no, not with the children coming up this weekend.

There would be lots of time to travel together later. She was looking forward to that. George had been depressingly unadventurous when it came to travelling. France was about as far as they ever got. He hated to take time off, that had been the problem and, even when he was away, he worried about his patients. One thing she already knew about Don. Away from business, he was away from business. Don had left it up to her whether or not she told the family this weekend. And she hadn't yet made up her mind.

'Now, Elsie . . .' she deferred the decision, returning to the job in hand, the making up of all the beds. Elsie was standing beside the linen cupboard, a very peculiar expression on her face. In her late sixties now, she still came along twice a week to help out with the housework. Through all the changes that over thirty years had brought, Elsie never changed. Small and rounded and a little puritanical in her outlook. She had told Laura quite recently that she couldn't be doing with all these modern ideas on marriage or rather lack of marriage.

Looking at the pursed lips, Laura resisted an impulse to smile at her indignation, to laugh it off. She mustn't forget that Elsie

had known the family for years, worse . . . that she had almost
worshipped George. It didn't matter that George had been dead
for years, behaviour like this was still akin to adultery in her eyes.
How could you, Mrs Howard, the look said. Quite plainly.

Elsie sniffed, picked up a pile of sheets. 'Miss Sonia and Mr
Matheson in the turret room, Miss Lotty in her old room and
Miss Beth and the vicar in *your* old room. Them lovely lads up
in the attic. Is that it?'

'That's right.' Laura decided to be brisk and businesslike. There
was nothing she could do about it. She was sorry to have upset
Elsie's sensibilities but there was really nothing she could do
about it. How was she to know that Elsie would take it into her
domestic head to get here early for once, her husband dropping
her off at the road, come quietly round the side of the house and
sneak in? She had surprised the two of them having breakfast
together, comfortable and happy, tousled and wearing dressing
gowns for all the world like an old married couple. They might
just as well have been in bed! Laura had been mortified, started
on the excuses immediately before Don took over, switching on
his charm of which he had ample and acting as if it was the most
natural thing in the world.

Which it was of course.

Oh well, what was done was done. She left a huffily silent Elsie
to the linen and went to make herself a cup of coffee. Guilt was
there somewhere but she pushed it aside. Don was quite right.
Why should she apologise?

She was a widow, Don a widower with no children of his own
and he wanted to make it official, was very keen to marry her.
It was she who was holding back. He was the first man since
George died in whom she had taken the slightest interest. Since
being introduced to him a few months ago at some function at
the Netherwood Hotel over in Grange, it had all gone so quickly.
It was indeed, for both of them, love at first sight. And she simply
had to get over the feeling that it was ridiculous at their age. As
Don was always saying, what the hell did age matter?

As for his proposal of marriage . . . well, it had taken her by
surprise, too, and that's why she was putting off telling the
family. It was nothing short of a miracle that she had managed
to keep his existence unknown to Beth, who popped in from

time to time to check on her. Poor darling Beth! She had let herself go a bit but was such a martyr to the cause of genteel poverty and refused to accept little gifts that would make life easier for her.

Laura was not looking forward to the weekend, her birthday weekend. She had already received her present from Don, a beautiful red silk blouse bought on his last business trip to the Far East. She had put his birthday card to one side until she explained to the girls.

The other cards were in the drawing room. Lotty's was on recycled paper, a picture of a yellow rose, Sonia's card was stiffly cream and expensive, enormous, roses again, and Beth's . . . well, it looked as if it came from a job lot she had acquired from one of her church jumbles. A picture of a galleon in full sail for some reason. Her grandsons rather endearingly had sent her a homemade card, another picture of a ship, more a rowing boat this time. There was no card from William. Yet.

She finished her coffee and went to check upstairs. Sonia's room was ready. A pretty room, the turret room, its walls covered in a tiny floral wallpaper, the dark polished furniture a lovely contrast, not quite Sonia's choice of course but Sonia's choice was bizarre. Sonia hated what she called wishy-washy shades. Bold primary colours in her rooms that made you flinch as you walked in. The huge wardrobe was empty waiting to receive Sonia's weekend collection.

Laura studied the room a moment, her eyes drawn as always to the view of the lake, the wooded island opposite very clear, smaller islands dotted here and there, the purplish hills beyond faintly clouded in a morning mist that was slow to lift. Already there was activity on the lake itself, the steamer chugging past, a couple of red-suited water skiers skimming by at the end of plumes of frothy water.

She sighed, smiled, never tiring of it. The first time she and George had walked into this room, that had been it. They had looked at each other, allowed the estate agent's frantic comments to wash over them and known that this was it. Their very first home, just about within their financial grasp, even though they were both from wealthy families. In the event it was to be their only home.

She ruffled up a bowl of rose scented pot-pourri and, satisfied, continued down the quiet corridor to Lotty's room.

It was Lotty's childhood room, looking very un-Lottylike now in its pristine freshness. When Lotty was away at university, it had been almost necessary to fumigate it every time she went back after the holidays and what havoc she would wreak on it before Monday morning was not worth considering. At least Max had been some kind of restraining influence on her, tried to make some sort of effort to keep the room shipshape.

Laura placed a yellow pot with white daisies in it on top of the pine dressing table, also placing an ashtray in a prominent position to encourage her daughter to use that rather than sprinkle ash all over the pale carpet. Why the child chose to smoke was a mystery and it had so annoyed George.

The single bed with its white lace coverlet was somehow significant that Lotty's marriage was all but over. They had been a volatile pair but Laura was still surprised that Max had walked out. Shame on him. Still . . . his absence did have some compensations as he and Sebastian had never got on so that was one less potential time-bomb.

Beth and Martin's room was next door, the large room she had shared all her married life with George. She always decorated it with colours of the sea, grey and blue, and she had picked out long-stemmed blue flowers and ferns from the garden for the tall vase on the table. On either side of it the same comfortable chintz armchairs where she and George had had their morning coffee together on their few lazy days and scanned the newspapers.

Briefly, she checked the attic room, the beds covered in cheerful striped covers, a couple of jigsaws and a few old boxed games awaiting the attention of Beth's children. Paul had his piano lesson this evening so they would be arriving later together with the dogs. Tomorrow morning, they would take a walk although Lotty would do her best to get out of it as always. Lotty was lazy. Sad but true.

For a moment, Laura hesitated outside William's old room. Pushing open the heavy cream door, she stepped inside. She tried not to come here too often because it upset her. William had been such a disappointment to his father, the much awaited son whom he had groomed, albeit subconsciously, for the medical profession from babyhood. A baby picture still remained on top of his bookcase and, with a sigh, she picked it up. A little angel with his mass of golden curls and big blue eyes. A pang hit her squarely and she clutched the picture to her bosom, tears springing to her eyes as she remembered the warm little wriggling baby squealing his delight as she tickled him, his head lolling against her shoulder, his hair a soft fluff. Glowing and smelling of clean baby. Sleepy. Skin like velvet. Her beautiful boy. After three little girls whom she'd passed over quite happily to a nanny, she had kept William for herself.

He really ought to be here instead of thousands of miles away and she knew in her heart that he would have forgotten her special day. Quickly, she put the picture down and went downstairs, avoiding Elsie who was now hoovering and dusting aggressively, and into the dining room.

It was dominated by the large oval dining table, poised now and expectant, a softly peach and cream room. Peach velvet drapes and cream festoon blinds at the two formal windows. Between them, on a low table, a toning display of fresh flowers.

There would be hand-embroidered mats, crystal goblets, silver cutlery, fine cream china at each of the eight place settings. Laura would make no allowances for the children and they would sit in equal splendour. She would enjoy preparing the meal later today and, if Lotty was late again and ruined the timing, she would strangle her. Lotty had no respect for the finer things of life and perhaps that was one of the reasons why Max had left her. Max was creative and people like that cannot exist on a diet of beans and toast, cigarettes and the cavalier manner in which Lotty conducted her life. Max worked in television, something to do with designing sets.

She must not forget that Martin would expect to say Grace. Such an embarrassment, but then having Martin as a son-in-law *was* an embarrassment. Sonia would try to look as if it were commonplace, Lotty would have that suppressed giggle look, and Beth and the boys would look suitably pious. Laura hoped to God the starter would survive in the meantime as it was one of her specialities, a walnut and stilton soufflé.

One final glance round the room and she nodded her satisfaction, recalling with a smile the cosy candlelit dinner she and Don had enjoyed last night at his home. He had gone to a lot of trouble and his expertise had quite astonished her. He had spent many years abroad, particularly in the Far East, and the oriental dish he had produced was something she had not tried before. Unusual but interesting. You didn't expect a high-powered man such as he to be handy at rustling up an excellent meal. George couldn't even boil an egg. She sighed, wishing she could stop this constant comparing of the two men. What did it matter? George had been George and Don was Don. She was so lucky they had met.

'It's a shame about Miss Lotty,' Elsie said, wiping every surface within sight in the kitchen when Laura got there. Laura regarded her with relief. Best if they said nothing. 'A shame that Mr Crabtree won't be here. Such a one he was. I always thought him and Miss Lotty were very well suited.' Her sniff was expressive. 'I hope you don't mind me saying that, Mrs Howard, but I have known Miss Lotty since she was knee-high. Always did have a mind of her own, didn't she? Still . . . I liked him and they did seem ever so lovey-dovey. But then you never really know with married people, do you? You never know what goes on behind the scenes.' The look she gave Laura was supremely innocent.

'It is sad but Lotty seems to be coping very well,' Laura said carefully, 'She has her career, Elsie, and that keeps her busy. Although why she has to make her life so difficult, I really don't know. If she lived a little nearer, I could help out a little. I can't imagine why she chooses to live in that town . . . there seems to be precious little to recommend it. And she chooses to live in a flat over a grocer's shop when she could afford something nicer. You should see the school she teaches at . . .'

'One of them inner-city things?' Elsie said knowingly, clicking her disapproval, 'And her doing so well at university too. Them kids won't want to know.'

'Charlotte regards it as a challenge,' Laura said brightly, determined not to sink into depression. God knows, she had enough to cope with this weekend trying to keep the peace. 'You know as well as I do what Lotty's like. She likes to think she can solve the problems of the world single-handed.'

'I'm just about finished, Mrs Howard.' Elsie shut the broom cupboard, sniffed again and smoothed her pinny. 'If that's all?'

'Thank you, yes.' Laura smiled. She really ought to say something about Don but she couldn't for the life of her think of anything.

Elsie could. 'I shan't say a word to a soul about him, that Mr Fletcher,' she said with a conspiratorial nod, reaching for her coat. 'After all, Mrs Howard, it's none of my business.'

'Quite right.' Irritated, Laura began to potter round the immaculate kitchen. She had always treated Elsie more like a friend than an employee, always been scrupulously fair, afraid almost to reprimand her for her terrible time-keeping and, more importantly, her tendency to clumsiness responsible over the years for the loss of some precious items of porcelain. Enough was enough. It was, as Don said, high time she learned to assert herself. 'It *is* none of your business, Elsie,' she said.

Dockside Comprehensive was in the Inkerman district of town, its pupils coming either from the rows of identical terraced streets that sloped steeply down to the rapidly declining docks or from the two tower blocks of shoddy sixties vintage. The pupils were largely foulmouthed, fond of a sly smoke, none too clean and aggressive and *they* were the girls!

That observation usually brought forth embarrassed giggles from guests at the media dinner parties Max had frequently dragged her to, over in the leafy affluent suburbs of rural Cheshire, where the notion that she taught at a run-down comprehensive was viewed as quaint and rather noble.

She didn't feel noble at all and it was a complete waste of time trying to explain her motives to that arty farty crowd. When she took the job at Dockside, she was also offered a cushy post at the up-market school in town, the former grammar school, and it was out of a sense of outrage that she accepted the lowlier position. Schools like Dockside had to put up with the scum of the teaching profession and they needed teachers of her calibre, with her commitment, to survive.

Years later, it was proving tougher than she thought. She was not yet completely disillusioned but in her fourth year History group for instance there were only half a dozen pupils who might pull through next year's exam with a decent grade, and that was painful. The present day was bad enough for them, their puerile pessimism depressing, and the majority of them couldn't be bothered with the past, particularly the Industrial Revolution which even Lotty had to admit didn't own many thrills.

It was ten times worse for Kevin. Trying to keep control in

his laboratory was a nightmare as the kids regarded any safety precautions as 'soft' and it was surely just a matter of time before some trainee terrorist blew the school to kingdom come.

With a sigh, Lotty pushed open the door of the staffroom with her knee and deposited a pile of books on the nearest surface.

'Ah, Mrs Crabtree, there you are at last.'

With a sinking heart, Lotty saw that she and Miss Finney were alone and the last thing she wanted was a heart-to-heart with the steely-eyed spinster, stiffly corseted under the tuttingly respectable summer frock and cardigan.

'Mr Dobson would like a word before you go,' Finney continued with a trace of satisfaction in her voice. Lotty was well aware what Irene Finney thought of her and therefore usually tried to confuse the woman by adopting a sugary sweet innocence. 'If you can spare the time that is?'

In her annoyance, Lotty forgot the innocent look. She glared at Finney as if it was her fault. 'Frankly I can't,' she said. 'I had hoped to get away promptly. I'm going away for the weekend.'

'Really? Anywhere interesting?'

Tired after an afternoon's double session with a bored fifth form who had seemed more dimwitted than usual, it took a moment to translate the odd note in Finney's voice. Of course! She thought Lotty was off for a dirty weekend with Kevin. Tired she might be but she couldn't pass up the chance of a little harmless fun at Finney's expense.

'The Lakes,' she replied, 'Although it hardly matters what the location is, does it?'

A flush spread over the other woman's face and Lotty was instantly ashamed. She hadn't meant to be a bitch and she found herself wanting to make amends.

'I'm sorry,' she said quietly, 'Forgive me. Irene, I . . . can I tell you something?'

She nodded, a very plain lady with kind eyes. 'Are you well, Charlotte? You look a little pale.'

'I'm just a bit off.' Lotty dismissed concern at her state of health. 'You know that Mr McBain and I have been seeing each other out of school . . . well . . . you might as well be the first to know it's all over.' She cast her eyes down, unexpectedly awkward. 'We've been stupid, both of us. Actually . . . I'm going to visit my mother this weekend. It's her birthday and we always have a family get-together. I have two sisters and a brother. One of my sisters lives in London, the other lives near mum . . . she has two children, two little boys . . . and my brother William . . . he travels. Last we heard he was in India,' she explained, thinking that at this rate she'd be confessing *all* in a minute. Irene Finney had quite a sympathetic air about her.

'How lovely! A weekend with the family. And what a lovely place to visit. I'm thinking of moving there when I retire. A little cottage maybe.' Finney had recovered her composure quickly, obviously deciding not to pursue the Kevin thing. Just as well. 'What have you bought her? Your mother. They're so difficult, aren't they? I know mine is.'

Oh no. A birthday present! She'd been so tied up with Kevin and her own problems that she'd completely forgotten about a present. Let's see . . . last year she had bought her a book, Daphne du Maurier's *Rebecca*, in a vain attempt to improve her mother's literary taste. Mother read crappy romances most of the time. She'd have to rush to the shops and get something before she set off. But what? She hated shopping in a panic. She hated shopping, come to that.

Sonia always spent a fortune on jewellery, Beth knitted something ghastly, so it was up to her to be less predictable, to buy mother something she might actually like. Slippers maybe? She said it aloud and Finney approved. She might have known. Finney would buy her mother slippers too, pink and probably edged with fur.

With Finney's mountainously boring alternative suggestions for a present ringing in her ears, Lotty excused herself. She popped to the loo first to check her appearance. God knows why but Mr Dobson made her extremely nervous. She looked pale. Finney was right. In fact, she felt pale, not her usual robust self at all. She hoped she wasn't going to start on this morning sickness thing as that would somehow make it all the more official. She applied another layer of pink lipstick but that only made it worse, made her look like a clown. She added a few spots of colour to her cheeks and smoothed them in. There! Artificially blooming! Her eyes were alert though, if a little anxious at what was to come. Mr Dobson did not summon members of staff in this way unless it was a matter of life or death. What could it possibly be? He'd better not criticise her work because she knew that it was up to scratch and more. She'd worked her knickers off to master this National Curriculum and, in some of her classes, there was just a trace of competitiveness creeping in and that had to be a good sign.

The headmaster's office was a small room overlooking the patch of rough ground they optimistically called the sports field. A straggly bunch were just visible on their way back, some of them already surreptitiously lighting up, looking about as fit as deskbound fifty-year-olds, accompanied at the rear by the perky track-suited figure of the head of PE.

'Nice of you to drop by . . . er . . . Charlotte. Do sit down,' Mr Dobson said, a tall slender perpetually worried man. 'Can I offer you a drink? Tea perhaps or coffee?'

She could hardly ask for a vodka and tonic which was what she could really do with. 'No thanks. Mind if I smoke?' she asked instead, waiting for him to nod a reluctant permission before she lit up. Sod him. It was her body and she could do what the hell she liked with it.

'May I begin by saying your work rate is excellent. You are to be congratulated on your efforts. Nobody quite realises the extent of our problems, Charlotte, in a school like this. We've got an uphill struggle in the PR department, haven't we? Somehow, we've got to make the school more attractive to parents . . . thinking parents. We've got to strive to get ourself up the league tables but it's not as simple as that, is it? The children, unfortunately, get little or no support from their families. No reading matter at home. Glued to the television every hour of their leisure time watching most unsuitable programmes. Sex and violence. Not getting to bed until midnight some of them.' He sighed and she wondered when he would get off his high horse and come to the point. 'However . . . on a personal level . . . I feel obliged to speak to you in view of . . . what I'm trying to say is . . . oh dear, this is so awkward.'

'Go on.' She smiled, drew on her cigarette, suddenly knowing exactly what he was trying to say. She had no intention of making it easy for him.

'It has been drawn to my attention that . . . er . . . certain members of my staff are conducting themselves in a manner not fitting to the profession. As you know well, Charlotte, we teachers have to set an example to the pupils and, regrettable as it may be, rumours are circulating. Alas . . .'

Lotty smiled slightly as she watched the gangly, well-meaning man floundering. She decided to put him out of his misery.

'My private life is my own concern, Mr Dobson,' she said, going for attack. 'It is no business of anyone other than myself and Mr McBain. We are adults and, as such, we can conduct our lives as we choose.'

He pursed his lips, cooled his eyes, and she recalled that he was a staunch Methodist, worse, a lay preacher, that his wife was equally po-faced and humourless and that they had produced a pair of like-minded Dobsons, both of whom graced the ex-grammar school with their presence.

'I beg to differ,' he said, his hands restless on the desk, not quite looking her in the eye. 'When it affects the morale of the school then I have to step in. I have to be seen to be doing something about it. I'm sorry but I regret it cannot be allowed to continue. As I see it, there is a solution. It really might be best if one or other of you thinks about moving on.'

'Have you spoken to Mr McBain?' Lotty asked, furious at what was emerging. If he imagined he could force her resignation, he could think again.

'Not yet.' He was uncomfortable but determined. 'I just wanted you to be clear what my position is. I wanted you to understand my dilemma. Believe me, I take no pleasure in saying this at all.' He hesitated as she remained silent, 'As I say, it's important that you understand my position.'

'What is your *position* exactly?' Lotty asked sweetly, feeling the familiar surge of anger beginning within her. She had the most God-awful temper when she got going as Max knew to his cost and, if he didn't watch it, Dobson here was going to feel the full brunt of it.

He sighed. 'Please don't make this any more difficult than it is already. If the staff talk amongst themselves, fair enough, but when gossip spreads to the children then I can't allow it to continue.'

'I see.' Lotty was so incensed that she forgot for the moment that all this was unnecessary. All she had to do was to tell the truth, tell him that it was all over, that she had given old Kev the push. Her reputation was at stake here and she had something to prove. She was miles better a teacher than Kevin would ever be but it looked like, when it came to the crunch, she would be the one expected to go. Dobson's wife had never liked her. What a wonderful excuse this was.

She stubbed out her cigarette on a wobbly metal ashtray. 'I'm not resigning,' she said coldly, 'You'll have to sack me and I shall claim unfair dismissal. I'll raise hell.' She watched his reaction closely. 'There'll be an almighty scandal, Mr Dobson. We might even get into the *News of the World*. They'd love it. I can see the headline . . . Teachers Sex Romp In Science Lab . . .' She stood up, pushing back her chair, giving him the benefit of a full-frontal angry stare.

'You're making a big mistake harassing me like this,' she went on, realising too late that she was doing herself no favours by acting like this. 'I'm one of the few teachers on your staff who *care*.' To her horror, she detected a tremor in her voice. Not only that, she felt hot and slightly sick. 'I've got a couple of youngsters in my sixth form group who might manage Bs. Christ! They might even scramble an A.'

'Language please, Mrs Crabtree.' He looked pained. 'That's another regrettable thing about your attitude. You know how I abhor swearing and yet you persist in doing so. It quite upsets some of the sensitive members of staff. We have to set an example to the children. There are more than enough words in the English language without having to resort to swearing.'

'Sod that. Who are you to tell me about swearing?' she said, knowing this was going from bad to worse, that she had to get out of here fast before she fell apart. 'I'll have you know that my sister is married to a vicar.' She was immediately aware of the idiocy of the statement as soon as she uttered the words but they were said. It was all too late. Mr Dobson was speechless it seemed and, excusing herself, Lotty judged it was high time she departed.

She met Kevin in the corridor making his way to the head-master's office.

'Well . . .' he queried anxiously, 'What did he . . .?'

'Oh, go to hell,' she said, desperate to reach the loo and privacy so that she could finally throw up. It was nothing to do with the pregnancy she decided as she leaned thankfully against the cool tiles, it was the vile pie they had served up at lunchtime. She waited a moment until she had recovered sufficiently, then splashed her face with cold water, rinsed her mouth, and walked down the corridor and outside into the fresh air or what passed for it round here.

'Mrs Crabtree . . .?'

'Yes. What is it?' She turned to see one of her third year group, an intense little girl with fine pale blonde hair and bright blue eyes. A strong nose and jawline saved her from being pretty-pretty. Lotty saw the droop of the child's mouth, the flush on her face, and softened her tone. 'What is it?' she repeated.

'I just wanted to say I really liked what we did this morning, I want to do that for my project if that's all right,' the girl said shyly, 'I like that kind of history. Henry the Eighth and all that. Rotten that beheading stuff. Imagine having to put your head on a block? I feel sorry for that Anne Boleyn.'

Lotty glanced round with a trace of suspicion but there did not seem to be any giggling accomplices nearby. She recalled the girl's work. Neat. Quite promising actually. Showed a thoughtful turn of mind.

'How can I help?' she asked, refraining from glancing at her watch.

'I'd like to read some more about it,' the girl said, managing at last to raise her eyes. Lotty believed her. 'But I can't afford them big books,' she went on with a theatrical sigh. 'The ones in the bookshop. I love going in bookshops, Mrs Crabtree, but you feel terrible when you want to read them and you can't afford it. And, if you're in there too long, they start looking at you, thinking you're going to nick one.' She sniffed and blew her nose with a tatty tissue. 'Got a bit of a cold, miss.'

Lotty smiled sympathetically. It seemed unnecessary to point out that, on a teacher's salary, she could rarely afford them big books either. The child probably thought she was a millionaire.

'What about the library?' She searched her mind for the girl's name, something extravagant, faintly exotic. 'That's what libraries are for ... er ...' the name jumped out at her, 'Jade, isn't it?'

The girl nodded. 'The library? You mean that place on Bridge Street?' She couldn't have looked more astonished if Lotty had said a sex shop. 'Oh, I don't know. I don't know anybody who goes to a library. I'd feel daft. I wouldn't know what to do.'

'Look, Jade ...' Lotty made a decision, probably foolhardy. 'It's on my way home. I can drop you off if you like. Jump in.' She opened the car door so that the girl could clamber in, complete with a sports bag that was dropping to bits. 'When you get there ...'

Lotty started the car and set off down Inkerman Street, left into Viaduct Terrace and then on to the main dock road, wide and shabby, looking less grim as the sun suddenly shot from a cloud and blazed out. Lotty shielded her eyes and concentrated on switching fearlessly to the lane she needed, ignoring startled hoots from behind, resisting a rude gesture because Jade was beside her. 'When you get to the library ...' she began again, as the traffic eased, 'Go inside and tell them you want to join. That's all there is to it. You'll probably have to get a card signed. Somebody at home will have to sign it. It won't cost any money,' she added quickly.

'I don't like to bother my dad with signing things,' the girl muttered uneasily.

'I can sign it. I think any adult will do,' Lotty said, trying her damnedest to be helpful as she signalled into Bridge Street. 'Here we are,' she said brightly, stopping on the double yellow line outside. 'Off you go.'

Jade stepped out with a whispered thanks and shut the car door, looking awestruck on the pavement. Lotty was tempted to get out and personally escort her inside and get the whole thing sorted out but she didn't have the time.

She really didn't have the time, she told herself guiltily, because she had to pick up her bag from the flat. She still had to pack it in fact before she set off. Why did she leave everything until the last minute? She dare not be late again. Her mother would not start the meal until they were all present and correct and it would mar the reunion if they had to hang around for her. She would throw a few bits and pieces in the bag and she could be on her way in fifteen minutes or so.

Bridge Street soared up to end at a difficult junction and, as usual, she was forced to wait in a queue of traffic. A confident driver, she pulled on the handbrake and tapped her fingers restlessly on the steering wheel. Come on!

Glancing in the mirror, she saw Jade lower down the street standing apparently glued to the pavement. A moment later, she turned and walked away. Damn. Anger caught at her, short and sharp, a physical pain. Anger and disappointment. If she didn't get off her backside and do something to help, that child would end up without hope. When she got back, she would sort through some of her old books and see if she couldn't find something to interest her. Not only that, she would try to make some private time for her, unpaid of course, for she now recalled that Jade's father was a single parent and wouldn't have any spare cash. She rather thought that Jade lived in one of the nicer streets of the area and to be fair to her father, she was always turned out okay. She'd met him once at a parents' evening although he hadn't made much of an impression. The strong silent type.

Jade was ripe for knowledge and if she could only whet her appetite . . . But the desire had to come from the child herself and no amount of parental or professional coaxing would help if that desire was not there.

Take her brother William. Easily the highest IQ of the lot of them and look where he had ended up, bumming and strumming his way around India or wherever he happened to be at the moment. Mum thought the sun shone out of him. Expected great things of him when all she seemed to expect of her three daughters was for them to be happily married. Lotty had had to work hard in school, university and teacher training college and all she had got from mother had been a muted 'well done, darling'. No enthusiasm. Dad of course had been peeved that none of them had wanted to study medicine. William had had a go at it actually but had fluffed the first year exams and not been sufficiently interested to repeat them.

That had been the start of his travels. Every now and then he arrived home, unexpectedly, smiling and suntanned, and was always welcomed with open arms, no questions asked. Lucky bloody William! No responsibilities. And when he was ready, mum supplied him with the funds for his next venture.

Why then should she feel the slightest qualm in asking for money? Mum . . . I wonder if I could ask this enormous favour of you? You see, the thing is, I've got into a bit of trouble with the credit cards and I really want to start all over again and not be so stupid next time. Would mother believe that? Credit card problem? She'd ask what she'd spent the money on but she could get round that. Or, should she be honest and come straight out with it? Mum, it's for an abortion. I'm in *that* kind of trouble, mum, at thirty five I'm up the spout and I need your help.

She couldn't. Her mother, bless her heart, was so blissfully innocent about such matters. To begin with, it would never occur that the baby was not Max's. Mother would assume they had tried a reconciliation and that the baby was the result. How could she possibly explain that she had been sleeping with another man, a married one at that? Mother would be quite shocked at such a thing. Dearest mother who had married, blissfully innocent, at eighteen, become almost immediately pregnant with Sonia and never known any man other than dad.

Thankfully, she turned the corner into Balaclava Street, parking her car in its usual place behind Mr Dassayaje's blue van and going through the shop rather than via her private entrance. The shop was crowded and noisy. Mr Dassayaje catered specifically for the needs of the Pakistani families in the area, which accounted for the wonderfully exotic smell of the produce. He was a lovely man, a born shopkeeper, ever keen for a chat and a laugh, helped in the shop by his calm beautiful wife who wore vivid saris that swished their silken way amongst the shelves of groceries.

Her arrival caused a lull in the chat as Mr Dassayaje smiled and greeted her with that polite nod of the head.

'I just popped in to tell you I'll be away for a few days. I'll be back on Sunday night. So . . . could you push the papers through the letter-box please and bring the milk in?' She grimaced her apology. 'Sorry to inconvenience you, Mr Dassayaje. I forgot to cancel them.'

'It is no problem. I will do that for you with the greatest of pleasures, Mrs Crabtree.' He beamed, apparently overjoyed that she should ask this small favour of him, 'A weekend break you are having?'

'Yes. I'm visiting my mother.' She smiled as his wife slid silently in. She couldn't see but she suspected she was barefoot under the folds of emerald silk. Barefoot with a thin gold ankle chain perhaps and scarlet toenails to match the fingernails. 'My mother lives near Bowness-in-Windermere. Her house overlooks the lake.' She felt obliged to prolong the chat as it was some time since they had exchanged words and, despite the green fingers, he was a considerate landlord. The customers in the shop were totally unconcerned at the time-wasting, looking at her rather with some interest. 'She has the most marvellous views from her windows,' she added, 'The lake and the hills and everything.'

Mr Dassayaje consulted the audience and joined them in a collective sigh. 'We are not so lucky. We have only the streets and the docks to look at.'

Lotty didn't bother to argue that it was only a half-hour drive to the river estuary and the open sea. He never took time off. Never.

Going upstairs to her flat, she noted the time as she picked up the letters from the mat. Not so bad as she thought and in fact she had time for a quick cigarette and a coffee before she need worry about packing. She had no idea what she was going to take. Sonia's suitcase would have been packed since mid-week. Clothes folded and wrapped in tissue paper. Hundreds of pounds worth of clothes. It was obscene the amount of money her sister spent on clothes. Some Italian designer or other. She had to hand it to Sonia, however, that she was damned successful. Straight after college, she had scorned a safe job, teamed up with a girlfriend who now seemed to have abandoned ship, secured a bank loan and dived headlong into business. She was original certainly, bold and original. Max had not liked her ideas. He was based in Manchester, working for one of the regional television networks, and he and Sonia used to argue, fairly amiably, about the merits of their respective jobs. Sonia's designs had to be lived with, she used to say, whereas Max's were dismantled once their purpose was served. You couldn't argue with that really but, of course, Max had.

Max had hated these weekends at Fernlands although in the early days he got on better with dad than either Seb or Martin. Dad had admired Max. For an awkward moment, just as she poured milk into her coffee, she felt an ache that she wouldn't see her father again. It had been such a shock it happening so suddenly like that. On the golf course just after he'd birdied the fifth and for some insane reason, that seemed to please everyone. How wonderful they said. What a way to go! It hadn't been at all wonderful, it had been the worst moment of her life, and even Martin's very moving conducting of the funeral service had failed to help. Mother had been in a daze, tearless, whilst she had wept buckets. Red-eyed, white-faced and utterly ghastly in black.

Lucky Max then that he was spared this weekend. Why they had to make such a damned fuss about mother's birthday was beyond her. You'd think mother would want to forget her birthdays from now on. Wouldn't it be nicer if they could be more spontaneous with their visits, pop in unexpectedly and perhaps find Fernlands in disarray for once. It was always so tidy.

Ignoring the mess all around her, she went to find something to put in the overnight bag. What? A dress for tonight of course. Her shocking pink number, strapless, that would make Seb sit up, Sonia jealous and Beth tut-tut. Beth could talk, she'd be jammed into that awful purple effort again.

She bunged the dress in the bag beside her relatively sober grey pinstripe suit which she was going to wear for church this year. She was going to be good. She was going to listen attentively to his sermon and then tear him to pieces later. A stimulating intellectual argument would do her the world of good and Martin was clever. Misguided of course but clever. She missed a good old argument now that Max was gone. All that volleying of heated words to and fro. Rattling him. Making him lose his cool.

What else did she need? Knickers and things. She picked up a handful from her undies drawer and threw them in without a second glance. In addition, she needed a waterproof or something for their jolly family walk by the side of the lake.

Hell's teeth! They did it whatever the weather just to please mother. When they were small, she'd always dragged them off on walks. Lotty had never enjoyed them, much preferring to remain indoors with a book.

The phone rang as she was struggling to zip the bag. She toyed with letting it ring but she couldn't. With a sigh of exasperation, she picked up the receiver half expecting it to be her mother checking up on her.

'What the hell did you say to Dobson?' It was Kevin's injured voice and she very nearly slammed the phone down. She did not, conceding that she probably owed him a few minutes listening time.

'Why? Did he give you a roasting?'

'I told him it was all over. He didn't seem to believe me because you hadn't said anything about that. He took some convincing and then he said that you'd seemed a bit odd but he's letting it pass because you looked peaky.'

'That's big of him.' Lotty sat down heavily on the chair beside the phone. 'Look Kevin . . .' She ran her fingers through her hair, 'I haven't time to talk now. I'm late already but when I get back, we will talk. No . . .' she went on hastily as she sensed he was going to take it the wrong way, 'You stick with Beverley from now on. You're not cut out for an affair.'

'Meaning what?' He was cool, distant, his pride no doubt hurt.

'Meaning you're too nice.' She bit her lip. 'Sorry Kevin. I feel responsible for all this. If it wasn't for me giving you the come-on, you never would have, would you? Be honest.'

'I've always thought you very attractive,' he murmured and Lotty smiled gently, feeling a momentary sadness for him. 'Are we going to be able to continue to work together?' he asked after a long pause.

'I'm not sure about that,' she said honestly, 'And that's what we'll talk about but not now. I have to go. It'll take me two hours to get there.'

'I'm not that happy at Dockside,' he said, reluctant still to let her go, 'And I've been thinking for some time that it's time to move on. I just can't seem to get through to the children here. I've seen jobs I fancy but it's Beverley, Lotty. She likes it here.

Her parents are here and you know that her dad's dying. She doesn't want to move. How do I persuade her?'

'You either tell her the truth,' she listened for his intake of breath at the suggestion, 'Or you make up some story about professional fulfilment, that sort of crap, wanting to spread the word of science into more amenable ears, wanting to teach kids who want to learn, or better still, go for a head of department somewhere. You've had the experience, you might swing it and the extra money might just persuade her.'

'I don't suppose you've been thinking of moving on?'

'Not yet.' It surprised her how quickly the response came. She wasn't finished here yet, not with kids like Jade hanging about. Not that she would ever say that to Kevin. 'I've got to go,' she said, putting the phone down on him.

Now ... was that everything? The washing up could wait until she got back. The letters were on the table and she rifled through them in case there was something of world shattering importance. Two bills. Gas and electricity. In the same day? Had these people never heard of customer's cash flow problems? She tossed them aside irritably. She would wait for the demands. She picked up the solitary white envelope and stared at it.

From Max. What was he doing writing to her personally? Any correspondence these days was addressed through their solicitors. She looked at the unmistakable handwriting and wondered. She was tempted to throw it away for he had no business, no reason, to write to her. Didn't he realise that just seeing his writing was enough to upset her? Stupid and irrational but true.

There was nothing more to say. He had walked out, well and truly burnt his boats, and it would serve him right if that woman turned out to have a mind like a marshmallow. There would be no stimulating arguments with her. My God, she and Max had loved their rows, sitting up into the small hours arguing until they were blue in the face before finally going to bed, all the differences forgotten as he reached for her.

She would take the letter with her and, if she had a minute, she might read it this weekend. She stuffed it into her handbag and picked up the car keys. There! That was finally it. All she had to do now was to get herself up to Fernlands.

She was heading north, on the approach road to the motor-way, when she remembered she still didn't have a present for mother.

6

Beth couldn't do up the zip on the dress. She lay down flat on the bed, breathed in and tried again. No. Damn, damn, damn! It was no use. Tears of frustration welled in her eyes. Now what? She had nothing else that would do for dinner this evening.

A fine time to find this out. If only she'd known, she could have bought some material and run something up on the machine although Sonia would turn her nose up at that. A home-made dress! She should have checked, of course, earlier in the week, but she hadn't realised she had put on so much weight since the last time she had worn it. She would have to lose about two stones. It was all very well for Martin to say it didn't matter but it did. It mattered when the children noticed.

John had brought some work home from school. A picture of her, her brown eyes prominent, a big smile on her face, her hair fluffed out. He had written in his careful printing: 'This is my mummy. My mummy is kind. My mummy bakes cakes. My mummy loves dogs. My mummy has brown eyes. My mummy is quiet fat.'

An essay no less! The word 'quiet' was corrected to 'quite'. No matter. *He* was being kind, bless him, in trying to qualify the statement but it was how he saw her. Kind, brown-eyed and fat. She had to do something about it.

Extricating herself from the dress, she stood undecided a moment before putting on a blouse and a skirt with an easy fitting waistband. She would have to buy something new. Quickly, she rummaged in the drawer that held her underwear and pulled out a small box. It contained fifty pounds, her emergency fund. It wasn't that she intended keeping it a secret from her husband, more that he wasn't really interested in money matters so there was little point in telling him. She shopped around. A couple of pounds saved on her grocery bill meant a great deal. All the loose change ended up in the box and gradually it grew. The fifty pounds was the start of her Christmas fund so that they could afford a few special things at what was such an important time of year for them.

Reluctantly, she put the money in her purse. She wouldn't do this if it wasn't important. Sonia had an unfortunate habit of looking at her as if she was kitted out in rags, mum just felt sorry for her and seemed forever on the verge of saying 'what did I tell you, marrying a vicar?' Lotty told her outright to do something for God's sake before it was too late. That was a bit rich coming from Lotty. Lotty's dress sense veered to the tarty. A couple of birthdays ago, she had appeared in a silver dress that had clung to her thin body like sellotape, slit to the thigh. She and Martin had, rather unkindly, laughed about it later. A stick of silvery rock.

So, this year, she would give the rest of the family no cause for comment. She would buy something flattering in blue, Martin's favourite colour, and she had an appointment to have her hair done too. She had nice hair. Thick and curly.

She glanced at the clock. She enjoyed her infrequent trips into town. She generally combined her hair appointment with a little window shopping, sometimes treating herself or the boys to a little inexpensive item, and Kendal was a joy to visit, one of her favourite places. She was giving Martin a lift but, if they set off now, it would give her time for a leisurely browse.

With Martin's bulky frame squeezed into the passenger seat, the dogs sprawled in the rear of the old estate car, Beth set off on time. She was looking forward to being at Fernlands again, if only for a few days, for in that odd way of childhood homes, Fernlands was still home. She loved its special waterside location and when they were little they had been quite keen on messing about on the lake in the family dinghy, a hobby that had escaped the interest of both Martin and her sons.

The house was too big for mum now but she had once said she would never move from there and Beth understood that. She was close enough to her and Martin, geographically speaking, for it not to be a problem. Mum need have no worries about growing old, although Beth sensed it did worry her.

She wished they were closer as a family. Beth had never felt, though Lotty would disagree, that her parents had been particularly close. Content enough maybe but not close in the sense that she and Martin were. She met Martin when she was only eighteen and working as a junior clerk in an accounts office. She still passed the very same office in Highgate every time she went to town. He was nearly thirty at the time and she discounted him as being too old for her but he wasn't having that as an excuse. He pursued her relentlessly, although it was not for some considerable time that she discovered he had a degree in theology. He had done other things for a while but he was at that time seriously considering entering the church. Called by God, he said simply and so seriously that she did not mock him. Martin was such a fun person when you got to know him and she had been captivated by him, he in turn absolutely determined to win her. She knew at once when he proposed marriage that that was exactly what she wanted too. She had, after a time, introduced him to her parents and he had, in that endearingly pompous way he occasionally adopted, asked her father for her hand in marriage.

Her parents were astonished. She had mistakenly thought they would be pleased but mum had protested that they didn't even go to church and that she had no intention of doing so. She was prepared to welcome Martin into the family on the understanding that he made no attempt to convert them. Martin never had. God would do it in His own time. There was a little stubborn streak in mother that showed itself occasionally.

Martin had kept his word. He was pleasant and courteous to her mother and it niggled Beth that she still held out on him. Refused point-blank to attend their church other than at Christmas, Easter and this coming special weekend.

'Do you think she'll like her present?' she asked as they neared their destination. 'It took me ages.'

'She'll love it,' Martin reassured her, shifting awkwardly in the confined space. 'And, even if she doesn't, it was given with your love. Be content with that.'

She glanced sharply at him. Sometimes he could be so irritating. Somehow his words didn't help at all for now he had put doubts in her mind.

'I shall have to buy a new dress,' she told him, changing the subject, 'I can't fit into that purple one.'

To her dismay, he laughed. 'Too many chocolate biscuits,' he said cheerfully. 'We'll make an effort together. Will that help? Chocolate biscuits are forbidden from now on.'

'All right.' She smiled, pleased to be doing something positive. 'Christmas will be my target,' she said, 'I aim to lose a stone by then.'

'Drop me off here, darling,' he said, as she turned into the site of the nursing home where he was to visit some patients.

She did so, shushing Ben and Dixie who wanted to get out with him, watching until he disappeared from view. He was very good at visiting the sick. A marvellous listener even if he didn't always listen to her.

Further down the road, there was a stretch of rough land and she spared the time to let the dogs have a run. She watched as they hurtled round just for the sheer joy of it. They came back to Beth as soon as she called them, tongues hanging out, delight in their eyes, collapsing onto their covers in the car and happy to wait for her.

When she had parked the car, she treated herself to a coffee and a cream cake in a little café in Stricklandgate, dallying a little over it, guilty about the cake, dreaming a bit, so that she had to rush, walking quickly, cutting through the cobbled alley of the New Shambles to arrive at the hairdressers with one minute to spare to her appointment. Red-faced and flustered.

'Sorry I'm late,' she found herself saying, even though, strictly speaking, she was not.

The girl, cool and blonde, with the perfect make-up of the make-up counter, asked her to wait and, thus dismissed, Beth took a seat and picked up a glossy magazine, trying to control her hurried breathing. What a rush! All because she'd been in one of her dozy, dippy moods in the café. It occurred to her that neither of her sisters would apologise if they were a minute *early* for an appointment. They wouldn't even apologise if they were genuinely late.

She was kept waiting. Deliberately or not, she wasn't sure. The girl who normally did her hair seemed to be doing nothing in particular, languidly sorting through hairbrushes, rollers and the like. Beth did not complain, glad of the opportunity to get her breath back. She looked through the magazine to find it faintly depressing with really thin models and lots of articles about resuming a career. Assuming you had a career worth resuming that is. Not for the first time, Beth found herself wishing she had trained for something worthwhile. She really would have liked to go in for nursing which would have pleased dad but somebody . . . she forgot who . . . persuaded her that she really didn't have a hope of getting the grades required in biology. Okay, so it wasn't her best subject but she could have given it a go. She should have insisted on trying.

She put the magazine down and found she was gazing at her reflection in the mirror opposite. She just had to face the fact that she was the plain one of the family. She had missed out on her mother's fragile beauty. All she had got from mother was a basic love of cooking and home-making. Sonia and Lotty couldn't bake a cake if their life depended on it although William, for all his faults, had quite a practical turn of mind. She smiled a little as she thought of her baby brother. Where on earth was he? Martin liked him, thought him such a troubled soul and was unfazed by William's experimentation with various religions. Why not, Martin said, that's the way he will discover his true self. Martin was extremely tolerant, more so than Sonia or Lotty who were totally irreligious.

'Mrs Bennett?'

The girl who did her hair, Norma, cutting it once every six weeks, was smilingly holding the pink striped overall aloft. Slowly, for she did everything at the speed of a snail with a limp, she draped the nylon cape round Beth's shoulders and tied it in an overly elaborate bow.

'The usual, Mrs Bennett?' she enquired, smiling, scissors poised.

Beth hesitated. The usual meant an inch off but the style remained the same. Longish. Curly. No style really. No proper style. 'I wonder . . .' she saw in the mirror that she was blushing and, as she was normally fresh-faced, she was now very nearly fluorescent. 'Could I try something different?' she asked, hesitating as she saw Norma's look of surprise. 'Shorter perhaps? With a fringe?'

'Shorter? With a fringe?' Norma frowned, pulling and prodding, bunching up Beth's hair as if it were already cut off. She pursed her lips in supreme concentration. 'Well . . . it would be such a shame to cut it, Mrs Bennett, after all the trouble we've taken to grow it. And your face is quite round . . . a short style would accentuate that. Of course if you really want me to . . .?'

Beth tried to hide her disappointment. Her colour was calming a little. 'I just fancied something different,' she murmured, by way of explanation.

'That's all right,' Norma continued with the pulling and the prodding before letting the hair fall heavily onto Beth's shoulders. 'The usual then?' She flourished the scissors once more, beaming.

She let Norma's tide of hairdresser trivia wash over her, relaxing her mind, dwelling on the good things God had given her. The boys. Martin. Good health. All the things that mattered. All the important things.

'Going anywhere special tonight, Mrs Bennett?' Norma enquired as she was brushing her hair loose.

It required a reply. 'To my mother's for the weekend. It's her birthday. We have a little family get-together.' She spoke quietly to make up for Norma's shrill voice. There weren't many secrets in this salon.

'How lovely.' She continued to fuss with Beth's hair and Beth tried not to fidget although she wanted to get away and buy the dress. Her hair looked nice. Dark brown with auburn glints in it that were more prominent in summer. Its natural colour. Funny that William should be so fair, almost white when he was a baby. He had been the most beautiful baby, she recalled, and mum had always looked as if she was anxious to get them off to school so that she could have him to herself.

Jealousy was a sin and yet William still managed to make her feel that way. She was envious of the free and easy life he led. Wouldn't it be wonderful to have no responsibilities?

She gave Norma fifty pence. Why she had no idea because Norma had been more irritating than usual today. She ought to start going somewhere else but she was used to this place and how would she tell them that she wasn't coming any more?

The boutique she drifted into specialised in clothes for larger ladies. It was lunchtime and crowded and it would seem from remarks she overheard that they were also short-staffed. The girl who stood by the fitting-room door was complaining bitterly that she still hadn't had her break, not even sparing the time to smile at Beth as she handed her the disc to take into the fitting-room with her.

'Four items,' she called out in a bored voice, 'Take cubicle two.'

Hot and flustered from being under the dryer, Beth carried the dresses she had selected into cubicle two. There was scarcely room to turn round, and she had to place her other shopping, two bags of groceries, onto the floor. A cheap-carpeted floor that needed a good hoovering. She drew the curtain across but it still gaped open at one side and she was in grave danger of showing anyone who cared to look everything she had got.

Was it worth it? By the time she had struggled out of her coat, skirt and blouse, found somewhere to hang them and extracted the first of the dresses from its hanger, she was totally fed up. The first dress, the cheapest, that had looked reasonable on the rack, was absolutely dreadful and she quickly slithered out of it. The next one she didn't even bother to try on at all. What had possessed her to bring that in? Number three was better.

She stepped out of the cubicle so that she could see it properly. As she looked at herself in the mirror, she noticed that the girl on duty at the entrance had disappeared.

The dress was red and she liked it. A shirtwaister style with a pleated skirt and a matching belt. She liked it and she thought it flattered her. She glanced at the price tag on the sleeve. A little nearer the fifty-pound mark than she would have liked but . . .

She quite liked the last dress too, which happened to be the most expensive. Perhaps a little dressier and more appropriate certainly for this evening in pale blue and cream silk. She sighed as it slipped seductively over her head. Martin would love this one. The trouble was she liked the red dress as well and she couldn't afford them both. She would have to make a decision.

Time was marching on and if she didn't get a move on, she

would be late picking up the boys from school. Damn. This blue dress was just a fraction tight. Perhaps if she tried a larger size?

She went to the entrance to ask one of the staff to get her another size. The shop had emptied considerably and there was only one girl she could see at the desk, engaged in a private phone call whilst surreptitiously eating a sandwich.

'Excuse me . . .' she called but the girl did not hear. From the speakers above her head, a piano concerto tinkled, reminding her of Paul's lesson this evening. She should have put it off for once, as it was going to cause extra hassle when they were all trying to get ready.

'Could you please . . .?' Beth gave up. It was okay anyway, and she was reluctant to have a size bigger. From painful experience, she knew that once you did that, there was no going back. She returned to the cubicle to sort herself out.

She paid for the blue dress.

She stole the red one, carrying it out neatly folded at the bottom of one of the grocery bags.

'What will we be having for dinner, mummy?' Paul asked as she drove him to his music lesson. 'Will I have to eat it all?'

'You certainly will, young man,' she said with a smile, 'Granny will have gone to a lot of trouble. You must eat it even if it's something awfully grown-up.'

He sighed. 'Like sherry trifle?'

She nodded. 'And you must be polite to your aunts, darling,' she went on after a moment, 'They're very fond of you and John.'

'Aunt Lotty says she doesn't like children,' he said doubtfully.

'She's just teasing,' Beth said, although she suspected it was true. Lotty was not the maternal type. Lotty was too clever for her own good. Sometimes she was glad she was the dimwit of the family. Well, not quite, merely academically less gifted. Nobody had bothered much, seemed relieved rather when she left school with just the barest of qualifications.

'Why does she tease?'

'I don't know.' Beth was finding the conversation a little wearing. Thank goodness they were nearly at the house where he had his piano lesson. She waited outside in the car while he was inside. It was a bit of a bore but she could always knit or take a book during the summer months. She had been invited to wait indoors but Mrs Miller kept cats and Beth did not like cats.

'Aunt Sonia says little boys should be seen and not heard,' he said soberly, not prepared to let the matter drop. 'What does she mean? Aren't we to speak at all? She's always talking. Doesn't she like us?'

'Of course she does. How silly!' Beth stopped outside the house, one of six in a new executive development. New cars in all the drives. Beth felt distinctly out of place, the poor relation, in their ancient mode of transport. The previous pupil was still there so they were obliged to wait. 'Doesn't Aunt Sonia send you lovely presents at Christmas and on your birthday?'

'Will granny have a birthday cake?' he asked, losing interest in Sonia. 'With candles on? I'll help her blow them out. I've got more puff.'

Beth watched as he disappeared indoors for his lesson. Mum gave the impression of fragility, she supposed, although in fact she was not in the least frail. Quietly determined was probably the best way to describe her. She rarely shouted in anger and she had never ever heard her swear. Not like Lotty who was absolutely outrageous.

Through the open window of the car, she could hear the laboured playing of her son. Martin was keen for him to play the piano so that one day he could progress to the organ at church. So far he had not rebelled being, for the most part, an agreeable child but Beth could not help thinking he lacked talent. She would be inclined to let him stop if it bored him but she knew that Martin would insist he carry on. The boys respected their father hugely and loved him too of course.

She had stolen the red dress. She was a thief. Thou shalt not steal.

Beth sighed and clasped her hands together. Oh dear, what had she done? I'm sorry, she said silently, offering up the apology to God if He was listening. She would never dare tell anyone and it would be a very long time before she dare go back to town in case they were on the look-out for her. The thing she couldn't quite get over was how very easy it was. If you picked the right moment then . . .

It would not happen again and, if she really wanted to make amends, she ought to find some way of returning the dress. Could she say that, when she arrived home, she found to her surprise that there were two dresses in the parcel when she had only bought one?

No. That was inviting trouble. In any case, she was hopeless at lying and her guilt would show. She had put the dresses away, both of them, knowing that Martin would not query her apparently buying two.

Stupid, stupid, stupid. She felt the onset of tears, blinked them furiously away. It was just a one-off. Most definitely a one-off. A momentary aberration, that's all. The unfortunate result of all the stress she was under to make ends meet.

She switched on the radio, trying to soothe away her fears with sweet music. Anxiety pounded from all sides, making her catch her breath, feeling the onset of panic.

'Mummy . . . let me back in, please.'

She breathed deeply, controlled it. 'Oh, hello darling. How did it go?' She put his music books into the back seat and waved at Mrs Miller through the window. 'All right today?'

'Great. I think I'll be a concert pianist,' he said brightly, 'I was very good Mrs Miller said. Can we have a big black piano?'

'No we cannot. We can't afford one, Paul, and if you can't afford things, you can't have them.' She tried to smile, starting the car and setting off, thankful to weave her way past the sparkling new houses, the shamefully new gardens, out onto the quiet road again. 'Now . . . we won't have much time when we get back,' she said, 'We have to get ready for granny's as soon as we arrive. Your bag's packed. You and John will be up in the attic. Won't that be nice?'

'Where will Ben and Dixie be? We'll have to take their baskets with us,' he said worriedly, 'They don't like different beds.'

It was the same for all of them, Beth thought wryly. She wished mum wouldn't always put her and Martin in the room she still thought of as her parents' room. It was disconcerting to say the least.

'Will Uncle Sebastian be coming?' Paul continued relentlessly. 'I like him. He goes on planes all the time. On his own. Aunt Sonia doesn't go with him.'

Seb hardly needed someone to hold his hand. Sebastian Matheson was the sort of hard-headed businessman whom she frankly despised although she knew that was a very un-Christian thought. Love thy enemies. Seb was not an enemy but his lazy charm was infuriating. A ladies' man. Lotty couldn't resist flirting with him, even when Max had been around but then she had a tendency to do that with any man apart from Martin. It was those big soulful eyes and that wicked grin of hers and that tendency to shock. Beth had caught her once or twice looking at Martin, weighing him up. If she so much as dared to make any move in Martin's direction . . .

She hurried Paul into the house when they got back. Everything was nearly ready. John was scrubbed, pressed and almost folded she saw, sitting on a chair in the hall where he had been told by Martin to wait and not move a muscle. The dogs were agitated, both at her arrival and because they sensed something was happening. She hoped they would behave this weekend. Sonia hated dogs and Lotty and her mother over-fussed them, gave them continual titbits and made them extra drooly.

Quickly, she went to get ready. Why was it, when they went anywhere together as a family, she always had to make do with the few minutes left available when all else was done? With the blue dress, she wore her cream shoes and pearls. Grandma Howard's pearls that had come to her when she died. Other items of jewellery had gone to mother, Sonia and Lotty.

The pearls looked especially lovely with the new dress and she took some care with her make-up, although she was still ready in fifteen minutes flat. A splash of last year's Christmas perfume and she was ready.

Martin was in the kitchen, smart in his suit, shining black shoes. Beth stood in the doorway a moment, watching him. What would he say if she told him? Should she? Dare she? He was her husband and he would not shop her . . . wasn't that the word? . . . to the police. He might insist she see a doctor though or, worse, a psychiatrist, and she had no intention of doing that. It felt suspiciously like temporary insanity to her but it was something she could handle.

'You look wonderful,' he said, turning and smiling, 'Nice dress. Is it new?'

She nodded. 'Do you like it? I got two actually . . .' she felt her smile freeze on her face. 'They were in the sale.'

'A bargain then? Well done. It looks expensive.' He lapsed into silence, looking at her with great tenderness. 'So . . . why the face? What is it, Beth? Are you worried about spending money? Is that it? I've told you, a little treat now and then works wonders.'

'I'm not worried about money, no more so than usual.' She wanted rid of this subject. 'If we're all ready then . . .?'

'Oh Beth . . . I've just realised what's bothering you. Seeing you dressed like this has reminded me.' He shook his head and she dare not meet his eyes for then he might very well read her mind. 'You shouldn't hide things from me. You and I don't have secrets, do we?'

Mouth dry, she couldn't even manage a smile in return. How could he possibly know? The shop couldn't have traced the theft back to her, could they? Perhaps the police were outside the house at this very moment waiting to arrest her. What a scandal! It would ruin Martin.

'I'm not trying to hide anything,' she said as calmly as she could. 'The very idea!'

'You don't want me to say Grace this evening, do you? You want me to skip it.' He came across and kissed the top of her hair, 'You should know better than that. I promise I'll keep it brief so they don't get restless. And we'll see what happens about Sunday, shall we? I would like them to come along. After all, everyone is welcome at church and they needn't be conspicuous. We can hide them away at the back.'

'Sonia won't sit in economy class.' Beth was still in shock, valiantly trying to get her mind into gear again, 'And neither will Lotty. We'll say nothing and maybe they'll decide not to bother.'

'Let's get ourselves over there.' Martin whipped the car keys from the table where Beth had dropped them. 'How did the lesson go?' he asked in a whisper, catching her arm before they went.

'He now wants to be a concert pianist.'

They exchanged parental smiles just as the doorbell rang and the dogs thundered through the hall to arrive at the door in a frenzy of barking.

'Who's that?' Beth asked with a click of annoyance, 'If it's a parishioner, darling, you'll have to put them off. Tell them we're just on our way out.'

Martin silenced the dogs with a single sharp command and opened the door. Lotty, in denim skirt and skimpy top, sailed past before he could register his surprise and rushed towards her sister giving her a hug.

'Have you any wrapping paper?' she asked. 'Thank God you've not gone yet. I've driven like a bat out of hell. I forgot mother's present and I had the devil's own job finding something. I spent ages in that motorway service shop bloody dithering. The choice is hardly inspiring.' She remembered Martin and turned to him, grinning. 'How are you, Martin?' she enquired, 'Still giving them what-for from the pulpit?'

Beth intervened. Martin took Lotty's teasing well but it irritated her. It was time Lotty started behaving like an adult instead of a cheeky overgrown schoolgirl. 'Are you all right?' she asked, 'You look very tired.'

'Tired? You'd be tired if you'd just done that trip. The traffic was an absolute bitch. I've never seen so many caravans and tractors. What the hell are tractors doing on roads anyway? They should be in fields.'

John and Paul were standing staring, overwhelmed by their aunt's sheer exuberance and her appalling naughty language. 'Would you see if you could find some paper, Martin?' Beth asked, 'In the cupboard in the sitting room I think.'

Martin went to find it and they stood awkwardly in the hall a moment. Beth couldn't get over how *thin* Lotty was. It only served to emphasise her own generous curves.

'Hi you two!' Lotty turned her attention to the boys, fishing in her bag and producing some sweets. 'Are you allowed these before dinner?' She didn't wait for an answer but tossed them over. Turning her back on the boys, she finally confronted Beth.

'You look blooming,' she said drily. 'How's mother? She's seemed a bit odd the last few times I've talked to her on the phone. Not that you can have a proper conversation with her. She keeps on at me about Max. She will not accept that he . . .' she seemed to remember that little boys have big ears and grimaced instead.

'Mother's very well,' Beth said with a little smile, 'Busy I think.

She's always dashing around whenever I call. Never has time for a sit down and a chat. Coffee mornings. That sort of thing. Occupational hazard for me too.'

Martin reappeared with wrapping paper and Lotty shrieked her delight. She opened her case and dug out the present, a slender vase. 'What do you think?' she said, 'Don't for God's sake tell her where I got it from. We can pretend it's from an up-market china shop.'

'She won't mind where it's from. It's lovely.' Beth was puzzled by Lotty. Something was wrong. She could tell by the forced gaiety. It was a family trait. None of them were any good at hiding their emotions.

She deliberately chose to go with Lotty on the drive to Fernlands. The little car was a tip, a continuation of the flat in Balaclava Street. Beth refrained from moving things but she had to sandwich her feet between various items on the floor. 'Have you heard from Sonia lately?' she enquired as Lotty led the way, Martin, the boys and the dogs following in the estate. 'She doesn't ring me very often. Apparently mother seems to think she might be working up to moving house.'

'Again? Where to this time? Is she ever satisfied?'

'Apparently not. What about William? Has he been in touch at all?'

'Not with me.' Lotty shook her head. 'Do you think he'll ever settle? Get himself a job for Christ's sake like normal people.'

Beth glanced at her. 'Lotty . . .?'

'Yes. Come on, out with it.'

Lotty would understand. Of all of them, Lotty would understand. She would not recoil in horror. She could tell Lotty what she had done and Lotty would not mind. Lotty would not mind in the least that her sister was a thief.

She hesitated. She could not tell her.

She could not tell anyone.

In any case, when she stopped being so selfish, thinking only of her own worries, she ought to spare a thought for her sister, try to find out what was worrying her.

As they turned into the tight awkward drive towards the house, they saw that Sonia had beaten them to it.

As usual.

7

Sonia had not driven straight to the house. She stopped just before the ferry crossing over to Hawkshead, pulling off into a little picnic area where the view of the lake was absolutely beautiful. She had forgotten quite how.

'Why have we stopped?' Sebastian stirred and yawned. He gave her a puzzled glance. 'We're nearly there. What's up?'

'Nothing.' Sonia stared down at the lake. When she was away from here, she rarely had time to think about it much. And every single time she caught her first glimpse of the lake and hills, she was struck as if by a leaded weight with its beauty. She and daddy had often walked along the lake shore, talking about this and that. Oh God, how she missed him. She could never come back here to live because the memories were too painful.

'Shall we take a stroll?' she suggested, 'A breath of fresh air. I need to talk to you before I face mummy.'

'I knew something was wrong,' he said, slamming his door and holding out his hand to her. 'Come on, let's walk through the woods.'

Sonia hesitated before following him. Her skirt had not been designed for clambering amidst woodland shrubbery but she knew it would only annoy Seb if she mentioned that. She did not want to annoy him because she had to tell him something that she knew he would not like.

At first a clump of trees and the slope itself hid Fernlands from view but then, a break in the trees and they could see a little of the house, essentially greeny-grey slate, imposing, glimpse its gardens, a blaze of colour amidst the green, and suddenly Sonia saw that it would be no easy matter to persuade her mother to leave all this.

'Seb . . .' she began, encouraging him onto firmer ground as her heels sank into the mossy dampness. 'Do you remember when you were away on business in Los Angeles? Last autumn, wasn't it? Well . . . whilst you were there, I had this phone call from a contact in the States. He's based in New York.'

'You never mentioned it.' He glanced sharply at her, his hair ruffled a little in the warm breeze from the lake shore. Above them, the sun relaxed and strengthened as the few clouds scudded off. 'Last autumn . . .? That's a long time ago.'

'Yes I know.' She took a deep breath, snagging her skirt on a sticking out branch. Hell! Fortunately, no harm done as she pulled it gently away. 'As I was saying, Seb . . . this contact has a friend who does the art work on *Quality Interiors*. That's an American glossy.'

'I know it,' he said to her surprise. 'Supposed to be up-market. Mainly California-based palatial mansions of the stars, that sort of thing. Vulgar. Why is it that film stars have next to no taste? You can't buy taste that's for sure.'

'You've seen a copy then?' Her heart sank. She might have known it. She supposed some of the houses featured were a touch crass but even so . . . she carried on quickly before she lost her nerve. 'To cut a long story short, they were interested in doing a feature, a four-page spread, on an English interior designer. Me as a matter of fact.'

He smiled. 'Marvellous. Just what you need to get yourself noticed. A bit of exposure even if it is a terrible magazine. How about this country house you're doing at the moment? They'll love that. It's got a nice bit of history attached to it, too. Drop a few aristocratic connections, that'll go down a treat.'

'It's too late.' From their higher vantage point, she stared at the lake, watching as the gentle waves rippled and broke to shore. 'That's what I intended to happen. But I invited the photographer and the journalist round for tea to discuss things and when they saw our house, they were thrilled. They thought it too cute for words. They called it *small*, Seb. A London town house. They so wanted to use it and I could hardly be awkward and say no, could I? And it would have looked ridiculous if I'd asked to have a word with you first. They were ready to start there and then and they work to very tight schedules. If I'd said no, they'd have just asked someone else. They have no loyalty.'

'What?' She saw and flinched from the anger in his eyes. 'Let's get this straight. You're telling me that our home, our *home* dammit, is blazoned across that magazine.' He turned to her, not caring that he was shouting because there was nobody to hear. 'Every bloody detail down to what lavatory paper we use. How could you, Sonia? You know how much I value my privacy. I don't want every Tom, Dick or Harry knowing that we happen to have the most disgustingly opulent bathroom in London. What the hell business is it of theirs? I hope you didn't let them anywhere near my study.'

There was a small silence. 'You did. Damn it, Sonia, you did. That's the last straw. You let strangers into my study, mauling around, snooping, let them photograph my desk, my bloody chair, without even bothering to consult me. I've got highly confidential papers in there, for God's sake.'

'Confidential papers? Who do you think you are, Seb, a cabinet minister? You've got a lot of car magazines as far as I can see. Let's walk back.' She set off without him, furious herself. 'I knew you'd overreact,' she said when he caught her up. 'Who's going to see it anyway? Certainly none of your wonderful business colleagues or any of our friends. Since when do any of them read third-rate American glossies?' She relented a little as she saw his face. 'Sorry. I know I should have told you at the time. I promise you'll be delighted when you see it. It looks charming. Stunning. It's easily the best feature in the summer edition. We should be proud of our home. It's not as if we live in a slum like Lotty.'

'Is it out yet?' he asked, his features losing a little of their initial annoyance.

'Yes it is. That's why I thought I'd better tell you,' she admitted. 'Just in case you saw it by accident.'

She was trying hard not to be intensely irritated at his attitude. Sometimes it seemed as if they were on a collision course. The old, old story of course. Sebastian didn't realise, even now, how important her career was to her. He still treated it as if it were a little pin-money part-time job when in reality she was ever expanding, with another shop in the offing specialising in their quality fabrics and wallpapers. More staff, more scope and also, more responsibility.

Just occasionally, like now, she wondered why they'd bothered to get married after years of living together. It had pleased Beth of course but you didn't get married just to please your sister.

'You've a nerve, Sebastian Matheson,' she told him coldly, 'Such a fuss! Do I ever complain about the things you do to further your business? All the time spent at the office, all these damned trips that leave me high and dry. What am I supposed to do while you're away enjoying yourself?'

'I don't enjoy myself on business trips and you've only yourself to blame,' he said, not giving an inch, 'You've never the time to come with me. You never help me a jot with my career so why should I bend over backwards to help you? We're on our own, Sonia. On this last trip, all the wives were there. I was like a lost soul at the receptions. It looks bad. It shows a total lack of support.'

'Didn't Jessica go along?' she asked sweetly, 'Couldn't she stand in?'

'She came along purely in the business sense. She's our Marketing Manager for heaven's sake. If you're suggesting that Jessica and I are anything other than colleagues, darling, you're way off the mark.'

'Am I?' She felt a moment's doubt. Had she been mistaken then? 'You can hardly blame me for thinking it, can you?'

The bitter words hissed between them, the calm beauty of the scene as they reached a clearing, saw the lake below, totally lost on them.

'You won't let me forget one mistake, will you?' he said, 'One bloody indiscretion with . . . Anne, wasn't it? I forget her name, that's how important it was . . . and you keep on about it. I don't know why we bothered to get married,' he went on, echoing her own thoughts, 'We were better off living together. Being married doesn't matter because you won't give me children. All that stuff in the marriage service about procreation. It's a sham for us.'

'We *agreed*,' she yelled, finally losing patience. 'We neither of us wanted children. We just wanted each other.'

'And I changed my mind,' he said. 'I'd like a son.'

'Oh come on, Seb . . .' she softened her voice, feeling, not for the first time, that their love was on shifting sand. It wouldn't take much for it to blow away on the wind. She didn't know why it was so important to her that it didn't. Sebastian was a difficult obstinate man to live with. 'You'd have been a hopeless father,' she said, unwisely perhaps but trying to smile him back into a happier mood. 'Just as I would be a hopeless mother. Babies are just sick and poo machines. Then they grow up into toddlers with tantrums and before you know it they're surly teenagers. You end up with your life revolving round them. It is not my idea of fun.'

'We could have a nanny,' he argued and Sonia looked at him, realising quite suddenly that this was the root of their problem, not the magazine article. This baby thing was beginning to obsess him. 'You're still young enough to try,' he added, 'Thirty five's not old these days for a first baby.'

'Thirty six. Thirty seven by the time I had it. I can't do it,' she said flatly, 'I am not prepared to bring a child into this world when I don't want one. You can't just change your mind, Seb, about something as important as that.'

'The sooner we get to France the better,' he said as they reached the car at last. 'It's nearing forty that does it. I suddenly feel bloody old.'

'What about poor mummy? Fifty five tomorrow.' Sonia sighed, deftly avoiding a patch of mud by the door of the car. 'She can't be too happy about that.' She eyed him closely. Thank goodness he seemed to have got over the worst as far as the article went, 'Sorry about the magazine thing,' she said quietly, 'My fault. I shan't do anything like that again without consulting you first.'

He grunted, climbing back into the car. They drove the remaining very short distance in silence, Sebastian irritating her even more by insisting on getting out to make sure she didn't bop the stone posts of the drive. He was likely to be in a baby sulk all weekend, Sonia thought unhappily. Most of their arguments these days were about their respective jobs. She knew he was under a lot of stress but then so was she. Of the two of them, she imagined she handled it better.

She believed also in thinking about the worst scenarios so that you were moderately prepared if they happened. She already knew what she would do if profits plummeted and it became necessary to close one of the shops and reduce staff, and, on a more personal note, she had often considered what she would do if Sebastian left her. Would she go to pieces like Lotty obviously had? Lotty had flapped about like a fish out of water, a foul-mouthed fish at that.

She thought she would handle it better, come out of it with some dignity. She had the business to keep her on track. But she would miss Seb. He was still capable of making her heart thud as in the way of romantic novels, could be amazingly gentle with her, make her feel pretty and feminine, and even the occasional rows injected her with a warm feeling. She loved him. However, she did not regret her stance on the baby. Under no circumstances was she ever going through that. Every time you switched on the television these days, there was some unfortunate woman screaming on a delivery table.

'No sign of Laura,' Seb observed as they stopped on the drive. 'Looks like we're first here as usual.'

'She's probably out on the verandah. She likes to sit out there. She'll have heard the car. Don't mention France,' she warned him, taking in her first sight of the house and garden with some pleasure. It never changed. She would miss it, too, when they stopped coming.

'Leave the timing of that to me . . . darling.' She tried the endearment tentatively to see if she was forgiven.

He said nothing, reaching into the boot for their suitcases. Leaving him to cope with the lot, Sonia walked to the porch, rang the bell, opened the door and announced that it was only them.

8 ∫

Laura had spent the afternoon relaxing on the verandah that stretched the length of the side of the house that fronted the lake. She loved the verandah with its wall of fresh air, ivy interspersed with clematis twisting round the stone pillars, and often in summer she breakfasted out here. With its cream rocking chair, her favourite, and other wicker furniture, bright cushions and hardy plants, it was where she liked to sit and while away sunny hours. Living so close to the lake when the children were small had, of course, been a hazard but George had instilled in them a respect for water and the dangers associated with it and, after all, they had survived. Slipping over the lake in their modest sailing dinghy had been one of their favourite pastimes.

Later in the afternoon, Don rang from the airport before he boarded and she was reminded by his voice just how much he had come to mean to her. He was everything George had not been. George had been a wonderful man of course. Didn't everyone say that? But . . . something was lacking and Don had succeeded in showing her just what. Excitement. Ardour. Humour even, for George had been quite an earnest sort of man.

It was ridiculous that it should have happened like this but there it was and one day she would have to break the news to the children, tell them about Don before they found out from another source, but not this weekend. This weekend must be got through with the minimum of disturbance. She was aiming fairly and squarely for harmony.

She roused herself at last from a pleasant slumber and went indoors just in time to hear Sonia and Sebastian arriving.

They had had a row. She could tell that from their posture, their bright eyes, their very cheerful voices. She told them that coffee and biscuits would be in the sitting room when they were ready, told them they were in the turret room and left them to it. She was not one to fuss.

Sebastian was first down, making his usual appreciative noises about the room and the view of the carefully tended gardens, taking a seat opposite her on one of the two pale lemon striped sofas, his arm casually stretched along the top.

'Nice to see you again, Laura,' he said with a smile, helping himself to coffee. 'Sonia won't be long, she's just finishing unpacking. As usual, she's brought everything but the kitchen sink.'

'For two days?' Laura demurred. She wished she could find it in her heart to like her son-in-law more. She couldn't put her finger on why she didn't like him. He was always courteous, handsome, successful. And he seemed to adore Sonia. 'How was your business trip?' she asked politely, 'Sonia said when I telephoned that you were away in the States again.'

'I only got back last night or was it this morning? Feels like I've lost a day out of my life. I'm feeling a bit whacked in fact, Laura. A successful outcome though. It went well, thanks.' His smile, polite enough, meant he had no wish to discuss it further. Laura did not mind. She was only making small talk and she found his kind of business, computer related, particularly boring. She was happy to leave her business affairs in the hands of her accountant, although now that Don had arrived on the scene, she might well let him deal with things.

'How does it feel to be fifty five?' Seb suddenly asked with a grin.

'Not until tomorrow,' she reminded him, returning his smile. 'Actually, Sebastian, it feels all right. At the moment I'm feeling rather pleased with myself.'

'Good. You don't look your age and I mean that,' he said in that easygoing way of his. He was a good liar if he was lying. If George were here, he could be relied upon to tell her the blunt truth. Not only had George not been one for the throwaway compliment, he had also been distressingly candid at times. Don never mentioned age. He just called her his lovely darling. 'Take

my advice,' Seb went on, 'See your birthday as a challenge. Do
something different. I always think birthdays are a good time to
sit back and take stock.'

'I may well do that,' she said impishly, 'I'll let you know later
what I decide.'

'Decide what, mummy?' Sonia asked, entering the room with a
flourish, a red chiffon scarf draped round the waist of a black linen
jump suit. Red flatties. A small red handbag. She had changed,
Laura noted with amusement, from the chic skirt and top she
had worn for driving. The first of many changes this weekend,
no doubt.

Laura ignored the question. 'You look very well, dear,' she
said. 'You obviously thrive on hard work. Sebastian says you are
extremely busy these days.'

'Yes I am.' Sonia sat down close beside her husband and,
perceptive as ever to moods, Laura noticed the friction that
fairly fizzled between them. A tiff that was all. Sonia was such
a sensitive child as befitted her creative leanings.

'Have you heard from William recently, mummy?' she asked,
accepting the cup Sebastian offered her with a smile. 'Thank you,
darling.'

'Quite recently.' Laura had no intention of quoting dates. Why
couldn't William write more? It was simply a question of putting
pen to paper and sticking a stamp on. 'He was on his way to
Australia.'

Sonia snorted her disapproval. 'I suppose he's still hanging
about with that funny crowd, is he? They are disgusting. Did I
ever tell you about the time he came to visit?'

Laura believed she had but she merely smiled, not wanting to
spoil Sonia's obvious glee in retelling the tale.

'It was the middle of the afternoon and I'd just popped home
to collect some papers when there was this ring at the door and
when I opened it . . .' her eyes glowed at the awfulness of it,
'there was this trio of tramps or buskers standing there. They
were carrying musical instruments anyway. I was just about to
get my purse to give them something when one of them grabbed
me and hugged me. William of course. Can you imagine what I
felt like?'

'He couldn't help it. He's hardly got en suite facilities when he's living rough,' Sebastian said and Laura could have hugged *him* for that small observation. She hated people to criticise her son. William adored his sisters and was so proud of them and, dammit, they ought to try to understand him more. Even Beth. Especially Beth. 'I envy him his freedom,' Seb went on thoughtfully. 'Working for your living can be a drag.'

'I've never had to work for my living,' Laura said before she could stop herself. 'Other than helping my father in the surgery for a short time when I left school. And then when I married your father . . .'

'You helped him in *his* surgery,' Sonia said with a sigh. 'How adventurous, mummy. A doctor's daughter marries a doctor.'

Laura frowned at Sonia's tone, tempted to tell her not to be cheeky. 'I suppose I've been lucky,' she said instead.

'Lucky? What are you talking about, mummy?' Sonia's voice had acquired the familiar cross tone. 'Don't you have *any* ambitions? I know it's hardly your fault you married so ridiculously early and started having us straight away. Obviously it put a certain restriction on your life but you could still do something even at your age. It's not too late.'

'Thank you, dear,' Laura said sweetly. 'You could say I have done something. I brought you into the world for one.'

'Oh that . . .' Sonia dismissed it. 'What I mean is that you could start afresh. Somewhere completely different. Give your life a completely new direction.'

'Have you ever thought of emigrating?' Sebastian asked and Laura was quick to notice the sly glance he and Sonia exchanged. What were these two up to? Sonia was blessedly devious and quite unscrupulous once she got an idea in her head.

'No, I have not,' she said. 'It must take tremendous nerve to do that. Pioneer spirit I suppose and I regret I don't have it. William has, doesn't he?'

'Have you ever thought of moving at all then?' Sonia asked, her hands casually folded in her lap, a quite innocent expression on her face. 'From Fernlands? It is a bit large for you, mummy, here all on your own.'

'It's odd you should say that, darling, because . . .'

Sonia looked at her, smiled encouragingly, but they were

interrupted by the ringing of the bell, followed immediately by the arrival of the others.

As Laura went to greet them, the dogs flew past her into the sitting room and Laura heard Sonia's cry of exasperation.

9

'Thank you for volunteering me to do the dishes,' Sonia said drily, glancing at Beth who looked much more at home in the kitchen than in the splendour of the dining room. 'Why doesn't she have a dishwasher? She's so out of date.'

The dinner had been lovely and even the formality of Martin saying Grace had been accomplished with slightly less embarrassment than previously when Sonia had forgotten to warn Seb about it and Seb had joined Lotty in a fit of giggles. Beth's boys had behaved admirably even though they said they preferred Instant Whip to the Mint Bavarois mummy had made. The dogs had had their dinners, too, and were now in their baskets, slumbering, although Sonia had a funny feeling they weren't really asleep and could spring into action at any moment.

'How quaint! I can't remember the last time I washed dishes,' she said as she plunged her hands into the hot soapy water, dallying with the first plate.

'Would you like me to do that? I have more experience than you. I don't have a dishwasher either,' Beth said, armed with clean tea-towel, hovering at Sonia's side.

'No. I shall do it.' Sonia smiled, trying to avert her gaze from the truly awful dress her sister was wearing. Quite a pretty blue but the style was too old for her. Frumpish. Beth should learn to steer clear of floral prints. They did absolutely nothing for her at all, other than emphasise her size. And she just had no idea how to wear Grandma Howard's pearls. The cameo brooch she had inherited was lovely but she wished she had had the pearls instead. She would have worn them with tremendous panache.

'Is Lotty all right, do you think?' she asked, reaching languidly for the next plate. 'I think she looks a little out of sorts. And she wasn't flashing her eyes at Seb as much as usual.'

'Really Sonia!' Beth flushed scarlet, barely able to control her impatience at the leisurely rate her sister was working.

'I think there might be a new man in her life,' Sonia continued, after a moment's thought. 'About time. She doesn't strike me as the sort of person who'll be on her own for long. Shall we ask her? I'm tempted but I know she'll bite my head off. It'll sound better if you ask. You're awfully discreet. You can make it sound as if you're concerned about her spiritual health. Something like that.'

'No. I couldn't possibly. It's a private matter. You know she's touchy about her personal life.'

'Oh . . . that. So is Sebastian. He won't let anyone set foot in his study. It's off bounds even to the cleaning lady. Such a nuisance. In fact, I've really put my foot in it, Elizabeth. He was in a foul mood just before we got here.' Sonia glanced at her, deciding that, as Beth was in the church, more or less, it would be a confessional experience to tell her about it. She explained about the magazine article and how upset he had been, although she refrained from telling Beth about the baby thing. That was indeed private, something she and Seb had to sort out. In any case, Beth would take Seb's side. The sanctity of new life and all that.

'As I see it, you've apologised and he's accepted your apology,' Beth said when she had finished telling the tale. 'It's regrettable but it's better that you cleared the air. There's a great danger in bottling things up.'

Sonia held a plate up for inspection. 'And I suppose you never do? Bottle things up?'

'Well . . . I never have in the past.' Beth looked round and lowered her voice, 'Martin and I don't have secrets. But . . . I do have a problem at the moment, Sonia.'

'*You* have a problem.' Sonia smiled affectionately at her. 'What hope is there for the rest of us then? You're happily married, you have two darling boys . . .' she hoped that Beth did not notice the touch of sarcasm, 'What then? Your weight, is it?'

Beth looked as if she was about to cry and, too late, Sonia cringed, aware she was occasionally insensitive particularly where her little sister was concerned. Surely Beth was used to it by now? She'd always been ... well ... the plump one.

'My weight does bother me a bit,' she said quietly restrained, 'But the real reason I worry is money. Martin just doesn't understand about money. He hasn't a clue, Sonia.'

'Vicars never do,' Sonia said, looking with disgust at the now distinctly grimy water. She let the plug out and smiled again at her sister. Poor love! She had only herself to blame, however. She might have known, marrying a country parson, she'd end up poor as the proverbial church mouse. She ought to have settled for a bishop at least. 'Vicars live on a different level than the rest of us, don't they? Too preoccupied with holy matters to worry about money.'

'That's uncalled for. Martin hates that kind of talk. He's a very down to earth sort of man. Oh, for goodness sake, let me do the rest of them or we'll be here until next week. You do the drying.'

Sonia was happy to agree, the novelty of washing up having rapidly lost its charm. They exchanged places and Beth rolled up her sleeves and set to work with a vengeance with the speed of the expert.

'Martin thinks money grows on trees,' she continued. 'We just about scrape the school fees together but it's such a struggle.'

'Oh I see. I'd forgotten about that.' Sonia took up her position by the steaming dish rack, fluttering a tea-towel. School fees must be horrendous. She and Seb would of course be able to afford them but it would mean a considerable dent in their income and fewer holidays. Last year, apart from Sebastian's business trips, they had had two major holidays and half a dozen weekend breaks. And there were the clothes. She'd have to kiss goodbye to the designer labels and Seb would have to start buying his shirts from Marks & Spencer like everyone else. 'Don't these places have discount schemes?' she asked helpfully, 'Does this school have a resident vicar or whatever? Can't Martin offer to be a consultant on religious affairs and, in return, bargain that the children go for half price?'

'Certainly not. He has no time anyway. Contrary to what people think, he is kept very busy. He gets very involved with his work, Sonia, too much sometimes. Very personally involved with his flock as it were.'

'Beth . . .' Sonia was losing interest in Martin's laudable and no doubt essential attributes. She would tell Beth about the chateau. She was less optimistic now than before she arrived. Mummy and Fernlands went together and mummy seemed remarkably cheerful and bouncy this evening. Springing on her the plans for her old age seemed dreadfully inappropriate.

'How much is this house worth?' she asked out loud, causing Beth to pause in her soapy endeavours. 'Do you think we could persuade mummy to sell?'

Lotty stood it for as long as she could. Then . . . 'Mind if I smoke?' she asked, the question directed to her mother because she knew that both Sebastian and Martin occasionally indulged. 'I've cut down,' she lied, seeing her mother's exasperation, 'Only ten a day. Less some days.'

'If you must . . .'

'Thanks. I must . . .' Lotty lit up, ignoring Seb's bemused glance. Thank God the meal was over. That mint pudding thing had made her want to puke and, if you didn't eat everything she put in front of you, mother got huffy, wanting to know what was wrong with it. Sonia had held court as usual. The business of course. The boring business of doing up the beautiful homes of beautiful, boring people who had nothing better to do with their time than flutter around with swatches of fabric.

And, during the course of the meal, someone, Seb wasn't it, had mentioned dad in passing and that always did things to her. She still half expected him to walk through the door, smile at her, ruffle up her hair. It was as if he was still here. She was half inclined to believe in the concept of ghosts and, if by some chance he was watching over them now, what would he make of it all? He'd be pleased that mother was bearing up so well, blooming in fact. Lotty could swear she looked younger and fitter than she had a year ago. Eyes bright. Hair in a new short and very classy style, freshly streaked surely. She was wearing a red silk blouse, an unusual choice for her, and with the long black crepe skirt it looked lovely.

Since Sonia and Beth had disappeared into the kitchen, mother had talked non-stop and then, quite casually, she had dropped the bombshell. She was learning to drive.

'I don't know what's put that idea into your head, mother,' Lotty said, crossing her legs and balancing the ashtray somehow on her knee. 'Learning to drive at your age? What a daft idea! You'd be best to leave well alone. You've managed all these years so why the sudden need?' She pulled a face as Sebastian laughed. 'Tell her she's being silly, Seb. The roads are deadly out there. The summer traffic round here is awful and she'll never be able to find anywhere to park when she goes into Bowness. Will she?' She looked helplessly towards the men for support, got none. 'You need all your wits about you to be let loose on these roads.'

'Are you suggesting I won't be capable,' Laura asked and Lotty sighed, recognising the stubborn sound in the voice. She could be just like Sonia sometimes.

'You're treading on dangerous ground, Lotty,' Seb said lightly, 'Martin and I are fully in favour, aren't we?'

'Indeed. I must say I'm surprised at you, Lotty,' Martin said, smiling in that irritatingly smug way of his. 'I'm sure that Beth will think it a jolly good idea.'

'Only because she acts like a taxi service at the moment,' Lotty said heatedly, waving a hand towards her mother who had reacted hotly too. 'Oh . . . all right . . . I can see I'm outnumbered but for God's sake get yourself some proper lessons. No tinpot amateur. Teaching anything is bloody difficult.'

'And there speaks the expert,' Seb said and Lotty could have hit him. Sarcastic sod!

Just at that moment, probably fortunately, Sonia and Beth returned from their domestic duties, flushed and triumphant. As soon as the driving was mentioned, they came down in favour as did Seb and Martin leaving Lotty alone in her opposition.

She supposed she sulked the rest of the evening, or at least she didn't take much part in what followed. Beth disappeared to get the boys ready for bed returning minus them but with the dogs this time. Why was it that Beth always seemed to be accompanied by others? Why was she so fat when she was forever up and down like a yo-yo? Lotty hated herself for thinking that. Could you credit it? Here she was, scraggy, more than happy to take on Beth's extra pounds . . . it didn't make sense.

Television was taboo on the birthday weekend, sitting sulking in the corner, so they played Monopoly which they'd played when they were children. It was dropping to bits but mother refused to buy a new one.

The game followed the usual pattern, good-natured to begin with before degenerating almost into a slanging match. Sonia, competitively honed and not giving anyone an inch, won, closely followed by Seb who was obviously irritated as hell. Martin looking a bit surprised was next, and Lotty only a bit behind him when she hadn't even been trying. Mother tried to cheat so that Beth was not last but of course she *was* last. Beth got herself in a complete fluster when it came to board games.

The hot drink ritual followed, the choice offered bewildering. Lotty excused herself and went up to bed, carrying her cocoa with her. She shut the door of her little room, the past closing instantly around her, stood a while looking out of her window onto the darkening hills. It was times like this when she missed Max the most. Max would have supported her about the driving idea. Mother was far too vague and polite to be put behind a steering wheel. The idea was preposterous.

She wanted to talk. Discuss the others. Quietly. Have their cocoa, a smoke, and talk.

She finished her cocoa, checked her watch and headed for the bathroom. The rota system was in operation as it always was when they were all here. One bathroom. An enormous house like this and one measly chilly bathroom. Lotty deliberately hijacked half of Sonia's allotted time causing her to rap agitatedly on the door. She took her time completing her ablutions, opening the door at last and sweeping past her silkily swathed sister totally unrepentant.

She left the curtains undrawn, wanting to see the moonlight slithering through trees towards the house. She could feel the presence of the lake, dark and forbidding now. Parts of it were very very deep. They'd dragged her along onto the lake, sailing, but her heart had never been in it and she had pretended enjoyment because her father and Sonia had loved it.

Sleep was long in coming, the bed too damned soft and comfortable. Poor mother was gutted that that thoughtless brother of theirs had forgotten to send a birthday card, unless one arrived tomorrow. If not, it would put the damper on the rest of the weekend.

Lotty plumped up the pillows on her narrow childhood bed, looked up at the familiar ceiling . . . no cobwebs there . . . and lay quietly, willing sleep. The summer air, with only a hint of chill, plunged in through the open window and she breathed it slowly until at last, just as her mother's birthday dawned, she fell asleep.

In the small room she'd moved into after George died, Laura, too, couldn't sleep for a long time. She tried to read a few pages of her paperback romance but her heart was not in it. She couldn't concentrate. She wasn't being overly sentimental about Don was she? Snatching at romance before it was altogether too late? She'd rather missed out on romance for George had been a bit shy about things like that. Oh . . . he had never forgotten her birthday but he had rarely surprised her as Don frequently did with little gifts for no reason. The red silk blouse, scented a little now with her favourite perfume, lay on the chair beside the bed, a reminder of him.

All in all, she thought it had gone rather well this evening. If George were here, he would of course be worried about Lotty. If George had been here, at the time of the break-up, Laura thought he might have done something about it. He and Max had got on quite well and George might have talked to him, persuaded him that Lotty was worth the persevering.

Gritty child. She always had been, the one who would not cry when she fell and grazed her knee. A trembling lip would be about it. Tough nut. The least feminine, she supposed, of all the girls, disinclined to wear the pretty little dresses she used to buy for them. Nowadays of course little girls seemed to live in jeans and the like, the frilly dresses appearing only on special occasions. She wished one of Beth's children had been a girl, a granddaughter, although of course she would never ever say a word. The likelihood of her having a granddaughter seemed to be getting slimmer. Beth couldn't afford another child and neither Sonia nor Lotty looked likely to have one. And, as for William . . .

She ought to have mentioned Don this evening. In passing. She had, as Lotty would have put it, chickened out. She could have broken it gently, so that they knew *of* him when eventually the true nature of their relationship was revealed. In the darkness, she smiled a little. She wasn't frightened of her own children, was she?

Not frightened.

But nervous of their reaction.

As Don had once said, quite bluntly, it didn't matter a damn what they thought.

But, of course, it did.

10

Lotty slept fitfully and awoke very early. She gave up all attempts to doze off again, tossing back the covers and leaping out of bed, putting a dressing gown over the old tee-shirt that was her attire when sleeping alone.

It was chilly and she realised why. A cool draught was blowing through one of the windows that had been left open. She ought to have shut it before she went to sleep. Her mother had this obsession with fresh air! Fresh air and minimum heating. This house was like a bloody fridge in winter. Shutting the window, she saw that it had started to rain, the kind of Lakes rain that looked set for the rest of the day. Good. That would put an end to the early morning walk or rather she would be able to get out of it more easily.

Why had her mother put her in here, her old room? Was it some sort of punishment for her marriage failing? She and Max usually occupied one of the little-used guest rooms at the side of the house with a pretty bay window and window seat. This room was making her tearful and it also made her feel sixteen again. Sixteen and full of hopes for the future. Sixteen and she didn't know Max Crabtree existed. Pity she couldn't start again and this time Max would definitely not feature. She ought never to have met his eyes across that crowded room at that party and certainly never have encouraged him to walk across to her, engage in that witty conversation he was so damned good at. He had hooked her in one!

Thinking of Max reminded her of the letter. Pushing at her dishevelled hair, she took it from her bag and opened it. Might as well see what the sod had to say for himself.

The first words made her heart skip a beat. She sank onto the bed and read it.

'My dearest Lotty,' he had written, 'I'm glad you decided to read this instead of throwing it away. I couldn't blame you if you had. What can I say, my darling? I made a mistake, a bad one, and I'm so miserable I don't know what to do. It's over with her and that must please you to know you were right and it didn't work. I know I've been a bastard, Lotty, and I know this will sound corny but I can't think of any other way of saying it.

'Here goes then. I'm sorry and I want us to try again. Please. It's not too late. Awkward and expensive but we can back out of things now and start again. I'll do whatever you want. Move up to Lancashire or you can move here. I've got this flat, not much, but an improvement on Balaclava Street. I'll let you think about it and then, some time soon, I'll call you. Okay? Are you going to be able to forgive me, my precious? I'm not sure I can go on without you. All my love, Max.'

She crunched the letter up, dropped it back in her bag. Who the hell wrote his scripts? Nevertheless, a perverse satisfaction settled on her. If he thought she would drop everything and go running back to him . . . A little sob caught at her throat and she stifled it. He had caused her such anguish. She wanted him back, of course she did, but how could she? How could she admit, without a huge loss of personal dignity, that she couldn't function properly without him either? He expected too much of her.

And now there was the baby. They were all looking at her oddly, especially mother. They suspected something was wrong but nobody was saying anything. Sonia and Beth were whispering together. And mother seemed to have taken leave of her senses. She was oddly skittish. Sparkling somehow. Eyes shining. She hadn't had a facelift, had she? Surely not. Mother wasn't the sort who'd pay out for that.

She went to the window and watched the day break. Such as it was. Gloomy. Pity that it should rain for mother's birthday. She got the vase out, ready to take down. They would hand over the presents after breakfast, another bloody tradition. The house was very quiet, still sleeping. Carefully, so as not to awaken anyone, she carried her clothes through to the bathroom and ran a steaming bath. Huge and old-fashioned the bathroom.

You'd think mother would have had a new suite. It wasn't as if she couldn't afford to make changes but she seemed reluctant to do so.

She threw off her nightwear and looked at herself in the mirror. She didn't look pregnant, not in the least, other than a slight change in her breasts. There was no reason why she should yet for the embryo was still minute, the diddiest blob. But it was growing by the second and the thought made her shiver. She had to get on with doing something fast. She had to speak to mother and get the money. Once she had done that, she could book the appointment and get it over with. She needed cash. It wasn't the sort of thing you could pay for by credit card. Perhaps it was but handing over surreptitious fivers seemed more appropriate.

She found herself clutching her stomach protectively as she lay in the bath. For the first time, something prodded at her, a feeling. She hastily snuffed it out. Now was not the time to start thinking about a baby, a proper baby rather than an embryo, a baby with fluffy hair and little fingers that curled round yours, a baby that she and Max had so wanted.

There was no time for doubts. She was doing the right thing. She would make a lousy mother.

The others, bundled up in waterproofs, were out of the house at eight o'clock for their walk. Lotty watched them go without envy, the dogs bounding gloriously ahead, and turned back into the sitting room where Sebastian was reading the paper.

'What was your excuse?' she asked him, 'I said I was just recovering from a nasty cold and couldn't risk getting another what with the exams coming up at school.'

He put the paper down. 'I'm expecting an urgent call,' he said with a grin, 'I've given them this number this week-end.'

'At eight o'clock in the morning?' Lotty smiled. 'I'm surprised Sonia went along so willingly. She had to wear wellies that didn't match her coat you know. The supreme sacrifice. Colour unco-ordination!'

'Don't be a bitch, Lotty. She wanted a chat with Laura,' he said, folding the paper in a very deliberate fashion. 'Come and talk to me . . .' he patted the sofa beside him, 'You and I haven't talked in a long time.'

She glanced wryly at him, before joining him on the sofa. Not too close.

'How are things between you and Sonia?' she asked abruptly, 'I hope you've decided to stay faithful to her in future, you swine?'

'That's none of your business, Lotty,' he said, not too offended, 'Did she tell you about that?'

'No. I guessed that's all.' She looked at him earnestly, 'Stick at it, Seb. It just causes an awful mess if you split up. Take me and Max for instance. Oh, by the way . . . he wants me back.'

'Does he?' He raised his eyebrows, 'Is that good or bad?'

'I don't know yet. I only read the letter this morning.' She took a cigarette from the packet, offering him one which he declined. 'You don't mind?' She lit the cigarette and tried to think it through. Calmly and sensibly. Max was right to give her time. Her first reaction was that she would not go back to him but now, mentioning it to Seb, was making her reconsider. She was pretty fed up with living alone in that crummy flat. Max had never actually lived there for she had moved out of their previous place but he had seen it once. He was right. It was on the edge of slumminess. The area was bearing up with more clean curtains than otherwise, but it was struggling.

'What do you think I should do?' she asked Sebastian, taking a sidelong glance at him. He was looking great this morning in tight jeans and a heavyweight dark sweater. Freshly shaved. Smelling very clean and very male.

'You really want my opinion?' he laughed shortly, 'That's funny. I can barely manage my own marriage let alone advise you on yours. And I'd have thought I'd be the last person to talk about Max. You know damned well we didn't get on. He was jealous as hell of my success.' His smile was irritatingly smug. 'Never really made the big time in his line, did he?'

'Don't push it,' Lotty said. She wasn't in the mood for an argument with Seb. 'Beth's the only one of us who has what you might call a good marriage,' she mused, 'Against all the odds. Mother was never keen on it. You know what she thinks about Martin and all that stuff. He's making absolutely no impression on her and he must be pig-sick. Did you see her face when he was saying Grace?'

'Certainly not. I had my eyes closed.'

They laughed and fell silent a moment, Lotty puffing enjoyably on her cigarette.

'I do wonder about it sometimes,' Seb said at last, 'The religion thing. Maybe there's something in it if it gives you peace of mind. Martin looks hellish relaxed. Sometimes I'm so damned busy I don't know what day it is. Deadlines. Everybody's so frantic in my business and you can't let your guard down or you might get stabbed in the back. You've got to be up to the minute, ahead of it if possible.'

'You should try teaching,' Lotty said with a short unconvincing laugh, 'It's soul destroying, Seb. There are kids out there, at Dockside, who have potential but, largely because their parents don't give a toss, that potential is going to be squashed flat. The parents don't even bother to turn up at parents' evenings that's how much they care. I have this girl in one of my classes . . . she's called Jade Entwistle . . .'

Sebastian laughed. 'Sorry . . . it's just the combination of names.'

'I know.' Lotty managed a smile, 'Jade Entwistle is bright, Seb. Quick to grasp facts. Desperate for knowledge. A teacher's dream. And yet . . .' she wanted to go on, but she caught his look, sensed he might be bored. Sebastian, after all, was singularly uninterested in children. 'Enough of that,' she said, 'Let's talk about something else. How's Sonia's business? Another shop I hear? Tunbridge Wells isn't it? I don't ask her myself, Seb, not because I'm not interested but because she's very suspicious of me, thinks I'm being patronising. She's awfully defensive about her job.'

'She feels vulnerable I suppose,' he said. 'I don't think she can quite believe how well it's all going. Our house is being featured in an American magazine.' Family pride surfaced. 'I have to concede that she's done it up well. It's got a very distinct style. It's very Sonia Matheson . . . hits you as soon as you walk through the door. *Before* you walk through the door. We're the only house with special effect lighting even in the porch.' He glanced round the room. 'This needs brightening up, don't you think? But then Laura likes pale shades, doesn't she?'

Lotty shrugged, noncommital. She quite liked this room.

'Should I commission Sonia to do up my flat?' she asked, smiling with him at the ridiculous notion. 'Assuming I could afford her prices that is.' For a moment, she thought she detected a spark of interest in those bold eyes of his and instinctively moved away. No further complications please.

'Sebastian . . .?' she stubbed the cigarette out before reaching a decision. 'You couldn't possibly lend me some money, could you? I wouldn't ask . . .' she went on, rushing the words before she lost courage, 'But it is very important. If I can't get hold of the money, God knows what I'm going to do.'

'I will have that cigarette, thanks.' He took one from her and she lit another immediately for herself. 'I thought there was something,' he said. 'Sonia said you were worried too. What is it? I might be able to help.'

'Can you lend me some money? That's the only way you can help.'

'How much, darling?'

She told him and he whistled. 'Lotty, you have to believe me that I would if I could. I'd really like to help because . . . dammit, I like you.' To her embarrassment, he leaned across and, a little absently, patted her hand. *Liked* her! Had she been wrong all this time? She'd always thought that Seb lusted after her. 'I know it might sound as if Sonia and I are rolling in it but, financially, we run a pretty tight ship. My own money's tied up in various stocks and shares. I can hardly scrape together fifty pounds ready cash at a time. Crazy, isn't it? I pay for every damned thing with plastic.'

She believed him. He wasn't just making excuses. She fell silent and they both gave a sigh and contemplated the quiet splendour of the room. Outside, the rain was persistent, a little heavier if anything, sweeping across the lawns, the lake itself scarcely visible in the wet gloom, the hills beyond not visible at all.

'Aren't you curious as to what the money's for?' she asked, resigning herself to having to ask her mother. 'It's the first thing mum will want to know.'

'I'm sure it's for a very good reason,' he told her, smoking the cigarette with enjoyment. 'Don't tell Sonia,' he said, indicating it with a smile, 'Our secret eh?'

'Of course.' Suppose, just suppose, she did go back to Max, would she ever tell him about the baby? Probably not. Oh, by the way, I've had an abortion since I last saw you. That would go down a treat. Despite his own indiscretions, Max could go all po-faced from time to time.

'Are you going to ask Laura for the money?' Seb enquired, glancing at the clock, as they were supposed to be starting preparations for the gigantic cooked breakfast when the wet and weary walkers returned.

'She's the last resort,' Lotty said. 'She'll give it to me. She always does. But that doesn't stop me feeling guilty about asking. It's like you're a little girl who wants more pocket money.' She smiled ruefully. 'I never could manage my finances even then. Beth could. That gives you some idea of the boring child she was. She had separate little boxes for the pennies and the twopences. William's just disappeared and nobody knew on what and as for Sonia . . . well, she saved hers and then had a binge.'

Sebastian smiled a little sadly. 'She hasn't changed,' he said.

Sonia deliberately let the others forge ahead into the drizzly distance, pulling up the hood of her bright yellow storm jacket and holding out a hand to help her mother over a rough bit. The murky weather closed instantly around them so that they could hear the others in the distance, hear the excited barks of the dogs. Sonia, not used to exercise of any description, found to her chagrin that she was panting with the exertion, more so than mummy who was striding along quite happily in her old walking boots.

Sonia stifled a sigh. Nobody in their right mind should be out on a morning like this, before breakfast too. She was rather glad Seb had opted to stay behind because that left her free to speak to mummy, get it over with, without his interfering.

'I know you don't like to speak about the future, mummy,' she began briskly, 'But Seb and I have been talking and we agree that it's time we discussed, calmly and rationally, what's going to happen to you in . . . say ten years or so . . . all alone here. I'm not happy about it, mummy. And neither is Sebastian.'

'Aren't you, sweetheart?' Laura smiled, peeping at her from underneath the rather chic souwester she was wearing. 'You have no need to worry. I have my own plans.'

'What plans? Paid help? That sort of thing? Don't you think that idea is a bit off when you have three daughters? One of us should look after you when you are old. I know it's an old-fashioned idea but I happen to think it important. You will not be dumped in some nursing home whilst I'm around, mummy.'

'That is comforting to know.'

Sonia glanced at her sharply. Why the sarcasm? It was most unlike mummy to be sarcastic.

'I don't wish to discuss it further, Sonia,' Laura went on firmly. 'Goodness, what are you trying to do? Make me feel a hundred? I am fit as a fiddle and I shall continue to enjoy life for many years to come.'

Sonia frowned. Her mother was in an odd mood, a touch defiant, unusual for her.

'We have to talk now,' she insisted, seeing the chateau slipping away. 'It's no use hiding away from the facts. I know you're a long way from being old but you're not getting any younger. What if you suddenly have a stroke or something?'

'That's quite enough.' Laura glanced sharply at her. 'If you're going to be so miserable, you can go back to the house now and I'll catch Beth and the others up. What is the matter with you? Everything's all right with you and Sebastian, isn't it? You are treating him nicely, aren't you?'

'Treating him nicely?' Sonia sniffed. 'We have an equal partnership, mummy. Something you wouldn't understand. I am not the "little woman" who stays home, makes the meals and looks after the children. That idea is so dated but of course you wouldn't understand.' She stopped and felt the borrowed wellington boots sliding into mud. She squelched them free. The rain had wickedly changed direction and was now hitting them squarely in the face, the hood no protection.

'Mummy, I have a proposition to put to you,' she said. 'I want you to think about it very carefully. Private nursing care when you get old is all very well, preferable I suppose to a nursing home, but you must be careful. After all, you are a wealthy lady . . .'

'What do you mean?' Laura laughed. 'You're not suggesting someone might murder me for my money?' She walked on at a cracking pace leaving Sonia to follow, gasping her discomfort. 'How ridiculous! You always did have an overactive imagination.'

'Seb and I are thinking of selling the London house,' Sonia persisted, wishing now she had waited until they were indoors to have this conversation. Out here, with the wind and rain, it was so damned uncomfortable. 'In fact, we may have a buyer. If you were to sell Fernlands, mummy . . .?'

'Sell Fernlands?' Laura glanced at her sharply, 'Has someone been saying something, Sonia? Have you been talking to Elsie?'

'I haven't seen Elsie yet,' Sonia replied, puzzled at the turn in the conversation. Had mummy already thought of selling? If so, then it would make things so much easier.

'Where are you moving to? I thought you were settled at last. That house was supposed to be the one you would end your days in, wasn't it? You've only just finished doing it up.' Laura shot her an exasperated glance, 'Really, darling! You're always doing this. Sebastian must be getting quite fed up. You're not thinking of moving back up here, are you? You wouldn't last five minutes without your theatres and your bright lights.'

'We want to move to France,' Sonia said, 'It used to be so wonderful when we spent our holidays there. Remember?'

'Of course I remember. We had some lovely times. But being on holiday's a bit different from moving there permanently. A different culture. A different way of life. You'd have to learn to speak French fluently.'

Sonia laughed, 'No problem at all, mummy. A lot of English people are setting up home there and there's a very lively English community. It's so much more relaxed. Warm and sunny. All that wine. And good food.'

'I'm fairly relaxed here,' Laura pointed out, indicating that they should retrace their steps towards the house. 'However, if you've made up your mind, then I wish you well.'

Sonia sighed. Mummy was missing the point. She was going to say no, she felt it in her bones. And if she did, then they would have to say goodbye or *au revoir* to the gorgeous chateau. It was in a rough state in fact and needed an awful lot of money spending on it to restore it to its former glory. 'This chateau that we want to buy is in Normandy,' she went on, slipping damp hands into her pocket. She would very likely catch pneumonia at this rate. 'Near Honfleur. It's beautiful. You'll love it when you see it. It's been on the market for about two years so it's at a knock-down price. It has the most gorgeous gardens . . . a bit neglected just now but they will be beautiful again. It's sticking because not everyone wants a house that size, you see.'

'Why do you? You're not suddenly intending to have hordes of children, are you darling?'

Sonia ignored the bitterness in the tone. Not surprisingly, mummy disapproved of her quite clearly stated reasons for remaining childless.

'It's a business proposition,' she said, casting an anxious glance round as she heard the dogs. They were running towards them and one of them, goodness knows why, had taken a special fancy to her. Last night, he had managed to dribble on her skirt whilst gazing up lovingly into her eyes. That stain had better come out or else!

'We want you to come in with us on the deal, mummy,' she said quickly. 'Sell Fernlands and we can sort out the financial arrangements with the others and then you can move with us to France. You will have your own suite decorated entirely to your choice. I will even allow you to have a pink bedroom if you like.'

'Are you out of your mind?' Laura laughed softly. 'I don't deny I have been toying with the idea of selling the house, Sonia, but for my own reasons. Reasons I do not wish to go into at the moment.'

Sonia pushed open the gate to the gardens and they stepped through. Everything was drenched, the flowers bowed down with raindrops. This was the wild bit of the garden where mummy allowed things to grow in haphazard profusion. Lots of tall grasses too and they somehow managed to shoot up her skirt and tickle round her knees as they scrambled onto the path. 'But wouldn't you like to live in Normandy?' she continued. 'The summers are better.'

'It's not so much the summers I mind as the winters here,' her mother said, after a moment, 'Such wind and rain. Last winter was particularly wet. The garden was absolutely sodden.'

'Exactly.' Sonia was triumphant, feeling her mother was giving just a little. 'Look at this rain just now. I bet it's not raining in France.'

'I like Normandy,' Laura said with a smile. 'Do you remember when we went camping? Before William was born and then nearly every year after.'

'I do. And, as I said, the chateau is near one of the campsites we went to. Oh, mummy, it will be so wonderful. Like being on permanent holiday.'

Sonia was reasonably satisfied as they neared the house. She had sown the seed. The next thing was to get mummy to visit the chateau at the earliest opportunity. Once she had seen it, she would be smitten.

'The postman's been . . .' Laura seemed distracted, stepping out of her wet things in the porch. 'I wonder if he's brought . . .' her voice tailed off but Sonia knew what she had been about to say. It was too bad of her brother. Totally selfish that was his trouble. Thankfully, damp clothing removed, she went through to the kitchen where Sebastian and Lotty were busy with breakfast, Sebastian doing the cooking, Lotty hanging about. Sizzling bacon and sausages. The big kitchen table set out with the red and white kitchen china. Quite a feast. Sonia eyed it grimly. She only ever had a black coffee for her breakfast.

'Enjoy your walk, darling?' Sebastian asked with a smile.

'Lovely, thank you. Very bracing,' she added with a grimace meant just for him.

'What'll you have?' he asked, looking pleasantly harassed as the sizzling preparations reached a crescendo. 'We can offer you just about anything?'

'Just toast,' she said, shuddering at the enormous fry-up, knowing she had to have something or mummy would force-feed her.

Behind her, the others were running through the garden, laughing, as a fresh, torrential downpour began.

The postman, thank God, had brought a card from William. William and a *Suzanne* to be precise. Nobody had the remotest idea who Suzanne was. It cheered Lotty up to see the sheer delight on her mother's face as she read it.

And that wasn't all! He actually rang during the morning, an almost unheard-of event. Lotty, from her position on the sofa in the sitting room, could hear the raucous telephone rendering of 'Happy Birthday to You' as her mother, with a ridiculous expression on her face, held the mouthpiece aloft so that they could all hear.

Good for William then. He had redeemed himself at the last stroke. It was also a stroke of luck for her for it would put mother in the good mood she needed her to be in. Feeling guilty to be taking advantage thus, but doing it nonetheless, Lotty finally plucked up the nerve to ask.

'What do you need it for?'

She had known that would be the first question.

They were alone in the house as Martin had gone off to officiate at a wedding and Beth and the children had taken the dogs out for a walk. Sonia and Sebastian were out somewhere, scouring antique shops for furniture.

Her mother was pleased with the presents. Delicate earrings from Sonia. A hand-knitted sweater in a mucky heather blue from Beth. And the vase from the motorway service shop of course. The price, dammit, was stuck to the bottom but, if her mother noticed, she did not comment.

The very vase, now containing flowers, was on the table in front of them beside a small collection of family photographs in silver frames. Lotty, feeling herself growing pink at the prospect of lying, dithered.

'It's so complicated,' she said, trying to avoid her mother's solid gaze, 'It's all such a mess. My finances are in a pickle and, on top of everything else, Max has sent me a letter asking me to go back to him.'

'I hope he hasn't been asking you for money,' Laura said quietly, hands clasped on her lap, looking very smart in black and cream. 'Because, if he has, then I'll have to say no. Your father wouldn't have wanted us to interfere. Didn't he always say that, once any of you were in a relationship, you had to sort things out for yourself?'

'I know. And . . .' Lotty hesitated, 'I never said thanks for *not* interfering with me and Max. You could have said "I told you so" but you didn't. It's nothing to do with Max, not the financial trouble. Max never had a problem with money. It's . . .' she knew she couldn't tell her the truth. She couldn't bear to see mother's face if she did. In a daft way, mother still thought of her as innocent. Never mind that she'd been married to Max, to her mother she was still little Lotty who couldn't manage money.

'It's credit cards,' she said, fussing with the belt of her jeans as she heard the sharp intake of breath. 'Yes, I know it's stupid. I know you warned me about them but there it is. I want to settle my debts and start again. Of course I could get another loan from the bank I suppose . . .' she paused, let that unwelcome thought sink in.

'Who on earth was unwise enough to give you credit cards?' Laura smiled a little. She was wearing a new fragrance, something flowery and lovely. 'And what, pray, did you spend the money on?'

Christ! This was like getting blood out of a stone. And this was mother in a good mood. 'Electrical equipment,' she said wildly, the first thing that came into her head. 'Video. Compact disc player. Microwave. It starts to add up. I didn't realise I was spending quite so much.'

'And you expect me to sort it out for you?'

Lotty stared at her mother, not sure if she had heard right. She wasn't going to say no, was she? What the hell would she do then? In another few weeks, this embryo would turn into a proper baby and then what?

'This is the last time, Lotty, and this time I mean it. Please don't ask me again.' Laura reached into her handbag and took out her cheque book. 'And, take my advice, cut up those cards when you've paid them off. How much do you need, darling?'

Feeling absolutely dreadful, almost reduced to that hopping from one foot to the other stage, Lotty kissed her mother and carried the cheque upstairs, hugging it against her. Here it was, the answer to her prayers. Why then, didn't she feel exactly thrilled? She could get the abortion arranged for next week, and, once that was done, she could get on with her life. She sure as hell wouldn't make that mistake again!

Max's letter had unsettled her, coming out of the blue as it had. She wasn't sure if her mother had ever approved of Max, just as she didn't quite approve of Sebastian or Martin. Could it be that, deep down, she didn't feel they were good enough for her little girls?

Pity the poor girl who hooked William. William and Suzanne. Who was she? Even mother didn't know. However, it sounded hopeful and he needed someone to look after him, a home-maker sort. They still existed, didn't they, albeit in a dwindling supply. Beth was one after all. What the hell was the matter with her? She had a shifty look about her which was quite absurd as Beth had never done a thing in her entire life that warranted guilt.

Lotty smoothed out the letter from Max and read it again. How much thought had gone into it or did the words just sound pretty to his sensitive ears. He could be quite poetical when the mood took him.

She still loved him. She lay on the narrow bed, listening to the rain pattering on the windowpane, and stared at the ceiling. She thought about the wedding Martin was officiating at. It had rained heavily on her wedding day too. It had ruined the photographs at church but it had cleared a little by the time they returned to Fernlands for the reception. There was a wonderful buffet, champagne and much laughter, and daddy made a speech to the assembled guests. Quite an event. To her relief, for she had worried about it, Max's speech had been eloquent and amusing.

She wore white, a frothy frilly dress that flattered her thin frame, and managed to look virginal which, under the circumstances, was quite an achievement. Max had looked terrific in morning dress, whispering sweet nothings when he thought nobody was looking, unable to take his eyes off her, thoroughly enjoying the day. She had changed into a suit, worn a hat of all things, and they had departed covered in confetti, the good wishes ringing in their ears for an idyllic honeymoon in the Bahamas.

Nothing to do for two whole weeks but relax in the sun, eat, make love. They had poured out their hearts to each other deciding they would have at least four children but agreeing that Lotty should continue her career. They would sort out the nannying arrangements later. She actually suspected she was pregnant by the end of the honeymoon from one of their earlier encounters but it was not to be.

Once, she remembered, cringing at the memory, she had made him promise, hand on heart, that he would never leave her. Of course, in the Caribbean sunset, he had promised.

Words were easy and words were as easily forgotten.

Oh what a bloody mess! Max Crabtree, I hate you, she said to herself, creasing up her face in her misery. Love, hate. What was the difference?

12

Sunday dawned bright and clear, the whole place sparkling after the day's rain. Laura allowed herself an extra hour in bed, luxuriating in the knowledge that the two men she most cared about had telephoned. Don had called, his call mercifully bypassing the rest of the family who were, at the time, having a heated argument about bathroom arrangements. Missing her like hell. Wanting to know what was happening. Had she told them? Perhaps it might be best if they broke the news together? She *was* going to say yes, wasn't she?

And the phone call too from William, her birthday call. He was happy. She knew that. It had been a brief call, of necessity, but it was long enough for him to pass on a current address and, when the girls had gone, she would take time to write to him. If she was brutally frank, she would not be sorry when they had gone. She could finally relax although, all in all, it had been a success, unless something went wrong at church this morning which was always on the cards with Lotty around.

They had been thoughtful this year about her birthday. Sonia's earrings were charming, Beth's sweater was pretty and Lotty's vase a bargain at ten pounds fifty.

Financially, it was less of a success in that she had parted with a substantial cheque to Lotty to pay off the dratted credit cards. She had a suspicion that was not the real reason as Lotty had looked distinctly shifty. As if that wasn't enough, Sonia was working up, in her ridiculously convoluted way, to asking her for a whole lot more. Her little scheme could have been amusing if it wasn't so deadly serious. Did she expect Laura to believe that the sole reason was so that she could fulfil her daughterly obligations? In any case, the chateau was regrettably a passing fancy just as the house in London and the former ones in Bath and then Chichester had been passing fancies too. It had to be said that Sebastian was remarkably patient. George would never have stood for it.

Against her better judgement and definitely for the last time, she would help. If only Sonia had been honest and asked outright for money instead of inventing the cock and bull story about actually caring what happened to her when she grew old. It was insulting and only confirmed Laura's long held but private belief that Sonia was the selfish one, Beth the meek one, Lotty the impulsive one and dear William the child.

She and Don had not yet decided where to live if, or more likely when, they married. He favoured her selling Fernlands and moving in with him and, indeed, it seemed the sensible option. She was fond of Grange-over-Sands, knew it quite well and his house off Fell Road, smaller than hers, was in an exhilarating perched-on-hill position. She would of course miss the lake here but there would be the alternative very attractive view of the sandy tidal reaches of Morecambe Bay.

The children would not lose out or only a little but she did intend to use a considerable portion of the money she would acquire from selling Fernlands for herself. It was time she treated herself to a little fun. They planned a round the world cruise as soon as Don retired and maybe they would also buy a place abroad, somewhere hot. Don had travelled extensively in his capacity as an importer of Far Eastern goods and wanted her to see the places she had dreamed of. George had been such a stick-in-the-mud. France, yes . . . but France in a tent.

Church beckoned and, with a sigh, Laura picked up her gloves and bag. She was wearing a fetching navy straw to match her plain dress. She didn't suppose the others had noticed but she was taking a new interest in her appearance. Don had done that.

She hoped Martin would take the hint and keep the sermon brief today. She was in no mood for a lecture and she was also suffering from a worrying lack of concentration. Funny . . . even Beth seemed to have taken to daydreaming and Laura had caught her once or twice this weekend gazing into space. Laura hoped nothing was wrong although, apart from perpetual money worries that she brought on herself, she couldn't think what else *could* be wrong. Martin and the children and even the dogs adored her. She was such an uncomplicated soul. She looked forward to the excellent lunch Beth was sure to prepare and also to spending some more time with her grandsons. They had been good this weekend, good but not that good and that pleased her.

Once, when John was being chastised by Beth for being rude to Sonia, she had winked at him over Beth's shoulder and he had grinned back, unfortunately receiving more sharp words as a result. Laura knew she ought not to undermine Beth's authority but it was nice to share a secret rapport with him and she found her heart warmed by it. Underneath that sober exterior, thank God, there lurked ordinary little boys. They must get to know Don. Because he had missed out on children of his own, he would especially enjoy being a sort of grandfather to them.

Sonia, Sebastian and Lotty were waiting patiently in the hall. Sonia lovely in peach linen with an upswept hat. Lotty had made an effort, neutral in a grey suit and pink blouse. She had swept her hair off her face and piled it on top of her head, her eyes large in her pale face, that little cloud of worry still encircling her. Laura glanced sharply at her. She should have personally insisted on cutting up the credit cards. Lotty had no sense about money and she had been in two minds to refuse her but she had looked so vulnerable, so sad.

'We're taking both cars, mummy,' Sonia said briskly. 'So that Seb and I can shoot off directly after lunch. We have a long journey home.'

'You come with me, mum,' Lotty said, hooking her car keys round her finger. She no longer wore her wedding ring, Laura noticed, surprised that none of them seemed to have noticed *her* new ring, a discreet single diamond that Don had given her. She wore it as a dress ring but she had thought one of them, particularly Sonia, might notice.

She sat beside Lotty in the tiny car amongst the debris of sweet-papers, cigarette packets and the like, wanting to know what was really wrong with her daughter but wondering how she could find out without giving offence. Lotty was apt to fly off the handle!

'I hope Martin's not going to bore us to death,' Lotty began as she started the engine. 'I was going to listen this year and have a real session with him afterwards but, to be honest, I don't feel brilliantly well this morning.'

'You don't look it, darling.' Laura eyed her with concern. 'You don't have to come to church. We can leave you resting at the vicarage if you like.'

Lotty shrugged it off. 'I can't miss it,' she said. 'They'll think I'm making an excuse and, in any case . . .' she turned and smiled, 'I've got my collection stuffed in my pocket so I'll have to go, won't I?'

She waited until they were soberly following Sonia down the road before she said an embarrassed thank you for the cheque. 'You don't know how much it means to me, mum,' she said quietly. 'You've saved my skin.'

'That's what mothers are for.' Laura waved it aside. 'Come on, Lotty, tell me about Max. That is what's bothering you, isn't it? Are you two going to try again?'

'I don't know.' Lotty sounded perfectly miserable. 'I don't know. Sometimes I want him back so much and other times I never want to set eyes on him again. We were forever quarrelling. Never a day went by without one or other of us starting a row.'

'Oh dear . . . I don't want to give you a lecture about marriage.' Laura glanced helplessly towards her daughter, 'There are ups and downs in any marriage. I know it's a cliché but . . . take me and your father for instance . . .'

'No comparison. You and daddy had a marvellous marriage,' Lotty said staunchly and immediately Laura hid her sigh. It was no use explaining to Lotty that George had, on the contrary, been extraordinarily difficult sometimes. His work, his patients, came first with him. Admirable, of course, and because it had seemed petty and selfish to quibble about that, she never had but it had left her feeling short-changed.

'Of course your father was a wonderful man,' she said. 'But he could be a teeny bit infuriating at times. I'm just trying to show that we're all human . . . All right, if I'm honest, then I never did get to know Max properly and I'm sorry about that. I would so love you two to patch it up, darling.'

'Mother, stop it.' Lotty stopped to check a junction before

proceeding, 'I don't need sensible advice thank you. I've got to make up my own mind about Max. I think I love him but this time I would want things to be different. More on my terms.'

'Perhaps if you'd had children . . .' Laura murmured, 'It might have helped.'

'We tried.' Lotty's voice was bitter. 'It was one of those things. Nothing ever happened.'

'Oh . . . I'm sorry. I had no idea.' There was a short, embarrassed silence. 'Why didn't you tell me? There are lots of things that can be done now, fertility treatment. Would you have liked children, darling?'

'I can take them or leave them. Especially the ones at school. I would definitely leave most of them. Preferably in the middle of the Sahara without water. That would test their ingenuity . . . not a bad idea actually . . . I might suggest it. Not the Sahara but some Outward Bound thing.'

'I wish you wouldn't talk about your pupils like that,' Laura said uneasily. 'You make them sound quite dreadful.'

'Most of them are, mother. You really have no idea, cushioned in your middle-class environment.'

'I beg your pardon . . .?'

'Sorry but it's true. Most of the kids have given up, more or less. At twelve years old, they know there's not a hope of getting any qualifications to speak of, no chance of a job. There are one or two exceptions of course . . .'

'I never know when you're joking,' Laura said with a little laugh, finding herself fascinated at the effortless way Lotty manipulated the gears. She was finding that aspect of learning to drive rather difficult. 'I admit children are hard work. Beth copes well of course . . . considering.'

'Considering what?'

'Well . . . for one thing, she looks after the house single-handed, does all the things she has to do for the church and also has to do that caretaking job just to make ends meet. Such a bore for her. Why they have to send the boys to private school, I don't know. Life would be easier if they didn't. She refuses help from me. You're a teacher, Lotty, why don't you have a word with her? The state school is quite satisfactory.'

'Oh no, don't get me involved. She loves it. Being the poor relation.'

'That's not quite fair.' Laura saw they were approaching the church on the hill. Bells were pealing out, the sun was shining, the sky was a watercolour mix of pale blue and pink. Sunday clothes and manners on display. Oh God, help us! She braced herself.

At the church door, wreathed in smiles, playing his vicar role to perfection, was Martin.

Beth wore the red dress. The stolen red dress. When she first put it on, her cheeks were very nearly the colour of the dress itself but by the time she arrived at church in time for the service, she had calmed a little.

After all, nobody would know. The boys had noticed the dress, bless them. Said she looked nice. Martin had said the same thing but then he never really saw *what* she was wearing. She took her place near the front beside Sonia and Sebastian. Ahead of them, in another pew, her mother and Lotty were sitting. Beth noted with surprise that, from this angle, Lotty looked quite reasonable this morning. Mum too. She'd been buying herself one or two new outfits recently.

'You're looking very . . . *bright*,' Sonia said in a whisper when Beth rose from her knees. 'What time are you planning lunch?'

'One o'clock.'

'It's not your usual dumplings and puddingy things is it? I have to watch my figure.' She did not add 'unlike some people' but the rapid glance said it instead. 'Have you thought any more about what we were discussing?'

'Sonia . . . please.' Beth frowned. Now was not the time to talk about what they had in mind. Persuading mother to sell the house. She was not sure yet that she would participate for it was surely a cruel thing to do. Mother loved the house. Such memories!

'We had a quick look round some estate agents yesterday to get some idea of local house prices. Fernlands will be absolutely top price. That view alone is worth a small fortune.'

'There are other things to consider . . .'

'Do you mind?' Lotty turned to glare indignantly at them. 'Do you realise where we are?'

They subsided into miffed silence.

The organ music faded prior to starting the processional hymn. Martin appeared walking up the aisle followed by the choir. As he passed by, she heard his deep voice raised in the triumphant sound of one of her favourite hymns, 'The Church's One Foundation'.

Beth had risen with the others. Her dress rustled as she did so and she was reminded of the awful thing she had done.

Her soprano voice, not so clear and precise as Sonia's, which soared above the rest, faltered a little.

Oh God, she prayed to herself, please forgive me.

'I can't help feeling Martin was having a dig at me,' Sonia said with a little frown as she and Sebastian drove the short distance from church to the vicarage. 'All that stuff about material things. I'm sure he was directing his remarks to me. I didn't know where to put myself. How dare he?' she went on, in full outraged flood. 'I give a share of my income to charity and I'm damned if I'm going to go round dressed in rags just to prove a point. I love beautiful clothes.' She glanced at Sebastian but he seemed unconcerned by her outburst. 'And did you see the look on Beth's face? She thinks the sun shines out of him. She's managed to convince herself that she believes all that tripe as well. And, as for that dress . . . well, I ask you . . . what a colour! Somebody should tell her . . .'

'My, my . . .' Sebastian said lightly, 'We are upset, aren't we? Take it from me, Martin was not having a dig at you, darling. It was just his standard sermon guaranteed to make us all sit up and squirm. Bloody good stuff. Martin's got something. Presence. Fire. Passion. Put him in a boardroom situation and he'd be dynamite. I'd like him on my team. Has he ever considered switching to finance?'

'He's hopeless with money. He leaves all that to poor Beth. Can't you see how harassed she is?' She glanced irritably at him, 'And he's hardly doing a job, is he? It's a vocation.'

She found her spirits lifting as Sebastian drove into the vicarage drive. An interesting approach via a curved drive and a dense bank of rhododendrons so that the stone house was but a tantalising glimpse until, at the bend, it was revealed in its haughty splendour. Covered in creepers, reddish gold now, that softened the stone, and, together with the backdrop of the gentle hills beyond, it was the stuff of romantic oil paintings. Sonia reckoned she could do things with a house like this, not that she'd ever consider living again in this backwater. Given a free artistic rein, the first thing she would do would be to get rid of Beth's frills and fripperies.

Luncheon was cold but there was a delicious home-made vegetable soup to start with crusty bread, and warm spicy apple and cinnamon pie and custard to follow. The dining room at the vicarage, despite its forbidding size, was, Sonia conceded, quite pretty if you liked that sort of thing abounding with Beth's frilly touches and masses of cut blooms from the garden.

'Can I have a word, Sonia?' Beth whispered as they rose from the table. 'Come and help with the washing up.'

'Again? Isn't it Lotty's turn?'

'Lotty doesn't look well and mum deserves a rest. Anyway I want to talk.' Beth's look was one of sheer desperation. 'You can stand and watch.'

The kitchen was big and square, islands of rugs on the cold quarry tiles, the dogs snoozing in their baskets, mercifully unmoved by their arrival. Sonia eyed them warily. This peach colour would not tolerate dog spit and hairs.

'What did you think of Martin's sermon?' Beth asked. 'He has such a way with words, hasn't he?'

'He certainly has,' Sonia said drily, 'I hope he wasn't getting at me. What is the point of trying to make those of us who are successful feel guilty? I noticed quite a number of people were looking very uncomfortable. I work very hard for my success, Beth, it isn't just handed to me on a plate. I don't clock-watch for goodness sake. If he went on like that in my neck of the woods, he'd lose half his congregation overnight. People don't go to church for that.'

'He was simply trying to make us all think about it. Being a Christian means trying to be humble. Trying to remember to be grateful to God for the good things we are given. Trying not to be jealous of others.' Her look was a shade defiant. 'I pray every day for all of us, Sonia. For Martin and the boys. For mum. For you and Sebastian. For Lotty.'

'Not Max? Has he slipped out of your prayers?' Sonia apologised for the cruel words with a grimace. Beth could be insufferable when she started going all religious. 'I must say that I still take exception to Martin suggesting that I am selfish. In this world, you've got to help yourself and it's no use praying for something and then leaving it to God to deliberate upon. He's not going to provide you with ready cash for school fees, is He?'

The dishes slipped into the sink with a nasty bang.

'That's despicable, Sonia,' Beth said, allowing her anger to show for once, 'You mustn't say a word to Martin about school fees. He would hate it if he knew I'd been grumbling to you. I can't think what got into me yesterday when I said I'd help you. That's what I wanted to talk about. I'm having nothing to do with it. Mum loves the house. Can't you see that?'

'But what about the money? You're desperate.' Sonia looked at her, astounded. All self-righteous fluster. 'Do you mean you'll forfeit the chance of solving all your problems on a point of principle?'

'Yes. If you put it like that, yes. Maybe it was never God's will . . .'

'You're such a fool, Elizabeth,' Sonia interrupted coldly. 'Doesn't your faith teach you anything about being nice to your own sister?' She threw the tea-towel down in a fit of pique. It was a waste of time trying to talk sense into Beth when she had her holier-than-thou cloak on. It looked as if she was going to have to go it alone. Seb was no help and she wasn't going to ask Lotty's help for anything.

She *had* to have the chateau. It was so beautiful bathed in sunshine as she had seen it that first time. It even had its own small lake, beside which she could hold garden parties in summer. A few local dignitaries. She could see people milling round, the tinkle of glasses, the laughter, the murmur of French . . . Perfect!

They'd even spotted a bargain yesterday in one of the antique shops, a pair of Louis XV giltwood bergère chairs almost hidden because they weren't the sort of thing that sold easily round here. They were superb and would fit in with her intended careful mix of English/French. A few sympathetic French pieces here and there. It was a wonderful opportunity for the business and all Beth could talk about was God's will. It was nothing to do with that. It was whether or not she, Sonia, had the guts to succeed. She had. Acquiring the chateau was crucial, however, and on their own, she couldn't quite make the sums add up. She needed her mother.

She frowned at Beth again through the sulky silence that followed. As a peace offering, she would give Martin a donation for the church roof and wondered would Beth be offended if she let her have a half dozen or so baggy tops she was frankly tired of wearing.

'Need any help? I seem to be getting off lightly this weekend.' A little belatedly Lotty appeared at the door to receive a rapturous welcome from the suddenly wide-awake dogs. 'I hope you don't mind, Beth,' she said, in between fussing them, 'Thanks for the wonderful lunch and you can tell Martin I'll speak to him later about that sermon but I'll have to set off home soon. I've got heaps of work to sort through before tomorrow. End of term exams looming.'

'Of course I don't mind.' Beth dried her hands and beamed, whipping off the apron to reveal the scarlet dress. 'It's been lovely to see you both again,' she said, her glance at Sonia wary but conciliatory. 'We should get together more often.'

For a moment, time jiggled and Sonia felt an aching tenderness for her sisters. Her little sisters. Impulsively, she found herself rushing forward to envelope each of them in a warm hug. Lotty was trembling slightly, her body slim and somehow fragile.

'Look after yourself,' she said, holding her at arm's length. She wanted to apologise for the fact that they rarely talked, that they were almost incapable of holding a conversation without bitching at each other. 'You look peaky,' she said instead. 'Are you going anywhere when you break for that long, long holiday you people have?'

'No plans yet.' Lotty managed a smile, even her eyes tired.

Sonia felt a sudden strange disquiet. She had no idea why but she had the distinct feeling that this weekend, this family weekend, was a turning point in their lives. A cold descended. She wasn't experiencing a terrible premonition of mummy's death, was she? No . . . she was just a bit down and sitting in that chilly church with Martin bellowing forth had not helped.

'Come and see me and Seb whenever you're in town,' were her parting words to Lotty. She hoped she would give her due notice if she did. What would the neighbours think if they knew she had a sister who taught in a comprehensive? It was bad enough they knew about William but she had laughed that off because all families have one oddity. She had upgraded Martin practically to the role of bishop and, in any case, the quirkiness of being in the Church was acceptable. 'You come along too, Beth,' she added, deciding she had better make some gesture towards forgiving her, 'Although you have a problem with the dogs, don't you?'

There was no way she was allowing those hairy slobbering monsters within casting and drooling distance of her rugs, her sofas, her polished furniture, her gleaming kitchen. The kitchen had been designed to the last millimetre. There was no place for dog baskets and tatty blankets.

Before she and Seb left, she arranged to be in touch with mummy very soon. Wisely she decided against pursuing the chateau further at this moment. Give mummy a little time to consider.

'Thank goodness that's over,' she said to Seb as they set off. 'Next year I hope we'll be in France.' She looked sharply at her husband as he merely grunted in reply. 'I've written a cheque for a hundred pounds for the church roof,' she told him, 'Martin was delighted.'

'Conscience money?' Sebastian laughed. 'That won't make the slightest dent in your funds, darling. If you really wanted to soothe your conscience, you'd have gone the whole hog and paid the lot. The remaining seven thousand or whatever.'

'And spare them the thrill of all that fundraising?' she smiled a little, 'Do me a favour. I noticed you only put a pound coin in the collecting plate. That was big of you.'

'I don't operate with cash,' he said, 'I was lucky I had a pound. What else could I do? Offer to pay by American Express? Lotty only put a pound in too but then she's broke.' He stopped, concentrating suddenly and intently on his driving.

Sonia stared at him a moment, 'She's been asking you for money, hasn't she? I might have known. What does she spend money on? Not on that awful flat and not much on herself either, judging by that suit.'

'She was sick this morning before church,' Seb went on quietly, 'It was my turn for that bloody stupid rota and I barged in the bathroom . . . she'd forgotten to lock the door . . . she was in no fit state to care. She looked ghastly. I got out pretty damned fast and I don't think she noticed me.'

'Sick? In the morning?' It took only a few seconds for it to sink in. 'You don't suppose she's pregnant, do you? Well, well . . .'

'And it's not Max's, is it?' His laugh rang out harshly, 'And, before you even think it, the answer is no.'

Part Two

13

Lotty tossed the old newspapers into the bin as soon as she got back to the flat, changed out of her suit into jeans and sweater. She was tired after the journey but somehow buoyed up too and, after the gracious quiet of Fernlands, the homeliness of the vicarage, she was able to view the flat through different eyes. My God, it was one helluva tip and she would waste no time. Start on it now, she decided, feeling a spurt of energy building up, then peeping into the kitchen and withdrawing hastily. After the immaculate state of her mother's and Beth's, it looked ten times worse. There was no excuse. It wasn't outside the realms of possibility that she could keep a place clean, was it? Nothing to it. Purely a matter of organisation.

She whisked into the bedroom, changed the sheets, got rid of all reminders of Kevin from the bathroom. She was feeling pleased with herself. She had got through the weekend without anyone guessing her interesting condition and, in addition, she'd got the means to have the abortion.

She was just making herself a cup of coffee when the phone rang. For a moment, she wondered and then immediately discounted that it was Max. Too soon for him. He would give her the time he had promised.

It was her wonderful, discreet friend Rachel who wanted to know what had happened this weekend. Lotty gave her a potted version, smiling as she heard the whoop of delight that she had the money.

'Have you booked yourself in yet?' was the next question.

'Not yet. I'll do it tomorrow,' she said, curling up in the chair for what could be a long session. Rachel was not noted for her short conversations.

'Do it as soon as we're finished. There'll be someone there. They operate a twenty-four-hour service.'

'I'm having second thoughts,' Lotty said, the words popping out of nowhere. 'I'm not sure any more. After all, you didn't have an abortion. You had your baby. You didn't chicken out, Rachel.'

'Charlotte Crabtree, I could throttle you! Stop it this instant.' The voice was vexed. 'And look how I've had to struggle. Being a single mum is damned hard and I wouldn't wish that on my worst enemy. You're not worrying about the op, are you?' The sigh was slight, 'There really is nothing to worry about. I'm told the staff are wonderful. It's a highly respectable clinic, hence the fees, not a back-street crone with a knitting needle.'

Lotty wished she hadn't said that. She couldn't stop a shudder. 'But it amounts to the same thing,' she said slowly as it dawned. 'When you get down to it, there's precious little difference. They just use a high tech knitting needle, don't they? They are still going to kill it, Rachel. Kill my baby.'

'The difference is . . . and I can't believe I'm saying this, Lotty . . . the difference is that this way you'll be cared for properly and come out of it undamaged. You'll still be able to have a baby some day but next time you can choose when.'

'Max wants me back. He wrote me a letter.' She listened a moment to the exasperated heavy silence at the other end of the line. 'I know . . . I said I'd fry in hell first but mother's been talking to me and I'm sure she thinks I should try again. Something about ups and downs. She never really understood him, Rachel. If dad was here, it would be different. He liked Max. They both liked golf.' She felt her voice give a bit, put her hand over the mouthpiece a moment.

'And you're letting her influence you? Lotty, are you listening? What does *she* know about it? Things were different in their day. They didn't have so much pressure. I bet she got married when she was about eighteen, didn't she, and never lived to regret it? Never had a cross word all their married life probably. People like that, smug as hell, make me sick.'

'But she did have a happy marriage,' Lotty said defensively,

'Don't go all snotty with me, Rachel. I only said I was thinking about going back to him. I don't know yet if I will.'

'How many weeks pregnant are you?'

'About eleven.' Lotty frowned. 'Why? Does it matter? Don't worry, if I'm going to have this done, I won't hang about.'

'You're going to talk yourself out of it,' Rachel said crossly, 'I can feel it in my bones. You've made the mistake of thinking about it as a baby. It isn't yet. It's just a bundle of cells.'

'We had to go to church this morning, usual summons,' Lotty said, suddenly thoughtful, 'Martin, my sister Beth's husband, stood there in the pulpit belting forth and, do you know, Rachel . . . the oddest thing . . . I wanted to ask him what I should do.'

'I'm coming over,' Rachel said, 'We've got to talk face to face. What is Max going to say if you turn up hugely pregnant? I can see I'm going to have to do everything for you, book the appointment, drive you there, everything. Otherwise, Charlotte Crabtree, you'll be blaming me in seven months time.'

Lotty sighed. 'You're pushing me. You don't need to come over. How can you, you'll have to get a babysitter. Look, I promise I'll ring the clinic in a minute. Put the damned phone down and I'll do it right now.'

'If you're sure . . . you still have the card I gave you? The number?'

It took some doing but she eventually persuaded Rachel that she was safe to be left to do the dirty deed personally. Even so, she did not snatch up the phone as promised. Sod Rachel. She would do it tomorrow in her own time. There was no rush. Another day would make no difference.

Rachel had succeeded in wearing her out and the flat would have to wait until tomorrow too for its spring clean, if she felt like it when she got in from school. Wearily, she carried her cold coffee into the kitchen. She would at least do the washing up left over from Friday. As she half-heartedly tackled it, she sensed something was wrong down there. Down in the pit of her stomach or in her womb to be accurate.

She was momentarily rendered motionless and stood awhile leaning against the sink, feeling the warm quite pleasant trickle deep inside. It couldn't be, could it? Moving slowly to the bathroom, she caught sight of her face in the mirror. She was ashen, eyes shocked.

She knew before she checked what she would find. Sure enough, there it was, a vivid scarlet stain. She stared at it and at what it meant, as she slid onto the floor.

No, she heard herself saying out loud. Please God . . . no.

'What have you done with Emma?' Lotty asked as soon as Rachel was through the door.

'She's at home alone, cooking chips,' Rachel quipped, her expression changing as she looked at Lotty for the first time. 'Sorry . . . just trying to cheer you up, love. Forget about Emma. She's fine, being looked after by my neighbour who spoils her rotten. You look bloody awful.'

'Thanks a million.' Lotty hunched her body, afraid to straighten up, afraid to walk about much, frightened of starting the bleeding off again. 'Did you phone the doctor? Did you explain that I'd tried to ring him myself but I'd come over all peculiar, couldn't get the words out.' She tried a brave smile as Rachel gave her a hug.

'I rang him and we're to get you into bed right away,' Rachel said, flinging her jacket onto a chair and rolling up her sleeves, 'Come on, no arguments.'

Too tired to argue, not even wanting to argue, Lotty allowed herself to be pampered, relaxing against her friend as she was helped into the bedroom. 'Sorry for the state it's in,' she muttered, wondering what the hell had got into her that she should even think of such a thing. It wasn't as if it was as bad as usual for she'd even dusted a bit when she'd changed the bedding. What the hell! Rachel was not exactly noted for her domestic skills either.

She allowed Rachel to fuss her, making no protest as she wrapped her in a big old crumpled nightie she found somewhere in a drawer. She tucked her in, probably unaware that she was making sympathetic maternal noises all the while.

Lotty waited until Rachel had finished fiddling with the bedcover before she asked the question that had to be asked. 'Am I going to lose the baby?'

It seemed her voice came from a great distance, detached

somehow. She waited anxiously for Rachel's reply as if she was some kind of consultant gynaecologist.

'What am I supposed to say to that?' Rachel asked with a wry smile, 'I thought that's what we wanted. After all, you were going to book an abortion. You haven't been trying anything, have you?'

Indignation flurried. 'I certainly have not. Damn it, Rachel, you don't seriously think I'd try a do-it-yourself job, do you? I'm too much of a coward. Believe me, it just came out of the blue.'

'I believe you. Sorry but what was I to think?' She patted her hand in apology, 'The doctor says it's probably just a little warning and that with care and rest, you'll be just fine.'

'Did he? That's a relief,' Lotty said with a big sigh. 'You can't know what a relief that is, Rachel.'

'I know one thing, you're going to end up having it, aren't you?' Rachel said, 'You big fool. I knew your heart wasn't in that abortion, Charlotte Crabtree.'

Lotty smiled, admitting to herself that that option no longer held any fears. She would cope. Others coped. Rachel coped. Her mother would be shocked but she would get over it. As for the father . . . she would tell Kevin it wasn't his in case he came over all protective. It would be a bit more difficult with Max but, if he really loved her, they would work something out.

'Although it was such a bugger finding out I was pregnant, in a way I suppose I was glad,' she said thoughtfully, 'It must be something to do with me not getting any younger.'

'You're hardly in your dotage,' Rachel said with a little laugh, 'For God's sake, there's no need for you to worry yet about your biological clock. You've got time to have half a dozen kids.'

'Not if I keep having miscarriages. Some people have lots, don't they?'

'Shut up. You're not having a miscarriage, just a little warning that you've been overdoing it.' She looked round the room, took stock of it. 'Do you want me to tidy up? Hoover or something?' she said, not very enthusiastically, 'In case we have to send for the doctor?'

'A spring clean going on round me?' Lotty spluttered, 'Oh yes, I really fancy that. Sod him. He'll have seen worse, Rachel.'

'Okay.' Rachel looked relieved. 'I'm staying overnight anyway.

I've to ring him again if . . .' she paused, flushed, 'Sorry, do you want to know the details or is it too horrific?'

'Yes I do,' Lotty said quietly, taking a deep steadying breath. 'I'm frightened, Rachel, and it's better if I know what's what.'

'Well . . . if the bleeding persists I'm to ring him. He says you might have some residual bleeding, brownish, from the earlier shock but that if it starts up again, fresh and red then . . .' she pulled a face, 'God, I hope you're not as squeamish as me. Has it stopped by the way?'

'Yes, I think so.' Gingerly, she moved in the bed, but, for the moment, she felt okay. 'I'll just lie here and keep still. All right?'

'Absolutely. Make the most of it while you can. Once you have a baby, you can forget all this lounging about in bed.' She smiled but Lotty could see the anxiety in her eyes that she was trying so hard to mask. 'I'm going to make us something to eat,' she continued, 'What do you fancy?'

'Nothing. I'm too wound up to eat. You have something.'

She lay very still as Rachel disappeared into the kitchen in a probably fruitless search for something edible. Outside the window, a wind had sprung up, quite strong for there was a sudden clang as someone's dustbin lid flew off. The tree made rustling, creaking sounds. She and Kevin had often lain here listening to the sound of that damned tree. Arms wrapped round each other after they had made love and before they started on the cigarettes. Just imagine . . . on one of those occasions, baby had been conceived. She told herself that she had loved Kevin in a way. And, if nothing else, he had given her this baby.

She wanted this baby.

'Hardly any food and you've no excuse, you live on top of a grocer's shop,' Rachel grumbled, coming back with a piece of bread and cheese. She sat beside Lotty on the bed, blissfully scattering crumbs and smiling. 'You feeling a bit better?' she asked, 'Do you want me to ring anyone else? The father for example?'

'Not likely.' Lotty shuddered. 'Absolutely not. If he enquires after me, he is not to be given any information. Information is to be given only to you or my mum. Will you make sure people know that if I'm in no state to tell them?'

'Meaning what?' Rachel asked with her mouth full, 'Don't start getting morbid, for God's sake.'

'Mother's number is on the pad by the phone,' Lotty said, 'You can ring her if . . . well . . .' A sudden sharp pain cut her short and she gasped, clutching at herself. Rachel clattered the plate down and reached for her hand.

'Bit of a pain?' she asked worriedly.

Lotty nodded. 'Should we tell the doctor?' she asked when it had subsided. 'He's not coming, I take it?'

'Fat chance. Bit laid-back if you ask me. He obviously operates a diagnosis by distance service. As I told you, I'm only to ring if we're worried.' She bit her lip. 'Are we?'

An after-twinge of almost comparable intensity snaked its searing path across her lower abdomen, shooting down to her thighs. 'I'm worried,' she whispered, feeling tears beginning and not wanting to cry in front of Rachel. 'It's losing its grip,' she said, fighting the sudden panic. 'Call the doctor again. Tell him I want him.'

She tried to relax when Rachel had gone out, tried to calm the anxious beating of her heart. Just a little warning, she told herself, that's all it is. What would she do if she had to spend the entire pregnancy flat on her back? She'd be bored out of her mind and yet, she knew, with an absolute certainty, that if that's what it took, she would do it. 'Well . . .?' she asked as Rachel came back in, 'Is he on his way?'

'Out on a call,' Rachel said flatly, 'Whoever I spoke to confirms what he told me though. At the moment, there's no need for you to worry.'

'Tell that to the marines,' Lotty said, pulling her hand away from Rachel's reassuring grasp in irritation, 'I have this bad feeling. I should be in hospital.'

'You can't go without a doctor's say-so. I'd drive you there myself but . . .' she stopped, sighed. 'I'm not being much help, am I? I always suspected I'd be a dead loss in an emergency.'

'I'll have to go to the loo, damn it to hell,' Lotty said as it dawned, 'Can you help me to get up?'

'Of course.' Rachel looked round, produced a dressing gown with the panache of a magician, 'Where are your slippers?'

'I don't wear them.' Lotty sat a moment on the edge of the bed, looking at her bare feet as they dangled. They felt curiously as if they didn't belong to her. 'I feel about ninety,' she said as somewhere another tiny twinge flickered. Again, the pain fluttered down to her legs.

She shrugged off Rachel's attempts to get her into the dressing gown and walked by herself, a little unsteadily, into the bathroom. 'You stay there,' she ordered, as Rachel threatened to follow her. 'I don't want you watching me.'

'If you're sure . . . don't lock the door whatever you do,' Rachel said, stationing herself right outside it.

Alone, Lotty slowly and carefully attended to her needs, shy of Rachel helping her, ashamed of the frail state she was in. It took a tremendous effort to do something that she didn't normally have to think about and she had to lean against the basin as she washed her hands. She studiously avoided looking at herself in the mirror. She knew from Rachel's face that she must look like death.

Rachel pounced on her as soon as she was through the door and she almost tumbled back into bed, worried at how much the effort had taken out of her. 'Cup of tea . . .' she found herself murmuring, amazed at how weak she sounded. 'Could you, Rachel . . . please?'

'Coming up.' Rachel bustled off, reappearing with the tea and even a couple of long-lost ginger biscuits.

'Let's talk about something else,' she said brightly, when Lotty was propped up, drinking her tea.

'Such as?' Lotty sipped the tea that Rachel seemed to have laced with sugar, 'Your love life?'

'Non-existent,' Rachel said, 'I haven't time. Would you believe it, I have not got the time for a man. The thing is I don't miss it either. I've got more important things to think about. Emma for instance.' A smile hovered.

'Men are not worth it,' Lotty said firmly. 'Not one of them. Take Max. I can't believe I said I might go back to him. Did I say that? How dare he write to me like that? Trying to catch me on the hop, I know his game. You'd never believe all that sentimental twaddle he wrote.'

'Wouldn't I?' Rachel moved things off the bedside chair, sat on it. 'Do you think we should try to get some sleep?' she suggested, 'It's very late.'

'I feel awful keeping you here. You've got a job to go to in the morning.'

'Oh . . . don't worry about that. I'm due a few days off so I'll take one. They're very flexible and used to me having time off.'

Lotty thanked her with a smile, handing her cup across, and relaxing against her pillows. 'What a good job this didn't happen this weekend at mother's,' she said, 'This would have completely cocked things up. Upset mother's carefully organised plans.'

'Try to sleep,' Rachel said, settling herself down on the chair, spreading the dressing gown around her. 'If you want me, just call out. I'm a very light sleeper. That's another thing about having a child. You never really sleep well again.'

They left a lamp on and Lotty dozed off too, dreaming of babies. When she awoke, she could hear Rachel making little snoring noises. 'Rachel . . . are you awake?' she asked stupidly, as she felt a sudden uncontrollable stickiness, a wetness in the bed. 'Rachel . . .'

'What?' She threw off the dressing gown, startled, 'Something wrong?' She was at Lotty's side instantly, moving back the covers as Lotty motioned what was wrong. 'Oh my God,' she said, 'I'm ringing that sodding doctor now. Stay here.'

Where would she go? She hung on as she heard Rachel's angry voice asking for, no, demanding, an ambulance. Hung on as two cheerful ambulance men arrived. Hung on as the ambulance bumped her at first over the cobbles before they reached the bliss of tarmac and a straight run through to the hospital.

'Should I be bleeding so much?' she asked the one who stayed in the back of the ambulance with her. He was a middle-aged man with a bashed-up face. She didn't know him from Adam, would probably never see him again, but she imprinted every detail of his face in her memory. She searched his eyes for comfort, *was* comforted by the fact that he looked relatively unconcerned as if this sort of thing happened every day. Nevertheless, she gripped his hand, not wanting to let go. 'I'm making a mess of things,' she indicated, clutching at the scarlet blanket they had put over her.

'Don't you worry about that, love,' he said, 'We'll have you there in no time.'

'A mess of things,' she repeated, and again her voice was from afar. From some distant place as if this was a dream or rather a nightmare.

It wasn't. It was stone cold reality as the ambulance braked and backed up to the entrance. Clatter of the stretcher and trolley. A final encouraging word from the ambulanceman and, confusingly, from a wild-eyed Rachel, who must have followed in her car. A maze of cream corridors, silent swinging doors, as she was pushed along. Being helped onto a hard-topped examination table.

Terror thumped her as the other sounds receded. How she loathed hospitals. The smell made her feel sick and she fought hard against it. Her heart raced in panic as a nurse with a gentle voice told her to take deep breaths and relax.

An admissions card to fill in. A bloody admissions card!

The gentle-voiced nurse, a redhead with freckles, apologised but it was the rules she said as she poised her pen.

'Name?'

'Mrs Crabtree. Charlotte.'

'Address?'

'3A Balaclava Street.'

'Your GP?'

She jotted it down, a little ponderously. Lotty watched, wanting to scream at her to hurry up. Her baby was fighting for its scrap of life! Didn't they realise that?

'Date of birth?'

The questions continued.

'Religion?'

'Christ Almighty!' She had had enough. 'Does it matter? C of E, I suppose.'

'All right, Charlotte. Sorry about the necessity for these questions. The doctor is on her way. Relax. You're going to be just fine. There's a good girl.'

The nurse with red hair smiled and held her hand.

Lotty held back the tears, felt about five years old again.

She wanted her mother.

Peace, perfect peace. Laura reclined on the sofa in the drawing room, Vivaldi's 'Summer' playing in the background, her book idly on her lap. If Don were here, he would be sitting opposite and they would probably be enjoying a glass of sherry. She chose not to drink alcohol when she was alone.

A Family Weekend •

She was oddly glad that he had gone away for a while and he was right, it had firmed things up in her mind. She missed him. Very much. His laughter and his love. She needed him to be here with her. And surely, that was all that mattered. The rest . . . what people might think . . . was nonsense.

When he got back, she would tell him that she was accepting his proposal, although she was reluctant still to tell the children. In some ways, it might be easier if she and Don presented them with a *fait accompli*. William in particular she worried about. What would he say?

She wondered who the Suzanne was, the girl mentioned in her birthday card. She would have to be a special girl to take on William. In the letter she had just written, she had asked William to pass on her love to Suzanne so that she felt she was holding out a long-distance hand of friendship and encouragement. Wouldn't it be wonderful if all the loose ends in her life could be tied up before she married Don? William happily married. Lotty reunited with Max. Beth didn't seem to have any loose ends thank goodness but Sonia . . . dearest, restless Sonia, whose own marriage looked just a little shaky.

She was going to see her accountant to arrange to deal in some shares so that she could make a gift to Sonia towards this infernal chateau. Perhaps she and Don might visit sometimes. It would be nice to visit.

The music was soothing and she closed her eyes. Fifty five years old and at last she felt in control of her life. She was pleasing herself by marrying Don. Mostly, before, she had tried to please others. In a way, she had married George because her parents had so wanted it, although the prospect of marrying a newly qualified doctor had not seemed such an unhappy one. George had been a kind man but she wished he had been not quite so wrapped up in his work, a touch more considerate.

Don was, on the contrary, a very considerate man as well as being charming and handsome and free to marry her, and she loved him. She didn't really mind that he seemed reluctant to talk about the past, about his wife of many years. Would that they had met when they were younger? Still . . . they had lots of time left and they would spend it together.

She switched off the tape and went upstairs. The house was

123 •

recovering fitfully, she felt, from its family invasion. Elsie would sort the beds out tomorrow.

She found herself peeping into the rooms they had used. Sonia's expensive perfume lingered. Charlotte's room smelt of cigarettes with the window tight shut and the ashtray brimming. Beth and Martin's room was prim in its neatness and Beth had removed the sheets, folded them. The boys' room, on the other hand, was a shambles. Beth must have forgotten that. Odd . . . but then Beth had been a little odd all weekend.

She was in bed, trying to relax herself by reading a little, when the phone rang. A worried sounding woman asking if she was speaking to Mrs Howard. Mrs Laura Howard.

Laura felt her heart thud. She knew at once that something was wrong with one of the children. She had had the funniest feeling earlier but had dismissed it as ridiculous.

'Laura Howard speaking,' she said calmly. 'What can I do for you?'

'Oh, Mrs Howard, you don't know me but I'm a friend of Lotty's, Rachel Green. I'm sorry to ring you like this but Lotty's been rushed to hospital.' The hesitation was minimal. 'I don't know if you're aware that she's pregnant . . . well, she is . . . and threatening to miscarry. I'm speaking from the hospital but I'm going to have to go home in a minute. They wouldn't let me go with Lotty. I'm sorry, I would stay all night if I could, but I have a young daughter and I think it'll be best to get back to her. I can't actually do anything here, you see.'

Lotty . . . pale, anxious Lotty. She might have known. Oh why hadn't she realised?

Lotty in hospital . . . the thought was appalling. Lotty couldn't stand hospitals.

'Are you still there, Mrs Howard? Only Lotty is asking for you.'

'I'll be there as soon as I can.'

At five years old, Lotty was adorable. A handful but adorable. Not easy to keep tidy like Sonia, and Laura soon abandoned what had once seemed a charming idea of dressing her two little daughters alike. It was amazing how identical dresses could look so unalike. In any case, little Lotty was happier in dungarees.

She was such fun. Bright as a button, quick to grasp things, unputdownable in other words. And when she was five, she and Sonia looked forward to the birth of their new baby brother or sister. It meant visits to the antenatal classes and, on one occasion, Laura had taken the children with her thinking the experience would be good for them, educational as it were.

What a mistake. Poor Lotty. Before Laura's eyes, all the bounce had gone from her and she became a clinging wreck, clutching her mother's skirt, trying desperately not to cry in front of her big sister.

'She's frightened, mummy,' Sonia said gleefully, 'Isn't she being silly?'

Laura adjusted the suddenly dead weight of Lotty against her, giving Sonia a 'look'. She spoke to Lotty in a quiet voice, 'There's nothing to be frightened of, darling. Why are you frightened? Everything's going to be all right. Won't it be lovely when we have the new baby at home? You'll be able to help me.'

Lotty nodded solemnly, tears welling up in her dark eyes, dribbling down her cheeks. Pale and quiet. 'I don't like it here, mummy,' she said, putting her face close to Laura's and whispering the words. 'Don't tell Sonia. I want to go home.' A little retching sound accompanied this observation, 'And I'm going to be sick,' she announced.

She was. In very dramatic fashion. It had caused quite a diversion and Laura had never ever taken her to hospital again.

'She needs me, Beth,' she said now, as Beth swept the car into the outer lane of the M6. 'She'll be so frightened on her own.'

'Mother really . . .' Beth finally allowed her exasperation to show. 'She's not a child. She's thirty five and she's going to be just fine. I wish you'd stop going on about it. How can you be to blame? How could you have known she was pregnant? I didn't.'

'But I'm her mother,' Laura said, realising as she looked down that she was wearing her old gardening trousers. What had possessed her to put those on? 'I did wonder this weekend about Lotty,' she said, 'She spun me this tale about needing money to pay off her credit cards. I didn't believe her at the time and I should have trusted my instincts. Don't you see what it was really for?'

'What?' Beth seemed genuinely puzzled.

'For an abortion.' Laura glanced sharply at her youngest daughter. 'What she's done of course is try to do it herself rather than go into hospital and she's ended up making a mess of it. She has an absolute dread of hospitals but then of course you know that. She wouldn't even visit you when you had the boys.'

'Abortion? I'm sure you're mistaken,' Beth said, 'She wouldn't do that. Not Lotty.'

'Oh Elizabeth, you're such an innocent sometimes,' Laura said, staring out at the traffic, wondering why there was so much of it at this time of night. 'How much further?'

'About three-quarters of an hour. I'm going as fast as I dare. I hate night driving.'

'You should have let Martin bring me,' Laura said, glancing at her with a smile, 'Although I really appreciate you wanting to bring me yourself. It was very kind of you, darling.'

She lapsed into silence, content to let Beth concentrate. If only . . . if only she hadn't been so wrapped up this weekend thinking about Don, it might have occurred to her how worried dear Lotty had been. She had thought about it once or twice but dismissed it, assuming she was still upset about Max. Whose child was this? In view of what Lotty had told her, about the problems she and Max had had, it was a very strange situation.

'The smell alone will make her feel sick,' she went on, ignoring Beth's audible sigh, 'She'll be a terrible patient. She can't stand needles or blood. How on earth she can be your father's daughter I can't imagine.'

'She'll be okay,' Beth said. 'You don't die from a miscarriage. The worst thing that will happen is that she loses the baby.'

'Or the best thing?' Laura said, quite prepared for Beth's indignant reaction. 'It's all very well, Beth, but how will she cope with a baby? You know what she's like. She might be a very competent teacher but in other ways she's completely dizzy.'

'You never worried about me coping with a baby,' Beth said.

'That's because you're you. Lotty's bravado is all for show.

Didn't she seem to be coping so admirably with Max leaving her, all that monumental cursing, but how do we know what she really feels? I think she is close to heartbreak about Max and I wish I could do something to help. He's written to her, did you know, asking her to think about a reconciliation?'

'Who is the father?' Beth asked, 'Do we know?' A little sniff accompanied the question and Laura sighed, as much at Beth's reaction as Lotty's predicament.

'Do try to be charitable, darling,' she said quietly, her thoughts returning to her middle daughter. 'Poor Lotty, she must have been out of her mind this weekend worrying about things.'

The baby . . . she found herself wondering about it. Contrary to what she had said, part of her hoped it would live, although she had a clear feeling that it would not, that it was already gone. She was sad about that and a little puzzled for she had always been bloomingly healthy herself where having babies was concerned, as had Beth.

Once, years ago, George had lost a patient when a miscarriage went wrong but she wasn't about to mention that to Beth. Why on earth had that popped into her mind? Of course Lotty would be all right. She had to be. She couldn't imagine life without her. Not bubbly Lotty, George's special little darling . . . she suddenly wished he was here. Comforting her.

'Mum . . . you're not crying, are you?' Beth glanced at her, 'Shall I pull off at the services and we'll have a cup of tea?'

'No.' She sniffed, 'It'll waste time and I want to get there as soon as possible. I wish I'd brought something to eat though. Anxiety makes me hungry.'

'Open the glove-box,' Beth said, 'Right at the back, there's a bag of sweets. My emergency ration in case I get stranded in a snowdrift.'

Laura managed a smile, did as Beth asked.

She opened the paper bag. A little treasure trove of Beth's favourites. Beth had always been extremely generous when it came to sharing her sweeties.

They survived the remainder of the journey on a heady mixture of fruit gums, sherbet lemons and jelly babies.

14

'That woman nearly killed me, that woman doctor,' Lotty said, her lips forming a kiss as Laura leaned gently over her. 'I shall sue.'

Laura ignored that. Lotty was distraught and didn't know what she was saying. There would be no medical sueing in this family. Poor Lotty! If she had looked unwell this weekend, she now looked dreadful, a drip in a vein in her arm with blood flowing from a bag above.

'Beth's trying to park the car,' Laura said with an attempt at normality. 'She'll be along in a minute.' She studied her daughter a moment, 'Oh darling, why didn't you tell me? Am I such an ogre? I wouldn't have been at all shocked.'

'Wouldn't you?' Gingerly, Lotty moved, wincing as she did so. 'I suppose blabbermouth Rachel told you. I wanted to pretend it was something else.'

'Don't be silly.' Laura glanced round the eight-bed ward. 'Are you comfortable here?' she asked, 'Or would you like me to ask for a private room?'

'No, I wouldn't. I like the company such as it is,' Lotty said. 'We're all trying to outdo each other with our horror stories. We've all been to the brink and beyond, mother. That woman in the corner . . . don't look . . . she's been having a stitch in her womb to try and keep the baby in this time. She's lost four already at about four months, isn't that awful? And the two opposite are both infertile and having treatment so it's hardly a bundle of laughs. We can't produce a proper baby between us.' Her lip trembled and Laura took her hand. Lotty didn't fool her one little bit.

She hadn't quite recovered from the shock of the phone call from Rachel. She had long anticipated a bad-news phone call but it never concerned Lotty who had seemed bomb-proof. William it would be, lost at sea, flattened in an earthquake or whatever. She wished George was here now for Lotty but then perhaps not. He had been inclined to be stuffy whereas she was doing her damnedest to be broadminded.

'We were talking in the car on the way over and Beth wants you to go and stay with her at the vicarage when you get out of hospital,' she said, finding her eyes drawn to the fascination of the dripping blood. 'It's something she very much wants to do so I hope you won't be difficult about it.'

'I'd like that,' Lotty said to the surprise of Laura who had expected opposition, 'If you must know, I wasn't relishing having to cope in that bloody flat. I feel terrible, mum. Sort of . . . flattened.'

'Beth will take better care of you than I can.' Laura felt obliged to explain why she wasn't doing the offering. 'She always had a hankering to be a nurse but your father didn't think she was bright enough.'

'Have you brought me any grapes?'

'Well . . . no.' She smiled, flustered. In the confusion, she'd quite forgotten about the niceties of hospital visiting. 'It's been such a rush. Beth had to make arrangements for the boys and everything. If I could drive, it would have been less hassle. Never mind, we're here now. I had this awful panic that you were in some sort of danger.'

'It's no thanks to that woman that I'm not in any danger,' Lotty said, mercifully lowering her voice. 'I told her afterwards that my father was a doctor.' Pain flashed. 'Dad would have had her guts for garters, mummy, for doing that to me.' Tears filled her eyes and she looked like little Lotty again, in some trouble with Sonia and aiming for the sympathy vote.

Laura squeezed her hand. 'Ssh,' she said, 'You mustn't go around making allegations like that,' she went on quietly, knowing full well that Lotty was just the sort of person who could and would. 'You're upset. Just relax and let your body recover. Do you want to talk about what happened?'

'I'm still going to sue,' Lotty said, 'There are principles involved so don't try to persuade me otherwise. I know you. You're frightened of making a fuss. Well, sod that!'

'You know how awfully busy the staff are,' Laura said, feeling her loyalty pulled towards the professionals, George's people. 'They're taking wonderful care of you so I think it's a bit ungrateful to be talking about sueing. There's no harm done.'

'No harm?' Lotty's laugh was not its usual robust self and she winced as a result. They waited a moment whilst a nurse came to check on her and then, to Laura's relief, Beth came in, red-faced in her agitation. As Laura had half expected, she burst into tears the minute she saw Lotty and even Lotty tried in vain to quieten her. Laura felt a moment's irritation towards her youngest daughter as a few heads turned sympathetically in their direction.

'It was what they call a spontaneous abortion,' Lotty said. 'A miscarriage. It just happened. The foetus . . .' her voice broke a little and Beth gave a hiccough as she tried to control her sobs, taking the handkerchief Laura handed her. 'It was grossly malformed that woman said. She didn't let me see it. Although the nurse told me it was a boy. A baby boy.' Again, her lip trembled and Beth, dangerously close still to heavy weeping, held her close.

'It's best you didn't see it, Lotty,' Beth murmured, 'That was why it aborted of course.' She looked earnestly at both of them. 'Sometimes that happens. God's way of dealing with mistakes as it were. By mistakes, I mean . . . well, I certainly don't mean . . .' she flushed, wisely stopped.

Laura shot her an exasperated glance, succeeding in silencing her. Lotty however didn't seem to notice, a faraway look in her eye, as she started to speak again.

'At first it was just a few spots,' she said, 'I managed to get to the phone and called Rachel. She called the doctor before she came over. He said to go to bed and rest and everything would be all right but then, quite suddenly and with no pain then . . . it just started to pour out. Rachel was frightened to death. She called an ambulance. When I got here they called in that woman, the one who nearly killed me. Incompetent bitch!'

'Oh dear . . . I'm sure she didn't mean to,' Beth said stupidly.

'Too right she didn't mean to but she nearly did,' Lotty went on, 'I was bloody scared and she did nothing to make me feel any better. Looked at me as if I'd done it deliberately. As if I would. Thank God that nice nurse was there, holding my hand, giving me some sympathy.'

'And then?' Beth prompted gently, eyes, beautiful eyes, luminous.

'Only tell us if you want to, darling,' Laura reminded her, stroking the slender bandaged hand, so very relieved that Lotty had not done this herself. As if she would . . . she felt a moment's guilt that she had ever doubted her.

'She never said a word, the doctor. She just pressed and prodded and poked and hurt me to hell. Then she walked out, leaving the nurse to clean me up and bring me up here. They told me to get some sleep but what they didn't tell me was that I shouldn't be bleeding like before. How was I to know? I don't believe I even noticed. When the nurse came to check me . . .' her smile was tremulous. 'She deserves an Oscar for best actress. "My, Mrs Crabtree," she said, "we are bleeding just a little bit, aren't we?" She took my blood pressure and then all hell broke loose. They sent for that woman again. If I'd had the strength, I wouldn't have had her near me again. She didn't get it all out you see, the afterbirth. Left a bit in. It's just as well I've got a common-or-garden blood group or I'd have been up the Swanee.' She gave a sob. 'I've had a proper scrape down in theatre and that's why I feel so bloody lousy. I'm whoozy from the anaesthetic. And I've been sick.'

There was an awkward silence. Nearby some visitors departed.

'Has mum told you the arrangements?' Beth said at last, 'She's going to stay at your flat for a few days until they discharge you and then I'll come back for you both. Don't worry, Martin and I will look after you. You can be a lady of leisure for as long as you choose. Can't she, mum?'

'Yes.' Laura smiled with difficulty, Lotty's harrowing time leaving its impression.

'Would you like me to arrange for the hospital chaplain to call and have a chat,' Beth said before they left. 'He'll be a great comfort.'

'Forget the chaplain,' Lotty said, her voice and manner a little stronger, 'I'd prefer to talk to Martin when I come up.'

She moved her head for Beth's kiss, 'I can say what I like to him.'

'Of course. He's unshockable.' Beth flushed, obviously struggling to keep a grip on her emotions. 'God bless, Lotty.'

Laura couldn't be sure but, as *she* kissed Lotty, she thought she found herself whispering those words too.

From the flat in Balaclava Street, Laura made several phone calls. She managed to get hold of Don at his hotel, delighting in hearing his very businesslike tones.

'Oh, it's you, darling,' he said with a laugh, 'Sorry . . . I'm expecting a call from someone else. How are you?'

'Fine.' She sat down, prepared for a long chat. She would of course reimburse dear Lotty for her calls later. 'How are you?'

'Busy.' The laugh was brief and she sensed, a little irritated, that he was in a rush, not exactly anxious to get rid of her but . . .

'Lotty's in hospital,' she went on, 'So I'm staying at her place for the time being. I'll give you the number in case you want to call me.' She trotted out the number assuming he was jotting it down.

'Nothing serious I hope?'

'No. Nothing serious.' She hesitated, wondering if he was family enough to be told. Deciding, awkwardly, that at the moment she would rather not tell him. 'Is your business going well?' she asked, determined to be cheerful for the last thing he would want was to worry about her.

'The usual . . .' The noncommittal tone annoyed her. Damn it, Sebastian was the same. As soon as business was mentioned, they assumed she was some moron who wouldn't understand. On the contrary, she would like to find out more about the business Don was engaged in as it sounded infinitely more interesting than computers. She could relate to the beautiful pieces of furniture Don acquired for his various outlets.

'Do you miss me?' she regretted the words, the silly little-girl enquiry and, thousands of miles away, he chuckled.

'Of course. I can't wait to get back to you,' he said. 'Celebratory meal when I get home, eh? Get your glad rags on.'

She started to tell him about the rest of the family but her sensitive ears detected boredom even before he pleaded that business was pressing and he really would have to go. They said their goodbyes a little hastily and, when she replaced the receiver, she found she was a little cross with him. She understood he was busy but you'd think he would be able to spare a few minutes to chat. And you would also think he could pretend a certain interest in her family even if, as was patently obvious, he had none.

Elsie, whom she telephoned next, was far more agreeable to chatter. Much too much in fact.

'I've been worried sick, Mrs Howard,' she said in her very loud telephone voice, 'Miss Beth told me you'd been called away urgently but she didn't say why . . .?'

The pause was expectant and Laura sighed. She would find out sooner or later and, all in all, she was discreet.

'Poor lass,' she said, when Laura had finished, 'Knock you back, them things. Miscarriages. She won't be right for many a month. Did I ever tell you about mine, Mrs Howard?'

'I think you may have mentioned it, Elsie,' Laura said but it was too late. Elsie was firing on all cylinders, relating the event with gusto, with the same absorbed attention to detail as Lotty. Strange, for she was describing an event which had happened thirty years ago.

Afterwards, weary of Elsie and guilty that she'd not thought of contacting her eldest daughter before, she tried to ring Sonia but she could only get the answering machine which she refused to speak to. How could you possibly converse with an electrical gadget?

Sonia would find out sooner or later and the most important thing now was to use the time at her disposal to do something with the dire state of the flat. It was quite some time since she had tackled cleaning on such a scale and she did not have Elsie's experience but she could learn. Quickly, she compiled a list of what she would need and went down to the shop. She didn't bargain for the rapturous reception she received from Mr Dassayaje. It involved going through to the private quarters at the rear for a cup of tea which she felt unable to refuse.

'How is Mrs Crabtree?' Mr Dassayaje looked most concerned.

'Emergency we understand? Ambulance in the middle of the night? Appendicitis?'

'A sudden haemorrhage and she's recovering well, thank you,' Laura said and thankfully he did not press the subject further, embarking instead on his favourite topic, gardening. Happier to be talking about non-controversial matters, Laura told him about her garden by the lake. 'I'm so lucky to live there, aren't I?' she said as she finished describing it. 'Look . . . why don't you and Mrs Dassa . . .?' she struggled with the awkward pronunciation and his smile broadened. 'You're most welcome to visit any time you are passing by.'

'It is most kind,' he said with a formal bow, glancing up as the shop bell rang out, 'Unfortunately, we do not have much leisure time . . . opening on Sundays now too . . . but, if we are able, we would very much like to visit the Windermere lake and Mrs Crabtree's mother's garden.'

Smiling, Laura returned with her purchases to the flat above. Starting work in the kitchen, she found the letter from Max crumpled in a corner. Not knowing what it was, she started to read it and then dropped it quickly. What had Lotty done about it? More to the point, what would she say if Max rang whilst Lotty was still in hospital? She would have to be very discreet. It wasn't up to her to tell Max about it.

She'd worked out a plan of the least said the better and when the phone rang, she was ready, breathing a sigh of relief however as Sonia's sulky voice came through, 'Someone might have thought to ring me,' she said. 'I've been ringing home for days trying to get hold of you. It was Elsie who told me. Honestly, mummy, it's a bit much when the cleaner knows more than I do.' She paused, obviously waiting for an apology.

'How dare you, Sonia! Elsie is much more than a *cleaner* as you put it. She thinks a great deal of all four of you,' Laura told her, waiting until she had the muttered embarrassed apology before she continued, 'You know how huffy you are if I call you at work, passing me from pillar to post, palming me off. And at home, all I got was your answering machine. Several times in fact. And I do not speak to them.'

'Why ever not? You're so old-fashioned, mummy. Everybody has answering machines these days.'

'I don't.'

'Exactly. How is Lotty by the way?'

'I thought you'd never ask. She is recovering, thank you. Why don't you call her at the hospital? She can receive calls.'

'I'll wait until she's at Beth's. I don't want to speak on a hospital line.' Sonia's sniff was very audible, 'Did you know she was pregnant, mummy? Seb and I guessed actually.'

'No,' Laura said wearily, sensing a lecture. Sonia was like George. Stuffy. She talked about *her* being old-fashioned!

'How could she have been so careless? Just like her, of course. Hang the consequences. Does Max know?'

'Not as far as I know. It's up to Lotty whether she tells him or not. I don't intend to. Nor must you, Sonia.'

'I never speak to Max these days. When are you coming to see the chateau?' Ah . . . at last . . . the point of the call. 'We're going over by private plane this weekend. Seb has a friend who pilots his own. Exciting, isn't it?'

'I can't leave Lotty, darling.'

'Why not? Beth's going to look after her, isn't she? And she isn't exactly at death's door either. Are you making an excuse, mummy?'

'Look, Sonia . . .' her irritation bubbled over, 'It will make no difference if I see the chateau or not as I have no intention of moving to France with you. Will you get that straight? I will help with the financial side of it if that's what's bothering you . . .'

'It's not *just* that,' Sonia wailed, 'Can't you see that? It may have started out as that if I'm honest but I do so want the others to see that I'm taking on the responsibility of looking after you. You never let me do anything. You always turn away from everything I suggest. Daddy would let me look after *him* when he was old if it were the other way round. You're coming to live with us, mummy, and that's that.'

'I am not and I resent you calling me old, Sonia. I wasn't going to tell you yet but I see I will have to to shut you up. I'm seriously considering getting married again.'

There was a short silence then Sonia laughed . . . unsure. 'You are joking, aren't you?'

'I am not. He's called Don Fletcher and he lives over in Grange. We met there at a do at the Netherwood. He's a widower.'

'Why didn't we meet him?' Sonia's amazement was obvious, her voice cracking. 'At the weekend?'

'He's away on business, dear. He was sorry he missed you all. However, he will be home shortly so you can meet him then if you wish.'

'Why didn't you tell us about him then? Are you ashamed of him?'

'Not at all and it's impertinent of you to say that, Sonia. It just didn't seem the right moment, that's all.'

'I don't see that there'll ever be a right moment. Do any of the others know? Does William know? Mummy, I can't believe it. Have you gone out of your mind?' Sonia's voice rose to a screech, 'How long have you known him? This *man*?'

'Long enough.' Strangely, Laura found she was rather enjoying this. Sonia's splutteringly indignant reaction was hilarious, just the reaction she might have expected. 'We enjoy each other's company immensely. He is quite charming. Tall. Grey-haired. Distinguished. Terribly successful. If we marry, then I am thinking of selling Fernlands in fact and moving into his house.'

'Mummy . . . hang on . . .' muttered voices in the background, Sonia's prominent, and then, 'Oh damn it . . . I have to go. I'm already late for an urgent business meeting. But I shall speak to you again.'

With that threat ringing in her ears, Laura replaced the receiver with a smile.

15

'We weren't going to tell you just yet until you were feeling a bit better,' Beth said, 'But then we decided that it wasn't fair to keep you in the dark and you are such a strong person, Lotty, so we knew you would cope with it.'

Lotty glanced at her. She was sitting in a chair in the room Beth had prepared for her, one of the pretty guest rooms at the vicarage. Old furniture and frills. Lots of frills. A predominantly pink patchwork quilt, no doubt made by Beth's fair hand, lay across the big comfortable bed. The walls were papered in a pinky stripe and, although a few weeks ago Lotty might have thought it twee as only Beth was capable of being twee, she now revised her opinion, found it relaxing, found the whole atmosphere of the vicarage warm and relaxing. Utterly peaceful.

Tired after the journey up, she had made no protest as Beth had cosseted her, fed and watered her and now she was content to sit and watch as Beth unpacked her belongings, feeding them reverently in turn into the huge old wardrobe and the chest of drawers.

'I can't believe it,' she said to Beth at last. The miscarriage seemed to have had the effect of making her a bit slow on the uptake for Beth had needed to tell her not once, but twice, before she could even begin to take it in.

'Nor can I. And as for Sonia . . . well, she's livid,' Beth said with a little smile. 'We must try to keep it in proportion, Lotty. Sonia may have misunderstood.'

'I don't see how. Mother said she was getting married again, didn't she? How can you misinterpret that?' Lotty felt her anger rising and anger was not good for her. 'Why didn't she tell us, Beth? Christ! . . . she had plenty of opportunity.'

'It wasn't the ideal moment,' Beth said gently, 'Perhaps she's still waiting for the right moment. You know what Sonia's like. I expect she wheedled it out of her. Oh dear, I find it all a bit upsetting. I suppose we're going to have to face him sometime.'

'What is she thinking of? How can she do this to dad?' Furious with the way the tears turned on like a tap these days, Lotty blinked them away. 'He was the most wonderful man in the world. I don't care who the hell *this* man is, he won't compare. Do you know anything at all about him?'

She shook her head. 'Martin thinks he may have met him. He recalls the name but can't remember what he looks like. Men are hopeless about things like that, aren't they? His name's Don Fletcher and he only moved into the area six months ago. Apparently he's bought the house at Grange ready for his impending retirement but at the moment he's still globe-trotting. He imports.'

'Imports what, for God's sake? Do we know?' The questions spluttered forth. 'Six months ago, did you say? You mean to tell me that she's only known him at the most six months and she's talking about getting married? Is she unhinged?'

Beth did not answer, fussing with the last of the items in the suitcase, Lotty's shoes.

'Where are your slippers?'

'I haven't any. And for God's sake don't take that as a hint. I don't want bloody slippers for Christmas.'

'Please, Lotty . . .' Beth frowned, enormous-bottomed in baggy trousers and one of her knitted sweaters. 'I don't want to sound priggish but I wish you wouldn't swear so much especially in front of the boys. They're at an impressionable age. And I particularly object to you blaspheming as it's not fair to Martin.'

'Okay, sorry . . .' she held up her hand in apology, 'I shall be sweetness and light. Can I smoke though? I can't survive without a smoke.'

'I suppose so.' Beth sighed and sat on the edge of the bed. 'Sonia's worried about the money,' she said, 'Our inheritance.'

Lotty grinned. 'I don't give a bugger about that,' she said, 'Money doesn't interest me, Beth, it never has. I'm more concerned about mother, about the mistake she's making. Don't you see? It's not her fault. This swine has conned her. Widower eh?

Well . . . it's obvious. He's about to retire and he wants to make damned sure he has a comfortable cushion . . . money-wise . . . do you understand what I'm getting at?'

Beth nodded, 'Yes I think so and I think you're being a bit mean, Lotty. We've never met him so it's a bit much to prejudge, isn't it? And I really don't think mum would be so easily taken in.'

'Stop being so bloody fair, Beth. Take it from me, he's on the lookout for a wealthy widow and mother fits the bill perfectly. Not only is she wealthy but she's pretty too. He's charmed the knickers off her.'

'Lotty . . . really!'

'I bet they're having it off,' Lotty said firmly. 'Bound to be. That's why she had such a secret look about her on her birthday weekend. I thought there was something funny about her but of course at the time I was a touch preoccupied myself . . .' she smiled sadly, 'I wish I'd told you Beth.'

'You should have. Still . . .' Beth seemed to make an effort, brightened up. 'I want you to put your feet up now and rest. Dinner's at seven. I'll feed the boys early so that we can eat in peace, just the three of us.' She smiled that gentle smile of hers as she went out. 'I'll be working in the garden. If you want anything, just open the window and yell at me.'

Lotty hadn't the strength to argue. She didn't want to be treated like an invalid. However, when Beth closed the door behind her, she moved over to the bed and lay on it. The memories of the hospital were still vivid and refused to go away, to diminish. She kept reliving them, moment by moment.

Dobson had been good about it. Surprisingly understanding. She was, at the moment, on sick leave and he had been at pains to tell her to make sure she was fit before she came back. There was no chance of her getting back to school before the holidays, not now, and she was irked about that as it would mess things up for the children but there was nothing she could do about it.

Dobson knew what was what but she knew she could rely on his discretion. As for the medical people, well, they kept saying that she could have another baby. The doctor, not *that* doctor, had told her that there was no reason why she shouldn't conceive again. And next time, he had said, brightly and confidently, they would keep an eye on her and there should be absolutely no problems.

There *was* a reason why she would not conceive. Max. She now knew that the only man she wanted to father her child was Max. And he still hadn't been in touch. He could pass a message on for God's sake. He knew her mother's number. He knew Beth's. Sonia's.

Perhaps he had had second thoughts. Oh Max, you sod, raising my hopes like that, she whispered into her pillow. Please ring.

16

Suzanne was exhausted as only someone who has not slept properly for several nights can be exhausted. She was also heavily pregnant and that did not help. It was debatable whether she should have attempted the trip at this stage of her pregnancy for airlines were a bit iffy about allowing pregnant women to fly. She had bluffed her way on board and was glad she was of such a stature that did not show her pregnancy to its full effect.

She was five feet eleven, well built, but even so the flight attendants had eyed her with some concern not relishing an emergency birth on the long-haul flight. It was all her own fault. She had dithered about leaving William but, in the end, she was determined that the baby would be born in England. She did not want an Australian baby. She quite liked Australia, city Australia, but William preferred the outback with its soul-destroying heat and flies, its sun-baked earth.

William had given her the instructions on how to find his mother but she had stupidly lost them in the hotel in Singapore and she could only remember a little of what he had written. Taking a bus north had been the first step but, dimwit that she was, she had got off at the wrong station and the coach was speeding off before she realised. The next one was tomorrow and she was rapidly running out of cash in any case.

The bus station could have been anywhere. She could write a book on the great bus stations of the world. Diesel fumes, litter, a film of grime everywhere, that peculiar smell, the resigned faces of the waiting passengers. At least the advertisements on the hoardings were in English so that told her something. She was home. Sort of.

What should she do? She held down the feeling of panic and struggled with her flight bag into the Ladies, gritting her teeth at the state of it. Lavatories of the world! That was another story.

She humped her overfull bag into the cubicle with her, pressing it against the door as there was no lock. She managed as best she could. She was needing to visit the lavatory frequently as baby pressed against her and she seemed to have spent the entire flight queueing for the toilet. Something to do she supposed.

Washing her hands with a sliver of green soap, she contemplated her reflection in the dingy mirror.

'Just take a look at us, Kate,' she muttered, moving her hands over her abdomen as she felt the baby kick. 'We are a mess. We have to look a bit more presentable before we meet your grandmama.' She bit her lip, rummaging in her handbag for a lipstick and hairbrush. She was not exactly pretty but, if she tried, she didn't look so bad. She felt awkward because of her height and was inclined to stoop. Dark blonde hair that needed a wash. There wasn't much she could do about that now. She combed it smooth, retied the ribbon that was holding it in its pony-tail and put on some lipstick, the only one she had, orangey pink that had looked fine in Australia, in that light, but looked utterly grotesque here.

She stepped outside into the waiting area and sat on a bench. She did not have enough money for a hotel and couldn't face a doss-house. In any case, it wasn't fair to Kate to take her to places like that. She supposed she could take a taxi but it was an awful long way to Windermere and it would be an unfortunate way to arrive. 'We've never met, Mrs Howard. I'm Suzanne . . . oh, by the way . . . can you pay the taxi?'

She had to make a better impression than that for she was about to throw herself on the woman's mercy. She hoped William was right and not viewing his mother through rose-tinted spectacles. She hoped she was as sweet and good-natured as he said she was. She would have to be if she was to put up with this wretched situation. If all else failed, there was an aunt of hers somewhere in Sheffield but she hadn't seen her for years and they didn't get on. With a bit of luck, Laura would be expecting her for she should have received William's letter of explanation by now. If he'd ever got round to writing and posting it, that is.

'We shouldn't have done it, darling. We should have stayed with your daddy,' she muttered, startled as her whisper echoed in the gloom of the concrete chamber. She had talked to the baby from day one. She had known immediately she was pregnant and she also knew that the baby was a girl. A blasé traveller, Kate, even before she was born.

A coach thundered in and disgorged a handful of weary travellers, pale and coughing and crumpled. The engine chugged and emitted a fresh supply of fumes in her direction. She felt her eyes water and stood up before she choked on them. She could hitch-hike. She had hitch-hiked worldwide, at first alone, and later with William and his friends. She felt safe with them. Alone, she had developed a fear that she had never felt in those far-off early days when she was fresh out of university, full of excitement and enthusiasm for travel.

What choice was there? She could kip here until morning but that was, on balance, more dangerous. There was an unshaven gent nearby giving her the once-over. Hell, he must be desperate! She wasn't afraid so much for herself for she had been in some pretty tricky situations but now there was baby Kate to consider and she daren't take any chances. She hoisted her bag onto her shoulder and stepped out into the cool of the night. This was home but it didn't feel like home any more than Australia.

The night was clear, the sky twinkling with a million pulses of light. Unwisely, for she was unbalanced with the bump, she stared up at the stars, reminded at once as she spotted particular familiar constellations that she was in a different hemisphere. She had left darling William behind. Tears threatened and she gulped a mouthful of cold air and steadied herself, moving to a spot under a street-lamp where she could be seen by passing motorists.

There was no option. She thumbed without expectation. She ought to keep moving. She supposed she could walk if necessary although it was foolish to try. She had one bar of chocolate left which would sustain her.

'What shall we do, baby?' she asked, 'Book into a hotel . . .?' And risk the wrath of not being able to pay the bill? Asking William's mother to fork out for a hotel bill was even worse. The baby turned a slow somersault fluttering against her and she smiled, huddled closer into her coat. Kate was going to be intelligent. Bright and beautiful with William's wonderful blue eyes. She and Kate had already discussed profound things and listened to music, not William's guitar stuff but her favourite Elgar and Bizet.

A dark car, big and sleek, drove past and she saw its reversing lights come on. Panic flooded her then, as quickly, subsided. Trust your instincts. At the wheel was a woman. She was alone. Frowning.

'You shouldn't be doing that,' she said, 'Don't you know how risky it is? I could have been anyone. Hop in and I'll take you wherever you want to go.'

'Thank you.' Suzanne climbed in, throwing her bag in the rear. The car was new and smelt of leather and a subtle perfume. She wanted to lie back and sleep but the woman, wanting company, was chatty and as it was her car, Suzanne felt obliged to return the small talk. By the time they reached a darkened Windermere, crawled hesitantly downhill towards the lake shore, they were almost friends.

'Are you sure you don't want me to drive you right up to the house?' the woman asked, stopping on the road. 'I can turn into the drive and help you with your bag.' She peered anxiously through the windscreen. 'It's pitch dark.'

'No, it isn't. It isn't so dark and I need a bit of fresh air. Thanks. You've come a long way out of your way.'

'That's quite all right. Good luck, dear.' She leaned across and touched her hand. 'Look after yourself and that baby.'

Suzanne waved her off. The silence once she had gone was immense. She needed a few moments to compose herself and she was stiff after sitting in the car so long. She rubbed at her back which was beginning to ache and looked at the house, checking on the gatepost that this was indeed it. She would be popular if she wakened some other poor soul at this time of night.

It loomed large, closer to the road than she had expected, as dark as the lake beyond was dark. Sensitive to smells, she sniffed the night air, a heady combination of garden and lake. She let it close over her. It was so fresh and cool. Nothing like Australia, the almost-desert vast interior Australia she and William knew. This felt good. Suspiciously like she wanted home to feel.

A spring in her step, she walked on. Nearly there darling, she said to the baby. What they both needed was a bit of comforting. A warm drink. A soft bed. Safety.

The thought kept her going.

Suzanne was installed in the sitting room, having a cocoa by the time a hastily summoned Martin arrived, accompanied by a panicky Beth. Laura apologised for dragging them out, saying she had thought Suzanne was a prowler.

'It seemed ridiculous to call the police,' she said, hanging on briefly to her son-in-law's hefty shoulder, still feeling a bit shaky. 'Sorry. I heard the noise of the gate opening and footsteps and I panicked. It was when she rang the bell that it occurred to me that prowlers do not do that.'

'Thank God you're all right, mum.' Beth's eyes were on Suzanne. 'We'll get back home ... we had to wake Lotty to tell her we were coming so she'll be worried.'

'Ring her if you like, darling,' Laura's eyes were also on Suzanne. 'We'll be fine. The two of us.'

'We'll just get back.' Beth kissed her and departed, shooing away the suggestion that her mother had been a nuisance. 'We've always said you could ring us if you felt at all worried,' she reminded her.

Returning to where Suzanne was sitting dazed in an armchair, the mug cupped in her hands, Laura assumed a brisk air, her initial surprise gone. At first when the girl had announced herself as Suzanne, she had thought that William was lurking around the corner but her disappointment was short-lived. Suzanne was the next best thing and judging by the state of her, she was very important indeed to her son.

'A warm bath I think and then we'll get you into bed. You look absolutely exhausted, dear.'

'May I sit a moment?' She had grey eyes and scruffy hair. A stronger face than she thought William's girl would have. A tall girl with big hands and feet. Laura felt an ache of tenderness towards her, for her awkwardness, the way she had blushed as Laura had taken in her ragged appearance.

'Do you feel like talking?' she asked, conscious of her own attire. With Don absent, she had resorted to an old familiar dressing gown over unflattering pyjamas. Neither of them would have graced a Paris catwalk.

'I can't believe that son of mine,' she said, 'Putting you on a plane in your condition. What was he thinking of?'

'Please don't be angry with him. He didn't want me to come but I insisted. I can be very pig-headed,' she said with a tired smile, huddled into the travelling rug Laura had wrapped round her until the fire took hold. It was blazing merrily now and Suzanne stretched out dirty bare feet towards the hearth. Her shoes, once white trainers, steamed gently beside her. 'I'll tell you everything, Mrs Howard,' she said, 'If you're ready to hear it?'

'Of course I am and call me Laura. Are you and William really married?' she asked, noting the thin gold band on the girl's finger. 'It's quite all right if you're not,' she added quickly, 'I'm very modern in outlook despite what my daughters think of me.'

Suzanne nodded, looking down at her ring.

'His idea,' she said. 'He got old-fashioned about the whole thing as soon as I was pregnant. I'm sorry we didn't tell you. I wanted him to tell you when he rang on your birthday but he wanted to surprise you later.'

'He's certainly done that. When is the baby due?' She smiled at the prospect. William's child.

Suzanne named a date, rubbing gently at her stomach. 'It's a girl,' she explained earnestly, 'I'd like to introduce you if I may. Kate . . . this is your grandmama Howard.'

Laura warmed instantly to her new daughter-in-law. Grandmama . . . she liked that. It had a lovely ring to it.

'We met in India,' Suzanne said with a little sigh. 'After I left university I decided to do some travelling . . . oh, I have a degree in English Literature . . .' she added with what seemed like an apologetic smile, 'The year I meant to take out just stretched on and on. Waste of time in some ways. I'm sick to death of strange places and everlasting sun. William disagrees. He loves the outback particularly but I've told him it's no place to bring up a child. He fancies getting our own place but I couldn't stand the loneliness and a child . . . children . . . need friends of their own age. The flying doctor marvellous as it is, solitary education at the end of a radio . . . well, I just can't cope with all that. I need a bit of civilisation. This sort of civilisation, the small town kind.'

'He isn't coming back then?' She knew as she asked the question it was hopeless. William would not be coming back. He really knew how to ditch his responsibilities, always had, but, under these extreme circumstances, with another grandchild in the offing, what could she do?

'I don't want to impose but may I stay here a while, please?' The question to which there was only one answer hung gently in the air. 'Until I get myself sorted out with somewhere to live?'

She thought of Don. This would play havoc with the plans they were hatching. Oh dear, just when they were hoping to get away for a holiday together, just the two of them, to relax and enjoy each other with all thoughts of her family taboo. That's what Don had said. 'Let's just think of ourselves for once, my darling,' he had said.

She looked at the girl and smiled.

'Of course you can stay,' she said.

'She couldn't get rid of us fast enough,' Beth said on the way back. The headlamps pierced the darkness as Martin drove them home and she rubbed at her eyes, tired.

She shivered and pulled her hastily gathered wrap closely round her. An hour ago, something like that, she and Martin had been tucked up together, fast asleep. The sudden urgent ringing of the telephone down in the hall had terrified her, cut through her dream and, heart thumping, dazed from sleep, she had shot downstairs to answer it before it woke everyone. Out of the blue like that, it had reminded her instantly of the phone call from mother on the day dad had collapsed on the golf course.

The whole house would likely be wide awake when they got back. She had felt it necessary to wake Lotty to tell her where they were going in case the boys woke and panicked that they were not there.

If it hadn't been so serious at the time, it would have been comic. They had charged over at full speed, outdoor attire over their pyjamas, Martin of all people driving like a maniac, terrified that mum would be in dire peril by the time they got there.

'I think she was embarrassed,' Martin said gently, easing the car a little more genteelly home. 'She needn't have been. It was a perfectly understandable mistake. After all, one does not expect visitors to arrive unannounced at one thirty in the morning, kitten.'

'Suzanne . . .' Beth curled the name round her tongue. William's lady. She would go over tomorrow and find out what was happening. She would take mum a sticky ginger cake and find out what was going on.

Lotty was up when they got back, smoking.

'The kettle's just boiled,' she said, 'Everything okay? The boys are fast asleep, not a peep out of either of them. I didn't know what I was supposed to do. I was going to ring the police if you weren't back soon and mother can't have put the phone back on the hook. I couldn't get through. I've been sitting here imagining the worst. Rape. Murder.' She shuddered, trying to laugh it off, but her eyes were still shocked. 'And those dogs of yours are useless. Dead to the world, the pair of them.'

'You're never going to believe this, Lotty . . .' Beth sank onto the sofa whilst Martin immediately bustled into the kitchen to make a pot of tea. 'Guess who's turned up? On the doorstep unannounced at half past one in the morning?'

'William,' she said at once. 'Why didn't he ring first? He has no common sense.'

'No, not William. Suzanne.'

'Suzanne?' Lotty stared a minute before the penny dropped. '*The* Suzanne? On her own?'

'Yes.' Beth removed the full ashtray, pushed another at Lotty, absolutely determined not to say a word about the smoking.

'I thought she was in Australia.' Lotty crossed her legs, her dressing gown sliding away to show off a good deal of bare leg. Beth glanced at Martin who had just come in with a tray but he seemed not to notice, handing out biscuits like there was no tomorrow. The chocolate ones reserved for visitors. Beth took one.

'She's just flown over,' she said, 'She took a coach from London and hitched the last bit for some reason. Mum says she hasn't a bean.'

'She and William both.' Lotty laughed, 'They sound a good twosome.'

'She's also pregnant.' Beth frowned and there was a short silence while they all digested this.

'Really?' If it bothered Lotty, she didn't show it. 'And what is she doing at Fernlands? Don't tell me she's intending to stay? For Christ's sake . . . sorry, Martin . . . that's all mother needs. She's being pestered non-stop by this randy old sod she's got involved with. She's had all this . . . my problems . . . and now Suzanne.'

Somebody has to go to Australia and drag him home. He can't shrug it off. Not this time.'

'Going to Australia is not very practical is it?' Beth said. 'What do you think, darling?' She looked at her husband who was pouring the tea.

'I know one thing,' he said. 'Your mother will of course do as she wishes but, if I know her at all, she will welcome Suzanne with open arms, looks as if she has already. The other matter will have to wait. Don't forget this child will be William's and your mother is especially fond of William.'

'That's true. He's her favourite,' Lotty said flatly and Beth flushed, not willing to admit it but knowing it to be true. 'He can do no wrong in mother's eyes,' Lotty went on, 'The fact that everything he does *is* wrong is conveniently glossed over. She'd better not put her in my room, that's all.'

'Don't be ridiculous.' Beth glanced at her, smiled. 'What difference can that make? You don't live at home any more.'

'No. And I don't live here either.' Lotty tossed the last of her cigarette into the ashes of the spent fire. 'Tell me, for God's sake, won't you, if I'm outstaying my welcome.'

'Of course you're not,' Martin said at once as Beth had known he would. 'You stay as long as you like, Lotty. Get yourself fully fit. Beth and I love to have you here, don't we?'

'I've got to get back fairly soon,' Lotty said, giving a huge yawn, 'I owe Mr Dassayaje money, although he's a love and certainly won't press me. But there are other bills to sort out. And Max is supposed to be phoning me at the flat. It might be a good idea if I'm there when he does that.'

Beth waited until Martin had disappeared into the kitchen before she asked Lotty about Max.

'Have you decided anything?' she asked gently.

'I can't make my mind up. I need to talk to him face to face. If I can manage to do that without swooning at his feet. He has an unfair advantage. He has this extraordinary effect on me, Beth. He manages to knock all the sense out of me. God, it makes me so angry with myself. I'm the last person you'd expect to go all fluttery and feminine, aren't I?'

'Not a bit of it, Lotty.' Beth smiled a little. 'I know exactly what you mean.'

'Don't tell me Max does it to you too? Does he do it to all women? I know he's an attractive so-and-so but I must say I'm surprised that you find him that way.'

'No. I meant . . .' Flustered, Beth declined to explain. She had meant Martin of course for he had that effect on her but she didn't care to talk about it with Lotty. She'd certainly never thought of Max in any sort of sexual way. He belonged to her sister for goodness sake, just as Sebastian belonged to Sonia.

'If you want to ring Max tomorrow, please do,' she said, by way of terminating the conversation. 'You stay up as long as you like . . .' she did not bother to stifle the yawn, 'Martin and I are going to bed. It's very late and we have to be up early tomorrow for the children.'

Leaving Lotty to her own devices, she and Martin returned to bed, trying to recall the slumbrous state they had been in before the frantic call.

'I wish Lotty would talk to me,' Martin said as Beth snuggled in his arms, feeling a little chill suddenly from the impromptu drive, 'I know she wants to, you told me she wanted to but she doesn't seem able to and I don't want to press it.'

'She seems different. The miscarriage has changed her, don't you think?' Beth said thoughtfully, her voice muffled against his shoulder. His body was warm against her. 'She came with me to church the other morning when I was doing the flowers. Supposed to be helping me. She just took off, wandered to the front and sat in a pew and do you know . . . I could have sworn she was praying.'

She frowned into the dark, aware that Martin was not really listening, beginning to drift off. That's what she ought to be doing herself, praying. The red dress, worn once, hung guiltily in her wardrobe. She had thought of trying to redeem the situation by giving it to Oxfam but worried that it might be on some sort of hit list . . . hot goods . . . and a policeman might pounce on it, ask who had brought it in. Oh God, what am I to do?

She would return it to the shop she had stolen it from. Somehow.

The guilt was starting to press down on her, stifle her, and she felt that if she didn't say something to someone very soon, she would burst.

She shifted a little in her husband's arms. He muttered something in his sleep. She sighed, tuned her breathing to his, and fell asleep too.

18

'Lotty? I just got back from France,' Sonia's telephone voice was harassed as usual, 'And then I had to go immediately to Bath for a meeting with a business colleague. Stayed over two days. Seb and I haven't managed to catch up with each other yet. It's been all go. I've never had a minute. Is Beth there?'

'No. Piano lessons or some damned thing. I never realised how much fetching and carrying there is to do when you have children. Just as well you and I don't, I suppose. Must you speak to Beth? Can't you tell me whatever it is?' Lotty pulled a face into the phone. No 'how are you feeling, Lotty?' . . . her sister was just self, self, self.

'I want us all to meet to discuss mummy and this man. Really, Lotty, it's too bad of her. It's been on my mind all the time. I've been frantic that she might suddenly sneak off and elope or something like that.'

'Hardly!' Lotty laughed. 'Is that likely, Sonia?'

'The way things are at the moment anything's possible. It can't be a menopausal thing, can it? Surely she's past all that.'

'That's not all,' Lotty said darkly, enjoying this moment, 'Remember Suzanne? The one on William's card? Well . . . she's arrived from Australia. Out of the blue. Middle of the night actually. Scared us all to merry hell. Mother heard footsteps on the drive, naturally thought it was a burglar and rang Martin and he and Beth had to go off, tyres screeching.'

'Where's William?'

'Still there. Refuses to leave apparently.'

'We'll soon see about that.' The sigh was deep. 'I don't know what the world's coming to when people think they can simply ditch their responsibilities. It is essential, Lotty, doubly so now, that we arrange a meeting at the earliest opportunity. I can fit you in on Wednesday afternoon, you and Beth, if you can get yourselves down here.'

'Like hell. We're not driving all the way to London, Sonia, to fit in with your schedule. You can come up here.' She smiled slightly at Sonia's cheek. 'In any case, I'm an invalid. I'm supposed to be taking it easy.'

'You don't seem to realise, either you or Beth, that I run a business. An international business. My presence is required. I can't just swan off here, there and everywhere because of a little family problem.'

'So it's just a little family problem now? I thought it was a matter of life and death. I don't want to meet you because frankly there's sod all we can do about it, Sonia. I'm furious with her too but short of dragging her away forcibly from him, I don't think we stand much chance of making her see sense. She's bloody starry-eyed. It's all those crappy romances she reads.'

'We have to try. I know you pride yourself, Lotty, on not being mercenary but is it fair on us? Would daddy have liked it? We stand to lose everything if she ups and marries again. He will become her next of kin, this man of hers, and we'll be second fiddle to him. William has to be told. We have his address, don't we? Let's write to him there initially and then, if all else fails, I see I will have to be the one to go to Australia and get him to come home to sort it out. Mummy will listen to him. You know she's always taken notice of what he says. Why I can't imagine but there it is.'

'Beth's back.' Lotty heard the car in the drive, 'Do you want to speak to her?'

'No. I have to go. Oh ... are you feeling any better by the way?'

At last. 'Okay, thanks. Beth's feeding me up on nursery food. Milk puddings and the like. By the way, did I mention that she's pregnant? No ... not Beth, Suzanne.'

Sonia's laugh was brittle, 'No you didn't. As if there aren't enough complications, she has to add to them. I'll be in touch later about meeting up although goodness knows when I'm going to be able to manage it.'

'Bye. See you soon.' Lotty replaced the receiver. She hoped to God not. Once a year was quite enough, thank you.

Don was due home and she had not told him about Suzanne staying. When he got back, he had suggested a dinner party at his place when he could meet some of the family. He wanted them to be together when they made the announcement. Side by side. She had spoilt things somehow by blurting it out to Sonia like that. A dinner party would be nice and Don's home was lovely. They would ask Beth and Martin and Lotty and Suzanne also . . . Sonia and Sebastian, too, if they were prepared to drive up.

Laura was aware that they were cool on the idea, all except Suzanne, who had reacted very positively. But then Suzanne was not her flesh and blood and, more to the point, Suzanne had no memory of George.

It saddened and disappointed her for she had foolishly hoped they would be as happy as she. She was lonely. She wanted company. Not only that, she wanted love and Don was the man she wanted. Simple.

Like a teenager, she crossed the days off the calendar before she would see him again.

She could hardly wait.

19

Lotty was getting used to waking in the room at the vicarage. Somehow the birdsong was welcome here or perhaps she had more time to enjoy it. She stretched luxuriously. It was past ten o'clock and the tray that Beth had brought earlier lay untouched on the bedside table. It still looked pretty even though the tea was stone cold in the pot. Beth spoiled her. With a sigh, she leapt out of bed and crossed to the window, drawing the pale yellow curtains and blinking at the sunshine. Beth was messing about down in the garden, hoeing the rosebed as if her life depended on it. Lotty watched her a moment with a little smile on her face. Dearest Beth. She looked as if she had the worries of the world on her shoulders sometimes and yet she had nothing at all to worry about.

Mr Dassayaje had kindly forwarded some mail. Some Get Well cards from school. One from Finney and one from Jade Entwistle. Lotty smiled as she saw them next to the breakfast tray, looking at them again. How sweet! A lump in her throat for ever thinking ill of Finney and as for Jade . . . as soon as she got back, she would get in touch with her privately, organise some tuition, let her have some books to read. She was determined she was not going to let that child slip through her fingers.

Back to family matters, Don Fletcher was on his way home, business concluded, according to mother. They were all invited to dinner at his home. Beth was in a tizzy about what to wear. Lotty was going to wear skin-tight satin trousers and a skimpy top just to test the old sod's reaction. How dare he get her mother into a compromising situation? Mother clammed up now whenever she tried to get her to talk about him saying she should reserve judgement until she had met him. Fair enough, Lotty supposed, but she wasn't particularly in the mood for being fair. When it came to Don Fletcher, she felt like coming up with all the tricks in the book to get the man to admit he was after mum's money. That had to be the only reason. It couldn't be sex surely?

Through the window, Lotty saw that Beth was returning indoors. Time she was up and about! She would have to think about leaving this little cocoon soon. It was not pleasant to think of returning to Balaclava Street but she had to resolve the Max thing, perhaps even get in touch herself. They couldn't leave it like this. Unsettled.

She would leave after the dinner party but before she did, she had to talk to Martin. She had been putting it off because it was embarrassing but she must talk to him, swear him to silence, for she wanted nobody else to know especially mother. At least she could trust Martin to keep his word.

Stripping off her sleeping tee-shirt, she stood naked before the mirror looking at herself critically. She was putting a bit of weight on, thanks to Beth's delicious home cooking, though her body did still have a bashed-up look about it. All systems go for a baby and then . . . wham. Next time perhaps, if there was to be a next time. She touched her stomach tenderly and choked back the tears.

'Aunt Lotty . . .?' The crash against the door and the instant opening of it had her grabbing a robe and slipping it on, turning away from John's innocent eyes as she tied the belt. 'Can I come in?' he asked, a bit late.

'Of course you can, John Bennett.' She collected herself together and smiled at him. John had a bit of a cold and Beth was insisting he stay indoors. Lotty thought Beth too soft by half. A blast of fresh air wouldn't do him any harm at all. It would do her, Lotty, harm because she wasn't used to it and her lungs were probably only working at half capacity. It worried her. The smoking. But there was sod all she could do about it. She had tried several times to stop. 'Where are the dogs?' she asked, resisting an impulse to light up in front of the child.

'Mummy's taking them for a walk in a minute.' He clambered onto the unmade bed and kicked off his slippers. 'When are you going home?' he asked.

'Why? Are you fed up with me?' She sat on the chair and pulled her robe securely round her.

'No. I like you,' he said earnestly. 'You swear a lot, don't you?'

'I suppose I do. I'm sorry. It's a silly thing to do but I bet you feel like swearing sometimes,' she said with a smile, 'You mustn't, of course.'

'Mummy says damn sometimes,' he said in a conspiratorial aside. 'Aunt Lotty . . .?'

'Yes. Fire away.'

'Some of the boys at school think it's funny. Daddy being a vicar. It's not, is it?'

She considered the question. 'It is a bit funny,' she said, wondering how best to explain to him. 'Vicars have a tough deal, John. They just happen to have the sort of job that affects the way other people think about them. Do you see? I'm a teacher. Some people think that's very strange. I don't care because it's what I want to do. Vicars are just terribly embarrassing to other people. People don't swear for instance if there's a vicar around.'

'You do,' he said promptly and she joined him in a smile.

'I'm different,' she said. 'What I'm trying to say is that vicars make people feel inhibited. Now there's a nice new word for you. Shall I write it down?'

He shook his head, losing interest in this tack. 'I'm going to be a doctor when I grow up,' he said stoutly. 'Like Grandad Howard.'

'Great. That would please him. Your Uncle William started to be a doctor but he decided he couldn't do it.'

'Why? Did he faint at the blood?'

'I don't know.' Lotty smiled a little. William just baulked at sheer hard grind, that was the gist of it. 'I don't suppose you'll faint at the blood,' she observed cheekily, knowing suddenly that John *would* be a doctor. Some people just made up their minds and stuck to it and he was one of those people.

'Do you say your prayers, Aunt Lotty?' he asked, dragging one of his socks off and picking very carefully at his toes.

'Do you say yours?' she countered solemnly, 'I hope you do. Tell me, who do you pray for?'

'Well . . .' he abandoned his toe picking and crunched up his little face in deep thought, 'Mummy and daddy and Paul. Ben and Dixie. Granny Howard. Grandad Bennett.' His intense look, the toss of the head, reminded her of Beth and something shattered inside. How wonderful to be able to recreate yourself in your own children and wasn't it just typical of her that she couldn't even manage that simple thing. 'And Aunt Sonia and Uncle Sebastian,' John went on, getting into his stride, 'And you and Uncle Max and Uncle William . . .' he paused, struggling at the end of the line, 'And anybody else who needs it.'

'That is a lot of people,' Lotty said, touched that he should still pray for Max. Still . . . it had got her over having to reply to his question. Did she pray? She hadn't since the far-off days when she had been at school and they had regular morning assemblies and even then she hadn't really prayed, only pretended. There was something though about church and silence. 'You'd better scoot off,' she said with a yawn. 'Put your sock back on and go. I'm going to get dressed and then I want a word with your dad. Is he busy?'

He shook his head. 'He's just writing his sermon,' he said, blissfully ignorant of the difficulties of doing that. 'I wish I was at your school,' he said as he climbed off the bed. 'I'd like you to be my teacher.'

'Oh no you wouldn't. I'm terribly stern.' She laughed as she ruffled his hair, 'You'd have to call me Mrs Crabtree. I couldn't be your Aunt Lotty if I was your teacher, could I?'

She found she was smiling as she dressed. She had misjudged the boys. When you got to know them, they weren't so bad after all.

She checked her appearance before confronting Martin. She was wearing one of her teaching outfits, a dark blouse and plain skirt, and she reckoned she looked relatively sober as befitted what she had to tell him. He probably wouldn't notice the little effort she had made on his behalf. He never noticed anybody except Beth. Those two had something going for them and she hoped they realised it. It was like it had been with her and Max, without the arguments though.

'I can come back later if you're busy,' she said, popping her head round the door of his study, 'John said you were in the middle of your sermon.'

'Come in, Lotty, I could do with a break. My ideas are drying up a little.' He pushed his papers aside and motioned her across to the window seat. It followed the curve of the window and they sat apart, at angles to each other, feet nearly touching. Close but not that close. 'This is better than facing you across a desk,' he said. 'Cosier. Although if you were one of my parishioners, I regret I would probably face you across the desk . . .' he pulled a face, 'Unwritten code of conduct. We have to be careful. We can be accused of sexual abuse at the drop of a hat.' His smile was sudden, unexpected, and very welcome.

She laughed, 'Oh, I see. You have the same damned problems in your profession as we do. The male teachers have to be bloody careful especially with some of the nubile wenches in the fourth form. Seriously though, Martin . . . I much prefer to gather the kids round me, chat to them like they do in the reception class but, as they get older, it's not so easy . . .' she paused, not really wanting to talk about teaching but not knowing how to bring up what she did want to talk about.

'The garden's looking lovely, isn't it?' Martin commented and she blessed him for giving her time to compose herself, 'Not as grand as Fernlands of course but we don't employ a full-time gardener like your mother. Or a cleaner either. Poor Beth, it would help a lot if we could afford to. However . . . we both enjoy the gardening and Paul's showing an interest. We've given him a small plot for himself to grow what he wants.'

'That's nice.' She looked down at her fingernails, ragged and bitten. 'Martin . . .' she saw and shrank from the sympathy in his eyes. 'Sorry, I don't know how to say this.'

The clock ticked solidly. Outside the garden slumbered in the morning sun. Opposite her, Martin was wearing casual clothes, one of Beth's appalling sweaters and cords. Oddly, and disturbingly, she found him sexually attractive in the get-up. It wasn't as obvious as Seb but it was there. He had nice hands too.

'Nothing you say will shock me, Lotty,' he said at last, breaking a silence. 'I've heard it all before. And you can be assured that whatever you say will remain confidential. I won't even tell Beth.'

'Are you sure?'

He did not bat an eyelid at the insulting question.

'Quite sure,' he said, pushing up the longish sleeves of the sweater, perfectly relaxed. No dog collar which helped. 'What's troubling you?' he asked. 'Please tell me. It might help.'

'When I had the miscarriage . . .' she took a deep breath for it was still painful to mention it. 'I don't know if Beth told you but there was a problem at some point and the doctor panicked. I overheard her say quite distinctly to a junior that this was an emergency and he'd to get the blood matched quickly. Well of course you can imagine how that consoled me. I was surrounded suddenly by anxious faces trying not to appear anxious. Talk about too many cooks . . .' she smiled as he responded by leaning over and patting her hand. 'I remember thinking sod this for a game of doctors and nurses.' Her smile widened. 'Sorry but that's exactly what I did think at the time.'

'It's okay,' he said, 'It must have been a harrowing experience.'

'Not half. I thought I was going to die actually.' There . . . she'd admitted it. She felt silly, overdramatic, saying it, and felt the colour flood into her face hoping he wouldn't laugh but, of course, being Martin he did not. 'I can't die I thought. There's too much to do. I've got to sort Max out for a kick-off and I want to achieve something at Dockside before I move on. There's this particular girl Jade who I'm determined to take under my wing. And I thought about mother and how she would feel.' She stopped, struggled a moment, not wanting to spoil this by weeping. 'I prayed, Martin,' she went on quietly, 'Don't you see? I prayed. I said something to the effect that if you get me out of this one, God, then I'll believe in you. Something like that.'

'It's not unusual,' he said. 'People often pray in situations like that and, as far as I'm concerned, that's okay too. If people want to use God in times of acute stress then so be it. I don't object.'

'But I do,' Lotty said. 'You can't switch on and off, Martin. You can't pray when it suits you, when you need to and then shrug it off later when all's well. That's cheating in my book. That's going back on your promise.'

'So what are you trying to tell me?' He leaned forward, intent. 'That you now believe?'

'I haven't finished yet.' Impatiently, she rose and strode across the room to his bookshelf. A surprising cross-section of books were crammed into it, mainly fishing and theology with some old school classics thrown in. 'Would you believe me, Martin, if I told you I had a sort of vision?'

'Go on,' he urged as she fell silent.

'It was when they were working on me, flashing lights up my nether region, that sort of thing, when I saw something at the foot of the bed urging me to keep on fighting, telling me to stay awake when I really wanted to close my eyes and go to sleep. Christ! I don't mind telling you I thought I was for it. I thought this must be how it feels to slip into a coma. It wasn't a figure I saw, nothing like that, just a sense of light, calm and peaceful. My fear just vanished. It was rather wonderful in fact,' she finished in a whisper, not sure if he had heard.

'Lotty my dear . . .' It was a gentle prompt and she sighed deeply, turning to look at him.

'You do believe me, don't you?' she asked. 'I'm not having you on. It really did happen like that.'

'Of course I believe you and I'm very happy for you. People who have been close to death have told me much the same thing. I don't think you were ever close to death, Lotty, but you thought you were. It's convinced me of one thing. We shouldn't be afraid of it. We are afraid because it's the unknown but I firmly believe that all our worldly cares will slip away at the moment of death and we will find a peace, an everlasting peace.'

'Don't preach at me,' she warned him softly, managing a smile, 'This is our secret, Martin. I've been bursting to tell someone.' She returned to join him by the window, 'Even if I do believe in God, in some spiritual being, I'm still not going in for all that stuff about church. I don't need that. In any case, I can't stand all the creepy bishops and the way the Church seems to delight in shooting itself in the foot. No . . . that's not for me. I can feel my feelings without all that middle-class crap.'

He laughed. 'We'll have another talk another time about that,' he said. 'I could have you hanged, drawn and quartered for saying that. Middle-class crap eh?'

'Thanks for listening.' She kissed him, missing his cheek and landing on his beard. He smelt faintly of soap. 'You're a love,' she added. 'Oh Martin, isn't life complicated? My life that is. After this dinner thing to meet you know who, I'm off home. I want to be there when Max rings.'

'Good luck. Get back in touch if you need help.' He turned his head as the outer door opened. 'There's Beth,' he said and his face lit up. It made Lotty ache. Oh that someone could feel that way for her. Had Max ever? Could they try again? Of course she'd never in a million years tell Max about the vision thing. He'd think she'd gone stark staring mad.

She might however tell him about the miscarriage. She couldn't carry that secret to her grave.

'Is she going home soon?' Beth asked, ashamed of the question, ashamed of the hope she would be. Lotty was her sister and she ought to enjoy her company but the plain truth was she did not. Lotty irritated her.

Lotty allowed things to happen to her and the miscarriage was just the latest in a long series of mishaps. She had allowed herself to be fobbed off with that difficult teaching job of hers that seemed from all accounts to be particularly unrewarding and she had also allowed Max to walk out on her. If she'd been softer, gentler, more thoughtful, he wouldn't have. Lotty should learn to practise some feminine wiles.

'She is talking about going home but not until we've met with Don Fletcher,' Martin said, resuming his seat at the desk and uncapping his pen, 'I hope she's not going to create a fuss. The poor man's obviously trying his best to win us over.' He turned to a clean page in his notebook, smiled, 'Sorry, darling, but I must get on.'

'I'll leave you to it then.' She was puzzled at the way he was dismissing her. He certainly did not wish to discuss Lotty and she wondered why not.

The thought occurred later as she was working in the kitchen, making pastry for a steak and kidney pie. Surely Lotty hadn't flirted with him? She wouldn't put it past her and, if she had, then of course Martin would say nothing. He would not wish to upset her. For all her thinness and Beth thought she was too thin, wafer thin, she was attractive to the opposite sex and it worried her more than she cared to admit. She trusted Martin, of course she did but that didn't mean she should stop trying. The answer was obvious. She had to smarten up, lose some weight and gain a bit of confidence.

She trimmed the pastry and popped the plate in the oven before starting on the sponge pudding. She was mixing with a wooden spoon by the time Lotty came through. She was, Beth was pleased to see, looking a lot better, a little bit plumper, in jeans and a sweater.

'I was talking to that son of yours this morning, to John,' she said, taking a couple of mugs from the rack and warming some milk for their coffee. 'He's bright, Beth. He says he wants to be a doctor.'

Beth smiled. 'And Paul's going to be a pilot. He changes his mind about twice a month.'

'I think John will be a doctor,' Lotty said thoughtfully, leaning against the table but making no attempt to help. 'I always knew I wanted to be a teacher. You wanted to be a nurse once . . . what happened to that?'

'I was told I wasn't clever enough,' Beth muttered, 'You forget I left school a pretty hopeless case.'

'You make me sick.' Lotty thumped the surface, sploshing the mixture, 'Of course you were clever. You're too easily swayed, Beth. By people, by events. I've a child at school who's going to go exactly the way of you if I don't take a hand in it. She's going to end up unfulfilled, having kids and making bloody puddings instead of doing something constructive with her life.'

'Somebody has to make the puddings,' Beth commented, managing a smile, knowing Lotty was trying to rattle her and not liking to show she was succeeding. '*And* have the children.' She stopped, remembering, wishing she hadn't said that.

Lotty chose to ignore it. 'Go and get yourself a proper job,' she said briskly. 'That cleaning thing you do is worse than useless. Oh . . . by the by, talking of cleaning . . . have you spoken to Elsie recently?'

'She's saying nothing.' Beth smiled, genuinely this time, 'She gets terribly confused when she's talking to me, probably because I'm married to Martin. It's obviously very difficult for her but she's being remarkably circumspect. It's also obvious she disapproves. Every time I go round, she finds an excuse to pick up father's photograph, dust it, draw my attention to it.'

They laughed. They knew Elsie. 'She disapproves of me too,' Lotty said. 'She's on Max's side. Max has this gift of being able to charm the older ladies and Elsie thinks he's lovely. All I can get out of her about Don Fletcher is that he spends a lot of his time round at mother's. A *lot* of his time. Do you think she was trying to tell me something I don't already know. This dinner party's going to be hell, isn't it? I'm not sure I'll be able to say a civil word to him.'

'We must try,' Beth glanced at her, 'Please, Lotty, don't make a scene. Let's try to be adult about it.'

'Are you for or against it? And come on, stop sitting on the fence.'

Beth considered. 'Against, I suppose,' she said at last, 'Mostly because I worry for mother. I think she has just been caught unawares. I'm afraid I suspect his motives too, like you. It's common knowledge round here that mum is . . . well, not exactly rolling in it . . . but she has considerable funds.'

'My point exactly. You're going to have to take charge of this, Beth, because I'll be going home soon,' Lotty said. 'I expect you'll be glad to see the back of me.'

'Why should we think that?' Beth murmured, washing her hands at the sink, 'We'll be sorry to see you go,' she said.

'Will you? Thanks anyway for letting me stay. It's given me time to think.'

'Have you and Martin had your little talk?' she asked, knowing she shouldn't really be asking. 'You did say in hospital that you wanted to talk to him.'

'We've talked, yes.' There was a surprising blush and a quick busy movement that did not fool Beth. If she suspected before, she was now convinced. Lotty was just a bit in love with Martin. Poor Lotty. She had to get herself sorted out where men were concerned. She couldn't go through the rest of her life alone, she wasn't the sort. She needed someone. A lover.

'When Max gets round to ringing me . . . are you listening, Beth?'

She nodded, giving her her full attention.

'I'm going to agree to see him. Max is a . . .' she paused and Beth knew she was substituting a milder word, 'He's awkward sometimes but I miss him such a lot and I do regret being unfaithful to him.' She lowered her eyes, her voice a blur, 'I know we were separated but it still feels like that.'

'I know,' Beth said sympathetically, not knowing at all. She felt awkward herself to be talking about adultery but, although she was curious about the other man in Lotty's life, she was not going to ask and she knew Lotty was not going to tell. It was finished. The baby had finished it.

She was still astounded that Lotty and Max had broken up. Despite the rows, they had seemed so suited, a couple. Sonia and Sebastian . . . well, yes . . . but not Lotty and Max.

20

Don was safely home but, with Suzanne hovering, his home-coming had been a trifle subdued. It just didn't seem right to sleep together, not with Suzanne in the house, Laura had pointed out to him, nor did it seem right either for her to spend nights away at his home. In any case, it wasn't fair to leave Suzanne alone at Fernlands. She was getting near enough to the end of the pregnancy for an early birth to be possible.

'For heaven's sake, Laura . . .' he was finding it hard to hide his irritation. 'You let them rule your life, that family of yours.'

'No I do not,' she said, impatient herself, 'I can't help the way I am, Don, and it embarrasses me, this side of it. The, the . . .'

'You can't even say it, can you?' He laughed but there wasn't much warmth in it, 'The sex, my darling. I really don't see the problem. Suzanne will be aware of it. She must realise what our relationship is. We're not that old, either of us, so it stands to reason that we're sleeping together.'

'We're not married,' she said unhappily.

'Whose fault's that?' he said, 'It's you who has cold feet.'

'Marriage is a big step,' she said, looking round anxiously, worried that Suzanne might hear if they raised their voices. It occurred, briefly, that, at eighteen, she had known without any shadow of a doubt that she would marry George directly he asked her. Why this soul-searching now? 'I know I said I might sell the house, move in with you but I'm finding it very hard to reach a decision.'

'You're putting them before me,' he said quietly, 'Your kids are grown-ups or hadn't you noticed? It's time you threw them over the side.'

'Don't you dare tell me how to handle my children,' she said, feeling a sudden cold anger. 'You've never had children. You wouldn't know.'

She sighed now as she remembered the row, their first real row. So . . . they had apologised to each other, put it down to frustration maybe, but some of the things he had said hurt her.

He was right. She ought to put him first. It ought not to make a difference what the family thought, she and Don were going to be married and the sooner the better. A long engagement at their age was ridiculous.

'How do I look, Laura?' Suzanne waddled into the room, tent-like in cream linen. 'On second thoughts, don't say anything . . .' she smiled, actually looking rather attractive for her skin was clear and shining, her hair loose from its pony-tail, newly washed and softly fluffed. Laura could quite see beyond the plainish features and see what had attracted her son. Suzanne was so very nice. Warm-hearted and thoughtful.

'You look lovely, dear,' Laura said happily, 'How do I look? When you get to my age, you have to be so careful.' She adjusted the belt of the dress, slipped a slender gold chain round her neck. Picked up a wrap.

Everything was organised for the birth. Laura had booked Suzanne into a private maternity clinic, she was in the care of Laura's own doctor and absolutely no complications were expected. Appropriately enough, they were turning William's old room into the nursery redecorating it in pink and white, the pink Suzanne's choice for she was of course convinced the baby was a girl.

William's letter had arrived a couple of days after she did. Laura dashed off a reply at once, regretting it directly she posted it because it was impossible to have an argument on paper. She said in her letter she hoped he was not thinking of abandoning his wife and baby. The girls, all of them, were up in arms about that too and for once she agreed with them.

'It's a shame Sonia can't manage it tonight,' Suzanne said as they checked they had everything, 'It would have been nice to meet her and it would have been nice for her to meet Mr Fletcher too.'

'Call him Don for heaven's sake.' Laura smiled at her, rather pleased in fact that Sonia had declined the invitation, pressure of work preventing it. It was bad enough that Lotty *and* Beth would be there. Lotty was rapidly recovering her tiresome candidness and would very likely show off, misbehave in her sister's presence.

She and Suzanne were taking a taxi to Don's home. It was a glorious evening and Laura sighed as she looked out at the colours of the lake as they drove by. She could never make up her mind which time of day she preferred. A spectacular sunset was on the cards tonight. Beside her, Suzanne sighed too and Laura reached out impulsively and caught her hand. At least she knew she had someone on her side.

'You'll like Grange-over-Sands,' she said, 'Do you know it at all? It's right beside Morecambe Bay. From it, you look across at Silverdale. It should be quite clear this evening. There is a walk you can do right across the bay but it's not without its dangers of course and you have to be accompanied by a guide who knows the movement of the tides. George and I once did it. Years ago. I shall always remember it.'

Suzanne allowed her a moment's reflection before saying that Elsie had told her it was a very quiet little town. 'I wasn't sure if she meant that as a positive feature or not. She says a lot of retired people live there.'

'Well . . . it has that reputation but it's a bit unfair, although I suppose that's what must have attracted Don,' Laura said. 'Lotty thinks it's very boring but then that's Lotty . . . I hope we arrive before they do. And I do hope it goes well tonight.' She couldn't help a little worried sigh. She wanted them to like each other.

'There he is at the door. That's him . . .' she felt a girlish glee as she heard Suzanne's faint murmur of approval. Yes . . . he was one of those sort of unselfconsciously handsome men with that easy confidence of the successful. He was casually clad but smart in black trousers and a fine-knit cream sweater. A smile broke on his face as she alighted.

'You look gorgeous,' he said softly, kissing her, then looking beyond at Suzanne. 'And you must be William's wife?'

'Yes.' Suzanne beamed, eyes on a level with his. 'And this is Kate.' She lowered her eyes. 'Laura's granddaughter.'

Laura had forgotten to warn him. She had grown quite used

to Suzanne's endearing way of talking to baby and it occurred it might seem a bit odd to others. To her relief, he grinned.

'Hello Kate,' he said as if it were the most natural thing in the world to greet an unborn child, 'If you're ready, we'll go inside. I expect the others will be arriving soon.'

Suzanne stood a moment, looking down at the little town huddled below and the sandy reaches of the bay, channels of water sparkling with spots of diamonds as the sun began to lower in the sky. A pinky gold sun. It occurred that she'd been all over the world in search of something like this and here it was on her doorstep.

'You two certainly know how to pick the views,' she commented drily.

Seeing how sullen Lotty was, Suzanne tried to make up for it. Beth was making an effort, mindful of her duty but it was only a polite attempt, and there was a certain tightness in her too. Suzanne knew and hoped it would not be obvious to Laura that Beth, despite some fluttery denials, disapproved of the prospective match. Lotty's disapproval was plain for all to see.

What was the matter with those two? Couldn't they see how happy their mother was? Were they so selfish that they would deny her that happiness?

It was an awkward meal. Don tried his best to be a good host and the food was excellent. Martin, too, was fairly fizzing with good humour at first but it was lost on the rest of the company. Lotty, clad in red pants, high heels and a little black top, scarcely bothered to pretend. She talked incessantly of her father in such a way that it would appear the man had been very nearly a saint. It was embarrassing and she surely realised as much. She rudely dismissed any attempts by Don to talk about himself or his work, and by the time coffee arrived, they were sitting stony-faced. Silent.

'Anyone fancy a walk?' Don rose to his feet, smiled at them, making one last stoical effort to save the evening. 'It looks beautiful out there.'

'I do.' Laura rose too, smoothing the folds of her black dress. Ash blonde, she particularly suited black. The tiny gold drop earrings Sonia had bought for her birthday showed to best effect with her hair swept off her face. 'Any of you care to join us?'

There was a muttered communal rejection of the suggestion and, collecting her shawl, Laura followed Don out of the room, turning to look at them all as she went out. The look said it all. A moment later, they heard the door close behind them and their steps on the path outside.

'That was disgraceful, Lotty,' Beth said at once, eyes flashing, looking quite unlike herself. 'You behaved abominably.' She tugged at the sleeves of her blue dress and looked to Suzanne for support. 'Wasn't it dreadful of her?'

Suzanne struggled for a safe reply, decided to say nothing. In any case, Lotty was up in arms, glaring at Beth, 'What are you talking about? You didn't exactly fall over yourself to be pleasant, did you? I'm just more honest, that's all.'

'I resent that. What must he think about us?'

'I don't very much care.' Lotty went over to the window, peering through the curtains into the gloom of the late evening. 'Can't see a thing,' she said, letting the curtain fall and turning to look at them. 'I'm lost for words,' she added helplessly. 'The first good-looking man she sets eyes on who shows her any attention and she goes all swoony. She's fifty five for God's sake.'

Suzanne sighed, moved a cushion a little further up her back. Baby was kicking, alive and kicking, and she hated to remind Lotty of that. She felt rather that she ought to keep apologising for the baby because of Lotty's recent bad luck, tried, even more foolishly, to hide the bump in Lotty's presence.

'I think he's a nice man,' she said quietly. 'And Laura obviously loves him.'

'What do you know about it?' Lotty turned on her. 'Mother still loves dad. How can she be interested in another man? It's absurd. And did you notice he said very little about his work, this dubious business he's engaged in. Importing indeed!'

'You never gave him the chance,' Suzanne murmured, colouring as she caught the full extent of Lotty's annoyance. She had to tread carefully here. They had all obviously adored their father and that was why they were being so awkward.

Lotty shuddered audibly, 'He's a charmer. Snake-charmer. I've met his sort before. Did you see the way he looked at *me*? His eyes nearly popped out.'

'If you must dress like that . . .' Beth said.

'Don't be such a prude,' Lotty slumped on the chair, reaching for her bag and cigarettes before she was reminded by Martin that Don had very firmly requested them not to smoke in his house.

'Would you like a mint instead?' Beth enquired, fishing in her bag, 'I usually have one.' She pulled out various items including dog biscuits before finding a packet of wrapped mints. 'There . . . I keep them for the boys in case they feel car sick.' She handed the packet round, all smiles again.

They all took one, something to do, chewing thoughtfully as the conversation stuttered to a halt. Don had told them to help themselves to more coffee, but the pot lay on the table untouched.

'We seem to have got off on the wrong foot as they say,' Martin said quietly, at last. 'We came here tonight determined, for one reason or another, not to like Don. I feel ashamed to admit my own views have been a little tainted by Beth's own feelings of disquiet at the situation.'

'Come to the point, Martin. Stop being so long-winded,' Lotty said with a sigh, fingers tapping on the chair, restless, exchanging a faint smile with Suzanne at Martin's brief excursion into pomposity.

'All right, I will. Lotty, you're being unreasonable,' he said, 'And so are you, Beth . . .' his glance at his wife was that of a parent to a naughty child and Suzanne saw her bristle. 'I can't believe that two grown women can be so unreasonable. Sonia's as bad frankly and I dread to think what would have happened if she'd been here. You're all acting like spoilt children.'

'Oh, shut up . . . she's not *your* mother,' Lotty sighed. 'Just as she's not Suzanne's mother. If it was your mother, Martin, acting like a silly teenager hell-bent on a daft marriage, it would be quite different.'

'My mother is dead,' he said softly. 'Nor would she have acted like this either.'

'There you are!' Lotty said triumphantly. 'You think it's a bit off too. It's all right for my mother to act like this but not your own. What's going on out there I'd like to know? For all we know, he could be seducing her. Assuming he hasn't already of course, which I think he has. This place might be the most boring dump on earth but I can see it might have its charms while walking on a beach in the moonlight. Did you see them at the table? If they weren't playing footsie then I'm . . .' She glanced at the clock, 'I'm giving them half an hour and then I'm going out to look for them. Mother will catch her death out there. She only had a thin wrap.'

Even Beth laughed. 'You sound like a mother hen,' she said. 'And . . . looking round here . . .' she looked carefully round the charming room, an unusual room filled not entirely unexpectedly with oriental treasures, 'It doesn't look like he's short of money, does it? Some of these things must be worth a fortune.'

'I think it improper to be discussing such things in Don's house,' Martin said, stuck apparently with the comic air of pomposity that had cloaked him this evening, 'It's abusing his hospitality.' He frowned at them and glanced at his watch. 'We must be ready to go, Beth, directly they arrive back. It's late.'

They subsided into a slightly worried silence. Suzanne felt the baby pummel against her but declined to mention it, respecting Lotty's feelings. She was concerned about William and his continued absence. However, he was right about his mother for she was sweet and good-natured as he had said and not once had she felt her presence an intrusion. She tried to help round the house but not all the rooms were in active use and the housework was therefore minimal. In any case, Elsie was not keen on her helping, urging her to sit and rest and take it easy. Laura was talking of engaging a nanny when baby arrived and Suzanne did not know how to tell her she didn't want that. She had to contact William. He had to do something for her and the baby. When Kate arrived, she would need a daddy too.

William doing a nine-to-five job was laughable. On the other hand, she couldn't stay here indefinitely in Laura's debt. Lotty and Beth were friendly enough but even Beth sometimes allowed her resentment to show and the sister she had not yet met, Sonia, sounded dreadful.

'There they are . . . about time.' Lotty sprang up as the outer door opened. 'Just listen to them. Laughing.'

Laura was first in, having discarded her wrap in the hall. Looking pretty and pink-faced, looking very much also as if she'd just been held in Don's arms.

'You should have come with us,' she said, puffing a little from the exertion of walking up the hill, 'We walked all the way down into town. Didn't we, darling?'

'We certainly did.' Don followed her in, looking pleased with himself. 'Now . . . what can I get you all to drink?' he asked, rubbing his hands. 'We're ready for a nightcap.'

'Nothing, thanks. We're off, aren't we?' Lotty looked towards Martin and Beth, who had the grace to look a little shamefaced as they retrieved their jackets and said their thank-yous and goodbyes.

'I'll drive you ladies home,' Don said to Laura and Suzanne when the others had gone. 'No . . . I insist. You're not getting a taxi back.'

'We are. You've had a few drinks.' Laura firmly refused the lift and Suzanne listened a while to their gentle conversation, accepting a mineral water as they had a brandy. Mention was made of their walk in the balmy evening, less said about the meal. The less said about that the better.

Suzanne was tired, desperately trying not to show it, for she did not want to spoil the rest of the evening, although she felt a little more relaxed now that Lotty and Beth were gone. Poor Mr Fletcher. He'd taken tremendous pains to make the dinner a success and it had been ruined by William's sisters. William wouldn't have allowed them to behave like that if he'd been here. She didn't know but she rather felt that William would be surprisingly cheerful about his mother's plans.

The mineral water was going right through her. She wanted the lavatory for the umpteenth time. She stood up, pushing herself into an upright position with her hands. She knew, although they were far too polite to say it, that they would much prefer to be alone and she was sorry that she was stuck here with them, a very awkward, very pregnant wallflower.

For the first time since she had arrived, she felt unwanted.

21

Flushed with guilt and embarrassment, worrying that she might end the day in a police cell, Beth carried the bag into the shop. A sale was on and it was packed with people. You'd think in a large-lady shop they'd have a bit more space between the racks of clothes. Beth squeezed her way to the rear and the pay desk. She had worked out what she was going to say on the way in but now, confronted suddenly by a red-lipped *thin* assistant, she forgot.

'I . . . er . . .' she smiled, catching sight of her pink face in the mirror behind, 'This dress . . .'

'Refund?' The girl whipped the bag away, opened it and retrieved the red dress in all its stolen splendour in a single graceful movement. 'Oh yes . . . we've had a lot of trouble with this design.' She flashed a look at a nearby sales assistant who was standing staring into space. 'Jenny? Another of them pleated things . . . do we need a receipt?'

'No.' Jenny woke up, appeared to be in charge, 'Not if the lady's lost it.'

'Have you lost it?' the girl asked, elaborately arranging the dress on the counter, pointing with a frown to the defect, a defect Beth hadn't even noticed.

'Lost it?' Beth repeated stupidly, recognising somewhere in the befuddled recesses of her guilt-riddled mind that she was being given a way out.

'The receipt?' the girl said with a suddenly patient smile, probably deciding she was dealing with a moron.

'I've lost it,' Beth murmured, putting a hand up to cover her mouth.

'You can still have a refund,' the girl said, pulling out a pad.

'Special circumstances you see. Do you want to get something else or do you want cash?'

Minutes later, clutching nearly fifty pounds and a belated apology, Beth walked out. Now she had fifty pounds that didn't belong to her but she couldn't have refused to accept it for that would have looked most odd.

On the way home, she debated whether or not the fifty pounds belonged to her. In theory, yes, because she had returned the dress. No, that wasn't right . . . she had never paid for it in the first place so how could it be hers?

There was so much she could do with fifty pounds. She could put it in her emergency fund to replace what she had spent or she could buy the boys something, a little treat, or spend it on Martin or on herself. She could buy something frivolous maybe. Or, alternatively, it would help very nicely with the electricity bill.

'Hello Beth. Thank God I've got you and not Lotty. I've never seen her in such a miserable state. You'd think she was the only woman in the world to have a miscarriage. All the fuss!'

'Hello Sonia,' Beth said wearily. 'How are you?'

'I'm fine. Did you meet him then? This man of mummy's? I believe you were going out to dinner. There was just no way Seb and I could get up there, not with all our business commitments. Such a bore. Anyway, what's he like?'

'Quite handsome, I suppose. A little older than mum. Tall.'

'Taller than daddy?'

'Yes I suppose so.'

'And . . .?'

'And what?'

'Oh Beth, are you deliberately obtuse?'

'I don't know what you want me to say, Sonia. He's all right I suppose.'

'I see. So there *is* a problem then?'

'The problem is mum loves him. I think he loves her. I have to say they seem very happy together. If that is a problem?'

'Are you being philosophical, Beth? It doesn't become you,' Sonia said sharply. 'I've been trying to get hold of William. My letter's been returned. He's no longer at that last address.

Nobody knows where he's gone. Isn't it infuriating? How can I go to Australia if I don't have an address? It's a big country.'

'I know. And I'm not sure it'll do any good either. She seems determined to marry him, Sonia. She hasn't actually said but I should think she intends to sell the house and move in with him. His house is smaller, probably more suited to just a couple. And then, when he retires, they plan to travel, maybe even get another home abroad . . .'

'They *what*? After all she said . . .' Sonia clicked her tongue. 'It sounds as if he's got expensive ideas. Another home indeed! Mummy's money. We'll end up with nothing, don't you see? She'll spend the lot, thanks to him. There'll be nothing left for us. Not a sausage.'

'But have we a right to expect anything?'

'Of course we have. Your boys have got something, haven't they, something to come to them later?'

'Yes but that was from daddy,' Beth said, feeling distinctly uncomfortable with this conversation. 'I've been thinking about it these last few days and, looking at it from mum's point of view, we're being terrible to her.'

'No, we're not. Someone has to save her from her temporary insanity. We know her better than anyone. The man can't possibly be serious . . . Lotty thinks he's a gold-digger.'

'He has money of his own,' Beth said carefully. 'He's spent a lot of time working abroad and he's acquired a beautiful collection of things from the Orient. You'd love it, Sonia . . . his home . . . it's very plush. Rugs. Wall hangings. Pictures.'

'Oh really? . . . Oriental items did you say? Interesting . . . Still, that doesn't mean he hasn't reached a difficult patch financially and he's desperately fishing round for sources of money or a comfortable base for his retirement. A rich widow being the obvious target. Unfortunately, mummy's fallen for it.'

'Sonia . . . let them be.' Beth was weary of it. If mum was going to make a mistake then so be it.

'Beth, you don't realise how finely tuned my business is. It's balanced precariously and I have always held onto the belief that one day . . . heaven forbid not yet awhile . . . that one day I would come into my inheritance. My long-term plans include that. Plans I certainly don't want to bore you with but with no inheritance that all goes down the drain. You don't realise how much it means to me. You have Martin and the boys. I have the business.'

'And Sebastian,' Beth pointed out, frowning into the receiver. 'Don't forget him.'

'Of course not. He would benefit too from the inheritance.'

'Mum's only fifty five.' It seemed worth mentioning. 'Unless you're thinking of bumping her off, you've got a very long wait.'

'Beth . . . you do say the silliest things sometimes.' There was a short pause and then, 'Is Lotty gone?'

'Just yesterday. Funny, I was sorry to see her go. I hope she'll be all right on her own. That flat won't be a very welcoming place to go back to, will it, and being there will bring back all the awful memories.'

'That's her own fault. She chose to live in that ghastly town, teach in that dreadful school. Can you seriously imagine her as a teacher? The clothes she wears . . . she does it purely for effect of course. The language she uses. Gutter language, Elizabeth. Where does she get it from?'

'I have no idea.'

'So . . . what are you doing with yourself these days?' Thankfully, she seemed temporarily to have dropped the subject of mum and Don and Lotty. 'Still doing that little job of yours?'

'At the moment, yes, but I'm considering applying for a job at a nursing home,' Beth said, delighting in surprising her sister, 'I got the application form this morning. A nursing auxiliary.'

'An auxiliary? Oh dear . . . you always choose such menial jobs, Beth. You'll be emptying bed-pans and things, don't imagine for one minute you'll be doing any actual nursing. Surely you can do better than that?'

'I *want* to do it, for God's sake.' Beth said, her anger unexpected, short and sharp, 'It's what I want to do, Sonia, so will you please respect that? I'm sick to death of people telling me what I want to do. Surely only I know that.'

'Of course . . . I didn't mean to imply that you were incapable. Goodness me . . . what is the matter with you? Sebastian's always accusing me of being touchy. It must run in the family.'

'I'm not being touchy. Just fed up,' Beth said quietly. 'Fed up with all of you telling me how hopeless I am. Fed up with you particularly, Sonia. We can't all be fabulous career women earning fantastic salaries and able to afford beautiful clothes. Or intellectually brilliant like Lotty.'

'Beth, dear . . . I'm sorry. Have I upset you?'

'Yes you have.' She felt stupid. Felt as if Sonia was patting her head long-distance. Big sister Sonia. 'You've made up my mind anyway. I'm definitely going to apply for this job.'

'Good for you. Well done.'

Beth listened for the sarcasm. Couldn't actually detect any.

'Oh by the way, Sonia . . .' she said, 'When you were up here, you were on about some of your charity connections . . .'

'Purely as a conversation titbit. I certainly didn't expect praise for my little efforts. I did give Martin a donation for the church roof although I swore him to secrecy. Has he mentioned it?'

'No, of course he hasn't, not if you swore him to secrecy. I seem to remember you telling us about some rescue kennels you contribute to . . .'

'Oh yes, that one. I have so many charity commitments, I quite forget just what. I can't think why I became involved with that. You know me, I have no great love of dogs. Why do you ask, Beth?'

'I would like to give you a donation for it. Fifty pounds.'

'Fifty pounds?' Her astonishment made Beth smile. 'Can you afford it, darling? Aren't you utterly broke?'

'Fifty pounds,' Beth said firmly and triumphantly. 'Will you pass it on as an anonymous gift?'

'Of course I will.' Sonia's amazement was complete. 'Anonymous or really anonymous?'

'What do you mean?' Beth asked, perplexed.

'Well . . . I usually donate anonymously but I make sure at least one person in authority knows who I am. Semi-anonymous if you like.'

Beth was bewildered. 'I don't understand what you're talking about,' she said flatly, 'I don't want anyone to know it's me. That kind of anonymous.'

'Oh, all right. And thank you very much. I must say, you have surprised me.'

Beth replaced the receiver, smiled. She had surprised herself too.

The money might as well go to the dogs.

22

'There! That's the lot.' Lotty handed the books over. 'I want you to read through the first chapter of the green one and then come round again and we'll have a discussion about it. And about anything else you want to talk about. Do you read newspapers, Jade? Good ones that is?'

'Just my stars, miss. And sometimes the problem page.'

'Well . . . try reading some of the leading articles as well. The political stuff. I know it may seem a bit boring but you need to know a bit about it.'

'I'll cut some out and bring them next time I come. If that's all right?' Jade looked at her earnestly and Lotty's heart ached. She was so keen to learn and having such a struggle with so many things against her. A parent who didn't care probably . . .

'It's a good idea to keep up with current events, serious events. Listen to the news too. Keep abreast of what's happening. It keeps your brain alive, makes you more aware and, above all, it stretches you. You'll find you want to ask questions and then I'll show you how to use reference books properly to find things out for yourself. We have to broaden your horizons as much as possible,' she said enthusiastically.

'Thanks, Mrs Crabtree.'

'That's okay.' She was a touch embarrassed by the child's gratitude. 'What does your father do, Jade?' she found herself asking as the girl prepared to leave, the books Lotty had found for her packed into a supermarket carrier bag. 'I think I met him once at a parents' evening.'

'He drives a lorry,' Jade said, blushing. 'Continental route. Belgium mostly or sometimes Scandinavia. He has to be away a lot.'

'Oh I see. And what do you do when he's away? Do you stay on your own?' She asked the question easily, deciding that Jade was probably just about old enough to be left on her own. In theory.

'There's an auntie I usually stay with,' she muttered, her sulky tone making it obvious she was not happy to be discussing private matters. 'My dad's sister. My dad doesn't like to leave me on my own. It's okay. You won't tell the social, will you? I don't want to get him into trouble.'

It dawned a little late that the child thought her father was about to be shopped for parental neglect. Lotty shook her head in irritation, tempted to tell the girl what she thought of local government in general and the social services in particular. It also irritated that Jade didn't quite trust her. She was still part of the establishment after all, a potential spy in high places.

'I'm quite happy about those arrangements, Jade,' she said, seeking to reassure her. 'Tell me some more about your dad . . . what does he do when he's home? Has he any interests? Sorry . . .' she realised she was being intrusive, 'You don't have to talk about it but I'm just interested that's all.'

'He's okay,' she said, a trifle defensively, 'My mum left us when I was four. Took up with another fella. My dad's looked after me okay, though he still doesn't know anything about going shopping and stuff like that. He won't let me do anything, Mrs Crabtree. He treats me like a child. If I go out, he wants to know where I'm going, what time I'll be back.'

Lotty smiled. 'I seem to remember my father doing the same thing,' she said, warming a fraction to Mr Entwistle. 'He's just concerned about you, Jade, and it's very sensible of him to insist on knowing where you are.' She couldn't believe she was hearing herself correctly. All this upstanding parent stuff! 'After all, there are some very strange men about and you have to be ery careful,' she added, making it ten times worse. She was beginning to feel hot and bothered. Christ . . . she'd be roped into telling the child the facts of life in a minute. Would she know already? Very likely. After all, some girls of her age were already on the pill. If she didn't know, she ought to know and poor Mr Entwistle would never get round to telling her.

She took a deep breath, braced herself. 'Er . . . you do know about sex and things?' She smiled a little, 'Because . . . if you do want to know anything . . . absolutely anything at all . . . do feel free to ask. I'll do my best to answer your questions if I can,' she added, amused to hear the vague note in her voice as if she didn't really know that much herself.

'I know everything about *that*,' Jade said solemnly with not a trace of embarrassment, 'Don't you worry, I know how to take care of myself. My dad's told me what to do if a man tries anything, I have to knee him where it hurts, miss, scream and run like hell.'

'Oh right . . .' Lotty was a bit stuck for words. 'Good idea!'

'It's not fair though, is it, the way he treats me like a child? I'm not supposed to tell anyone but my dad has a tattoo, miss, and he still won't let me have my ears pierced . . .' she said miserably, 'And you know, Mrs Crabtree, how everybody in school has their ears pierced. Even their noses. Kids of three, they have their ears pierced. Some babies even. Can you tell him? Can you come and tell him that it's okay? He thinks it's common.' She eyed Lotty's hooped earrings with envy, 'When he sees you've got yours done, miss, he won't be able to say no, will he?'

'I haven't the time at the moment but when I see him, I will mention it.' She smiled, knowing it was an adult excuse and hating herself. She felt quite sure, however, that Mr Entwistle would not care to have his authority undermined or, to be more accurate, pierced and she was damned if she was going to do it. At least the child had not gone off and had it done anyway. Didn't one of the more enterprising young ladies in the sixth form operate a cut-price ear piercing service? Bloody dangerous that but she was a sly madam and they'd never actually managed to catch her at it.

Not knowing Mr Entwistle at all, she felt suddenly sorry for the man. Another poor soul whose partner had walked out! All in all, he had managed to bring Jade up nicely. A polite child in a school where politeness was in short supply. That and brains!

A certain satisfaction settled on her as she watched Jade leave. The interest was kindled and all that remained was to make damned sure it caught hold. Jade had a bright intelligent hopeful air about her and could go far. She *would* go far if Lotty had anything to do with it.

In a strange way, she was glad to be home. Beth's cosy comforts and home cooking had begun to pall and she was happier stabling in her own muck as it were. The flat was already slipping back into disarray after her mother's futile attempts to clean it up. Not so bad yet but scruffiness was just waiting on the sidelines.

This morning before Jade arrived she had made an effort. Tidied. Stuffed things in cupboards. Dusted around with an old tee-shirt because she couldn't find any dusters. Yesterday, Mrs Dassayaje had come up to the flat, shyly bringing her fresh flowers from the garden as well as a card and a box of chocolates.

Lotty had asked her in for a cup of tea and they had wolfed the chocolates but the conversation had been stilted, consisting mainly of much smiling and talk about the shop, with one dark indecipherable reference to her stay in hospital. The slight language difficulty Mrs Dassayaje experienced was hard to penetrate and Lotty wished they could be friends, real friends. Apart from Rachel, she was a bit short on them.

There had been a spate of family phone calls. Beth was excited and girlish about a new job she had landed herself. The way she talked about it you'd think she was the matron or whatever they called them nowadays of this nursing home, instead of a skivvy. She seemed happy though, content even. She earned a little more and it would make *all* the difference, she said. She didn't want to bore Lotty with details but things had reached a pitch lately, financially speaking, and at last she could see a way out.

Sonia was still beavering around trying to locate William. If weddings were as much as hinted at, she was to be informed immediately, she said, and she would fly up to intervene. Mother was still half dazed with love for Don bloody Fletcher, annoyed at the way the dinner at his house had gone and tightly uncommunicative as a result. And Suzanne had rung too. Carefully trying not to talk about the only thing she really wanted to talk about, the impending arrival of the baby.

Lotty didn't mind. Sometimes she thought about her own baby and it was some comfort now to know that she had not gone through with it. Killed him herself. Ghoulishly, she found herself wondering what the doctor had meant by malformed. Perhaps if she had seen him . . . and then, perhaps not. As it was, with the pieces stuck together in the wrong places, he had just given up on life . . . poor little sod.

Despite the phone calls batting to and fro, the one she most wanted did not materialise.

Max had not rung.

23 ∫

Suzanne watched Laura depart for a meal out with Don and turned back into the house, smiling. Laura was looking very happy and it was infectious. She had never known William's father George but she was sure he couldn't have made Laura any happier than Don.

William was temporarily out of touch. Typical of course and Suzanne was not unduly worried for she knew he would write as soon as he was settled at another address. William and pen and paper were unfortunately not compatible. Communicating at all come to that. She did not know if he had received her last letter in which she had brought him up to date with the news about his mother.

It was difficult to gauge how he would react. William was close to his mother despite his casual approach but she didn't know how close he had been to his father. He didn't talk much about his father. Poor William. Perhaps only she really understood him. He had tried so hard with the medical course and walking out on it had been the hardest decision of his life, he told her, not in the least impulsive. He would settle down one day but in his own time and he would not be jostled. Suzanne was wise enough to know that if he was determined to stay in Australia then she and Kate would go back to him.

Kate was going to be a large baby, a nine-pounder the doctor said with relish. Suzanne was scared stiff. Blast William. It might have helped if he was there to hold her hand. All the other girls at the antenatal classes had their husbands or partners with them and she had nobody. It wasn't fair. Both Laura and Beth had offered to stay with her during the birth but she wasn't sure if they meant it or were just being polite, nor was she sure she wanted them.

Restless, she tried in vain to get comfortable on the chair, propped with cushions. She couldn't remember now what it was like to be normal, unpregnant, slim . . . well, comparatively so . . . and without a boxing match constantly going on inside. 'Kate . . . keep still, darling,' she said, as the baby slowly tumbled.

The phone rang and she cursed, having to struggle to her feet. The voice at the other end was cool, crisp, clipped.

'Who is that? Where's mummy?'

'Oh, hello. This is Suzanne speaking. You must be . . .?'

'Sonia. That's right. Is mummy out?'

'She's out to dinner. With Don.'

'Is she now? Really! I particularly wanted to speak to her. Why hasn't she rung me? I think she's frightened of speaking to me actually. Guilty I suppose. And not surprising.'

'I'm sorry she's out,' Suzanne said, beginning to feel personally responsible for Laura's oversight in not being here every minute of the day, 'I have a number where she can be contacted if you wish.'

'Don't bother. It can wait. So . . . you are Suzanne, are you? How do you do. You gave mummy such a shock turning up like that. I've tried to get hold of William but he's disappeared by all accounts, no doubt having washed his hands of his responsibilities. Typical. He's so selfish. I assume he has bothered to tell you where he is.'

The pause was distinct, inviting comment, but Suzanne was unable to say anything, her heart thumping at the words. Sonia was mistaken. It wasn't true. William would get in touch. Very soon.

'I hope you're not planning too long a stay at Fernlands,' the voice continued, 'Quite honestly, you couldn't have timed your arrival to happen at a worse time. Surely you can see that, one way or another, mummy will be selling up. Once she's seen sense and got rid of this man, she'll be coming to live with my husband Sebastian and myself in France. We're lined up to buy a chateau. And, even if, God forbid, she marries this man, she'll still be selling Fernlands and moving in with him.' A sniff accompanied this last observation.

Suzanne stared into the receiver, blankly. 'Selling the house? But nothing's been said. Surely she would have told me so that I can think about what I'm going to do.'

'Obviously she's not going to throw you into the street, not with you having a baby, but you have to understand it's not a long-term arrangement.' A cool laugh rang out. 'I see nobody's had the decency to tell you. Mummy will certainly never get round to it until she's forced to. Somebody has to tell you and as usual I can see it's fallen to me to break the news. Don't you see? She can't possibly sell the house or make arrangements to do so with you and a baby *in situ*. You're an acute embarrassment.'

'I'm due to have the baby soon,' Suzanne said hesitantly, 'I'm booked into a clinic and I had thought that I would be staying here a while longer. Until William comes home at least.'

'Can you honestly see that happening? I'm sorry to be so blunt but you're going to have to face up to the fact that you'll be going it alone.'

'We've decorated the nursery,' Suzanne sighed, 'In pink.'

'A pink nursery? Typical mummy! I don't know why she doesn't ask my advice. After all, it is my job and I wouldn't do a pink nursery even if a client got on her knees and begged me.' Again, the laugh tinkled. 'I do hope I haven't upset you, Suzanne, but I've always found it best to be honest. It's kindest that you are aware of the position. It's up to William to look after you, not mummy.' She brought the conversation to an end quickly, 'Good luck with the baby. I do hope you don't have too terrifying an ordeal and I hope it's a girl.'

Wondering why Sonia should care one way or another what sex the baby was, Suzanne sank down beside the fire, feeling suddenly alarmingly chill, and considered the position. She ought to have realised that, of course, Laura was too nice a woman to tell her to get lost even if she might think it. She had seemed so welcoming but, in reality, she was anxious to get the house sold.

They must be talking about her now at dinner. Wondering how to get rid of her. She had never been one to stay where she wasn't wanted. There was therefore only one thing to do and she would do it. She would leave promptly before they got back. She would go to Aunt Margaret's in Sheffield. They may not have hit it off in the past but there was no reason why they shouldn't make it up.

The decision made, she moved quickly or as quickly as her ungainly body would allow. She gathered a few things together, had a final wistful look at the nursery, wrote a note and was out of the house within half an hour.

She did not look back. Too late for that. Funny thing but of all the many places she had lived in over the last few years it was Fernlands that felt most like home. William's old home and, even though he had not lived in it for years, there was still a hint of his presence. He had talked about it a lot and Laura talked about him too . . . this was William's favourite room . . . William used to sit just there and read . . . William used to have posters all over that wall . . . that sort of thing.

'The point is, Kate, that we will not stay where we are not wanted,' she said, deciding a brisk approach was best. Now that she had made up her mind, there was nothing to be gained from floundering like a fish on dry land. Principles were at stake and William, although he pretended otherwise in his laid-back way, was a great believer in principles. That's why he'd insisted they get married as soon as she told him about the baby. 'You don't have to,' she had said, fully prepared for him walking away, 'I don't want you to think I'm trying to trap you.'

'You? Trying to trap *me*?' He had laughed and drawn her close, 'Suzanne darling, don't you understand? Haven't you understood a word I've said? I want to marry you, my big beautiful lady.'

The house was out of sight now even if she had wanted a final peep at it and she sighed, drawing her jacket closer round her. After the warmth of the living room, it felt chill out here and there was a dampness in the air, a threat of rain. There was just a shaky slice of white moon appearing from time to time but mostly it was hidden by clouds, making it a very dark evening, and she couldn't see the lake, although she could hear its night ripples. She was walking at the edge of the road farthest away from the shore, facing the small amount of oncoming traffic. The proximity to the woods at the roadside was a little frightening and her ears were alert for the slightest sound. A few unexplained scurries must be nocturnal creatures going about their business, she told herself, for what else could they be? She'd walked the world, very nearly, trekking through unbelievably dangerous countries with bandits lurking round every corner, any number of insects and snakes just waiting to be stepped on, and she was scared *now*?

The first drops of rain fell, tentatively, and she looked up in annoyance, walked faster. After each car passed, the silence was exaggerated, and she was aware only of her own ragged breathing and shuffling footsteps. Laura had tried to throw these trainers out and she had retrieved them in the nick of time from the bin bag. They'd been through a lot together, walked all the way from Australia in a way, and, more importantly, they reminded her of William. William had a thing about old familiar shoes.

Another car. She squeezed herself as far into the side as she could get, uncomfortably aware that she was camouflaged beautifully in her woodland coloured jacket. The car shot past, the driver probably never noticing her, and she dusted herself free of some sticky feathery plant, hooked her bag further onto her shoulder, and carried on.

'We're going to stay in a hotel tonight, darling,' she told Kate, tugging at her collar as the rain started in earnest. 'And then tomorrow bright and early, we'll get ourselves over to Sheffield to your aunt's. Actually, she's your Great Aunt Margaret.' She checked that the purse was still in her pocket containing some money. A little gift from Laura. She had felt badly about taking it at the time for she certainly had not earned it but Laura had cheerfully ignored her misgivings and insisted. Think of it as a loan, if you must, she said, William can pay me back later.

At least it meant this journey could be accomplished in relative comfort, once she had got herself to Windermere that is. She had thought of ordering a taxi but, stupidly, it seemed no distance at all and, prudent nature to the fore, she had decided to save money and walk. No distance in a car that is, with Beth at the wheel chattering non-stop and those daft dogs gazing adoringly at her from the back seat. No distance then.

It suddenly occurred that she would look most odd trying to book herself a room in a hotel at this time of night. A pregnant wet rag. And people were apt to be sniffy about dog-eared trainers. Oh why did she never think things through? She ought to have stayed at Laura's, had it out with her in the morning, instead of behaving like a baby herself, a child in a tantrum, running away.

She was getting soaked. The moisture was penetrating under her collar, cold drops landing on top of her head and her trainers were indeed on their last legs, letting in water. The occasional houses loomed, sometimes lit and welcoming, and she did consider sneaking up one of the drives and finding temporary shelter in a shed or something but she couldn't get Kate arrested for breaking and entering before she was even born.

'William Howard, I could kill you having a sister like that . . .' she muttered fiercely, knowing full well that if he were here, he'd just laugh. Catch Sonia ever worrying *him* to this extent! Too late, she thought of all the things she should have said to Sonia but she'd always needed time to think about things, had never been one for a quick retort. She'd been sleepily sitting by the fire, pleasantly relaxed, thinking about the baby and she'd been taken by surprise by the venom of Sonia's attack.

She stopped dead, having stepped in a deep muddy puddle. She squelched first one foot free then the other as the wet seeped into her socks. She was tired, fed up and a fool. Who in their right mind would do this? Laura had to be given the opportunity to give her side of the story. Running away was stupid. She turned, looked back, and dithered. The rain decided it for her, seeming to change a gear, great sheets of it falling so heavily it bounced off the road. Suzanne stuck cold, damp hands deep in her pockets, squared her shoulders, blew strands of hair off her face. Shivered at the cold horror of all this.

'Right, Kate. Change of plan. We're going back,' she said, walking across to the shore side of the road and starting off. It wouldn't seem so far going back. It never did. Going back was easy, it was the going on that was always the challenge. If she'd been on her own it would have been different but there was the baby to think about.

With a bit of luck, she might get back before they did and then they need never know. She would have a warm bath when she got in and be tucked up in bed asleep when Laura arrived back.

'It'll be our secret, this little escapade,' she said to the baby. 'Although I don't think you've listened to a word I've said tonight. It's all right for you, you're nice and cosy in there. Lazy-bones.'

Right on cue, Kate fluttered and punched her playfully as if in reply.

24

Lotty had insisted on giving her mother the cheque back and now wished she hadn't. She should have done what her mother had wanted and spent it on a holiday, the first for years, to somewhere hot and distant. Somewhere where she could laze by a swimming pool and do nothing except reread some of the classics she had been promising herself she would read again for some time.

Moorside Park, on the Kev and Bev side of town, worlds away from Balaclava Street, came a pretty close second to the Bahamas when the sun shone. When the sun shone, you could close your eyes, feel its heat, see the glowing red-gold image and forget where you were.

Lotty was wearing a scarlet bikini under her cotton top and trousers. She had peeled off the outer layers ignoring the glances from a group of frumpish women nearby and was now stretched out, fully oiled, glistening, on the grassy slope beside the cricket field, listening to the insects at ear level and the oh-so-English sounds of bat on pad sprinkled with the occasional shouts of 'Owzat'. Heaven indeed!

She was feeling very much better. Not quite up to tackling a marathon but reasonably fit with the remainder of the school holidays dallying before her. She had heaps of work to do before term time but it could wait a little longer. She would make time for Jade though whenever the child needed her. She was sponge-like for knowledge, absorbing it, retaining it and with ample space for more. She was coming on in leaps and bounds.

She was grilling nicely, almost too sleepy to turn over and do the other side when she heard the sound of approaching footsteps rustling through the grass.

'Well, this is a coincidence,' the voice said, 'Mind if I join you?'

Damn and blast!

'Hello, Kevin.' Lotty reluctantly opened her eyes, propped herself up, squinting as she adjusted to the glare, 'What the hell are you doing here?'

'Some welcome,' he grumbled, flopping down beside her, wearing shorts with white socks and sandals. 'I'm trying to get the old legs brown,' he muttered, following her glance.

'Not succeeding are you?' Lotty said tartly, reaching for her oversized white top and slipping it over her shoulders. She couldn't carry on a serious conversation as this threatened to be with him studiously avoiding looking at her breasts. 'I forgot you live round here,' she said, accepting a cigarette from him with a thank-you, 'Having a good holiday?'

'We've been to Cornwall,' he said, 'Near Looe. Five of us in a tent.'

'Sounds great. Like an Enid Blyton title.' She grinned at him, surprised to find she was in fact quite pleased to see him. 'I would never have guessed you were the outdoor type, Kev.'

'I'm not.' He managed a rueful smile, 'Too primitive by half for me. It was Beverley's idea. She thought it would be good for the kids. Back to nature and all that. They liked it, nearly set us on fire one night when they tipped over a candle. They missed watching the telly though.' He drew on his cigarette, shuddering at the memory. 'If you've not been stuck in a tent in the small hours during a thunderstorm, you've not lived. The kids loved it. The highlight of the holiday. Me and Bev were petrified.' He smiled, staring at her intently, 'What happened to you? Bit of a shock you being whisked off to hospital. We thought you'd looked a bit ropey. Miss Finney said she thought it must be gastric trouble. Doing the rounds she said. Must've been bad to get you into hospital.' He eyed her with what she felt was suspicion and Lotty wondered if Finney had guessed and had tried to act therefore with demure discretion. 'I would have come to see you . . .' he shrugged, 'Believe me, I did think about you but, under the circumstances, I thought it best to stay away. I did the right thing, didn't I?'

'Oh yes.' God, that's all she would have needed, the father

of the child no less. He would have put two and two together then. She volunteered no further information but the curiosity remained, burning in his eyes.

'Was it gastric trouble then?'

'It's none of your damned business,' she said, pretending great irritation. 'If you must know it was one of those bloody embarrassing things that we women have to put up with. Dobson knows all about it. If you want details, ask him. I've been on a waiting list for ages. I got a cancellation for a D and C and I'm not going to explain what that is.'

'Oh?' He eyed her closely. 'It wasn't an emergency then? Sorry, you know how these rumours get started . . .' he was flustered, flushed. 'Sorry, I didn't mean to pry. I found out you were in Ward 2 though and Bev was in there before our first was born. Bit of a scare with her blood pressure.'

Lotty was silent, feeling her own blood pound. Phew! Dangerous that. She'd reckoned on something like that. Ward 2 equals gyny ward, does not equal gastric trouble. He was a sly old fish was Kevin. The partial lie seemed to satisfy him for he too fell silent.

'I've been talking to Beverley about moving,' he said at last, his attention distracted a moment by a triumphant shout from the cricket field. 'I think she's going to be okay about it. Surprising really. She seems quite keen. I did what you suggested, told her I needed a new challenge and I've got an interview for a job down south. Head of department actually. A couple more on the cards if that doesn't come up trumps.'

'Good for you.' She turned to watch the batsman on his way to the pavilion, wondering why Kevin's news was a bit depressing. If nothing else he was an ally. Most of the other members of staff couldn't stand her, and without him life would be pretty unpalatable.

'We are doing the right thing calling it a day, aren't we?' he said. 'We were discreet, Lotty. Okay, so Dobson had got wind of it but I don't honestly think Bev ever suspected anything.'

'Forget me, Kevin,' she said quietly, the sadness she felt making her slump a little, 'It's best this way. Best you leave and start afresh. Seeing you every day . . . well . . . it's difficult isn't it?'

She smiled, feeling a need suddenly to make it a little easier for him, 'It's difficult for me anyway.'

'Bloody difficult.' He was looking at her smooth tanned legs stretched beside him. 'I'm still attracted to you, Lotty love.'

'Just as well then that you're planning to leave,' she said crisply. 'As a matter of fact, Kevin, I may be getting back with my husband.' She stroked her slightly damp hair off her neck in an effort to cool herself down. 'Max has been in touch and we're meeting next week to discuss things.'

'Oh . . . that's a surprise! Bit of a cheek, isn't it, after what he did to you? Do you want to go back to him?'

She hid her irritation. 'I don't know,' she admitted, 'After my . . .' she stopped dead having very nearly blurted it out. 'Lately, I've had time to think whilst I was staying over at my sister's and perhaps we were a bit hasty, me and Max. We strike sparks off each other, you see . . .' she did not finish, not wanting to have to tell him that, as a lover, Max won. Kevin would not appreciate such frankness. 'And that blonde bimbo threw herself at him,' she added bitterly. 'And we all know how good men are at resisting, don't we?'

'Always one for the jibe, Lotty?' He was surprisingly restrained, succeeding in making her feel ashamed. Why the hell did she say these things to hurt people?

'I hope it works out for you, if that's what you want,' he added stiffly and she knew it was hard for him saying goodbye. She was his first and probably last fling outside marriage. He'd plod on with Bev for the rest of his life. Bev and the kids. And wise Bev would keep a tight grip on him from now on, yank him back to heel if he so much as looked at another woman.

'Was it just coincidence our meeting today?' she asked, looking at his worried face, 'Or have you been following me, you twerp?'

He didn't answer for a moment and they watched as a fielder ran full pelt towards them chasing the ball, slipping near the boundary as he retrieved it. Demure applause broke out round about.

Half-heartedly they joined in, their minds on each other.

'It was a coincidence,' he said at last, 'Beverley's taken the children to the dentist's and I thought I'd get a breath of fresh air, watch a spot of cricket and lo and behold there you were. You're not exactly camouflaged.'

She took the point. Scarlet bikinis do not merge well into backgrounds of cricket white and green. Just for a moment, as he stood up and dusted down his shorts, she wanted to tell him about the baby, his baby. She wanted sympathy. She wanted to tell him what she'd gone through. He ought to know if he didn't already.

Thank God the moment passed.

25

'It's nice. Just the two of us, isn't it?' Don said, bringing in coffee. All smiles. They had dined at a hotel but had declined coffee in the lounge, preferring to go home to Don's and take it there.

'I enjoyed the meal. It was lovely. Thank you,' Laura said, realising she sounded a little formal, a little stiff, wondering if he had noticed her preoccupation this evening.

'Good restaurant isn't it? One of these days I'm going to show you some of my favourite restaurants abroad. Treat you to real Oriental cuisine. Fantastic.'

'Are you settled here?' She didn't know why she asked the question, saw the surprise in his eyes. 'Here in Grange?'

'Settled? I've bought this house, haven't I?'

'Yes but . . . you talk of buying a property abroad and I wonder . . .' she smiled, wished she hadn't asked, looked round the room at his treasured mementoes of time spent far far away.

'Okay.' He put his coffee cup down and looked at her seriously. 'Since you ask . . . I'm having a few doubts. I'm not so sure it was a wise move. I got it by accident almost, a colleague of mine was selling and I came along, liked it, and . . .' he laughed shortly, 'I'm a bit impulsive sometimes.'

'Impulsive with me?'

'No.'

'You sound a bit doubtful.' Laura laughed nervously, wondered where on earth this conversation was leading.

'This is not an easy decison, Laura, but there's going to be no point in hanging onto this house when we might only be using it for a few weeks a year. I want to sell up and move abroad permanently. How would you feel about coming to live with me?' He let the question sit on the air a moment, 'I know you'll miss your family but we can come back to visit any time you like. Hop on a plane and be back in a few hours or so . . .'

'Where abroad?' she asked in amazement.

'Somewhere in the Far East of course. It's what I know best, where I've spent most of my life come to that. Okay, so the situation in Hong Kong for instance is a bit volatile at the moment but I'm happy to take a chance. I feel pretty optimistic about it. It feels like home whenever I go back, Laura.'

'It's not home to me. God, Don, why can't you make up your mind?' she asked him, suddenly angry. 'One minute, you're trying to persuade me to sell my house, move in with you here, and now . . . you're talking about selling this and want me to traipse off with you halfway round the world. Just like that. I have commitments. My children to think of. How can I go off and leave them?'

'I take it the answer is no then.' He stood up, cleared away their coffee cups. 'Come on, I'll run you home.'

'Don't be like that,' she said quietly, 'Outraged and huffy. Let me think about it at least.'

'What is there to think about?' he said, 'You either come with me or you don't. Forget your children. It's whether or not *you* want to come that counts.'

'Give me time. Please.' She was close to tears, fearful that she might lose him.

'Of course. Come on . . .' he stifled a yawn, 'I need to get to my bed. Have you forgotten I'm off again tomorrow. Crack of dawn. Morning flight.'

His goodbye kiss at the door of Fernlands was restrained. Both saddened and annoyed at the way he thought he could spring things on her, she clicked the door shut on him, standing in the empty hall, listening to the silence. He was off again tomorrow, back to his beloved Hong Kong and normally, he might have wanted to stay here tonight with her. If it hadn't been for Suzanne, she might have wanted that too. He hadn't said as much but she knew he thought she was being stupidly modest, shilly-shallying, shy of him staying over, sleeping in her bed, because Suzanne was in the house and she was worried what her daughter-in-law would think. At fifty five years of age, it was ludicrous!

She took off her shoes and went quietly upstairs, listening a moment outside the door before knocking gently. Suzanne was not sleeping well in this latter stage of pregnancy and, if she was still awake, she might like a cup of hot milk.

The door swung a little to her touch and she realised, with surprise, it had not been closed. She peeped in.

It took a few seconds to realise that Suzanne was not there, that the bed was still tidy, morning smooth. Laura snapped on the overhead light and the room flooded with a soft glow. 'Suzanne . . .' She hurried down the corridor to the bathroom but the door was open and the room empty.

Worry, akin to what she had felt when the children were small and momentarily lost, swept through her, rising to panic when she returned to Suzanne's room and saw the note propped on the dressing table. She read it twice. Suzanne, for reasons that weren't entirely clear, was on her way to Sheffield. Surely she wasn't hitch-hiking again in her condition? The poor girl must be deranged to consider such a thing. She couldn't have got far. Or could she? It depended if anyone had taken pity on her and picked her up.

She snatched up the phone and tried Don but of course he wasn't yet home. Oh God . . . Martin and Beth again but then she remembered that they were having one of their very rare evenings out together. Twenty minutes or so and she would try Don again or should she call the police?

She couldn't. Suzanne had left of her own will and, after all, she was an adult even though just now she wasn't behaving like one. Nothing must happen to Suzanne and the baby. What would she tell William if something did? She'd never be able to face him. It was something to do with Sonia. Sonia had telephoned this evening for there was a note to that effect on the pad from Suzanne. What on earth had Sonia said to her?

After eighteen minutes, she tried Don, leaving the phone to ring and ring and ring, willing him to answer.

'Hello . . .' he had obviously run to answer it for he was out of breath. 'Laura! What's wrong now?'

* * *

She made herself a cup of sweet tea, relit the fire, whilst she waited for Don to return. A chill was penetrating deep, curling towards her heart, like the day his golfing partners had come to tell her about George. She had looked at them stupidly. 'But it's tuna quiche . . .' she had protested, 'His favourite.'

Don's car was crunching to a halt on the drive. She flew out of the house, into the rain, running towards him and landing squarely in his arms.

'Relax,' he said in that quiet voice of his, 'She'll be fine. Hey . . . your heart's pounding fifteen to the dozen. Calm down.'

'I'm sorry.' Shakily, she let him lead her back indoors. Immensely relieved by his solid presence, she took him into the sitting room. The fire had taken hold and they sat close to it. 'She's pregnant, Don,' she told him as if he wasn't aware of it already. 'She should be in bed asleep and look at her . . . where the hell is she? She could be dead in a ditch.' She took a deep breath, holding back tears.

'No she isn't,' he said firmly, 'How long has she been gone? Any idea?'

'I don't know,' Laura said, twisting her hands on her lap. 'I thought she was already in bed when I got back. I was going to make her some hot milk . . .' she gave up on the tears, allowed them to seep over and trickle down her cheek. 'Damn. What a thing to happen.'

'It's all right.' He nestled her against his shoulder. 'Can I see the note she wrote?'

'Yes. Silly girl.' She rubbed at her face with her sleeve, sniffed. 'I'll go and get it,' she said, 'I've left it in her room.' A thought occurred as she was on her way out, 'Oh, I'm sorry, Don, you have to be up so early tomorrow. I'm sorry, too, that it turned out as it did. With one thing and another, it's been a night I'd rather forget.'

'Go and get the note.' His smile was a little forced, her worry probably catching at him. 'Maybe it'll give us a clue.'

'Shall we call the police? Do they deal with things like this?'

He shook his head. 'Let's try to sort it out ourselves first. Do you have an address for this aunt she talked about in Sheffield?'

'No, I don't think so. But I know her name,' Laura said, suddenly remembering, 'We can find out her phone number maybe. Ring enquiries and get them to look in the Sheffield directory.'

'Whereabouts in Sheffield? It'll cover a big area, won't it?'

'I don't know exactly but they can look up the name, can't they?'

'What is it?'

She saw the impossibility of it even as she spoke.

'Smith,' she said quietly, 'Margaret. And she has a husband so it's probably under his initial. I don't know what that is.'

They did not laugh, nor even smile.

'I'm going out to look for her,' Don said, grabbing his car keys, 'You'd better stay here in case she comes back.'

'No, I'll . . .' she hesitated, wondering what was best. They had to do something. They couldn't just sit here and twiddle their thumbs. 'Where will you go?' she asked, 'Which way would she go? She's hopeless with directions and things. God knows how she's managed to travel all over the world.'

'I'll drive towards Windermere first,' he said, 'I didn't see her on the road in from my direction but then I was concentrating on getting back here as fast as I could.' He was off, shrugging into his coat, kissing her a little absently on the cheek.

Laura stood in the porch, the rain slanting at her, watching as he ran towards the car, clambered in. As he switched the headlamps on, a figure was revealed just turning into the drive, a bedraggled figure scarcely able to lift one foot in front of the other.

'Don . . . wait.' Relief and anger in equal measure. Don getting out of the car and rushing to help Suzanne, everyone suddenly talking at once, nobody making any sense.

'I'm sorry,' Suzanne said, standing in the kitchen, still and unhelpful as a shop-window dummy, as they shrugged her out of her jacket, tugged the trainers off her feet, peeled off her wet socks. 'We've been out for a walk. Thinking and walking. I suppose you must have read the note. Sorry about that too. I've decided we should talk about it. You weren't too worried, were you?'

Laura picked up the sodden clothes, dangled the disintegrating trainers by their knotted laces, said nothing. She gave Don a warning glance, seeing he was about to burst a blood vessel. 'Take Suzanne through to the living room,' she said sweetly, 'Sit her by the fire, get her a towel so that she can dry her hair and I'll make cocoa and we'll have a talk.'

Don reappeared when she was pouring milk into the cups.

'She's lying tucked up on the sofa, very nearly asleep,' he said, 'Exhausted. You're not going to get much sense out of her tonight. If I were you, I'd just get yourself to bed. It'll wait until morning. Don't worry. She is not going anywhere except that sofa.'

'I'm so sorry, dragging you into all this,' she said, laying a hand on his arm, 'It's not fair on you. What time are you setting out tomorrow?'

'Today . . .' he corrected amiably, 'Six-thirtyish.'

She passed him the cocoa, smiled, 'Drink this before you go home,' she said, giving a little shudder as the events of the evening finally caught up with her.

'Go?' He put his arm round her. 'If you think I'm leaving you tonight after the shock you've had . . .? I'm staying, Laura. And what's more, I'm sleeping in your bed. To hell with Suzanne.'

They peeped in at her, at the lumpy softly breathing shape underneath the blanket on the sofa, before going upstairs.

26

Max's phone call, despite everything, still managed to catch her unawares. Hearing his voice after so long quite literally rendered her speechless which, over the phone, is desperate.

'Hang on,' she managed to croak at last. 'You caught me at an awkward moment,' she said with an unconvincing laugh, 'Pots boiling all over the stove.'

'That doesn't sound like my Lotty,' he said lightly, 'Domesticated you are not.'

True. He had an uncanny knack of mind-reading. 'It's good to hear you,' she said, unable to stop herself, unable to hide her delight, 'How are you, Max?'

'As well as can be expected.' His laugh was confident, sure of himself and of her.

'And the job? Going well?'

'Great. How's yours?'

'Oh . . . everything's fine.'

A little silence. Then . . . 'You read my letter then?'

'I did.'

'So . . . what's the verdict? You've had your time to think by now surely?'

She could see him clearly. A broad-shouldered man, chunky, not terribly tall, blue-jawed because he was forever in need of a shave, tough, hot-tempered. Dark. Hairy. Sexy. With a smile to kill for.

'The verdict?' she said vaguely. 'Well . . . I've been thinking a lot lately.'

'So have I. What can I say, darling? If only I could turn the clock back. I wish I'd never set eyes on Loretta.'

'She's given up on the sweet, domesticated bit then?'

'Forget her. Lotty, darling . . .' there was a pleading in the voice that she recognised from long ago and it very nearly brought tears to her eyes. Damn him to high heaven! After all this time, all the horrors, the humiliation, she still loved him. It beggared belief. For God's sake, wasn't she supposed to be an independent soul? She was going to carve a niche for herself in her profession, do something, help children like Jade Entwistle, and a man would just cramp her style, get in the way.

'We've got to talk,' he said urgently, 'We can't talk over the phone. I want to see your face when I talk to you, my love.'

'Cut the crap, Max,' she said sharply, 'It's not that simple. You can't walk out on me and then expect me to come running back, just like that, whenever it's convenient to you. I don't know if I can ever trust you again.'

'I know.' He was subdued, unlike him, and the reaction surprised her for she could have coped better with an outburst. 'Don't you understand? Didn't it get through to you? I'm trying to do things right for once.' His sigh sailed down the line and she felt herself wavering. His voice mesmerised her. It always had. She was listening to the wonderful sound of it at the expense of the words. 'I meant every word of that letter,' he went on, 'I can't carry on without you, Lotty. Life doesn't seem to have any meaning. I miss you. I miss you so much. I miss everything. Holding you. Touching you. Making love to you. Everything.'

She gulped. Him and his bloody sweet talk! 'I miss you too,' she said, horrified to have finally admitted it. 'Do you want to meet then?' she asked, astonished at how childlike and hopeful she sounded. Had she gone out of her mind? A small part of her was telling her to slam the phone down before it was too late.

'I'm working in London just now but I've got next week off. How about meeting halfway? I can drive up the M6 and you can drive down. In fact . . . I've just had a thought. How about meeting at the Queen's Arms?'

She collected her emotions together before she fell apart. 'How corny can you get?' she asked, resorting to what she was best at, sarcasm. 'I don't think that's a good idea at all. In fact, it's a lousy idea.'

'Why is it? Just because we spent our first dirty weekend there? My God, do you remember that?'

'Of course I remember it, Max Crabtree, and let me tell you, it was a mistake. I did not intend that to happen on our third date. You conned me with all that romantic crap.'

His laugh made her smile. 'Still the same old Lotty,' he said easily. 'You never could resist me, could you? One touch from me and you're like putty in my hands.'

'Don't flatter yourself, buster.' She was still smiling. They were good at this, the slick repartee.

'Don't worry. I'll book separate rooms if you want.'

'Like hell you will. If I know you, you'll book the honeymoon suite.'

'Maybe I will.' He chuckled and she was suddenly so comfortable and happy. 'Shall we say next Wednesday then? We'll stay over Wednesday and Thursday night for starters and by then we should have worked something out. Okay?'

'Okay.'

'I love you very much, Lotty. Remember that.'

She tried but she couldn't quite bring herself to say that she loved him too.

'My dad's brought me round.' Jade smiled nervously as Lotty opened the door. 'He says he wants a word.'

'Ask him to come in then.' Lotty stood aside as Jade walked through, her arms full of books. 'We can talk here. I'll put the kettle on,' she added, feeling a domestic flurry coming on.

'No. He says down in the street. He probably wants to talk about me,' she added, flushing her dismay. 'He says quick because he's on double yellow lines.'

Lotty refrained from cursing. Max's phone call had had a strange effect. It had given her an enormous surge of energy and she had been in the middle of cleaning the flat, forgetting Jade was due until she actually stood at the door. Everything, including herself, smelt of Dettol and some lemony flavoured furniture polish she'd found in the cupboard. Mother must have bought it. She was wearing her very oldest jeans whose button had pinged so that she had to pin them at the waist and a tee-shirt that had started the day white. She supposed she could change into something glamorous but why the hell should she for a lorry driver with a tattoo?

'Wait here,' she said to Jade. 'Start on some reading. I won't be a minute.' She tugged at the ribbon that had been holding back her hair and fluffed it round her face.

'Mrs Crabtree . . .?'

'Yes?'

'If you get a chance, ask him why I can't have my ears pierced, will you?'

Lotty smiled. Made no promise as she made her way downstairs.

She expected to see a lorry parked there occupying at least three spaces but there was just a car. An oldish model in good nick. Recently washed and polished. My God, she couldn't remember when she'd last washed her car. Had she ever washed it? The window wound down as she approached warily.

'Mrs Crabtree . . .?'

'Mr Entwistle, I presume?' They shared a quick smile. 'This is not very convenient,' she said, 'Why don't you come up to the flat? I can make us a cup of coffee. You can park round the corner.'

'I'd rather talk here if you don't mind. Don't worry, I won't keep you long.'

She shrugged, climbed into the passenger seat, realised the car was very clean and tidy inside too which made her feel ten times worse. 'Excuse my state of dress . . .' she muttered, noticing in one brief glance that he was clean and tidy himself, jeans and a check shirt unbuttoned at the neck. 'Now and again, I succumb to a house-cleaning bug. Not very often actually.' Her smile was rueful this time. 'What can I do for you, Mr Entwistle?'

'I want to say thank you for what you're doing for Jade,' he said and, glancing again towards him, Lotty took in a strong face with straight fairish hair. 'I know what you're doing is outside the realms of your job description,' he went on, 'In my book, it counts as private tuition so I would prefer to come to some arrangement . . . I'm quite capable of paying you for your time.'

'God, no,' she said hastily, feeling her cheeks redden, 'This is strictly a one-off, Mr Entwistle. Just me and Jade. I shall be very offended if you offer me payment.'

He nodded. 'Sorry. I wasn't sure. Under those circumstances then, thanks once again.' He had a quiet way of speaking. Also . . . and she was ashamed of the assumption she had made . . . he sounded educated and intelligent.

'That's okay. I don't mind.' She turned in the seat so that she could look more closely at him. 'I told Jade I'd met you at a parents' evening,' she said, 'But I was mistaken. I had some other man in mind. Sorry . . . it gets a bit confusing trying to match parents to children.'

'I haven't been to a parents' evening,' he said and the regret was obvious, 'They always seem to be on a Thursday evening and as often as not, I'm not around. Awkward. I did once speak to the headmaster . . .'

'Ah yes, Mr Dobson. He does a good job,' Lotty said carefully. 'Although I always feel it's better to talk to a child's teachers. For what it's worth, Mr Entwistle, I'm terrifically impressed with your daughter. If we can get her motivated, she'll go far.'

'I feel I've failed her,' he said quietly, 'You know my circumstances and, believe me, it's been very hard since her mother left. I do my best but . . . well, I have to be away a lot with my job and I can't help feeling I'm neglecting her. Not physically, God forbid, but . . . intellectually.'

'You've done a pretty good job,' she said, 'Jade is one of my pleasanter pupils. Some of the girls of her age are already hooked on smoking and they're already . . .' she hesitated, not sure if she should tell him of her suspicions. As a caring father, he would be horrified.

'Sexually active?' He seemed amused at her discomfiture. 'It's okay. I am aware it goes on and at her age too. How can I help her? That's another reason I wanted to talk to you, Mrs Crabtree, to find out just what's acceptable at her age and what isn't. What time should I reasonably expect her to be in if she goes out? Is ten o'clock reasonable for instance? That sort of thing.'

'I don't have children of my own,' she said brightly, 'So of course I'm the last person to offer advice but . . . if anything worries you, ask her to talk to me about it. I've told her that too. I think I'm beginning to gain her confidence.'

'Thank you. That's what I hoped you'd say.' He tapped fingers on the steering wheel, seemed oddly embarrassed. 'Sorry, you must think me a fusspot of a dad.'

'Not at all. It's very good that you care enough to fuss,' she said, thinking that Max would fall about laughing if he could hear her. Parent counselling now! He'd never understood her enthusiasm for her career. Always ready to ridicule. 'Oh . . . could I say just one thing?' she asked as she remembered. 'It's about ear piercing actually. Just a thought but I think it's quite okay for Jade to have her ears pierced. If you like I can take her along into town on Saturday if she doesn't mind meeting me that is . . . get her ears done, have a browse in the bookshop maybe.'

A moment's reluctance, probably acknowledging, correctly, that he was being manipulated by two women, and then he nodded.

'I'll let you get on with the lesson then. Nice to have met you, Mrs Crabtree,' he said, reaching round to shake her hand.

'Nice to have met you too, Mr Entwistle,' she said, closing the car door and smiling back at him.

27

Lotty drove down the M6 in heavy traffic. Roadworks every-where. Irritated faces. She was glad to be off it at last onto the quieter roads leading to the country hotel. It was one of those old coaching inns with a discreet new bedroom wing at the rear. Stepping out of her car, the silence was immense. Just a few country sounds, the chirping of birds okay in this context, the roar of the motorway light-years away.

She pulled her overnight bag out of the boot, excitement in every pore. She had told nobody about this because she wanted the announcement of their reconciliation to be made jointly. They had been fools, she and Max, tormenting each other like this, he a fool for running off in the first place, she a fool for not forgiving him sooner. When you got down to it, that was a weakness of the male species and had to be recognised as such. Martin apart of course, but then Martin was Martin.

She carried the bag into the inn. She hoped he had booked the honeymoon suite because it felt like a honeymoon, a second chance, and she was determined not to fluff it. There was no sign of his car yet, assuming he still drove the BMW and she was glad because she needed time to get ready for him.

Her bag was stuffed full of new clothes. A spending spree she could ill afford. She had spent the money vaguely put aside for the phone bill on herself. Sod BT. There was a new dress for dinner tonight, sapphire blue, Max's favourite colour. It had a deep vee back and front and two cute little bows on each shoulder. It was far too short but Max had always admired her legs. The crimson silk for tomorrow night was longer and she loved the colour herself. Two new nighties. A crisp Anne of Green Gables, stiff white cotton and broderie anglais, and a complete contrast, a black slinky. To wear very briefly, of course, just to get him started. Not that he needed much starting off. They wouldn't be able to keep their hands off each other. Darling Max. Her skin was tingling already for his touch. How she would last out until after dinner she did not know.

'Good afternoon, madam.' A receptionist stood behind the old dark desk. Horse brasses, old maps and hunting prints hung on the walls. The carpet was thick and dark red. Through a door to the right, a waitress was visible laying tables in the beamed dining room. It was just as she remembered. Quiet, thank God, no piped music.

Max *had* booked the honeymoon suite which was part of the old building. A pink and gold fourposter bed dominated the room. Lotty was glad she had popped her wedding ring on again. Not that it mattered a fig and she was astonished she should even think of it in this day and age. A welcoming bottle of champagne, fresh fruit and flowers awaited them. Perfect. If the girl thought it a bit odd them arriving separately, she was far too discreet to say anything.

The adjoining bathroom did not belong to an old coaching inn. It was bang up to date with a huge corner bath, acres of white tiles and masses of fluffy white towels as well as two bathrobes. His and hers. Left alone, Lotty giggled at the opulence. A bit of a far cry from the shambles at Balaclava Street.

Wandering back into the bedroom, she pulled aside the heavy curtains and looked down into the rear courtyard, extra parking space amidst raised flowerbeds. Charming! Lotty gave a sigh. Max would be late. He was late for everything.

She slipped off her jacket and lay on the bed. Above her head, the silk folds of the canopy were elaborately frilled. Everyone should make love in a fourposter, she decided, with a smile. Physically she felt fine now so she could presumably have sex without it having any funny effect. Get pregnant again even. For some inexplicable reason, she had felt shy when she had gone for her check-up and been unable to ask such a question. The doctor who had dealt with her at the time of the miscarriage no longer seemed such a monster, just an ordinary woman tired at the end of a long day, making a mistake, and it wasn't worth the hassle of sueing when there was no harm done. In any case, she ought to behave a bit more like Beth when it came to doling out charity to others.

Would she tell Max? Certainly not yet, not tonight. She didn't want to spoil things tonight. The thing that might really upset him, his masculine ego, was not so much that she had had a relationship with another man but that she had become pregnant as a result. He would find that hard to take.

She would not let him so much as touch her until after dinner. They would dine leisurely in the candlelit dining room and then they might take an after-dinner stroll in the gardens that lay off to one side. A moonlit stroll with the right person at your side was not such a daft idea after all. Only when they had done that would she allow him to take her to bed. The anticipation would drive him wild.

She must have dozed off for, when she awoke, startled, it was past six. Where the hell was he? Even Max should have been here by now. Not too worried, she had a shower and changed into skin-tight leggings and a baggy top. God, she was getting more like Sonia every day. She'd be changing for dinner in a couple of hours. Refreshed, she brushed her hair and put on some light make-up. She'd racked her brains to remember what perfume she used to wear in those far-off days when they'd first met and it had come to her in a sudden inspiration. She was wearing it now. Max was a romantic. Max would remember.

She went down to the reception desk to enquire if there had been a message. It was the same girl on the desk and, after Lotty asked the question, she hesitated, sweeping long blonde hair off her face and tapping the register with a slim gold pen. 'Is Mr Crabtree driving up the M6?' she enquired.

'Yes he is,' Lotty replied with a smile, 'We've been living at opposite ends of the country,' she added, for some reason feeling her smile falter, 'I've driven down and he's driving up from London.' She stopped. It was nobody's business but their own but the girl had a similar sympathetic look to Finney. It came to Lotty suddenly. He'd stood her up. He'd backed out. The bastard had backed out. She'd kill him for this. 'Is there a message?' she repeated, deciding she would be ice-cool.

'I'm sorry, Mrs Crabtree . . .' The girl's lobby composure was cracking, 'There's probably nothing to worry about. In fact . . . I feel quite dreadful for mentioning it . . .'

'Mention what?' Lotty felt the blood drain from her face as time slowed. The grandfather clock nearby ticked. Ticked. Mouth suddenly dry, she moistened her lips with her tongue, scalp tingling. Something had happened. 'What is it?' she asked aggressively, as the girl seemed to clam up.

'It's been on the news. There's been a terrible pile-up on the motorway, ten miles south of here. Field smoke across the northbound carriageway they think. Anyway . . . six cars and a couple of lorries are involved. The emergency services are still there, clearing up . . .'

'Anyone hurt?' It was a ridiculous question and they both knew it. Lotty physically felt the waves of the girl's sympathy. It was suddenly necessary, however, to put a hand on the desk to steady herself.

'Six dead already.' The girl whispered, casting her eyes down.

'I see. Thank you very much.' Lotty wondered why, under the most impossible of circumstances, you could still manage the basics of politeness.

She had just thanked the girl for telling her that Max was dead.

He was dead.

Dead.

She knew.

28 ∫

No matter how tired she was, Sonia never neglected her late-night beauty routine. How you looked was so important in her profession. If you couldn't turn yourself out superbly, how could you do justice to an interior? Her clients expected it of her and they also expected imaginative ideas. Luckily, they were not the sort of people who baulked at the cost for imaginative ideas do not come cheap.

It had been a dreadful day. The client she was dealing with had proved singularly awkward, uncertain and quibbling. Frankly, she was beginning to think it might be better if they went their separate ways. She hated working with clients who doubted her.

After the difficult working day, the promise of a dinner party at the gracious home of their friends Caroline and Rupert looked to be a way of soothing her nerves. Caroline was a wonderful cook, good company and their dinner parties were generally rather special.

Not so tonight. For once, it was not the relaxing, harmonious happening it usually was. And it was all Seb's fault.

Furious, she eyed him through the mirror of her dressing table as she took off her make-up. Jars of expensive creams stood ready. The night cream for her face. The one for her neck. The eye lotion. The hand and elbow cream. And the soles of the foot cream.

'You'll slide into bed one of these days,' Seb muttered, stripping off his cream dinner jacket and tossing it carelessly onto a chair.

'Hang that up.' Sonia continued to apply cream to her neck, trying to calm herself down. She was proud of the smoothness of her neck. It ran in the family for mummy had a good neck and marvellous skin for her age. Quite honestly, she would be more than pleased if she looked as good as mummy at fifty five.

She glanced at Sebastian who was undressing with the careless ease of a husband of ten years. He was down to boxer shorts now, naked from the waist up, trim from his sessions at the gym where he worked out twice a week. He seemed in a funny mood recently. Had been for a few weeks.

'As if I haven't enough problems with this thing with mummy,' she hissed at him, as he stepped into grey silk pyjamas. 'I can't get hold of William . . . God knows where he is . . . and all the time mummy and this man of hers are getting cosier and cosier. Something will have to be done. And then there's the chateau . . . we can't put them off for much longer. And now . . . you . . . well, I just hope you're satisfied, that's all,' she finished, recapping the jar. 'How childish can you get? Look at my gown. It's ruined.' She was already in her nightwear, not daring to look at the gown which was hanging forlornly on its hanger. 'It wasn't as if it was just any old gown either. It was my special investment gown from last autumn.'

'You think too much about clothes, darling,' Seb said with a smile, 'Remember what Martin said . . . beware of idolising material things.'

'Don't bring that up. It was an Yves St Laurent!' She almost screamed the words at him. 'It cost a fortune.'

'It's time you got your priorities right, Sonia.' His expression was sober. 'What if you had to economise? Would it be too much to ask you to buy your stuff at Marks & Sparks like everybody else?'

'Don't be flippant. You can talk!' Satisfied she was adequately creamed, Sonia screwed the rest of the jar lids on, 'We don't have to economise, do we, so don't play silly games. If I choose to spend a few thousand on a single item, I see it as money well spent. It's good for my business image. I have to wear originals. These things last. Pale lemon chiffon . . .' she cried out, remembering. 'All over the bodice. He was sick all down the front and it has tiny pleats and beading. Handstitched. A work of art no less.'

She turned on him, dragging the folds of her negligée off the dressing table stool. 'You planned it, didn't you?' she said, 'Admit it. You asked Alex and Maggie to bring the baby along in some fool attempt to make me feel maternal. Didn't you?'

'Actually no. It wasn't my dinner party.' He looked at her with innocent eyes. 'Maggie must have asked Caroline if she minded. It had nothing to do with me. Why is it upsetting you so much? Is it getting to you, darling?'

'Imagine bringing an eight-week-old baby to a dinner party? It reduced the conversation to a nonsense. Childbirth. Breast-feeding. Nappies. Who wants to talk about that? I certainly don't. If that's what happens when you have a child, then I'm glad I'm not having one. Maggie used to be such fun.'

She glared at Sebastian, slipping off the negligée to reveal a softly green nightdress. Pretty, semi-transparent material with tiny rouleau straps. As she caught his glance, she suddenly wished she wasn't wearing this particular ensemble as it was not easy to control an argument with her nipples on show. On this occasion, however, it seemed not to matter for, other than the quick glance, Seb seemed preoccupied, propped against pillows, not really looking at her, not properly looking.

'Women are beautiful when they're pregnant and when they've just had a baby,' he said at last, as she climbed into bed beside him. 'Maggie's still got a sort of glow about her and that little chap was beautiful too, wasn't he?'

Sonia sighed. Not again. He was not letting go of this insane idea. They had agreed, dammit. His obsession was becoming almost amusing. He would remark on it whenever they saw what looked like a happy family. Mum, dad, a couple of angelic-looking children. He never noticed the yelling, screaming, snotty-nosed variety as she did. It was starting to get her down and was succeeding in putting her off sex well and truly.

She had nearly died tonight when she had seen Maggie arrive clutching the infant to her. Glamorous as ever with her figure almost regained, Sonia had to concede that she looked beautiful. Eyes shining. Alex was besotted with the pair of them, his wife and the blasted baby. The infant had been passed round like some sort of pass the parcel game and, to her horror, she had found herself holding it. Awkwardly, slightly away from her body, so that it screwed up its face and squirmed uneasily. Wise already, it had looked towards the source of the strange nervous voice and then, with a total disregard for logic, it had lolled its head towards her breast in a vain search for milk. Good God! It was just then as the others laughed at her incompetence that it gave a sort of cough and threw up a gush of milky substance. All over the bodice of the Yves St Laurent. Unbelievable!

'Are you still thinking about it?' Sebastian was watching her closely, 'Maggie was mortified about the dress. She did offer to pay for the cleaning.'

'It's not that . . . oh, forget it, will you?' She picked up the novel she was half-way through, the new one from an acquaintance of theirs. She wasn't going to admit to anyone, least of all Seb, that she didn't understand a blessed word of it. She had to finish the damned thing so that she could offer up some careful thoughts when they next entertained him to dinner.

She glanced at Seb who was doing the *Telegraph* crossword. He liked to keep his brain sharp and it was a challenge to complete it in the fastest possible time before he went to sleep.

'Do you think I should give mummy another ring about the chateau?' she asked him, trying to put the dress to the back of her mind.

'I wouldn't if I were you. She's off you. She rang me at the office to complain. Said she couldn't trust herself to keep her temper if she spoke to you.'

'Rang you? Really! She's getting worse. I blame this man's influence.'

'She had reason to be upset.' Deliberately, he put down his pen, tossed the paper aside, 'What the hell did you say to Suzanne? After your call, she only upped and set off in the middle of the night hot-foot for Sheffield for some reason. It was pouring down. Laura says it's surprising she's not got pneumonia.'

'That's hardly my fault.' Sonia drew in her breath, 'She's good at the theatrical gestures, isn't she? And mummy's fooled by her just as she's fooled by William. She had no intention of going to Sheffield but it did the trick, didn't it? Mummy's letting her stay for goodness knows how long and the whole thing's made me out to be some kind of unfeeling monster. My name, should I ever succeed in finding William, will be mud from now on.'

'Did you or did you not tell her she was in the way? Not

wanted. Well . . .? Laura's furious with you and you can forget the chateau.'

'There you go again! The first setback and you give up.' She slipped a bookmark into the book and put it on the table beside the bed. 'I am determined to have the chateau.'

'She's not going to sell. Or, if she is, we're not going to benefit at all.'

'Mummy can be persuaded.'

'You think so?' His laugh was harsh. 'Can't you see you're turning her towards this man of hers? What must he think of us?'

'I don't very much care.' She thumped her pillow, lay down, heart thumping too with her anger.

'I'm bloody exhausted.' Seb turned from her. 'I don't suppose I can persuade you to come with me to New York next week? . . .' His tone was strangely wistful and she glanced sharply at him.

'I can't. Utterly impossible. In any case, I'm not very good at playing the dutiful corporate wife am I? I tend to tell them what I really think and that doesn't go down well generally.'

He made no comment and it left her with an uncomfortable feeling. Did he seriously expect her to drop everything, cancel all her meetings, and go with him? Seriously? Maybe there was an ulterior motive to this baby thing. Maybe if he got her pregnant, maybe if she had to take maternity leave, maybe then she would find it more difficult to pursue her career?

No. He wasn't that mean. She had seen the look in his eyes this evening when he watched Alex holding his newborn son. It had hurt. For a moment, dangerous, she had thought how nice it would be to see Seb looking down at his own son. At their son. Sentimental twaddle instantly squashed when the dratted child disgraced himself in the most flamboyant manner possible over the most expensive dress in the room.

If Sebastian had wanted a mother-earth figure, he should have opted for someone like Beth or Suzanne. Beth suffered most stoically in the pursuit of a happy husband and family. Poor Beth.

She could not sleep. She knew Seb was not asleep either but she was damned if she was going to speak to him. Let him stew!

Or perhaps . . . she debated whether or not to be the first to forgive. He was putting pressure on her and she hated that. All she had to do was have a baby. *All*? Maggie had not helped. They had all the details over the main course. Progressive sorts, Alex and Maggie, and they had gone for some horrific new mode of giving birth, partly submerged in water. Something ghastly like that. They had . . . and this had really killed conversation . . . they had passed round the photographs. Colour photographs. For goodness knows what reason, something about family bonding, Alex and Maggie were apparently naked in the water together, a couple of midwives in attendance. The pain, Maggie said, looking at Alex and clutching his hand, had been glorious.

If she ever had a baby, she was having none of that. Sebastian would be miles away. Whatever happened to the idea of the father pacing the corridor? So much better. Nowadays, it seemed you were practically forced to have someone with you. She didn't want Seb to see her like that. She would have private treatment and get them to do a Caesarian or whatever so that she wouldn't know a damned thing about it. The baby would be cleaned up by the time she set eyes on it.

She had thought . . . if . . . if I have a baby. Was he wearing her resistance down?

'Sonia . . . are you awake?' his voice cut through the darkness and startled her.

'Yes.' She edged a fraction nearer but, to her dismay, he drew away. 'What's wrong?' she leaned across and switched on her lamp.

'We have to talk.'

'Oh Seb . . . I know how you feel. I do know,' she said quietly, 'But the truth is, I really do not want a child. I married you on the understanding that you didn't either.'

'I don't know how I'm going to tell you . . .' he hesitated, most unlike him, looking drawn and haggard and all of his years. 'I've got to tell you. I've been putting it off for weeks but it's not going to go away. Jessica's right. It's not fair on you.'

Her heart pounded. She gasped. She knew what was coming. She knew exactly what was coming. 'Tell me,' she said, 'Get it over with.'

'I didn't mean it to happen. Please believe that. And, when it did, I thought we would be able to sort something out but of course that's stupid.'

She felt his pain. They had gone through a lot, building up their success, their early time together had been very happy.

'I'm nearly forty, Sonia, and what do I have to show for it? I could have a couple of sons at school now. My old school. I could have a daughter, beautiful like you . . .'

'You still can,' she said, making one last desperate effort as the gravity of the situation hit her. He was going to leave her. 'I'm still young. We can have two children, one after the other. Shall we try?'

'It's too late.' He snatched his arm away and, although he may not have intended the gesture to be quite so dismissive, it was. 'Jessica thinks she's pregnant.'

'Is it yours?' She didn't know why she was bothering to ask. Clever Jessica. Sweet, wide-eyed Jessica. She had her sights set on her husband for a long time.

'Of course it's mine.' His anxiety seemed to have fallen away now that he had confessed all. There was instead an air of pleased resignation about him. 'I've said I'll stand by her.'

'Bully for you. You can get the hell out of here then. Now preferably. This minute. Go to your precious Jessica.'

'Be reasonable, Sonia . . .'

'Reasonable?' She laughed, reaching for her negligée. 'You can contact me through my solicitor. Oh . . . and by the way . . . the chateau's off. Just as well. French is such a pain of a language to learn.'

'You must understand that it's been on the cards for a long time. We've been growing apart . . . can't you see that?'

She flounced off before he could try to stop her. He didn't.

In the privacy of the spare room, she felt the tears coming and made no attempt to stop them. She would ring mummy tomorrow. Mummy always knew what to do.

All his stuff was in the apartment he had in Manchester. Somewhat sniffily, Max's mother let her have a key, although the inference had been she was not to touch anything. Max's mother, cool-eyed at the best of times, positively stony-eyed at this worst of times, would deal with the disposal of his belongings later. Lotty suffered the accusing silence. There was no point in explaining that they were about to be reconciled. Possibly. Who would believe that? Lotty was uncomfortably aware that it was only her word now, for there was no Max to back it up. Let them think what they would. It made no difference. It wasn't as if there was a huge inheritance to fight over. It wouldn't have mattered if there had been. She only wanted him, not money nor property.

She had never been here to this flat. This was somewhere he had lived without her and it showed. It was very tidy. Masculine. Rather like one of his stage sets and just as impersonal.

She was reluctant to do things like look in the drawers, peer in the cupboards, and, now she was here, she didn't know why she had bothered to come. All it was doing was turning the screw on her grief one more notch. Tightening it so that it couldn't possibly go any further.

She hadn't bothered to explain anything to that tight-arsed mother of his. Why should she? Some things were still private even though Max was dead and she had no wish to discuss them with any of the Crabtrees. There was no point in the 'what might have beens'.

His clothes were hanging in the wardrobe. She ran her hands along them. Laid her face against them. Sniffed his tweed jacket, the one he'd bought when they'd once been asked out for a country weekend. He liked to look the part, did Max. Oh yes, there were the golfing sweaters, teamed up with the trousers. Bit of a dandy, Max. She looked quickly through the drawers where his underwear and socks were neatly folded. He'd always hated the way she'd just bunged them in, all mixed together. She smiled at the thought of him standing in front of her, wearing one sock, asking her what the hell she'd done with the other one. It had been the start of many an early morning row. After all, why should she be responsible for his bloody socks!

She frowned at the black sheets on the big bed, the stark black and white striped quilt, cast aside a quick vision of Loretta in there with him. In the drawer of the bedside table, there was their wedding photograph, face down. She saw what it was, did not look at it. So that's where that had gone . . .

Papers were in the desk. In date order. Oh well . . . of course. It occurred to her that, if it was her, if she had died in the crash, someone would have their work cut out trying to sort through *her* paperwork. She kept unnecessary things, had an envelope stuffed with newspaper and milk bill receipts from the year dot, but, come to think of it, had no idea where her television licence or car insurance documents were hidden. Every year it caused havoc when she had to find them. Every year she vowed she'd put them somewhere obvious for next time. Every year she forgot.

She put Max's neatly clipped documents to one side and shuffled through the remaining files. All numbered and named. Except for one.

A plain pink folder.

She dropped it on the desk, opened it.

An envelope inside it and, inside the envelope, photographs. Of her. He must have nicked them out of the photograph album, at the same time he'd sneaked the wedding picture out. One or two of her baby pictures, plump and unsmiling, Lotty as a child sitting beside a sweetly smiling Sonia, Lotty as a teenager. And then some of her and Max together, smiling into the camera, Max's arm round her shoulders. Very proprietorial and they'd only known each other a few weeks. But then, they'd known from the beginning of course.

'Sentimental sod,' she said softly, replacing them in the envelope with a little sigh. There was a notepad too and she opened
it. Drafts of a letter. Started. Crossed out. Started again. Crossed
out again. Several pages of it.

'My dearest Lotty . . . I'm glad you decided to read this instead
of throwing it away . . .' Pretty much the finished version
that one.

She wouldn't let his mother get her hands on these. She tipped
the rest of the papers out and something dropped, rolled, and
slipped off the desk. She bent down to retrieve his wedding ring.

Held it solidly in her hand a moment, closed her fingers round
it. The screw tightened even more.

Max Crabtree . . . why the hell didn't you slow down? Didn't I
always tell you you drove too fast? Too close? Why did you never
listen? Or were you so excited and happy to be meeting me again
that you were just careless for a split second?

It mattered that he had been happy at that moment. It mattered
to her a lot.

As she drove away, she realised with a grim satisfaction that
there was not a trace of Loretta anywhere in the flat. It was as if
she had never been part of his life.

And that's how it should be.

Lotty retreated to her flat in Balaclava Street, shutting herself
away with her thoughts. She waited until after the funeral
before contacting her mother or her sisters because she did
not want them along. It was bad enough coping with the
daggers-drawn looks of the rest of Max's family. They could
hardly bring themselves to speak to her and the fact that she
had been totally unable to drum up any tears only cemented
the impression that she didn't care. How could she, for hadn't
they been separated? The fact that Max had left *her*, that he had
been the guilty party, was conveniently glossed over.

When she did get in touch with her mother, she was out. She
spoke to Elsie who announced that she was out for the day with
that Mr Fletcher and wouldn't be back till late. If then, she had
added darkly and with much meaning . . .

She talked instead to Beth who said she would break the news.

She was prepared for the immediate shock and tears. Martin would come over at once, she threatened between sobs, but Lotty told her she didn't want Martin. She couldn't face Martin and his consoling-the-bereaved crap at the moment.

Kevin had been round, embarrassed, to offer his condolences. How the hell he knew she didn't enquire although there had been a lengthy report in the nationals and names had been mentioned. There couldn't be that many Max Crabtrees in this world, she supposed, and now there was one less. Seeing Kevin only confirmed that he meant nothing to her, that he never had.

There was only Max for her and now there would be nobody else. She was finished with all that. She felt like shutting herself away in a nunnery, something suitably mind-boggling like that, but on second thoughts she couldn't stand the grim grey uniform they wore nowadays and would opt for a personal crusade instead. She laughed bitterly. If she could help one child and one child only . . .

Her mother rang, awkward, subdued, holding back tears, seeming relieved when Lotty refused her offer to come over. Would she like Martin to come then? God . . . no . . . she'd already told Beth no.

Martin, of course, ignored her plea and arrived by first-class post next day, mercifully in plain clothes clutching flowers and a card. A religious card edged in black. 'May God be with you in your time of sorrow.'

'You'd better come in, I suppose,' she said ungraciously, 'Although I thought I told mother and Beth I didn't want you.' She propped the card next to Kevin's on the fireplace. 'I'm okay. I'm not going to cut my throat or anything. Can't stand the sight of blood.'

'Of course you're okay.' There was no trace of sarcasm but she eyed him with suspicion. She was ready for him. If he dared start on the mysterious ways of God . . .

'Find a seat.' She could see the place was rapidly reverting to its former state. 'Move that stuff. I'll see if I can find a vase.' She watched as he sat on the sofa, laying the flowers on the table. Ignoring them because she would never be able to find a vase and he might be offended if she stuck them in a milk bottle. She offered him coffee, which he refused, and lit a cigarette, wishing she was wearing cleaner jeans and had bothered to put a bra on under the tight tee-shirt. It was not entertaining the vicar garb, too sluttish by half.

'Why didn't you tell us right away?' he asked. 'We knew about the accident on the motorway but we didn't bother with the details, didn't read the names. It upsets Beth, that sort of thing. We just never thought.'

'I know. Accidents always happen to other poor sods, don't they? I've told you now, haven't I? I was waiting until after the funeral until I felt more composed.' She glared at him defiantly. 'I don't know why I said that, Martin. I have been bloody composed the whole time. I can't cry. I've tried and tried but I can't. I wonder why not. I disgraced myself crying at dad's funeral so why can't I cry now? Max's family all managed to weep buckets and I just stood there, not quite smiling but serene. Hellishly composed. I feel . . . sort of . . . stoppered.' She touched her heart, 'It hurts here,' she said, not quite daring to look at him, 'I know I'd feel better if I could let it out. Mr Dassayaje tells me I should scream and wail.' She managed a smile. 'They've been wonderful, and Rachel of course. When something like this happens, you find out who your friends are. I shall be sad to leave here.'

'You're moving then?' he coaxed gently.

'Not far. Just to the other side of town. I have things to do yet at school. Children I'm not giving up on.' She sighed, thought of Jade and her bright eyes and hopes. Thought briefly of Jade's father and his anxiety. 'It'll be a fresh start, won't it, moving to a new place.'

'Do you want to talk about Max?' Martin asked. 'I liked him incidentally and I'm not just saying that. He was frank and intelligent. Of course we didn't see eye to eye on God but then I'm used to that.' A smile flitted across his face, 'How can a bloke like you be so bloody stupid, he once said to me, can't you see it's all mumbo jumbo.'

Lotty nodded. That sounded like Max. 'He rang me, Martin,' she said, drawing deeply on her cigarette. 'After I got back here, he finally rang and we were going to meet to talk about things. That's why he was on the motorway coming to meet me at a place we once knew.' She felt herself blush as if he were aware of the circumstances. 'I don't know if we would have worked it out but I like to think we would. We never got the chance. The last thing he said to me . . .' she heard her voice shake, controlled the spasm, 'was that he loved me and I couldn't even tell him that I loved him too. He died not knowing that.' She looked at him, the thought hard to bear.

'Ah . . . but words aren't always necessary are they?' He leaned forward, patted her hand, withdrawing at once as if he sensed her reaction. 'It's tough. You must be wondering what God's playing at? On the one hand, He gives you faith and on the other He takes away someone you love.'

'Three people. Max. Dad. And my baby.' She pulled at her tee-shirt, realising too late that she was drawing unfortunate attention to her nipples. Martin seemed not to notice, presumably above such things. 'The night after Max was killed . . .' she hesitated, 'It was a dream I suppose.' She flicked at some ash that had fallen on her jeans. Something to do. 'Christ, Martin, I'm forever talking to you about these things.'

'Who else?' he said with a smile.

'I just hope to God you don't tell anyone, not even Beth.'

'Trust me,' he said, his voice a whisper. 'This is between you and me, Lotty, and, of course, God. Your faith's been badly dented, hasn't it?'

'Too bloody true,' she said vehemently. 'And yet . . . maybe it was a dream but it didn't feel like one. Max sent me a message.' She dared to look at Martin, gauge his reaction, but he was wearing a carefully neutral expression, 'He said he was fine and that it was okay where he was and that it was just sod's law, something like that.' She shrugged. 'Now you think I'm completely daft, don't you? Visions. And now messages from the other side.' She managed an uneasy laugh, 'What is the matter with me? Max was bad enough at communicating even when he was alive so why should he bother now?'

'You're a very sensitive person, Lotty,' Martin said, 'Sometimes you like to pretend otherwise but you don't fool me. Or yourself. And sensitive people can stretch out to the limits of our under-standing. Max was sensitive too so why shouldn't there be some means of him communicating with you, the woman he loved?'

'Because it's creepy that's why,' Lotty said, a shudder running through her. 'It makes me doubt my sanity.' She raised annoyed eyes to him, 'Why did your God do this to me?' The hurt in her heart was numbing her, 'Explain that if you can. Why? Okay, so I swear a bit and smoke a lot but I'm not that bad surely?'

'It's *my* God now, is it? Don't tell me you're a fair-weather Christian, Lotty.' He spoke calmly but she felt his underlying anger. She had rattled him. 'I have precious little patience with people like you,' he went on, surprising her by allowing his anger to show, 'A believer when it suits you but, when the going gets tough . . . don't you think there have been times when I haven't questioned God? Last week I had to officiate at a funeral of a child. A little three-year-old boy. What do I tell the parents? I'm supposed to understand.'

'I expect you thought of something. You've got all the glib answers,' she said bitterly, 'But it's not good enough, Martin. Not for me.'

'It will help if you believe,' he said, 'It will give you the strength to cope.'

'Spare me the sermon.' She gave an impish smile as she caught him looking at her breasts. Yes, anger aroused her. Max had always known that.

He looked quickly away. 'Come back with me,' he said, 'Beth wants you to.'

'No, she doesn't. She thinks it's her duty but she doesn't want me there. She feels insecure when I'm around.'

'In what way?'

She laughed. 'Must I spell it out for you, Martin?' She was behaving badly and she knew it. She was flirting with him. Flirting! The hurt in her heart was unbearable. It was moving upwards. Becoming a sort of sob. 'I'm not welcome up there. Mother's distraught. Blaming herself for some daft reason. Sorry she wasn't there when I called. And Seb's left Sonia too, although you know that of course. It's as if two of her little darlings have fallen down at the same time and hurt themselves. She wants to pick us up and kiss us better. I know her.' She turned away and stubbed the cigarette out viciously. The sob pounded and made a very small sound. She had to get him out of here.

'I'm here if you want to cry on me,' he said and touched her shoulder. 'Nothing else, Lotty. I love Beth, you see.'

'I know you do. I'm sorry.' She was desperately ashamed of herself. The sob gushed out, a heart-rending sound. 'Oh, Martin . . .'

'Cry, Lotty,' he said gently, opening his arms to her.

'I feel guilty,' Laura said. 'It was bad enough what happened to Sonia, Sebastian walking out, but now poor Lotty losing Max like this.' She glanced quickly at Don as she heard his sigh. 'I ought to have gone to see her myself but Martin . . . well, he is a professional, isn't he?'

'And you are her mother,' Don said, raising his eyebrows, 'You're always going on about that. I wouldn't have thought wild horses would have stopped you from going to her in her hour of need.'

'Are you being critical of me?' she snapped, 'Or merely unpleasant?'

'Neither.' His smile was forced. 'What's the matter with you? I know you've had your share of shocks recently, darling, but you all seem to be glossing over the fact that Lotty was separated. Surely that makes a difference? To me, it hints, just a bit, of hypocrisy.'

'She might have been separated but she still loved him,' Laura said quietly, 'She can't hide things from me. And that's why I know exactly how she must be feeling.'

'It's reminded you of George, hasn't it? All this?'

'Of course it has. And poor Lotty doesn't even have any children to help take her mind off it.'

'I didn't have children either when my wife died.'

'Oh . . . I'm sorry, how thoughtless of me,' she murmured, making a little conciliatory gesture. 'I'm being selfish I know but I can't help it. It's how I feel.'

Don came across, sat beside her, reached over and took her hand. 'This is a terrible thing to have happened,' he said, 'But there's no point in letting it get you down. Other than being sympathetic as you've been sympathetic to Sonia, what can you do? You can't bring Max back. You've got to be strong for Lotty's sake . . .' He tried a smile, 'Isn't that what they advise?'

'They? Who are they? Spare me all that counselling nonsense,'

Laura shook her head in exasperation. 'You just don't understand the mother-daughter relationship do you?' she went on. 'Max was my son-in-law. I didn't particularly like him if you must know but that doesn't make any difference. I am feeling this way because of Lotty. I spoke on the phone, heard her. It doesn't matter a damn what she said . . . words don't matter. She was trying to be brave, you know her, but Lotty is very very sad and that makes me sad, too. Sadder, if that's possible.'

'Oh come on . . . she'll get over it.' His laugh was brittle. 'Looking like she does, she'll soon find another man.'

Intensely irritated at the remark, she brushed him aside as he tried to draw her near to him. 'Leave me,' she said. 'I want to be on my own for a while.'

He nodded, stood up and left her.

She sat quietly, wondering what George would have felt. George had liked Max, perhaps understood him more than she. She wondered what they'd said to each other on the golf course. George . . . she said to herself . . . what *are* we going to do with Lotty? If it's not one thing, it's another with her. Always has been.

Please don't let anything else happen. Nothing nasty that is. Lotty is strong but not that strong.

Beth was knitting. Fine white wool, a matinée jacket, mittens and bootees for Suzanne's baby. The movement of her fingers along the needle soothed her and it was a simple pattern so that she could do it without thinking and carry on a silent debate with herself.

She couldn't quite believe her luck in landing the job and Martin was being so wonderfully supportive. Of course she must do it, he said.

Succeeding at the interview, against all odds surely, had given her the boost she needed. She could still remember the interview, word for word, and how nervous she had been. She could remember the joy of being offered the job, there and then, and she could remember going into town to celebrate.

She had gone into *that* shop again but this time there had been no straying from the path, nor would there ever be again. It had been for a purpose, she decided, so that she would be better able to cope with people like that when she came across them at her various voluntary agencies. Someone had asked if she would do some visiting at a Young Offenders' Centre and she had agreed at once. There but for the grace of God . . .

She felt calmer now than she had done for some time. Whoops! A stitch dropped and she fumbled a minute with the needles, picking it up and concentrating again, finishing the row as Suzanne appeared with a tray, having insisted on making a pot of tea.

'You're so clever, Beth,' she said admiringly, glancing at the tiny garment. 'Isn't she clever, Kate? I don't know one end of a knitting needle from the other.'

'It's not clever,' Beth said, feeling obliged to point out the obvious, 'Being nimble with your fingers is just one of those things.'

'You do yourself down,' Suzanne said, sitting opposite, heaving herself into a comfortable position. They exchanged a smile, enjoying these little get-togethers that had become quite a regular thing recently. Thank God the little upset with Sonia, misunderstanding they preferred to call it, had been forgotten. Suzanne was staying with her mother for the moment but not for ever. William would turn up trumps. Suzanne was certain he would and so was Beth. Let the others have their doubts. 'I've met a lot of academically gifted people who are absolute idiots,' Suzanne went on cheerfully, 'Sometimes people who think too much have no common sense.'

Beth beamed at her. She hoped that by now William would have received the letter she had sent him soon after Suzanne's arrival. She and William were the two younger ones and when they were little it had sometimes meant ganging up on Sonia and Lotty. They had enjoyed little conspiracies together and it had to count for something. Quite often in the past, William had done what she asked and this time she had simply asked him to come home.

'Beth . . . I know it sounds stupid but . . .' Suzanne nibbled a biscuit and Beth put down her knitting and sipped her tea. 'I'm scared stiff of having the baby.' One hand circled the bump. 'Every other thing on television seems to consist of watching a woman giving birth and it's really putting me off. Hours and hours of pain. I don't know if I can cope with that. I'm a big softie,' she added with a smile, 'William knows that. Oh . . . I wish he was here, Beth.'

'Don't worry. He will be here as soon as he can manage it,' Beth said with a smile, a reassuring smile she hoped. 'And stop worrying about the birth. Things are improving all the time, better now than when I had the boys. Nobody expects you to bite on the bullet. If it gets too much, you get help. You must talk to the doctor. Tell him.'

'Should I?' She sighed, 'All the other women are having their second or third so they know it all already. Oh Beth, I so envy you.'

'Envy me?' she asked in astonishment, 'Whatever for?'

'You've got Martin and the boys. Your home is so lovely. You're so relaxed. So comfortable with life. It's the God thing I suppose. It must help.'

'I suppose it must.' Beth smiled slightly. 'Come on, let's go for a walk. We'll take the dogs.'

Wellied up, they set off. The path skirted fields and the dogs bounded ahead, leaving her and Suzanne treading more warily. They chatted, mainly about William and the things he had got up to in Australia, and, as they walked, the sun struggled through broken clouds at last, gently steaming off the effects of a heavy shower. A smell of damp, green earth, lakeland, the very special smell of home.

Elizabeth Bennett, be thankful, she told herself, helping Suzanne over a stile, giggling with her in the process. So . . . she didn't have Sonia's figure or Lotty's razor-sharp mind but look what she did have.

The path petered out and the view of the hills, their peaks purpled as they shook off the clouds was breathtaking. A still strong wind battered her face and lifted her hair into wild tendrils as the hood of her anorak slipped free. She turned to look back towards the village, the spire of the church clear against the sky.

A great contentment settled on her.

She had all this.

31

Sonia had been shopping. Two new suits, a dress and a couple of beautiful blouses helped. That, and a brand new hair-do. She felt completely different with the new cropped style.

It wasn't so much Seb leaving her, she realised now, as the humiliation that it brought upon her. All their friends knew, probably had known for a while, and they would be talking about it behind her back. After all, why did a man leave his wife? Because she was in some way inadequate, that's what they would be saying.

She would show him and them. She would get herself a new partner as soon as possible and with her looks it shouldn't be too difficult, although she had precious little appetite for it. Impatiently, she tossed the samples of fabric aside and sat hunched at her desk. Even the super country house commission she was engaged on at the moment had lost its appeal.

The truth was she didn't know quite what she was going to do. The rehearsal was different from the reality. There'd always been someone to grumble at and it wasn't so much fun grumbling when there was nobody to hear. And, if she was honest, she did spend money like a drunken sailor and she needed someone to remind her of that occasionally. Designer clothes were a drug though and she didn't know how she would cope with lesser creations.

The first time she'd tried to phone mummy, she was away. It was a bit off, particularly as she was by all accounts out with that man of hers. God knows where . . . Everybody knew about Sebastian now, the whole family, and, sensing an uncharacteristic coolness in her mother's response, she no longer wished to discuss him with anybody. Surely mummy wasn't blaming her in some way for Sebastian's departure? In any case, Lotty's coup had upstaged her own problem, made it pale into insignificance. Trust Max to get himself killed like that. She was sorry, of course she was sorry, for Max and for Lotty but the timing had meant mummy had to dole out her sympathy to both of them and she felt she got the lesser dose.

Sebastian was gone and the house was empty. A big empty house and his leaving had left it ghost-like, her design work no comfort. Some of her more outlandish designs were beginning to jar even on herself. She was going paranoid. She felt a change coming on her, a pastelly change, even yearning for mummy's ghastly pink. She needed to be soothed. She looked round the stark black and white room that was her study and frowned.

The doorbell ringing made her jump. Sebastian? She had insisted he hand over his key so he would need to ring the bell. The financial arrangements of the divorce would take an enormous amount of sorting out and she was damned if she was going to make it easy for him. Jessica was supposed to have money so let her spend some of it.

It rang once more and she rose, knowing she had to answer it. If it was Seb, how should she play it? If he had come to his senses and wanted to come back, she would stop short of asking him to go down on his knees but not far short.

She clattered across the hall and opened the door with a flourish.

'William!'

'Sonia!' He was beaming, eyes bright in his tanned face, hair even blonder than usual, bleached by that everlasting Australian sun. 'How's things?'

'You haven't got a heap of friends lurking somewhere?' she asked suspiciously.

He shook his head, 'What a welcome!' he said drily, 'Nice to see you, Sonia. Nice to see you too, William.' He looked at her closely. 'You look great. Stunning as usual.'

She hugged him, a little surprised to see how pleased she was. 'When did you last have a bath?' she wrinkled her nose, studying him closely. 'I've been trying to locate you, you big clown. You don't exactly make it easy, do you? How on earth have you got here?'

'By plane. A great big jumbo.' He grinned, dropping a large sausage-shaped bag onto the floor and Sonia fussed round, showing him to the bathroom, finding him some clean clothes . . . Sebastian's left-overs . . . and left him to it.

'What do you eat these days?' she asked as, shiningly scrubbed, he came through to the kitchen. 'Are you still vegetarian?'

'On a cattle farm? I eat anything. Where's Seb? Still ducking and weaving through the stocks and shares?'

'He's not here at the moment. He's away on business,' Sonia said coolly, preparing his meal, avoiding eye contact. William could find out from someone else. 'Aren't you going to ask how your wife is? She's about to give birth any time so you'd better get yourself up there fast. You can borrow my car if you like.'

'Thanks.' He stretched out Sebastian-jeaned legs, wearing unbelievably tatty trainers. Blonde-haired. Blue-eyed. Tanned. Healthy. No worries. 'It's good to be back in England,' he said. 'That first glimpse of little green fields can still bring a lump to your throat. Home I suppose.'

'For how long?' The egg broke in the pan and she cursed silently. Cooking was not her forte. She and Seb had usually eaten out and on the occasions they had stayed home, he had done the cooking. 'Do you want chips with this?' she enquired, 'There should be some frozen things in the freezer.'

'Sure.' He watched with amusement as she struggled gamely on, 'How is Suzanne?'

'She's fine. We're all fine although . . . well, first of all Max is dead. Yes I know . . . it was a big shock to us all. Car crash.' She fell silent a moment as he digested this. 'Lotty's very upset of course even if they were separated.'

'Hell . . .' He seemed more upset than she would have expected, pounded his fist on the table in sudden anger, 'I'm really sorry to hear that. Great guy, Max. Poor old Lotty.'

'And the other thing is that mummy's taken leave of her senses and is seeing another man. That's what I've been trying to get hold of you for, to explain.'

'Seeing another man?' He tucked into his poorly prepared meal with vigour. She remembered that he'd always enjoyed his food.

Seb was so damned picky, worrying about cholesterol and the like, afraid of gaining an ounce, terrified of getting a paunch. 'Obviously it's not really serious,' she went on, passing William a big mug of coffee, 'She must miss daddy such a lot but it's so silly of her to do this. You'll have to talk to her. She'll listen to you.' She sighed her exasperation, 'She's always ignored me. She still treats me like a child sometimes.'

'That's because you behave like one,' William said amiably, wiping up the last morsels of the fry-up with a piece of bread. 'Playing at houses . . .' he glanced wryly round, 'Buying pretty dresses.'

'How dare you!' she whipped the plate from him, finished or not. 'If anyone in this family behaves like a child, you do. You show no responsibility to your wife and baby. I hope it's damned well occurred that you'll have to provide some means of support, somewhere to live. You can't sponge off mummy.'

'I don't intend to.' He smiled, so like his mother just then that Sonia stared. It wasn't only the wonderful blue eyes, but also the expression, the stubborn tilt of the chin. Any resemblance to their father had totally passed him by. 'Suzanne and the baby are coming back to Australia with me,' he said, 'I've got us somewhere to live. You're sure she's okay?' A little uncharacteristic worry seemed to flutter about him. 'I did write but I don't know that I ever got round to posting them. There isn't a post-box on every corner out where I was.'

'According to Beth, Suzanne is perfectly all right. A bit scared perhaps but then who wouldn't be?' Sonia looked at him and smiled. 'She even wanted reassurance from me about the birth and I ask you, what would I know about it?'

'A baby would cramp your style. You and Seb's.'

She ran her hands through her hair in agitation, forgetting it was cropped. It felt odd. She felt odd. Seb would hate it. 'You'd better get yourself up to mother's,' she said, 'Are you going to ring first?'

'I want to surprise her. Suzanne. I want to see her face when she sees me,' he said, that easy, eager smile flashing again, 'I've missed her. I don't mind telling you that I was irritated as hell that she wanted to come back here but she can be stubborn.'

'That makes two of you.' Sonia managed only a tight smile, trying to recall the last time Sebastian had bothered to delight her with a surprise, a nice surprise that is.

'Why did you come back, William?' she asked curiously.

'Beth asked me to,' he said. 'Her letter finally caught up with me. Lucky because I was just about to move on. You know me, I've never been able to resist little Beth especially when she's brimming with indignation and she certainly was.'

'Little? She's the size of a house. She's too caught up with her infernal good works and that family of hers to bother about herself.'

'There's nothing wrong with Beth. She could teach you a thing or two about family values,' he said with that quiet dignity she had forgotten he possessed.

'Don't let's quarrel,' she said with a little smile, 'Although you're a fine one to talk about family values,' she added, not able to resist the dig.

'Touché.' His smile was wary too. 'I'm here now, aren't I? A bit late, I grant you, but I'm here now.' There was a silence and then they each gave a sigh for their own reasons. 'One of these days, Sonia, you'll discover there's more to life than this . . .' he looked round, shaking his head in wonder, 'I don't know how you can live in this show-piece. I know it's your job but I like a house to look lived in . . .'

'Lived in?' Sonia laughed shortly, 'That's a euphemism for messy in my book. Like Lotty's flat.'

But he had struck a nerve and perhaps he had a point. Maybe Seb had felt the same. No matter that it had looked so wonderful in that magazine.

She watched through the window as William set off erratically, weaving his way past the parked cars. She wasn't too sure of the wisdom in allowing him to use her car. The remains of his meal were in the kitchen and she tidied things uncertainly away, looking for items that were her cleaner's domain. Everything shone. The grey marble worktop. The black and grey tiles. The shiny cupboards. The white tiled floor.

She thought a moment of Lotty and Beth's kitchens. Lotty's

was a disgrace as she herself was. Beth's was clean of course but hardly *Homes and Gardens* material either, not with those two disgusting unhygienic dogs camping out in it.

It was home.

She so envied her that.

32

'He's away again then, that Mr Fletcher.'

'Yes.' Laura glanced at Elsie, as she finished off the morning's cleaning. They were alone in the house as Beth had taken Suzanne to the clinic for a routine check. 'Would you like a cup of tea?' she enquired with a smile, 'We can take it through to the verandah as it's such a nice day.'

'Lovely. I'll make it, Mrs Howard.' Elsie beamed, all their little differences of the last few weeks forgotten. 'You go and put your feet up. I'll bring it through.'

'And some of those chocolate biscuits, perhaps?'

'Right you are. Coming up.'

Laura wandered off to the verandah. It was early and quiet yet on the lake, the boat traffic limited to a couple of small craft. The water was unruffled, dark, and the morning sky pressed against the hills, blue green hills rimmed with sunshine. After all these years, it was still capable of catching her unawares. George, despite his practical turn of mind, had felt just the same.

'Here we are.' Elsie reappeared with the tray, sat down opposite. They usually managed a cup of tea together when the work was done but not always. Today, however, Laura wanted to talk and Elsie was as good as anyone. Very discreet in fact despite the disapproving mutterings. Despite the barrier that their employer/employee relationship created, Laura knew that, when it came to the crunch, she could count on Elsie far more than some other of her so-called friends.

'You remember when the children were small, Elsie . . .' she began, as Elsie fussed with the cups and the pot. 'Once, around Christmas time, George and I were invited to this extravagant function in Grange. At the Crown. A dinner dance and an overnight stay.'

'Can't say I recall that exactly,' Elsie said uncertainly, 'He wasn't one for dancing and that, was he, not the doctor?'

'No.' Laura smiled. 'Well . . . I'd bought this beautiful gown. Deep blue, floaty material. I can remember it perfectly well. As you say, we didn't get out much and I was very excited about it. The day before, I'd had my hair done and my nails manicured and George's dinner suit was pressed and ready.'

Elsie nodded, waiting for what was to come, sipping her tea in a very genteel fashion.

'And then, guess what? Sonia developed this high temperature. Followed by Lotty then Beth and even little William. George was very concerned about them for there was no rash or sore throat. We cancelled. We couldn't leave them like that, could we? Even with a nanny at hand, we couldn't go off and enjoy ourselves. It wouldn't have seemed right.'

'No. You did the right thing, Mrs Howard. You were good parents, you and the doctor.'

'Were?' She laughed, reached for a biscuit, took a dainty bite, 'I still am I hope. Or rather, trying to be. Can you believe what's happened to Lotty and Sonia?'

'Poor Miss Lotty her losing Mr Crabtree like that. Dangerous things cars, aren't they? You still learning to drive, Mrs Howard?'

Laura nodded. 'My test's coming up soon,' she said, 'Don't say anything to Lotty, but Max was a very fast driver, an accident was on the cards. Too late now, of course. As for Sonia's problem . . .'

'She can't help it,' Elsie said stoutly, and looking at her, Laura recognised that what she had long suspected was true. Elsie had a soft spot for her eldest daughter. 'It's not her fault that that Mr Matheson's left her.'

'That's debatable,' Laura mused, 'She's taken Sebastian for granted for too long and you and I know, Elsie, that a man needs to be cossetted a little.'

'Ah yes . . . that!' Elsie sniffed. 'I hope you didn't think I was sticking my nose in, Mrs Howard, over that business with Mr Fletcher. You do what you want. Don't let anybody tell you what to do.' She poured them more tea, lowered her voice, 'If you ask me, them children of yours are going to see sense eventually. Mark my words, they'll be giving you their blessing before long.'

That evening Suzanne went into labour. As previously arranged, Laura rang Beth who was to drive them to the clinic. Everything would be fine, she assured her daughter-in-law who looked frightened to death.

'You'll sail through it,' she said cheerfully, 'I had four so it can't be so bad, can it?'

'That's what everyone keeps saying,' Suzanne said, attempting humour. 'I'm not convinced. I think it's a gigantic conspiracy not to admit the truth.'

They were on their way, negotiating the gateway, sharing the car with Ben and Dixie who, for reasons known only to herself, Beth had brought along. As Beth swung into the road, she braked so suddenly that the dogs landed in an indignant heap on Laura and Suzanne.

'For goodness sake, darling . . .' Laura protested to Beth, shoving the grumbling animals out of the way and checking that Suzanne was all right. A moment later, she saw the reason for the abrupt halt. Sonia's car was a mere few feet away, signalling to turn in, and at the wheel . . . 'William . . .?' She tugged at her seat belt in her excitement, 'Girls, it's William.'

Suzanne was momentarily engaged, breathing through a contraction. 'I'll kill him,' she said as the contraction waned. 'Wouldn't you just know he'd get here on time? Doing this to me. Letting me think he didn't care.'

'We're holding up the traffic,' Beth said worriedly as an impatient hoot sounded, 'Shall I reverse and then William can bring the car in? Or shall I set off and stop up the road and he can catch us up. The trouble is it's so narrow and I won't be very popular if I do that. What shall I do, mum?'

'Stop fussing for a start. Reverse, Elizabeth, and let William in,' Laura said impatiently. 'And be quick about it.'

With Beth dithering at the wheel, a certain amount of jiggling and juggling of vehicles followed before they were finally able to set off. Only a mile up the lane Beth stopped suddenly again with a look of panic, speedily reversing and diverting to a sleepy garage. The pump attendant accomplished the filling up of the tank at an infuriatingly sedate pace, quite astonished when Laura thrust a twenty pound note at him and told him to keep the change. 'Sorry about that, everyone,' Beth said with a little laugh, climbing back into the car, 'But it would have been a fine thing, wouldn't it, if we'd run out of petrol. It's Martin's fault. He never ever looks at the petrol gauge when he's driving. He has supreme faith that the car won't let him down.'

Laura laughed, glancing quickly at Suzanne and William in the back. 'If I'd said something like that about his faith, you'd have told me off,' she said amiably. 'It's all right, William, we've got ages yet. First babies are so slow.'

She lowered her voice as Suzanne's shaky rendition of 'Waltzing Matilda' heralded the onset of yet another contraction. 'They're coming too fast and furious for my liking,' she whispered to Beth, 'I don't actually think we have that much time.'

'I can't drive any faster,' Beth said, 'You seem to think I'm some sort of miracle worker when it comes to getting you from A to B. We'll be there soon enough, don't worry.'

'Keep on singing, sweetheart,' William was urging from the back, as Suzanne faltered in her efforts, 'Sing through the contraction, isn't that what you're supposed to do?'

'If you'd been with me at the classes, you'd know,' Suzanne said, uncharacteristically cross, 'It hurts like hell and now I feel sick.'

'We're well equipped,' Beth said, 'Little red bucket under the seat. I can pull off if you like.'

'No . . . oh God . . . another one.'

Couldn't she have chosen some other tune? Laura thought, as the tortured singing began again, Suzanne yelling out that it wasn't working. Tune or no tune, she could feel the pain. Contraction, William corrected, to be practically thumped by his wife. He'd been reading up on childbirth on the way over, he told them, and he reckoned she was at the transition stage so they'd better get a move on.

'I didn't have a tune to sing when I had the boys. Did you,

mum?' Beth asked, ignoring William's panicky tone, determined to keep calm and cheerful.

'No. They hadn't thought of that then,' Laura said thankfully, as the singing began once more. Worse, William had decided to join in.

'At least the dogs have behaved, bless them,' Beth commented still plucking nonsensical statements out of nowhere, as if they were out for a Sunday afternoon drive. She slowed as she came upon a cyclist. 'Oh dear, what a nuisance.'

'Get past, dear . . .' Laura craned her neck to see what was happening in the back. Suzanne had quietened and had a worryingly earnest look on her face, lying half on the seat with William squashed at the edge. Four babies to the good, Laura knew precisely what that look meant.

To her relief, Beth had managed to overtake the cyclist, was approaching the gates to the clinic at last.

Laura reached over to the back seat awkwardly, as her daughter-in-law turned crimson in her exertion. 'Try not to push yet,' she said, knowing it was the most ridiculous thing to ask of a mother at this stage in her labour. 'Until the doctor checks you're fully dilated. Pant instead . . .'

'Mum . . .' William looked at her in something approaching horror as it dawned they were unlikely to make it.

'We're here.' Beth said triumphantly, stopping right outside the entrance before leaping out, saying she would get someone.

Her leaving was the signal for the dogs to bark.

'Shut up, you two,' Laura said, scrambling out at her side to help.

'She can't have it yet,' William said, big and awkward and getting in his mother's way as she tried to push past. 'There's no room in here.' He spoke frantically to his wife, 'Hold on. Hang on a minute.'

Laura shot an exasperated glance at him as there was a final grunt from Suzanne, accompanied by an anxious whine from the dogs. With a slither, baby arrived, just seconds before Beth and a hastily acquired midwife.

Amazed and delighted that it had been so easy, Laura straightened up and beamed. A granddaughter at last. Her first granddaughter.

'I'll move the car in a minute,' Beth, flushed from her mad dash, apologised with a smile to a porter, 'Sorry but we've just had a baby. Would you believe it, she was actually born in the car. In my car.'

We? A collective birth?

Letting out a huge sigh of relief, Laura had to acknowledge that it felt exactly like that.

33

She had to eat. She supposed.

Lotty trailed the supermarket trolley in an anti-social direction round the shelves. School had started again and she was tired after the strain of the first week. The news about her loss had spread and awkward condolences were uttered. More awkward than normal because everyone knew she was separated, weren't sure therefore if they should be *too* sorry. Finney, bless her, had hugged her, with tears in her eyes. She'd once met Max, in the early days, on a rare occasion he'd picked her up from school and he'd said something to Finney that had made her blush and smile. Charm the water off a duck's back, Max. Whatever it was, Finney hadn't forgotten.

'Hello, Mrs Crabtree. The new term's started I see. Must be keeping you busy?' Mr Entwistle loomed suddenly beside her, his trolley full of tins and frozen packets. Rather like hers. He was taller than she had thought. Taller than he had appeared sitting down in his car. Taller than Max. She wished she was wearing heels. She didn't go in for the cute little woman thing and it irritated that she had to look way, way up. 'Jade usually helps with this,' he said, 'But she's at the library doing some work she says.'

'Good. She's coming on very well.' Lotty smiled, wished he would go. She didn't know if he knew about Max, too, everybody else did but she was in no mood for explaining. My ex-husband, actually, but we were on the brink of a reconciliation. People might think she was making that bit up to get extra sympathy or something. As if it mattered now. As if anything mattered.

'I was wondering . . .' he hesitated and they parted momentarily as an overflowing trolley accompanied by a harassed shopper clattered through the gap. 'Jade's birthday's coming up and I was thinking of a surprise party for her. She hasn't had a proper birthday party for years and well . . .'

'I'm sorry,' Lotty said flatly, 'Don't look at me. I know nothing about parties for youngsters. Isn't she a bit old anyway for jellies and pass the parcel?'

'Not that kind of party,' he said, heading round the corner towards the cereals. She had no option but to follow. 'More sophisticated. Teenage stuff, you know. Records and things.'

'I *don't* know.' Lotty was determined not to be helpful. 'It's a helluva long time since I was a teenager.'

'Not that long surely?' The smile was brief, flashed, the eyes suddenly and unexpectedly interested.

'Haven't you anyone else you can get to help?' she said, desperate now to get rid of him. God, if he thought she was in the market for a bit of . . . Hell's teeth, it wasn't as if she'd done anything to encourage him. She was always dressed practically in rags when she met him and this evening was no exception. She'd torn off her working suit directly she got home and grabbed the first thing that came to hand. Oatmeal-coloured dungarees, crushed linen, fussily gathered at the waist, that managed to make even her look like a bloated dumpling. With them, for God knows what reason, she was wearing a high-necked sweater in a shade that could only be described as puke.

'There's nobody I can ask. My sister's moved down to Nottingham.' He dropped a packet of cornflakes in his trolley, sighed, 'Sorry. I am imposing. I didn't mean to.'

This was the time to draw a line under it, under any possibility of anything happening. If she had any sense, she would do it. But . . . she never did have much sense where men were concerned and he had that expression on his face that always got her.

'Have you time for a coffee?' Lotty said, indicating the little café by the entrance as they waited at the check-out. 'I see we need to talk, Mr Entwistle.'

'I'm going to get Jade some earrings for her birthday,' he said.

They were squeezed at a table, together with the trolleys. Lotty had made sure they were in the tiny smoking section, just in case.

'Earrings? That's nice.' Lotty smiled. 'She'll like that. She was delighted to get her ears pierced by the way. Thanks for that.'

'Thanks to you for taking her. She was a bit apprehensive, as if it was a major operation.'

Lotty regarded him calmly. 'It is a bit nerve-racking,' she said, 'Although I should imagine having . . . say, a tattoo . . . must be ten times worse.'

Did she imagine the very faintest of smiles? She couldn't be sure.

'Mind if I smoke?' she asked, fishing for her cigarettes.

'Go ahead.' He held up his hand, shook his head, 'No thanks, I don't smoke.'

Nor had she ever heard him swear. What else did he *not* do? She was under no illusions. As men went, she'd seen worse. For a lorry driver, and she rather regretted the assumption she was making, he was perceptive and intelligent. She wondered about the tattoo but it would be too rude to ask outright. Something he'd done in his youth that he probably now regretted.

'How did you get to be a lorry driver?' she asked, deciding on a direct approach.

'I worked my way up to it.' He grinned and she felt herself flush.

'I'm not for a minute suggesting there's anything wrong with being a lorry driver,' she said hastily, 'Christ . . . I hope to God I'm not a snob. One of my sisters is snob enough for the whole damned family. It's just . . . that you're obviously a bright bloke. So . . . I wondered why you haven't done something else?' She smiled slightly, 'If I'm being a nosy cow, tell me to shut up, won't you?'

'You don't talk to the kids like this, do you?' he asked with a little lift of his eyebrows, 'Look, Mrs Crabtree, I'm happy enough doing what I do,' he said, still smiling to show he was not offended, a little surprised maybe by the language. 'My wife leaving me meant it knocked me back a bit, hit my ambitions on the head. I had to give up some plans I had . . .' he did not elaborate and she thought it unwise to ask. 'What else could I do?

Someone had to look after Jade. Her mother washed her hands of her so there was no choice. My mother used to help out at first but she died when Jade was seven so . . .' he shrugged, 'I was really on my own then. Maybe driving sounds a funny choice but it's not worked out too bad. I enjoy it, it pays well and, when she was little, she used to stay with my sister when I was on a job.'

'Does she keep in contact at all? Your wife?'

He shook his head, 'My ex-wife,' he corrected her, mildly. 'Any news I get is from a third party. Last I heard she was in Australia with the bloke. I think they have another child.' He looked away and Lotty fell silent, allowed him a moment's reflection. 'I can't get over how she just lost interest in Jade. At four years old, she wasn't much more than a baby. How do you explain it to a child without making her hate her mother? I've tried not to be bitter but . . .'

'I have a brother in Australia.' Lotty smiled, steering the conversation away from Jade's bitch of a mother. She finished her cigarette. Smiled again. Hesitated a moment, almost on the verge of telling him about Max. 'I'll do a deal with you, Mr Entwistle,' she said, watching as he tackled a cream cake. He'd offered to buy her one too but she'd refused. She would not be accused of accepting a bribe. Across the table, he was really enjoying his cake and she was suddenly surprised to see she was enjoying watching him. Jade was damned lucky to have this man as her dad. He was wearing a blue denim shirt, crisp, clean. The sleeves were pushed up to reveal strong hairy arms.

'The deal is this,' she went on, 'I'll help you with the party but, in return, you have to help me with my move.'

'You're moving?' He could not hide his dismay and she was oddly flattered that he should care one way or the other.

'Just from one side of town to the other,' she explained, 'It's a bigger, better flat with a nice view of the park. Not that I'm particularly fussy about views,' she added with a shrug. 'However, I was thinking of hiring a van to move my bits and pieces and I need a man.' She smiled, never able to avoid this wicked tendency of hers to flirt. 'What do you say?'

'Okay,' he said at once. 'It's a deal. If you can prepare a list of what we need for the party, I'll get it. Just sausage rolls and things. Definitely not jellies, she's no sweet-tooth. And if you'll let me know the date you plan to move, I'll be there to help. I'll bring a friend along if you like. We'll get it done in no time.'

'Thank you.' Lotty wasn't sure who was getting the better deal. All he had to do was lift things but she'd landed herself with the job of entertainments manager. Sausage rolls and things sounded awfully ominous. She was a dead loss at any sort of catering. Max had always ended up doing both the shopping and the cooking at the few dinner parties they'd hosted.

They parted company at Lotty's car but not before he helped her unload her shopping.

'By the way, I'm James . . .' he said, his sudden embarrassment showing in a faint flush. 'I hope you don't mind but it seems daft being so formal.'

James? Not Jim, or Jimmy?

'And I'm Charlotte.'

She watched as he strolled off, pushing his trolley in a cavalier fashion with just one hand. Was it her imagination or was there a new confidence in his step.

She got into her car, smiled to herself, watched through the mirror until he reached his car.

Buster, you can forget *that*!

34

In the cool of the ancient church of St Mary's, Kate Howard sneezed, a delicate baby sneeze, dispatching a minute spray over the cream lace of the family christening gown. Uneasily, Sonia held her, reminded of another baby and another gown. This time, in view of the autumnal weather without, she was wearing a camel-coloured woollen suit with a dark trim that would absolutely not tolerate baby sick. Obliged as one of the godmothers to hold the infant, she looked anxiously towards Beth who was so much more accomplished at these things.

Beth gave her an encouraging smile. What had happened to Beth? The nursing job seemed to have changed her drastically. She was looking confident and a little slimmer in a grey dress with a white collar that quite suited her for once.

Kate, two months old, seemed surprised at the sneeze, looking up at Sonia with astonishing blue eyes, the eyes of her father and her grandmother . . . the family likeness . . . wise beyond her tender years. She was one of those rare things, a contented baby, who slept and cooed and generally displayed a good humour, destined no doubt to be one of those fearsomely good-natured women in due course. Sonia silently willed the child not to disgrace herself by doing something outrageous, fully aware that babies, even angelic ones like Kate, were dangerously unpredictable.

Interpreting Beth's glance, she snuggled the infant closer to the expensive wool of her jacket, immediately feeling the little body relax against her. To her amazement, it occurred that she had been rocking the child, quite subconsciously. A fluff of palest blonde hair escaped the lace of the little bonnet that matched the elaborate gown, the same hat that William had worn, that they had all worn. It was an elegant baby outfit, one that Sonia thoroughly approved of. She was determined to take her duties as Kate's godmother seriously. Kate Howard would grow up to be an elegant young miss if it killed her.

She would have to be subtle for, as parents, William and Suzanne were singularly lacking in elegance. She had started off as she meant to carry on, buying Kate a selection of French-designed baby garments from an exclusive boutique in Kensington. She had already established a rapport with the owner, so important if you wanted to be classed as a serious shopper, an important client. Kate was not going to look like a common-or-garden baby with those ridiculous popper outfits that most infants spent their entire social life wearing.

She chanted the responses soberly, reflecting that Martin took the part of vicar very well, striking a happy balance between joviality and earnest intent. He had been nice to her, to be honest, about Sebastian's sudden departure but she could manage without his sympathy. She had reached the conclusion that Seb wasn't worth the hassle and worry played havoc with her complexion. Let him have his fling. Let him discover that life would be no bed of roses living in Jessica's much humbler abode with their offspring. She had grown quite used to being without him and she wasn't sure she wanted him back any more.

She hid a sigh as she caught sight of Suzanne, still a bit lumpy from the pregnancy, wearing a loose front-buttoned dress from which she cheerfully dislodged her enormous breasts from time to embarrassing time when it was Kate's wish to be fed. William displayed the same sentimental characteristics as Maggie's husband towards the baby, a more mature William as befitted his new role.

Thankfully, she relinquished the baby to Martin's capable hands so that he could perform the necessary water sprinkling. Again, a faint air of surprise passed over Kate's face but she did not cry. A murmur of pleasure was gently eased from the small congregation as they watched. A lighted candle was handed over and it was all strangely moving, especially when John and Paul came shyly forward to plant kisses on their new cousin's cheek.

Autumn, the first nip of it, was in the air as they gathered outside and leaves were beginning to yellow and crisp, a few lying in the churchyard. Sonia felt a sudden desire to pay homage to daddy's grave but she refrained from suggesting it in case it upset the mood. Her emotions whirled, happy and sad, and she stood alone a moment, hardly listening to the elaborate arrangements that were taking place as to who was travelling with whom back to Fernlands for the christening party. Missing Seb suddenly for hadn't he always been here on these family occasions, Sonia hastily composed herself and hurried to the Saab, finding her mother standing beside it clutching a couple of L plates.

'Can I drive back?' she asked with a smile, 'I'm perfectly capable, Sonia. I only just failed the test last time.'

'Well . . .?' Sonia eyed her doubtfully and then, not wanting to be accused of thwarting her confidence, she handed the keys over. 'You will be careful,' she said, 'This is a bit different from the one you're learning in.'

'My instructor says that once you can drive a car, you can adapt to any car,' Laura said, settling herself in the driving seat and pausing a moment to familiarise herself with the controls. She set off very smoothly, taking up the rear of the convoy of vehicles, including a recently acquired heap of William's, heading for Fernlands.

They settled to a modest speed and Sonia tried to relax.

'I wanted the opportunity of talking to you privately before we arrive,' Laura said, 'So this has worked out well.'

'What about?' Sonia glanced at her suspiciously. 'I don't want to discuss Sebastian if that's what it is. I have nothing to say. I'm over it and he can do what he likes. By the way, I call myself Miss Howard now.'

'So I've noticed. You've taken off your ring too.' Laura sighed, her own wedding ring and sparkling engagement ring still firmly on her finger. 'What am I to do with you two girls? You and poor Lotty?'

'Please don't feel sorry for me,' Sonia said quickly, 'There's no need. I absolutely refuse to see it as the end of the world. As a matter of fact, it's given me the chance to start afresh without worrying about Sebastian's business interests. When I think of the number of times I've propped him up financially . . . The chateau is off, of course, it was always a silly idea if I'm honest but I am thinking of moving abroad.'

'Where to?' Disconcertingly, Laura took her eyes off the road and looked at her, 'Where to this time?'

'I've been talking a lot to William about Australia,' she said, 'I like the sound of it. Not the outback of course, neither Suzanne nor I could stand that and it's not the right environment to bring up a fair-skinned baby like Kate.'

'You're thinking of moving to Australia?' Laura did not hide her surprise, shuddering to a halt at a junction, perilously close to the rear of William's junk heap as it signalled to turn, 'With William and Suzanne?'

'Not with them exactly,' Sonia said, 'I shall buy my own place, of course, but reasonably close by probably so that I'll be on hand if Suzanne needs a friendly chat . . . that sort of thing . . .'

'You and Suzanne? A friendly chat?'

'Don't sound so surprised. I admit we started off badly but we've recovered from that. We like each other. I'm going to help her with her image. She's big, yes, but she must learn to make the best of that. I shall set up business over there and my interiors will go a bomb . . . you know what Australians are like, mummy? . . . totally lacking in any sort of style. Primitive. Years behind. They need advice, some flair. And the colours out there are fantastic, William says. A different hemisphere, you see, calling for a completely new outlook. What a challenge for me!' she finished enthusiastically, not bothering to say that it was also thousands of miles away from Seb and dear Jessica and the baby they would be producing. She didn't say that. Maybe it was an escape route but it was still a challenge and, more importantly, she would be on hand to guide Kate. Kate might unfortunately grow up with that Australian accent but she would at least be stylish.

'You have taken me by surprise,' Laura said, driving quite neatly, handling the big car competently, 'If you're sure you're doing the right thing, then I'm pleased for you. What about me though?' she asked and Sonia glanced at her quickly, sensing the irony in the voice, 'What will happen to me when I'm old and doddery? I thought you were going to look after me.'

'I thought you had that all mapped out,' Sonia replied, 'Aren't you going to marry Don?'

'Possibly . . .'

'Only possibly?'

'Things have been a tiny bit strained lately.' Laura glanced at her, managed a smile, 'I decided I would accept his proposal if he were to ask me again, but so far it has not been forthcoming. So we must wait.'

'Ask him yourself,' Sonia said, 'There's no need to be coy about such things nowadays.'

'There is every reason for me, dear. However, the longer he leaves it, the more doubts I have.'

'Really? . . .' Sonia glanced at her mother with interest, 'They call it cold feet, mummy. I had cold feet before I married Sebastian. With hindsight, of course, I ought to have taken notice of the doubts. Did you have cold feet when you married daddy?'

'No. And I don't wish to talk about it further. I must concentrate on my driving now.'

Sonia let her do just that, letting her mind drift. The colours at this time of year were glorious, copper and bronze and gold. The sky a smudged palette of darker blues and greys. The lake as she caught glimpses of it was taking on its wintery hue as summer drifted away. Sonia liked autumn but this year the falling leaves seemed to have a deeper meaning, indicating a new season in her life. A life without Seb. She would never forgive him this time. How had Lotty managed to forgive Max? Lotty was certainly acting the part of bereaved widow rather than a woman whose husband had walked out on her. Lotty needed a new direction in her life too.

'I was thinking in church about some of the other times we've been there,' she said softly, forgetting that her mother was supposed to be concentrating. 'Strange, isn't it, that Martin took over as vicar there? I was thinking about . . .' she heard her voice catch and coughed to cover it up, 'about getting married there. Daddy was so proud. And Lotty and Max. And Beth having the children christened and daddy's funeral.'

'Yes. So was I.'

There was a moment's pained pause before Sonia cheered up

with an effort. 'Wasn't Kate beautifully behaved?' she said with satisfaction, 'I've never met such a perfect baby. She seems to successfully accomplish all the messier baby habits in private.'

'She is sweet.' Laura's voice was full of grandmotherly pride. 'Of course William was always a good baby, quite unlike you three.' She laughed as Sonia protested, 'It's true. You were horrors in your different ways.'

Sonia was relieved to see Fernlands approaching.

'Well done, mummy,' she said now they were on relatively safe ground. 'You should pass your test next time with no trouble.'

'Did I mention that I've decided to go away for Christmas? If not with Don, then alone,' Laura pulled the car to a halt beside Beth's. They waited a moment until Beth and her family had climbed noisily out before doing the same. 'It'll make a change for me. What will you be doing at Christmas, darling?'

'I'm not sure yet,' Sonia said brightly, the awful thought occurring that she had no one to go to. They'd always come up here for Christmas, grumbling at the necessity to do so, but perversely enjoying themselves once they were here. It was very inconsiderate of mummy to go traipsing off elsewhere.

She watched, irritated as Laura ushered the others in. What was she supposed to do at Christmas then? Off to one side, Lotty stood by herself, looking a little underweight again, rocked by Max's death. She was wearing jeans and a bright polo-necked sweater, incredibly casual for so important an occasion. Suddenly Sonia's heart went out to her sister. She needed help. She needed someone to advise her on the finer points, someone to break the news gently that you simply did not wear jeans to a christening. She went over, smiling.

'You okay?' she asked.

She nodded, 'I was just thinking . . . that church. It brings back all the memories.' Her sigh was deep. 'Max and I were married there,' she said.

'I was there. Matron-of-honour. Remember?' Sonia touched her arm briefly, 'You looked lovely,' she said, 'A dream of a dress.' A lump in her throat, she wanted to hug Lotty but something held her back. 'I understand a bit more now,' she went on, 'Now that

Sebastian's left me. I understand what you went through and I'm sorry I never sympathised.'

'Men are pigs,' Lotty said dismissively, 'All of them. Give or take. Come on, let's go and start on the buffet. Beth's looking well, isn't she? Nursing suits her.'

'At least she can rely on Martin.' Sonia slipped off her jacket to reveal a finely pleated cream silk top. 'What are you doing at Christmas?' she asked, very casually, 'I thought it might be nice if you and I spend some time together. William and Suzanne are going to her aunt's in Sheffield and mummy's going off somewhere so . . . what do you think? It will be my treat. Anywhere you like.'

Lotty flushed. 'That sounds marvellous but the thing is that Beth's asked me over. She can't have realised that you'll be on your own too. Why don't you mention it? The more the merrier at Christmas for Beth.'

'I'm not on my own,' Sonia said hastily, 'Did I give that impression? God no, I have plans but they could have easily fitted you in, Lotty, if you were stuck.' She beamed, not sure if it had worked or not. Christmas at Beth's would be pretty horrific. They would be expected to be in and out of church the whole time. Whilst she and Seb liked to enter into the spirit of Christmas with one outing to church on Christmas morning, there was a limit. You could have too much of a good thing. Christmas was about listening to a CD of Christmas carols, giving presents, holly and mistletoe, decorating the tree . . . that sort of thing. Seb always bought her a bottle of her favourite Estée Lauder perfume as well as her Christmas surprise.

Seb always . . . close to tears and hating her vulnerability, she excused herself as Lotty went to face the buffet. She wandered into the calm of the darkened drawing room where Kate was asleep in her cot. She stood a moment, unobserved, feeling her face, her whole body, soften as she looked down at the sleeping babe. She was breathing very gently, eyelids closed, a fist of a hand with tiny pink fingernails just brushing her face. Thank God, she did not seem to need one of those awful dummy things. What on earth was going through her mind? What could she possibly be thinking? She knew nothing about anything. All she knew was that she was warm, well fed and loved.

Wanting urgently to pick the baby up and hold her close, Sonia gave a deep shuddering sigh.

When you got down to it, what more was there to life?

35

Corny as it might sound, losing Max had given Lotty an entirely new perspective on life. She felt like a rag doll who'd had the stuffing shaken out of her and hastily stuffed back.

Kate's christening had done her good in that it had stopped her feeling sorry for herself as she had transferred those feelings to her sister. Poor old Sonia! She was doing her best to pretend she was coping with Seb leaving her. Funny business that! Of course he was an attractive bastard but even so he and Sonia had seemed okay together. She hated to think of Sonia being alone at Christmas and it had been a terrible embarrassment to fob her off. She would be discreet but she was going to ask Beth to issue an invitation. They would have to stick together as mother had decided to abandon them. Going off somewhere, she kept saying vaguely. Going off where?

They had always spent Christmas at Fernlands. It was family tradition for Christ's sake. Turkey, presents, silly games, stuffed to sickness with chocolates, sozzled with booze. Wonderful. Even the obligatory carol service had been tolerable and Lotty remembered she and Max singing the carols with gusto. This year Fernlands would be empty, shuttered, and it seemed like a turning-point.

After the christening, she had stayed overnight with Beth and was taking a morning stroll, trailing in their wake as usual, deep in her own thoughts. She was off men. James bloody Entwistle was circling her, chomping at the bit, but she wasn't having any of that. Jade had noticed, coloured up a bit when she mentioned him, but Lotty thought she had handled it well. Calmly. Cold-shoulderedly. If he didn't let up, she'd have to resort to telling him to sod off.

She admired Martin though. Beth was lucky there. Martin was one hundred per cent out of bounds but Beth had somehow got wind of it and it had worked wonders. She was looking good, pretty, hence the we're-still-in-love look, obvious even from a distance.

Closer to Lotty, Paul was messing about in the stream, attempting to create a dam with some sticks. He was intent on his task as the dogs waited patiently, wanting him to throw the sticks. John had also been involved but, looking up and seeing Lotty alone, he came across, suddenly and unexpectedly putting his hand in hers, taking exaggerated steps to keep up with her easy strides.

'Aunt Lotty . . .?'

'That's me.' She gripped his hand, smiled down at him, 'How are you, John Bennett? You and I haven't talked in a long time.'

'Are you sorry about Uncle Max?' he asked in that fiercely direct way of children, 'Are you sorry he was killed?'

She nodded, shocked by the question. Adults didn't do this. Adults dodged the issue.

'Yes I'm sad.' She felt the warmth of the small hand, taken back to when he was very tiny and she had held him at his christening, his baby fingers curling round her finger, perhaps even then trying to forge a link, a link that had never properly been there. Not until lately.

'When I say my prayers, he goes at the end with all the other people who are in heaven,' he said, quite matter-of-factly.

'Does he? That is nice.'

'Why do you think God made the car crash?'

Oh lord! Beth would go daft if she knew this conversation was taking place. John would be told to be quiet and stop upsetting Aunt Lotty at once.

'I have no idea,' she said calmly, 'Have you?'

He shook his head, kicking at a loose piece of tree stump. 'Granny Howard might be going on a ship,' he said instead, 'At Christmas.'

'She told you that?' Lotty marvelled that John had managed to wheedle that much out of her. 'Who is she going with?'

'Might be with Mr Fletcher,' he said, 'He goes to China, places like that.' He looked up at her, grinned. 'If she marries him, will he be my new Grandad Howard?'

'No he won't.' She felt a tightness in her chest at the very idea. 'How can he be?'

She talked to Beth later about it. Beth dismissed it as childish chat. Nothing to worry about.

'It's lovely to see William back again,' she said, changing the subject, 'For once this weekend it was like old times. Kate's a lovely baby, isn't she? Makes me quite broody.' There was a small pause, 'Oh sorry, I . . .'

'It's okay,' Lotty said impatiently, 'You don't have to wrap me in cotton wool. I'm over it. I'm even getting over Max. More or less . . .'

They were passing the church.

'You go on to the house,' Lotty said, trying to keep her voice casual. 'I'll catch you up. I just want to pop in whilst it's quiet. Just to sit a minute that's all.'

'Of course.' Beth smiled, fiddled with her hair, stared a moment, 'I'll leave you to it. See you back at the house and do take your time.'

36

Beth kept in touch with Lotty when she got back, was pleased when she moved out of Balaclava Street into something nicer, said they would come to visit as soon as possible. William and Suzanne seemed to be having an extended stay in Sheffield, prior to spending some time with Sonia, but were also in touch, tentative plans being made for their return to Australia. Sonia had sold her house, settled up supposedly amicably with Sebastian and was never off the phone, checking up on the latest situation with mummy and *that* man as she persisted in calling him.

As for mother, she was preoccupied, still seeing Don according to whispers from Elsie, but no word yet of marriage or moving house. Elsie rather felt, though she was at pains to say it was no business of hers, that the whole thing was fizzling out. Mrs Howard would never leave Fernlands, she told Beth sagely, and that was the sticking point.

On a particular morning in early November, Beth woke and lay quietly a moment, instantly remembering what day it was. She told Martin and he agreed it would be nice if she popped over to Fernlands to see mum. 'I may stay for lunch,' she said, over breakfast, 'She's on her own just now.'

'Give her my love, kitten.' Martin came round to her and put his hands on her shoulders, gently kneading them. 'It's nice to be on our own again, isn't it?' he said, 'Of course it was pleasant having Lotty to stay but . . .'

'I know.' She tipped her head back, looked at him, 'Lotty's getting very dependent on you, darling. Sure you can handle it?'

'Don't worry about her. She's working it out in her own way.'

He kissed the top of her head. 'I love you,' he said, raising her to her feet and patting her comfortably on the bottom, 'You'd better get yourself over to Fernlands and give Laura my love too.'

Laura was alone, baking in the kitchen, a batch of cakes for some charity function. Beth settled herself on a chair and waited, making no mention of the date. She certainly wasn't going to mention it if mum didn't.

'You're not on duty today then?' Laura looked at her and smiled. 'Are you still enjoying your job?'

'Really enjoying it, mum,' Beth said happily, 'I don't like to say it because it sounds trite but I do feel I'm doing something worthwhile. And it isn't a problem, not really, fitting in all the other things I have to do.'

'Good. You look well. I'm glad you came over,' Laura said, spooning out the gooey mixture into the tins. 'I knew you would have remembered.'

Beth recognised the tone. She smiled sympathetically and waited.

'Want to lick it out?' She held the mixing bowl towards Beth, 'You always did when you were little.'

Beth shuddered. 'I'm not little now,' she said. 'And I have to fit into my purple dress for Christmas. I've still got a way to go.' She helped clear away the baking dishes, feeling awkward at having reminded her, if she needed reminding that was. 'I thought you might be a bit down today.' She glanced at the clock and looked squarely at her mother.

'It was sweet of you, darling. You're very thoughtful.' Laura hugged her and Beth felt the slightest tremble. 'It's eleven thirty,' she went on, 'Almost the exact moment. Funny, isn't it, how anniversaries of birthdays and deaths take on such a strange meaning. I'd rather forget it because it's just another day but I've found myself thinking about it all morning . . . that's why I did the baking . . . to take my mind off it.' She wasn't too far away from crying, 'I know I've been seeing Don and that must be hard for you all to understand but you mustn't ever think I'd forget your dad.' A tear slid down her cheek and she pushed at it impatiently, 'Don't you dare start,' she warned as Beth's lip wavered.

'Have you and Don decided anything?' Beth asked when she,

when they both, had recovered. If it was vaguely obscene to be discussing another man on this day, they neither of them seemed to mind.

Laura looked out of the kitchen window which had a view of the side beds. Seasons just ploughed on whatever, she reflected soberly, winter beckoning and she had a decision to make.

'Decided anything?' she murmured vaguely, 'Not yet. I've been thinking, Beth ... we ought to have a little celebratory weekend before William and Suzanne go back to Australia. I must arrange something.'

'I shall miss them,' Beth said. 'Is Sonia really going to go with them?'

Laura nodded. 'So she says. What do you think of that, Beth? What is she doing it for? You know Sonia, she never does anything without an ulterior motive.'

'I suppose it's to get away from Sebastian,' Beth said thoughtfully, 'And to be with Kate. Have you seen the way she looks at Kate? I should think those are the two reasons. All that talk about shaking the Australians out of their lethargy and hitting them with her designs is just nonsense.'

Laura smiled. 'Beth, darling ... has anyone ever told you that you are very astute.' Her eyes were still a touch watery but she was quite composed, 'I always knew there was more to you than meets the eye. Your father thought so too.'

Beth beamed. That had to be one of the nicest things her mother had ever said to her.

Lotty woke to silence. She listened for a moment, hardly believing it. Where were the birds? Alone in the bed, she stretched luxuriously, reached for the radio button and switched on some gentle waking-up music. She was wearing striped pyjamas and socks because, when she slept alone, she suffered from cold feet.

The new flat was on an avenue that edged the park, a big studio flat in a big comfortable house. The apartment smelled of fresh paint. It was bright and clean and there were no curtains at the window, just blinds, so Lotty had a clear view of the parkland opposite, most of its trees November naked, silhouetted against the grey sky.

James had helped her decorate, ably assisted by Jade. They'd spent quite a few enjoyable weekends painting and the like, James driving off to get them fish and chips at lunchtime which they ate out of the paper. It was perhaps getting a little too cosy and she would of course have to watch that. They were starting to act like a family and that would never do. If you weren't careful, things drifted and before you knew where you were, that was it.

Her few pieces of furniture had looked odd, small and insignificant, and she had started to replace them with heftier items. Rachel had been a big help with choosing the soft furnishings, new bed linen and pretty cushions. It amused Lotty that some of Beth's influence was creeping into her choice. Why not?

Wide awake, she jumped out of bed and went over to the window, leaning on the sill amongst the jungle of potted plants Mr Dassayaje had given her as a parting gift. She was feeling happier than she had done for some time and, as long as she held on to the belief that Max's death had been for a purpose, had had some divine point, then she was reasonably okay about it. Martin was right. Her faith was a pivot. A secret too. She still did not attend church, happy to leave that to those who possessed best suits and could sing. But she believed. She said her prayers if you could call them that, each day, at odd times, and never on her knees. She preferred to think of it as a quiet reflective chat with Max maybe listening in. She was not only happy, she was content. It was amazing how little she thought about sex these days, channelling her energy into other things.

Luckily, James Entwistle had finally got the message. He seemed happy enough to be celibate too. She had baulked at telling him to sod off because he was so nice but she had made it perfectly clear where she stood and he had smiled, accepted it, agreed he wanted to be just friends. He was very wary of another serious relationship, he explained earnestly, and he was sorry if he had given her the wrong impression.

She was also making an effort not to swear so much or smoke because James did neither. Losing on one count, she thought irritably, as she lit her first cigarette of the day. She really needed this first cigarette!

She had talked to Sonia, Beth and William on the phone last night about the coming weekend visit to Fernlands. Grudging resignation was how they were going to play it. Mother would have their blessing . . . well, sort of. A little oddly, for none of them were shrinking violets with the possible exception of Beth, they had agreed that it would be best if William was spokesman. He would adequately say what needed to be said. When he took it upon himself, William could be rather dignified. One of dad's attributes that had somehow slipped through.

None of them would dare to say what they really felt. They none of them liked Don Fletcher simply because he wasn't George Howard but how could they say that?

How could they be so incredibly selfish?

How could they?

'Mum . . . what are you doing here?' Lotty looked at her mother in amazement, still recovering from the surprise of hearing her mother's voice on the flat intercom. 'How have you got here?'

'I drove, dear.' She smiled. 'You must come and see the car afterwards. It's brand new. I'm parked very nicely on the avenue. I've done a beautiful parallel park. Oh . . . didn't I tell you? I passed my test on Monday.'

'And you've driven all this way? In fog? Was it foggy? Honestly . . .' Lotty clicked her tongue, stood aside so that her mother could enter the flat. 'It's nice to see you, of course, but I'm surprised that's all.'

'You are alone?' She hesitated, casting a nervous glance around as if a half-naked man would suddenly appear.

'Yes.' She tugged at her dressing gown. 'I'm alone, mother. I'm always alone now. Look . . . come on through and sit down. I'll fling a few clothes on and we'll have a cup of tea and a natter. I was going to do absolutely bug . . . nothing at all . . . this weekend.'

Proudly, childishly, she showed her mother the living area. Compared to Balaclava Street, it was like a palace. 'Look at the view,' she said excitedly, 'Not like yours but not bad eh? You can see right across the park.'

'It's very nice.' Laura took off her jacket, wandered over to the window to examine the view. Murmured approval. Told her the plants needed watering.

Lotty was quick. Dressed in dark leggings and a red top, her hair pulled up on top of her head and fastened with a narrow red velvet ribbon, she returned with a tea tray, cups *and* a milk jug, finding her mother relaxed on a sofa, shoes kicked off.

'I hope you were careful driving,' she said, wishing she hadn't bothered as she saw the quiet resignation on her mother's face. Sorry, she wanted to say, but Max's accident has made me nervous. If I told him once about driving too near the car in front and too fast, I told him a thousand times . . . the accident had caused her to drive like a sainted aunt these days.

'This is wonderful,' Laura said, as they sat drinking their tea. 'I feel such a sense of freedom for the first time in years. Not that I was ever imprisoned of course but I always had to rely on someone else. Beth, or Elsie's husband or a taxi, to take me places. Now . . . well, I can just hop in my car and go anywhere I like.'

'What does Don think about it?' Lotty smiled, feeling the familiar tightness as she mentioned his name. 'I suppose he's thrilled.'

'He doesn't know yet. He's away for a few days.'

'Again? He's never at home,' Lotty muttered, watching her mother carefully. 'Has he got itchy feet or what?'

'Business, dear. He has a nephew who's going to take over but there are a lot of loose ends to tie up and, between you and me, I'm not sure he's ready yet to pass it on. But yes . . . you're right, he is away such a lot. And even when he retires, he's talking of travelling. He'll move from Grange of course sooner or later. He's not the sort of man who will ever be able to put down roots, is he? Not like your father.'

They fell silent. Lotty wondered if her mother was trying to tell her something, couldn't for the life of her think what, so decided not to pursue it.

'I've got a friend, mum,' she said at last. 'A man friend. No . . . just a friend. That's all he is. He's the dad of one of my favourite pupils. A lorry driver. He helped me do up this place.' She looked round happily, still not quite able to believe how at home she felt here.

'I'm pleased for you, darling,' Laura said. 'Let me know how it goes . . .'

'It's not going anywhere, not in the way you mean.' Lotty smiled. 'I'm finished with all that.'

'Funny . . . that's what I thought.' Laura put down her cup, folded her hands, twisted the rings on her fingers. 'I only made up my mind to come and see you this morning. Spur of the moment thing. That's why I didn't even telephone. I just wanted to surprise you.'

'I'm glad you did. I hate all these organised weekends. Is it wise to have a get-together for William? We'll only end up rowing. I'm violently opposed to Sonia going with them. Sticking her nose in, telling poor Suzanne what to do with the baby. I'm surprised Suzanne hasn't told her. What the hell is Sonia playing at, mother?'

'I've had this conversation before with Beth. Leave Sonia to sort herself out . . . I think that's what we decided.' The movement of the fingers was brisker, troubled. 'Lotty, can I tell you something?'

Lotty nodded. 'Of course. You can tell me anything, mum.'

'Like you tell me everything?' she said drily, giving a sigh before proceeding. 'The thing is that for a long time I've had this recurring dream . . .'

'I have dreams, too, mum. If I've had a heavy supper, they're really vivid.' She grinned, tried not to recall her dream and the retelling of it to Martin.

'In the dream, I'm trying to get in touch with your father. Trying to get him on the phone and he's never in. I keep having to leave messages. Rather like Sonia. She's never in when you phone.' She smiled a little, 'But in the dream . . . George is never in either.'

'Oh . . . well, that's obvious, isn't it? Frustration.'

'Last night, Max answered.' She looked at Lotty, 'Asked how I was, said he'd put me through. He sounded very bright, quite like his old self. I was tremendously pleased to hear him. I sort of knew he was dead . . . you know how you can be aware in dreams that you are dreaming? It felt a bit like that.'

Lotty joined her in an uneasy laugh, 'Did he ask after me?' she asked jokily.

'Yes he did. I told him you were fine.' She bit her lip, looked across at Lotty, any hint of humour gone suddenly, 'And then I spoke to George. He sounded younger somehow, as he used to sound when we first met. A young man.' Her sigh was slight, a faint flush on her cheeks, her blue eyes looking beyond Lotty towards the past, 'It was all very matter-of-fact,' she went on in wonder, 'I told him about Don and he said I must do what I wanted.'

'You were just needing reassurance, mum,' Lotty said softly. 'A dream is just a way of solving things that are troubling you. Don't you see that?'

'But it didn't seem like a dream exactly. Oh . . . I can't explain.'

'I think I know what you mean. Have a biscuit.' Lotty shoved the plate at her. 'When you spoke to Max . . . in your dream,' she added hastily, 'You didn't tell him about my miscarriage, did you?'

Laura took a biscuit, looked at her oddly.

'No,' she said. 'It *was* just a dream, love.'

'I know.'

'Will you be able to get over for the weekend? I'm so looking forward to having you all together again. William as well this time and baby.'

'But not Seb,' Lotty pointed out sadly, 'We keep losing one of the men off the list. It only remains for Martin to leave Beth . . . which of course will never happen.'

'It's going to be quite informal,' Laura said, 'And Don might be around if he's home. If he is, then I would like you all to make more of an effort this time to make him feel at home. I want to make it a memorable weekend so that William and Suzanne and Sonia of course will remember this last visit to the house.'

'They will be able to get back from Australia,' Lotty said with a laugh, 'You talk as if they're going to another planet.' She hesitated a minute, 'Or are you talking about Fernlands? Mother, you're not seriously thinking of selling it?'

'I am seriously thinking about it.' Laura smiled a little, 'And about Don and me, our future. I know you don't approve, none of you, and that hurts me, darling. It's as if all your doubts have filtered through to me. As I said to Beth, I've been thinking a lot lately. I never had these doubts with your father. But now . . . maybe it's because I'm older or because none of you are happy about my remarrying.'

'You would put us before him?' Lotty asked as it dawned what they were asking of her. 'You would really do that, mother?'

'Yes.' Laura smiled. 'If you'd had children, darling . . . perhaps you still will, of course. Then you would understand. It's children first. Husband second. If George had ever asked, I would have lied, told him the other way round so as not to upset him but now, I'm being honest with you. The maternal bond is fearsome. Perhaps that's not the same for everyone but that's how I've always felt ever since Sonia was born.'

'Baloney!' Lotty said fiercely. 'Where do you fit in that equation? You? Yourself? For God's sake, mother, do what *you* want. Whether we like it or not is sod all to do with it.'

'But that's dreadfully selfish, dear.'

'So what? Be selfish. We're grown up. We don't need you any more.' She regretted saying it, not really meaning it, but knowing it was for her mother's own good. If she wouldn't push them out of the nest then, by God, they'd have to push her out.

'So you won't be asking me for any more loans then?'

They looked at each other a moment and then laughed.

38

It was, literally, a flying visit. Home.

Don was off again, the next day, another plane, another destination, but he found time to drive over to Laura's. They talked excitedly, very pleased to be with each other again, and he was, as Lotty predicted, delighted that she had passed her test, now had a car. He dutifully inspected it, admired it, then, arms folded round each other, they went back indoors.

'It's beginning to wear me out,' she told him, 'All this travelling about that you do. You need to relax more, Don, or you'll wear yourself to a shred.'

'Get your bag packed and come with me this time,' he said, 'I've had enough of this. I've let you off too long. I've bought a ticket for you.'

'But I've got the family coming for the weekend, arriving tomorrow,' she said, taking him through to the drawing room where a fire blazed in the hearth. A cool mist hovered over the lake and the hills were blurred. A heavy overnight frost still lingered on the grass. A little winter colour was provided by some flowering shrubs and heathers.

'Cancel them,' he said abruptly. 'I've got this double room booked in the airport hotel for tonight. I've left Nigel to deal with the business, it's about time I let him handle things. You and I are going off somewhere else to enjoy ourselves. Just the two of us.'

'A holiday? It sounds lovely.' She poured the tea from the silver pot. Passed him the sugar and milk. Wondered how she was going to tell him.

'God, I've missed you, Laura,' he said, 'For the first time ever, I didn't really enjoy this last trip. My mind wasn't on the business in hand. The more I'm away, the more I miss you.'

She smiled at that, her thoughts still on the coming weekend. 'William's off to Australia soon,' she said quietly, 'And I really would like to see my granddaughter one last time before she goes away . . . this weekend's the only time we can all of us get together. A little farewell party. It's a pity you won't be around. I'm sure they would love to see you.'

He smiled ruefully. Sipped his tea. Looked at her and didn't say a word.

She glanced at him before turning to look through the windows at the lake, sombre in its winter hues. If she went with Don, things would never be the same again. It would be like closing a chapter of her life. She didn't think she could do it. She was suddenly quite terrified of doing it.

'It's all arranged,' she said helplessly, 'They're all coming up. The beds are made up. I've got the menu planned. And I've promised Martin we'll go to church on Sunday. God knows why I do these things but Martin always makes me feel extremely guilty . . .' She looked at him. 'What will they do if I'm not here?'

'They'll manage without you. Laura, we've been through all this.' He laughed but she could not, a chill seeping through her as she realised she was going to lose him. She knew with an absolute certainty that this was her last chance. He would not wait forever.

'Ring them all now. Cancel the weekend. Explain that we're going to the Bahamas, that we're getting married.'

'Bahamas? Getting married?' She laughed. 'Don, I can't possibly go to the Bahamas, just like that. You have to give me time to think about that.'

'No. You've had time. You've had all the time you need. You're coming with me.' His smile was gentle, as he very deliberately put down his cup, came over to her, lifted her to her feet, drew her to him. 'You are going to marry me, aren't you, my precious? You're not going to break my heart?'

39

'My mum might be coming back to England,' Jade said, dropping the bombshell as she gathered up her books after their hour-long session. 'Look . . . she sent me a note.' She fumbled in her bag, extracted a crumpled bit of paper. 'All my love, mum . . . it says.'

Lotty did not look at it, couldn't believe it. The mother who had dumped her when she was little? The same woman now daring to say 'all my love'?

'Coming back?' she said, alarmed at how the news had affected her. Bopped her one. 'Coming back just like that?'

Jade nodded. 'Dad's had a letter too,' she said with a slightly worried smile, 'I don't know what his said. He pretends he's not bothered but I know him. She's beautiful, my mum.' She fished again in the bag, came out empty-handed, 'Thought I had a photo somewhere. Not a recent one though.'

'You can show it to me another time,' Lotty said inanely. 'In that case . . .' she found she was momentarily lost, unsure, 'We had this party arranged for next Wednesday at your house . . . when is she coming back?'

'I only said she might be coming. That's still on,' Jade said, picking up books, stuffing them in the bag, wearing her hair off her face to show off her birthday earrings. 'He says sorry but can you get the food as he's not going to have time. He has to take an urgent load down to Southampton on Sunday. He'll be back Tuesday afternoon. I'm going to stay at my friend's.'

'Right. Tell him that's okay. I'll get the food.' What was it about this man that he seemed to think she was some kind of catering consultant? What kind of food? For how many people?

He was setting up his own business, a bit risky she felt, but what did she know about it? At any rate, he was excited and optimistic and reckoned it merited a celebration. The people coming were mainly prospective customers and she knew sod all about his business, would be no help at all, but here she was being dragged along, roped into doing the whole damned thing herself. Who did he think she was? Didn't he know she was hopeless at the domestic lark?

She waited until Jade had gone before she allowed her feelings to show.

Blast and bugger it.

Who did this woman think she was, swanning off, leaving a little girl for her dad to bring up and then just coming back when it suited her?

She had a nerve.

Not that it really bothered her because she and James were just friends.

40

Sonia had been entertaining William, Suzanne and Kate for a few days and they all intended to travel up to Fernlands together for the weekend.

The plans for Australia were under way.

Sonia had organised a little PR event on their arrival in Sydney. A photographer friend was going to be there and she had prepared a little item for him so that he could get her some publicity. She rather thought a photo of her dangling Kate on her knee might go down well. A caring image. Doting aunt. That sort of thing. And darling Kate could always be relied upon to behave beautifully and look adorable.

Or rather she used to be.

The last few days had proved a little wearing and had finally, regrettably, brought to a head the doubts that had been swirling round in her mind for some time. Kate was teething and, red-faced and frequently yelling, she was proving just a teeny bit tiresome. It seemed to be affecting her . . . well, her bowels . . . and Sonia had found it necessary to leave the room if Suzanne was changing her nappy. She was dribbly too and some of the gorgeous little dresses were having to be dry cleaned too often. Suzanne, showing a blatant disregard for the fine material, had actually washed some herself. Put them in *water*!

'It'll be strange going up to Fernlands again,' William said, as they relaxed over dinner. Kate was asleep, worn out poor darling with the sobbing, and Suzanne, up and down all night apparently, was looking a touch weary. 'Perhaps for the last time . . . who knows? Has anybody any idea what mum's going to do? Is she going to marry this bloke?'

'Of course she isn't,' Sonia said briskly. 'She's passed her driving test.'

'What's that got to do with it?' Suzanne asked and Sonia looked at her sharply. Really! Suzanne could be quite brusque occasionally. With William around, she seemed different. She supposed they complemented each other. Suzanne became less malleable and William less awkward. 'What's passing her driving test to do with getting married?'

'Because it gives her freedom,' Sonia pointed out, pouring coffee, 'She doesn't need him to ferry her about now, does she? If she'd been really serious, she would have done it by now. Can't you see she's dithering because she isn't sure? She told me she had cold feet.'

William laughed. 'Sonia . . . I thought we had agreed our strategy this weekend with Beth and Lotty. If Don's around then we are going to offer them our best wishes aren't we? I've got the speech prepared.'

'Yes,' she said doubtfully. 'Of course. We have no alternative but to wish her well if that's what she wants although nothing will change my view that she's making a mistake.'

'You've never met him,' Suzanne said, eyes bright with annoyance, 'I have. And I like him. He adores your mother.'

'More coffee?' Sonia heard Kate yell out a fraction after Suzanne was already on her feet, muttering 'excuse me'.

She waited until she and William were alone. Smiled at him.

'William, I have something to say to you,' she said.

'That sounds ominous. Something you don't want Suzanne to hear?' he asked in that mild way of his. Not really minding.

'No, it's not that. Or at least . . . perhaps it might be best if you tell her yourself. I don't want to see her upset. I have no wish to be accused, yet again, of upsetting her.'

'What's up?'

Sonia took a deep breath, suddenly remembering Sebastian's awkward confession of a few months ago. Moments like this were hard. Agonisingly difficult decisions. Once you'd said it, it was too late.

'I can't come with you,' she said, 'To Australia. I'm so very sorry to mess up the arrangements at the last moment and the decision has been heartbreaking for me. But . . . I have to stay here in England.' She was aware of his silence and rattled on, 'I was never happy about the arrangements I'd made for the business here and I have one or two plans that I shall have to instigate myself and also . . . well, this place is sold as you know and I've seen a new property. Absolutely fantastic country house in the Cotswolds. The most beautiful mellow stone and it's in a couple of acres. I'm teaming up with a landscape gardener.'

'I see.' If he was upset, he didn't allow it to show too much.

'I'm so sorry. I know you and Suzanne were looking forward to me coming with you, helping look after darling Kate . . . that sort of thing. Of course I shall still visit as often as I can. What's a few hours on a plane? I want to see my god-daughter grow up. I want to make sure she remembers me.'

'I'll make quite sure she doesn't forget you.' His smile was slight, 'It's not every little girl who has such a stylish aunt.'

Sonia beamed.

'I'll leave you a minute to tell Suzanne,' she whispered as she heard the footsteps outside and Suzanne appeared with Kate. A hot and bothered little baby, emitting a snotty sneeze just as Sonia was about to offer her a soothing word.

She was saved by the bell. The telephone.

'I won't be a moment,' she said, directing a knowing smile at her brother. 'I'll just get that.'

Suzanne cuddled the baby to her, wiping the little nose, murmuring soft words of comfort. 'What was all that about?' she asked William with a smile, 'She's got a very secretive look about her, that sister of yours.'

William tickled the baby's toes, was rewarded by a grumbly sort of chuckle. 'Now darling . . .' he said to Suzanne, 'You've got to promise that you're not going to break down in tears? I'm afraid I've got some bad news for you.'

They were trying not to laugh, trying to appear suitably saddened by the announcement that Sonia was not going to grace them permanently with her presence in Australia, when she reappeared.

'You'll never guess,' she shrieked. 'That was mummy. You'll never guess what she's going to do?'

* * *

The weekend was cancelled.

In a daze, befuddled after phone calls from Sonia, Beth *and* William, Lotty unpacked her bag, the one she had hastily packed twenty minutes ago. Could you credit it? When she had told her mother to be selfish for once, she had never seriously thought she would take her up on it. Mother had always put them first. Always. Forever and ever.

She rang James, told him.

'So . . . with my weekend cancelled, I'm at a loose end,' she said. 'Does Jade want to come round for a chat? I've got a couple of books I'd like her to look at with me.'

'She's out. At a friend's for the entire weekend. But I'm not doing anything,' he said, 'Until Sunday evening that is when I have to take a consignment to Southampton. By the way, you still okay for the party next week? Did Jade give you the message about the food?'

'Yes she did.' She smiled sweetly into the phone, tempted to tell him where he could stuff the food. 'I'm not a party person, James,' she said, 'I hate the forced laughter, all the bitty food, trying to be friendly to people you don't have a thing in common with.'

'You should have said,' he said huffily. 'How do I know what you like if you don't say?'

'Can you believe my mother?' she said, thoughts of parties vanishing, as it hit her yet again. 'I can't stop thinking about it. The Bahamas? She'll hate the heat. She's got very fair skin and it will do her no good at all. I went there for my honeymoon actually. With my husband,' she added stupidly.

'I went to Eastbourne for mine,' he said, 'With my wife.'

They laughed.

'Where do you fancy going then?' he said after a moment and, just for a moment, a bit slow on the uptake, she thought he was proposing marriage in a roundabout way, asking where she wanted to honeymoon.

'Tonight,' he said, his voice amused, making it crystal clear. 'Where do you fancy going tonight seeing as we're both at a loose end?' His voice, too, had a mesmerising edge to it. Not as mesmerising as Max's of course but close. 'I haven't offended you, have I?' he went on as she said nothing, 'Surely we can go out once in a while, just the two of us, without it meaning anything? After all, we are just friends, you and me, Charlotte. Aren't we?'

'What's this about your ex-wife writing to you then? What's happening there?'

'Ah . . . Jade's told you. I told her not to mention it. It doesn't mean anything at all. Now and again, she does things like this. Fit of conscience I suppose. Drops me a line, all friendly and sweet. She shouldn't have written to Jade though. It's upset her a bit. Raised her hopes when it's hopeless. She'll never come back and, even if she did, I don't want her back. It's all over, Charlotte.'

Lotty nodded at the phone. Satisfied. She had to trust him. 'Why don't we have an evening in?' she said, 'Come round and we can watch a video or something.'

'Sounds nice. And you can make us a meal maybe?'

'Sod off. You can make us a meal, James.'

'I can't cook.'

'Then we'll have to starve, won't we? Or better still, get a takeaway.'

She smiled as she replaced the receiver. Got ready for him. Took a little extra care with her appearance, wearing a new dress, black and white, smart and simple. She washed her hair, left it loose, thinking he might like it like that. If she got him in the right mood, she reckoned she could get James Entwistle rattled. She'd never seen him lose him cool. Unfortunately, he seemed remarkably even-tempered and tonight, for any number of reasons mainly concerning her mother, she felt like letting off steam, having a really good old-fashioned row.

She'd ask him where his tattoo was. Or better still, ask him what it was a tattoo of? Apparently, he was very touchy about it. Or she'd start on about the number of lorries on the motorways, how they always drove right up your rear end, moved out without signalling. She could talk about motorways now, without getting upset. She knew he was a very good driver himself and that should get his back up. There were one or two other possibilities if that failed to ignite him.

And afterwards . . .

Arguments always had a funny effect on her.

Max had known that.

And James was about to find out.

'It's all right, mother,' Lotty held the receiver close, smiled. 'You have no need to apologise. I've spoken to Sonia, Beth and William. We're all delighted for you. No . . . honestly! Didn't I tell you to do what you wanted to do? Stop having doubts. Off you go to the Bahamas, get married and have a lovely time. Come and see me when you get back.'

'Good. I hope I haven't disturbed you, darling, ringing so late. I just needed to hear your voice.' Laura sounded happy, distant as if she was already in the Bahamas instead of a hotel near Gatwick. 'Don sends his love by the way.'

Her hesitation was minimal. 'Give him mine too,' she said.

She replaced the receiver. Was suddenly very glad that her mother was happy. It was possible then to lose someone, like she had lost Max, and be happy again someday. A different kind of happiness, a smudged kind of happiness.

She smiled into the darkness, alone in the big bed in the new flat.

The evening had gone well. It was a comfortable sort of relationship, hers and James's, and she saw that it would be different from the one with Max. Neither of them had admitted it yet, that, in a way, they loved each other, but it was only a matter of time. Damn it, she had failed to get him rattled. He had seen through her, laughed instead at her attempts. And she still had no idea where the damned tattoo was but she intended to find out.

She smiled into the darkness and, as she often did in the silence of the night, had her little personal chat with God. After all, He deserved a bit of credit surely for letting Jade and James into her life. If she hadn't offered Jade a lift to the library that Friday afternoon . . .

This evening, at the door of the flat, James had kissed her goodnight for the first time. He had drawn her to him, pushed her hair gently away from her face, drawn a finger down her cheek, looked into her eyes and kissed her. Given a little sigh of pleasure. And then he had gone.

It had left her in a dizzy, dozy daze, walking on air, a feeling she remembered from long ago, from Max. So . . . it was going to be like that, was it? Of course, she had to recognise that he was a bit behind the times. Didn't James know that courtships, as such, didn't exist anymore? People didn't do that sort of thing, that creeping around on the verge, those meaningful looks, the gentle touches, the flowers, the engagement ring. That joyous anticipation. Wooing didn't they used to call it?

Romantic nonsense in other words. James was very nearly as bad as Max.

Okay . . . if that's the way he wanted to play it, she would go along with it.

She touched her cheek where he had touched it.

She stretched out her hand towards the empty place in the bed.

Entwistle? Charlotte Entwistle . . . God, it was truly awful, it was worse than Crabtree. She could always refuse to change her name. Now *that* would get him rattled.

Sleep beckoned and she let it drift towards her.

She was so contented.

She could wait.